Queen of Swords

Saga of the Swords Book 1 (Tales from the Tarot)

Christine Cazaly

Lo, the Queen of Swords,
bedecked in austere yet regal
raiment, stands as a paragon
of intellectual prowess and
unwavering discernment. Her
blade, not wielded with haste,
but as an emblem of her
insightful wisdom, gleams with
the brightness of a sharp mind.
Her gaze, akin to the blade's
keen edge, pierces the veil of
obscurity, and her countenance
reveals the strength born of
trials endured with unwavering
resolve. In her presence, one
discovers guidance through
profound contemplative
wisdom, though her relentless
pursuit of truth may sometimes
render her aloof,foor the
journey to enlightenment often
demands solitary, unyielding
diligence.

PREFACE

Dear Reader,

Welcome to *Tales from the Tarot: Volume 1 – Saga of the Swords!*

This series was inspired by my fascination with metaphysical fantasy and the profound symbolism of the Tarot. Within these pages, you'll journey through Arcanis, a world where magic and myth meet medieval intrigue, with each book following a different character whose story embodies one of the Tarot's court cards. You don't need any knowledge of the Tarot to enjoy these stories—the archetypes are woven seamlessly into the narrative, enriching the journey for those familiar with them while remaining completely accessible to everyone.

The Saga of the Swords is told through three distinct voices—three perspectives on one epic tale. Following key members of the Court of Skies, these interconnected stories delve into a land of ancient prophecies, hard-won power, and magic that walks the line between salvation and ruin. In the kingdom of Epera, destinies are forged in the heat of conflict, and even the most unlikely heroes must rise to meet the shadows of their time.

Queen of Swords begins with Petronella—the overlooked daughter who becomes a queen fighting for justice. But her story is only the first card drawn. As the saga continues, you'll walk alongside Dominic Skinner, Joran, and others whose fates are inextricably woven together. Each perspective reveals new layers of the kingdom's struggle, and by the final book, you'll understand why each voice was essential to the whole.

At the heart of this saga are characters who resonate with universal struggles: courage tested by fear, loyalty strained by ambition, the cost of sacrifice, and the redemptive power of self-belief—all underpinned by the enduring themes of the Tarot. While each book shifts its lens to a new protagonist, the story is one vast, interconnected tapestry. Trust the journey. Stay with them. The threads will come together in ways you won't see coming.

I hope these stories transport you to a world where magic and history intertwine and that you'll find as much wonder in reading them as I did in weaving their tales.

The adventure begins now—are you ready to draw your card?

Warmest blessings,

Christine Cazaly

LOOK OUT FOR THE NEXT SERIES IN TALES FROM THE TAROT:

'Way of the Wands'

Book 1: *The Unbound Flame* is available now!

A NOTE FROM THE AUTHOR

The Saga of the Swords is an epic fantasy told through the eyes of three different characters, each representing a card in the tarot's suit of swords.

While Petronella's journey begins here, the fate of the kingdom rests in the hands of all three. Each book shifts perspective to follow a different character's arc—but the story is one vast, interconnected whole.

Trust me. Stay with them. By the end, you'll understand why each voice was necessary.

— Christine

Contents

Prologue

Epera, From the Journal of Briana, Lady Falconridge, 1585

The news arrived from the Castle of Air last night: Darius has secured a betrothal with Prince Arion. For Petronella. She will take her older sister's place. Become Epera's queen. King Francis has agreed to wait until she comes of age. We have eight years in which to prepare her.

How my husband managed it, I will never know. My mother has aged over the last fortnight since our great hope for the kingdom, Jana, died. Deep lines score the sockets under her weary eyes. We were just days away from the long journey south. We'd packed Jana's bags. The grooms had brushed her horse's coat until it gleamed like molten gold. Her coronation gown took up the whole of one trunk. Jana knew our plans, of course. Her role in the revival of our kingdom's magic. My mother refused to send her south without knowing what she faced. My Jana, always a warrior, from the moment she opened her mouth and squalled. And look where all that bright energy has ended. She lies in Falconridge's family tomb, her life over. Her laughter a silent echo in her empty chamber. How long will her shade linger there, I wonder?

My youngest daughter is abed. Apprehension twists her fine white brow. She clutches her doll tight to her narrow chest. She cannot sleep without the herbs Felice de Winter mixes for her, and she has yet to speak since the accident. Her eyes follow us as we creep about her chamber, filled with loss. Without her sister, she's a puppet with cut strings. Felice has to sit with her and feed her soup, sip by sip, warm her cold feet. Tend her nightmares.

Petronella. Ever the quiet one. The fragile bird, as likely to take flight as to roost. She loves her books, as much as Jana avoided hers. A creature of ink and water, not flesh and blood. I look at her, lying there, trying to understand the shifting of her world without Jana to explain it to her, and I'm terrified for our kingdom's future.

My mother wants to prepare her for the role we had expected for Jana. I can't let her do it. Not Petronella. She hasn't the strength of her sister. Nor her courage.

So I have instructed Felice to give her the Heartsease Tea. Three doses, every day, without fail. Together, we will crush her magic. Together, we will keep her safe. My mother and I will teach her everything she will have to know to survive the Court of Skies. And I pray to the Mage that he blesses her with a child.

Because without a child, we are all doomed.

Chapter One

Epera, Castle of Air, Court of Skies 1603

Candlelight glinted on the remains of the evening meal. A warm glow lingered on the greasy legs of gnawed fowl and made shining puddles of spilled wine that pooled the boards like old blood. Members of the nobility, clad in velvet and fur against the weather, crowded the four long central tables in the Great Hall. Courtiers toasted each other with clashing tankards and tossed gnawed bones aside, ignoring the hopeful dogs and skinny peasants who watched for scraps. Voices swollen with alcohol echoed around the Great Hall like the raucous chatter of crows.

Old Girdred with his harp warbled almost unnoticed in his usual corner by the massive fireplace while a troupe of jugglers performed a series of lacklustre tricks to the less than attentive audience. Smoke, burnt meat, stale ale and rotting vegetables formed a pungent backdrop to the poisonous gossip that coiled through the air.

Clad in sumptuous blue velvet and crowded between the men at the top table, Petronella, Queen of Epera, massaged a dull headache as she regarded her meal. Her stomach begged for food, but her throat had constricted along with the rising tension in her shoulders. Picking a morsel of stale bread from her silver plate, she placed it in her mouth and chewed, trying to ignore the speculative glances that rained on her from the feasting nobility.

She shifted to her right as her husband, King Arion, leaned into her. His eating knife waved perilously close to her ear as he argued his point with the oily and war hungry Count of Dupliss on his left. Dupliss perched in his chair like a stork, a stick like dapper figure dressed in black. He trimmed a piece of meat from the bone, cut it into precise pieces, and arranged it in its own gravy as he listened with courteous attention to the king.

"What can Oceanis expect other than war if they persist in raising their prices? We cannot feed our people with what we now produce. The granaries are almost empty, and all Merlon does is sit on his plentiful arse while we fight for scraps in the rain."

Dupliss replied to his king, his lowered voice unheard in the din. Petronella turned her own blade in her hand, handle over tip. War. Still. Arion thought of little else these days. For a clever man, his mind ran on one extremely well-oiled track. Or two, if she included his obsession with her ability to bear a child. The thought of her failure in that regard made her stomach clench.

Stifling nausea, she waved away a tray of gilded partridge offered by the skinny serf who bowed in front of her. Her husband glared at her. She shrank away, refusing to meet his gaze.

"That's the last of the partridge. You should eat it."

Arion stabbed his knife through one skinny bird and transferred it to his plate where it languished, uneaten, as he turned back to his councillor. The servant slunk away with his burden to the lesser tables. Petronella's lip trembled as she marked his progress across the room, scanning vacuous faces as they ate and drank.

The Lady Violet de Grym, dressed in red velvet and ermine, was already drunk. She swayed as she leaned over the board, fumbling for the nearest flagon of Argentish. Her copious bosom swelled from her bodice. As she had undoubtedly intended, her charms had attracted the besotted attention of several gentlemen, none of them her husband. The closest nudged the decanter nearer to her with a flourish and a leer.

At another table close by, a sweating governess struggled to remove the king's ten-year-old bastard son from the company. He resisted her, fists flailing. Blood bloomed from the woman's nose as he scored a direct hit. Petronella glared at him, but the boy continued his campaign until Arion snared his attention and nodded at the door. The child tossed his blond head and left the room with his narrow shoulders squared and his governess scuttling in his wake, a kerchief held to her bloody nostrils. The noise level in the room intensified with their exit.

Petronella's father, Lord Falconridge, a long-standing senior member of the King's council and his former tutor, leaned across her into the argument. His broad shoulders crushed her against the hard back of her wooden chair. She inhaled the familiar scent of musk and dust that lingered in his robes as she tried to avoid him, and squashed her anger as his furs tickled her nose. Her eyes bored his powerful back with disgust. His disrespect would change soon enough if she bore a child. Her mother, Briana, would have delighted in a grandchild, but she'd never properly recovered from the shock of Jana's death. The Falconridge family crypt claimed mother and daughter both. Only Petronella remained to take her sister's place as queen, and provide the heir to the throne.

Huffing a sigh, her mind drifted to her bedchamber where an old copy of *Ye Arte of Conceivinge* lay tucked under her pillow, awaiting her attention. Her tutor, Mistress Eglion, had sourced and smuggled the volume to her under a mound of Arion's shirts awaiting embroidery. The sense of failure tugged at her once again, and her listless spirit drooped as the meal progressed and the din increased. If Jana sat here as queen, babes aplenty would crowd the nursery by now, all bearing her russet hair and their father's black eyes. The kingdom would be thriving. Perhaps the book held something to help her. Something she had yet to try.

Lost in her thoughts, she snapped back to bitter reality when a tremendous scream filled the air. Drowned out, Old Girdred fumbled mid phrase and dropped his harp. A distracted acrobat landed on the feet of his partner and they both crashed to the stone flags. Props spilled with a clatter.

In the sudden quiet, curious eyes turned to Lady Violet and the unfortunate servant with his empty platter. The rest of the fowl jutted from the well of her cleavage and oozed a sticky trail of grease down her bodice. A snicker of laughter, soon hushed, snaked through the company.

Cheeks scarlet with anger, Lady Violet plucked roast meat from her bosom and threw it at the man who grovelled on the stones at her feet. He snatched at the spoiled food. She kicked him, and he staggered upright, stammering ragged apologies. Fear paled his narrow face. Dark eyes surrounded by shadows. Already a skeleton.

"Your ladyship, I am so sorry, I tripped."

His voice trembled forwards, aimed at the floor. His hands shook so much the gathered food spilled once more onto the flags. Knees knocking, bladder clenching, Petronella tried to rise from her seat. She shoved at her father, but he braced himself against her, one heavy arm pinned across her lap to ensure she kept her place. The carved wood dug bruises into her spine. Arion stood. His towering form cast shadows across the boards in the flickering light of the torches.

"We do not waste food in these hard times. Bring him here." His command rang like iron wrapped in ice.

Lord Falconridge sat back in his chair, a tight smile on his thin lips. His snapping black eyes bored a warning into hers. Petronella pressed a boneless hand to her chest, where her heart beat an erratic tattoo. Goose flesh pricked the hairs on the back of her neck and her constant headache intensified. The lash of rain against the stained-glass windows dominated the sudden, enthralled silence as the courtiers froze. Half in terror, half in fascinated interest at the spectacle. Content to ignore the drama now she'd created it, Lady Violet picked up a discarded rag and dabbed furiously at her ruined gown.

Two of the king's men at arms shouldered their way to the servant and dragged him, like a sack of second-hand cloth, to the dais. The king looked down his nose at the man as he hung between them, his eyes narrowed on him like a hawk on prey. The young man's eyes darkened with terror as he struggled, his puny strength no match against the men who held him. His terrified gaze roamed the ranks of the highborn arrayed in silent judgment before him and snagged with hers in mute, desperate appeal. Petronella knew, suddenly, exactly what would happen. Her head thumped. She swallowed, her throat dry as ash.

"My Lord," she said. "Show mercy to your people."

Arion turned to her, raking her with his glare. His eyes sparked like dark jewels in the candlelight. "You go beyond yourself, Petronella of the Falcons."

His hand lifted. A flick of a wrist, a flash of shining silver across the gap between them, and the young man stared with horror at the blade embedded with pinpoint accuracy in the spoon of his fragile chest. A drawn breath from the avid courtiers and the guards let go. The unfortunate attendant crumpled to the floor.

Arion gave them a curt nod. "Take him away." He glared at the blade buried in the dead man's chest. The slim handle protruded. A thorn, badged in blood. It bloomed on the serf's tunic like a poisoned rose. "And someone bring me another knife."

Heads down, his subjects obeyed.

The king remained standing, cold as a statue, as his men dragged the former servant out, still twitching. The courtiers drew away from the grisly procession and returned to the meal, picking up goblets and refilling their cups. Conversation swelled once more and Girdred reclaimed his harp.

Face frozen at the king's right side, Petronella's hand shook as she raised the dark, dry wine she favoured to her lips. The goblet knocked against her teeth. Heart drumming, her eyes scanned the crowd. Another eager suitor aimed an intrepid cloth at Lady Violet's stained bodice. She batted him away. The acrobats picked up their juggling tools and resumed their routine.

The table lurched as her husband regained his seat, claiming her attention. The familiar scent of decay surrounding him twisted her stomach. Eyes narrowed with spite, he turned to her. Rancid with stale wine and herbs, his breath enveloped her as he hissed in her ear. Stifling nausea, she turned her face away.

"You dishonour me," he said. "Queen of this kingdom for ten years and yet to bear me a child. I will give you one last chance. Do not believe you are any safer than he."

Petronella's hand sprang to her mouth. Tears blurred her eyes as she forced herself to look at her husband.

"Forgive me, your majesty," she said, "I suddenly feel ill."

She scraped her chair from the table. The king dismissed her with a bored wave of his hand, barely glancing at her as she withdrew, accompanied by the ladies of her household.

Chapter Two

The court, who should have honoured her departure with bent knees, managed a few spare nods of deference as she hurried by. The wine, rich, dark and prized from the fertile fields of the Argent, had taken hold of the courtiers. Their glazed eyes and frenetic conversation, punctuated by shrieks of high-pitched laughter, painted a thin veneer of normality over their fear. Only the king's most favoured generals and advisers looked him in the eye.

Her father threw her a contemptuous nod as she left the chamber. Even Lady Violet appeared somewhat chastened by the events of the evening. Tonight, she satisfied herself with one admirer and glanced up with the contented eyes of a cat from the love seat by the hearth as Petronella swept by. Her sombre ladies-in-waiting trailed her like a wilting bouquet, forming a guard of their own as they hurried with her to the Queen's Chambers.

The stark stone corridors of the Castle of Skies echoed with the sound of their footsteps. Hollow-eyed servants scurried in tight-lipped silence about their usual evening chores. Word must already have reached them of the death of one of their own. Petronella closed her eyes to their stony glares, steeling herself as she stalked past, flanked by her ladies. Her rank made her untouchable, and she understood they must hate her, a useless, barren queen, just as they hated the king.

Her shoulder blades clenched as she marched along passageways lit by flaming torches and decorated by huge tapestries. She couldn't help but expect a knife in her back at any second. A quick flick of a blade and none the wiser. Arion had withdrawn her personal guard following her failure to become pregnant last month, as though he could scare her into conceiving. Without their solid presence, the journey from the Great Hall to her chambers seemed to take forever, with a potential assassin lurking behind every corner and decorative suit of armour.

The Castle of Air stood sentinel at the head of Eagle Pass, the narrow valley leading to the heart of the kingdom's wealth hacked from the mines and quarries of the Iron Mountains. Originally a simple keep, succeeding generations of monarchs had added to the castle until its grey shadow dominated the lower slopes, flanked by moats and buttresses.

Petronella now inhabited apartments in the bright southern wing in the most recent section of the residence, built by the late King Francis for his beloved bride, the late Queen Gwyneth. At her request, he had given her a splendid set of rooms overlooking the busy courtyard. From here, the former queen enjoyed the view over the battlements west to her homeland of Oceanis and south to the home of the gods at World's Peak.

The queen's suite included three interlinked rooms. An outer chamber for those requiring audience, an inner solar, where Petronella and her women congregated during the day, and her bedchamber. Her junior ladies had rooms leading off her suite, whilst her senior ladies occupied smaller apartments of their own in the same wing. Decorated in her house colours of grey and blue, her sanctuary offered blessed privacy away from the prying eyes of the Court.

Petronella sank to a cushioned footstool by the fire, holding her icy hands to the blaze, whilst her four ladies dispersed around her to begin their evening tasks. The songbirds in their cage in the corner fell silent as her third lady, Domita Lombard, darkened their shelter for the evening.

Lady Felice de Winter, the nurse of her childhood and now the most senior member of her household, clicked her broad, jewelled fingers at the most junior member of her ladies, Princess Alice of the Court of Waves in Oceanis, who clapped her hand to her mouth to stifle a yawn.

"Warm Western wine for the queen and prepare her bedclothes."

Young Alice, a pretty fifteen years, hurried off, her sea green skirts rustling, and Felice knelt by Petronella's side, stretching her own hands out to the hearth. The firelight glinted on her rings and gilded her dark skin with rich gold.

"Are you well, my queen?" she asked.

Petronella nodded, taking comfort in the earthy perfume Felice always wore that spoke of lands both warmer and more fertile than the ever-chilly Kingdom of Epera. She cupped her hands around the thick glass of mulled wine the young princess brought her and inhaled the familiar, sweet aroma of Heartsease and Dragonseed. Her startled stare sought confirmation of her nurse, whose grim expression and sympathetic eyes told her more than she wanted to know.

"Surely not tonight?"

"The Moon is full. Easy, my lady. Drink up."

Felice nudged the goblet to her reluctant lips and Petronella took a shaky sip, followed by a larger gulp. The wine slipped down her throat like warm silk and she sighed, dropping her head to her lap as a welcome warmth flowed through her icy body and her muscles relaxed. Her first lady caught the tilting cup and stood over her as she swallowed the rest down. The drug left her still alert but removed a degree of fear. Soon, her skin would lose sensation. A temporary effect but necessary for her sanity.

Domita helped her off the stool, and her ladies prepared her for the night. Her mirror reflected her anxiety. Her dark blue eyes held shadowed secrets. Despite her youth, silver strands already rippled like moonlight through her once black hair. Arabella of Wessendean, Mistress of the Wardrobe, handed her a night rail of white silk, imported from the Argent at substantial cost and trimmed with Northern lace. The material slithered down her body and raised goosebumps on her skin. Pinched with nerves, her face as pale as her gown, she already resembled the ghost of herself.

Dark hollows shadowed her cheekbones. Her companions persuaded her to take a little food in the privacy of her chamber, but she usually managed nothing whilst in the king's company. Her stomach closed like ice across the lake in winter when she had to chew with him, glaring at her like a hawk, waiting for her to make a wrong move.

Once dressed, her women handed her into the high bed hung with grey and blue velvet and embroidered with silver falcons, the symbol of Petronella's house. She sighed as her body sank into the warmth of a mattress stuffed with goose feathers and her mind lifted into the mental freedom of a clear, cold sky. Barely aware of the rich silk sheets against her skin, her mouth relaxed in a relieved smile.

Her husband might use her as he willed for the next few hours, and she would not feel his touch. The King of Epera enjoyed inflicting pain as punishment for failure. If Arion found the concoction her old nurse made for her, drawing on the ancient medicinal skills from Argentia, her home in the East, he would kill them both himself.

Felice chivvied the rest of her ladies into tidying the bedchamber for the night under Petronella's drowsy gaze. Young Alice, dead on her feet, stifled yawns as she cleared away the remains of the food and drinks. Lady Arabella, a thin, sour faced cousin of Arion's choosing, inspected her discarded gown for soiling and damage. A skilled needle woman, common amongst the women of the North, she enjoyed hours of quiet embellishing punctuated with sharp tongued gossip. Also embellished.

Lady Domita Lombard of Battonia, perched herself like a sentry at Petronella's window and swiped condensation away with her fist as she scanned the rain drenched courtyard for action. Her red hair blazed like a torch against the darkness of the night.

"Someone's coming," she said, clambering up on the cushioned seat and stretching to her toes to peer through the smoothest pane of glass.

Arabella crossed the room to join her. "Who?"

Petronella's concentration blurred. Their figures swum in and out of her focus in the candlelight and she clenched her fists into her palms. Her nails indented her flesh, but the potion numbed her skin.

"Not sure. Flying the colours of Oceanis. Guarded."

"He is either brave or stupid. Come down before someone sees you," Petronella commanded.

"He's riding a Batonnian Stallion." Domita jumped down from the window, her brown eyes entreating. "We have finished for the night, haven't we?"

Petronella rolled her eyes. "Go on then. You can find out what's happening. Do not steal the horse."

"Done."

Domita remembered a curtsy to Petronella and disappeared through the door in a flurry of russet, snatching up her cloak as she left.

"Alice, Arabella, thank you for your service. You may retire now."

Petronella spoke through semi-numb lips, reaching out her hand for her nurse, who joined her at her bedside. Felice laced her warm fingers into Petronella's and squeezed.

"Is the potion working?" she asked, her voice dropping to a whisper as the door closed behind them.

Petronella nodded. "Yes, thank all the gods. "

The First Lady's lips thinned, and she shook her head. "A drug should not be necessary. Gods blast him. They would strip a man doing this to his wife in my country and send him naked into the wilderness to learn how to treat others with more kindness."

"Arion is angry with me. He would be different, perhaps, if we had sons and heirs to the kingdom. Problems beset him from every angle."

"Don't you defend him, my lady. We both know he brings his troubles on himself with his war mongering and cruelty to his people. Things were better under King Francis. A hard man he might have been, but at least he did not murder his servants between courses."

Petronella allowed herself a small smile. "He wasn't always like this. The fault is mine."

Her hands left Felice's and twisted together in her lap. Her coronation ring winked up at her. The piece formed a heavy, strangely dull diamond supported by a thick, angular band. The setting clutched the jewel with possessive gilded talons. Legend said only death would remove the band from her finger. Like her marriage, it offered only a tight and cold embrace. Her fingers played with the circlet of gold as she talked, trying to work it free. She always failed.

"I can't bear him children, and now he's a monster." Her tired voice notched just above a whisper.

Felice frowned. "That is not true, my lady." She shook her head and patted Petronella's hand. "A brute he may be, but your ability to birth a child has no more bearing on the situation than one acorn to an oak tree. The man was born cruel, and I blast the gods for it."

Petronella's face twitched as she tried to lift an eyebrow. Her First Lady had never cursed her religion or her husband in such blunt terms before. The silence stretched out as they regarded each other with increasing alarm.

"I am here to do my duty as a queen. Tonight, at dinner, he gave me one last chance. What more can I do, Felice? The kingdom needs an heir to the throne. He may be a brute, but that is still a fact."

Felice stared away into the depths of the fire. Her shoulders slumped as she sighed.

"There is nothing else you can do."

"I pray every day for a child. I've consulted the physicians, the wise women, the libraries..."

"I know."

They both started as the heavy door banged open and Arion marched in, alone and unannounced. Tall and dark, lean and well-muscled, his face held an angular quality with a strong, predatory nose and a neat black goatee. She had once thought him attractive until she experienced his personal brand of cruelty. A pungent scent of cinnamon accompanied his progress across the room, but did nothing to mask the sickly essence of decay that clung to him like a poisonous shadow. His familiar, angry presence shattered the calm of her bedchamber. Heart pounding, she shrank into protecting silken sheets that were no protection at all.

"You. Get out."

He jerked his head at Felice, and she gave Petronella's hand another quick squeeze before she curtsied and left, careful to take the flagon of drugged wine and the empty glass with her.

Petronella flinched as the door slammed closed, leaving her alone with her husband. He divested himself of his steely crown, placed it with drunken precision on her dressing table, and glanced over at her, a tight smile lifting the corners of his face. The sight of his dagger glinting in his hand dispelled any remaining hope Petronella harboured the night would pass without violence.

"Well met, wife."

"Husband."

Despite the drug, her breath clogged with panic. Ashes dusted her throat.

Arion stalked across the rich carpet, removing his robes as he came. He manipulated both clothing and knife with wary ease. Never unarmed, even against her. Never surprised, not for a moment. He reached the bed and leaned over her. She tried not to inhale his stench. The point of the knife grazed her face as he traced a pathway down her cheek. The edge followed the line of her jaw and lingered at her slender neck before slicing through the fragile silk of her nightdress to expose her small white breasts to him. He knelt over her, one knee on the silken coverlet, and blew out the candles.

In the darkness, she caught her breath as his hand twisted in her hair, pinning her to the mattress, imagining the blade as the metal skated across her chest, over her stomach, down to where her empty womb remained unfilled and disappointing.

"This, wife. This is what you are for," he said, his breathing unsteady, already aroused. "Breeding is your one purpose and your only value to me. This night is your last chance. The kingdom can no longer wait. If you cannot produce an heir, then you are of no further use to me."

Petronella's numb body froze further at his words. The blade kissed her skin, and she felt the warm trail it left behind, a line of pain buried under the numbness. He needed no more than that. Not to remind her of her place. He ripped off the rest of her clothes and entered her. She struggled to breathe. His wine-soaked breath, the sweet scent of decay and the insufferable weight of his body as he slid on the blood between them made her want to vomit. She clamped down hard on her fear and remained passive beneath him. The drug ensured her compliance and her stillness.

There was no point in screaming. Help would never appear. She turned her face into her pillows to avoid his breath and thanked all the forbidden gods for the combined potions of Heartsease and Dragon-Seed that prevented the pain from reaching her, at least until tomorrow. But she couldn't prevent the horror, or the anguish, or the knowledge that tonight represented her last hope to do her duty as a queen.

CHAPTER THREE

"By the Gods."

Petronella bit down on a groan as Felice peeled the covers off her. Arion had tried three times to make a child on her over the course of the night and now the drug had worn off, she hardly dared move.

Blood still leaked from one savage cut across her belly, though the first two, less deep, were mending already. A dull ache between her thighs and the musty reek of spent male seed exposed to the chilly morning air made her retch. Stomach twisting, Petronella heaved up the little remaining in her belly into a small bowl Felice held ready for her. She laid back with a gasp of pain and Felice sprang into action, ordering a hot bath, cloths, bandages and healing salves in quick succession.

Her ladies scuttled to do her bidding. Young Alice took one appalled look at the long lines of additional damage on Petronella's white skin coupled with the blood on the sheets and turned bone white. Petronella gripped her hand before she darted away.

"Say nothing. Do you understand me, Alice?"

"But my lady!"

Petronella gave her a little shake, forcing the girl to meet her eyes.

"This is important, Alice. Promise me. Not. One. Word. To anyone."

The princess bit her lip. Sympathy flooded her face and Petronella forced a smile. The girl was so young, with a tender heart. She shouldn't be worried about this.

"Will you do me a favour?" She asked.

Alice gave her a slow, uncertain nod, eyes wide. Unshed tears still sparkled in the turquoise depths.

"Will you sing to me? One of your ocean songs? Your voice is so pure."

Face clearing, the maid claimed her lute from its carrying case, and the room filled with the liquid, supple melodies of the West, blessed by the magic of a true-born daughter of Oceanis. Petronella's fragile spirit revived as the sun teased an appearance from behind the iron-grey clouds, flooding the chamber with a rare, bright light.

Domita fidgeted her way through her tasks until the last note sounded and Petronella had clambered from the bath and dressed before she shared her news.

"Doesn't anyone care what I found out?" She demanded.

"Forgive us all if we had other things on our minds, Domita." Felice said, drying her hands.

"What?" Smelling gossip like a bloodhound, Arabella's long nose rose from her embroidery.

"The man who arrived last night. He's an ambassador from Oceanis. He's come to treat with the King for a lasting truce."

"From Oceanis?" Alice put away her lute, folding the decorative ribbons and giving the instrument a last pat. Shadows darkened the room as the weather closed in again.

"Didn't we have a treaty?" Arabella asked,

Petronella gave a hard laugh. "No longer, judging by the discussion at dinner yesterday," she glanced at her youngest maid, "I'm sorry, my dear, but Arion wants to go to war with Oceanis. Apparently, they are cutting us off from valuable resources and not treating us with the respect we deserve."

Alice brought her hand to her mouth. Petronella avoided her reproachful gaze, hating the instant guilt that shot through her.

She sighed. "It is not my wish, but what can I do?"

The girl blinked. "You're the queen. Can't you stop him?"

Petronella laughed. The abrupt bark sounded nothing like her. "You saw the type of justice His Majesty served to our servant last night, did you not? I cannot counsel the king. No-one can." She said, loathing the sarcasm in her own voice. "What do you imagine will happen if he lets our army loose in your kingdom? I'm sure your countrymen will compose songs about the invasion of the Cups for centuries ever after."

Alice's small chin jutted.

"In my land, we are equal, both king and queen. Man and woman. If the queen says something, the king attends her words. He's good at listening. If he says something, she waits him out. She's good at listening. That's why we enjoy music and singing. Everyone can speak. Everyone has a voice."

"The Court of Skies no longer works like that, Alice. Now we obey the king." Petronella shook her head in defeat as she turned away, avoiding the scornful glare Arabella threw at her.

Her mind replayed the events of the previous evening. The terrified expression of the doomed serf. He knew the moment his blasted platter collided with the noble lady's bosom what his fate would be, and she, his queen, did nothing. Her nails dug into her palms. Jana would have done something. Mind you, if her sister reigned, her children would play in the nursery, the servant would be alive, and no-one would be starving.

Her tortured gaze clashed with Alice. She stood with her small fists clenched, blue eyes blazing, ready to take on the world. Domita's hot brown eyes sparked with expectation. They appeared to be waiting for something.

Brow quirking, Petronella wondered what they expected her to do. She had no power of command here. The realm had no use for her if she did not bear a child. A babe would give her status and power. Without one, everyone regarded her as a useless ornament, a broken vessel, and Arion would set her aside and take another wife.

Unable to stand the accusation in their eyes, she limped to the silver cage in the corner that housed her songbirds. Alice's father had gifted the mated pair to her when she took the girl into her service.

She opened their shelter with gentle fingers and took some grain in her hand.

The braver of the two hopped onto her palm, regarding her with wise, avian eyes. He took the food and pecked at her wedding band, cocking his head, looking as quizzical as Alice. He performed the action twice more while she stroked his soft feathers with the tip of one finger, admiring wings shimmering red and purple in the morning light. His companion, drab by comparison, regarded the intruder from a wary perch at the back of the cage.

These songbirds were the last of her permitted pets. Arion had forbidden her the companionship of her magnificent Peregrine Falcon, The Grayling, six months ago. Now he languished, trapped and bored in the falconry. She missed him more with every passing day, his empty perch in the corner by the window a constant reminder of her disgrace, though she could not have said why the loss troubled her so deeply. His empty perch in the corner by the window was a constant reminder of her disgrace—and of something else she could neither name nor forget.

Making up her mind, she lifted the metal enclosure from its hook and shuffled across the room to the casement window. She forced the swollen frame open, shivering as the cold, dank air rushed in to claim territory from the hearths. The heavy curtains snapped like sails. Felice uttered a cry of protest and caught a toppling candelabra before it could scorch the carpet. Ignoring her, Petronella opened the bird house.

"Go on," she said, "You don't belong here."

She gave the cage a small shake, and the songbirds swooped free, the female in the lead. She followed their darting flight against the lowering sky until they disappeared in the distance. Leaning on the sill with drizzle on her face, she wished with all her heart for the freedom to fly after them into the fresh morning air.

A brief tap on the door interrupted the women from their accustomed tasks later that morning.

The ladies exchanged glances. Petronella put down her book and nodded for Domita to admit the visitor. Much to her shame, her fingers crossed for luck in the folds of her skirt as she prayed the King wasn't the person standing outside.

"Lord Colman."

A portly man in middle age, the Chamberlain managed the household and court affairs with one eye on efficiency and the other on his pocket. He lowered his head in a stiff bow, less than courtesy required, but all his bulk would allow.

"My lady. The King requests your presence at his side. An emissary from Oceanis has arrived, and His Majesty wishes you to attend the audience."

Petronella arched an eyebrow. Arion rarely requested her attendance in matters of state politics.

"Tell my Lord I will be along presently," she said.

The man nodded, sketched another bow, and withdrew. Petronella gained her feet, and her ladies cast their needlework aside and went to their tasks with a will, glad of the interruption to the dull monotony of their days.

Fingers and feet flew as they found Petronella a more suitable gown, braided her hair and polished her skin with cosmetics. Arabella's sallow face glowed when Petronella complimented her on the delicate lacework trimming her grey skirts. In minutes, Petronella's everyday self disappeared. Transformed by the ceremonial garb, a queen appeared.

"That will do." Felice placed a last pin and stood back. Petronella groaned to her feet, one hand protecting the wounds on her body, decorated like a butterfly, and pinned into place with costly satin, a diamond ring and a delicate filigree crown.

Guards in the blue and silver livery of Epera stood sentry on each side of the towering carved oak doors that warded the Throne Room.

They bowed her through, and Petronella led her entourage into the crowded chamber. Fur-clad gentry wearing their best velvets pressed to the front rows. Scholars and scientists, in their motley choice of stained and tattered robes, huddled at the back, discussing their latest theories.

Always ready to put on a show when necessary, everyone bowed.

Petronella kept her face fixed ahead, trying not to look at Arion, who dominated the proceedings from his throne, dressed in his habitual black tunic and hose. Luxurious dark ermine trimmed his velvet cloak and blurred his narrow outline. The familiar steel circlet crowned his brow.

A royal blue velvet canopy hung over the dais, and her heels tapped across intricate tile work in the shape of clouds and swords, interspersed with a repeated curving figure of eight. Tapestries of hunting scenes and ranks of polished weaponry filled the walls. No comfort here. Only the King and Queen could sit.

Setting her jaw against the pain of her abused body, Petronella glided to the dais, stopping to perform the traditional obeisance to her husband before she ascended the steps. Her ladies followed suit, their skirts billowing like blown flowers behind her. Arion frowned as she took her seat on the smaller throne at his side. Her women fanned out behind her in order of precedence. Petronella assumed her habitual stony mien, noting expressions, faces, who stood with whom. Alliances, rivalries, truces. Awareness of her enemies came naturally to her now.

Her father held his position near the throne in the first row, with Count Dupliss next to him. The two men conversed in soft voices as they waited. Tension, more tightly strung than Domita's treasured bow, radiated from Arion on her right. More guards than usual dotted the room. All armed. A chill crept over her.

A loud trumpet blast announced the diplomatic party from the Kingdom of Oceanis, and the Court herald introduced him.

"Hail to the King of Epera in the Court of Skies. We present Lord Joran Weir of Oceanis, Emissary of the King of Oceanis in the Court of Waves."

The heavy double doors of the throne room opened to reveal a group of four men. Their leader captured attention with nonchalant ease.

A tall man with an imposing physique, he wore a dashing cloak of aqua over a steel breastplate. The light armour covered a broad chest covered by a blue silk tunic, long, saddle-hardened legs clad in tight hose, and close-fitting riding boots. A jaunty hat in the same turquoise as his outer garment completed the ensemble, but his eyes attracted her attention the most as he strode towards them. Aquamarine eyes, unusual in a man. Tanned skin, honey brown hair and a wide mouth made for smiling formed a favourable first impression. Behind her, Alice gave a delighted gasp, quickly hushed.

The stranger glanced at her once but then gave his sole, solemn attention to the king, who waited like a predator for his prey to move.

Petronella pressed a hand to her head, where a sudden pulse of pressure lanced straight between her eyes.

Lord Weir swept off his hat and bowed, showing an elegant leg. Petronella gave Lady Violet a stern look. The woman wore her lowest-cut gown and pushed her way to the front row of courtiers, level with the delegation. Her flimsy husband tried to manhandle her backwards with little success.

"Your Majesty. Greetings from King Merlon. May we present a gift?"

He gestured to one of his fellows, who handed the administrator an ornate wooden casket.

Arion lounged on his throne, unimpressed, but gestured his man forward with a bored wave of his gloved hand.

The Lord Chamberlain opened the container with a flourish for the King's inspection. The box held two further abalone shells, packed to the brim with precious Oceanis blue salt, a rare commodity, obtainable only with much bravery from the centre of the Marshes across the Western Wash. A prize fit for a monarch indeed.

Arion raised a dismissive eyebrow.

"A handsome present, Lord Weir. I wonder what your master can want in exchange?"

The emissary took a breath but held his gaze steady. "King Merlon requires the immediate return of Alice, Princess of Oceanis, and the withdrawal of your forces on our northern border." His voice, pleasant and melodious, almost distracted his audience from the impact of his message.

A ripple of well-bred shock ran through the ranks of nobility, and Petronella schooled her face to impassivity as her mind raced. Both matters were news to her. The murmurs from the courtiers and the sight of them straining forward for more information reminded her to keep her chin up and her expression impartial. Her stomach twisted at the added embarrassment in front of the court. Merlon's request for his daughter's return from her service demeaned her. And their armies lingered at the border of Oceanis? When had that happened?

Arion settled back in his seat, his dark eyes snapping danger. One hand toyed with his dagger. The edge flashed as it revolved butt to blade on the arm of his throne.

"You ask much for a little seasoning. What else will you give?"

Petronella tightened her fingers in her lap, toying with her ring, her thoughts in turmoil. *He thinks he can bargain with Alice's life like a chip on a gaming board. What is this? He flies in the face of all precedent and decency.*

Her stare narrowed at the man in front of them. His composure was complete. Elegant, handsome, the perfect courtier. He bore no arms. She cursed her ignorance of the politics of the Kingdom as she wondered at his bravery and the other forces at work.

"I am instructed by His Majesty, King Merlon, to offer a revised price on our wheat and fish until the rains cease and your crop yields recover, thus enabling you to more easily feed your people."

Arion tapped his dagger against his teeth as he considered his reply. His guest waited with the utmost courtesy, although the courtiers were already debating matters among themselves. A hush of conversation whispered around the room, with many a scornful glance tossed Petronella's way as she sat on display, struggling to keep her face impassive.

"We will meet with your party later today to discuss this matter in more detail, and you will, of course, join us for our meal tonight. We thank you for your generous gift. Please remain here and enjoy the hospitality of my court."

He stood, and the courtiers sank to their knees. Arion held his elbow out for her, and Petronella placed her reluctant hand on his velvet sleeve, walking with him the length of the room, followed by her ladies and Arion's council and gentlemen of the bedchamber.

He dropped her arm and gestured to Alice as soon as the throne room doors slammed shut behind them.

"You will keep her close, Madam. I am not finished with Lord Weir yet, and I don't trust him. Make sure rooms are ready for him and his men in the east wing."

Petronella frowned, confused. "I do not understand, sire. Why should Merlon wish for the return of his daughter? She is perfectly safe here with me."

Arion bared his teeth in a wolfish grin. "He is not a stupid man. He is worried at the thought of our troops near his borders, and he can only guess at our other plans. I can send my forces to take what he agreed to sell at extortionate prices, and he wants his precious daughter back home where she belongs. So, I refuse to let her go. He can want all he likes. The child will stay here, a hostage against her father's good behaviour, and if he refuses to give us his produce, he will never see her again. I will kill her if I must and send my troops to take what I need anyway."

He sauntered off whistling, well pleased by the turn of the day.

Mouth agape, Petronella whirled to her ladies. Her generous lips compressed into bare winter twigs, Felice appeared to be lodged in place like a tree. Cinnamon eyes flashing, Domita paced in a furious, aimless circle. Face wild with fear, tears streaked Alice's cheeks as she lunged at the door of the Throne Room, where the guards greeted her efforts with lowered pikes and mute defiance.

With some dim thought of offering support, Petronella reached for her, but her arms returned to twist at her waist as her blurred gaze clashed with Arabella's. The blonde woman regarded her with distant disdain, grey eyes hard and uncompromising. Petronella clutched the folds of her gown, her fingers digging into her own abused flesh as she bit down on the urge to sob. What comfort would she be? What must they all think of her? A failed queen and now the unwilling jailer of a terrified fifteen-year-old princess.

Chapter Four

In the event, the diplomatic party did not stay for the promised banquet.

Arion met with Weir and his contingent later in the day. Before nightfall, the grim-faced Oceanis delegation collected their horses, mounted and rode off with all speed into the damp gloom, the jeers of the Eperan courtiers ringing in their ears.

Lord Weir did not ask to see Alice, and fury gripped the girl. She paced the length and width of Petronella's chambers, demanding Petronella find her a horse now, this second, and let her go after him. The sky darkened, and a growling storm accompanied by lashing rain howled over the mountains to add another layer of drama to the dismal day.

"I hope he gets soaked and dies of pneumonia. I want my father," the princess wailed, before collapsing onto a brocade sofa and sobbing her heart out.

Exhausted, Petronella sent her to bed with a sedative of Felice's devising. Within the hour, her junior lady slept, the storm abated, and the two women shared a goblet of wine before the hearth in her bedchamber, discussing the events of the day in hushed voices.

"I still can't believe what Arion's done." Petronella turned the ruby liquid in her glass, watching the swirling patterns. "This has never happened in our history. What is he thinking, making such an enemy of Merlon? Our four nations rely on one another. Our world works with all quarters working together, each in its own manner."

Felice took a deep draft of the rich wine as she considered her reply. "Our world is not as balanced anymore. The man who rules Epera is unlike the other kings before him and faces unique challenges. Arion is doing what he believes he must to protect his kingdom. His sentiment is sound, and he is a man of logic, but his methods are harsh. What he cannot achieve through diplomacy, he will take with force. Why else did the gods' gift him a country rich in mines, factories and raw minerals and a nation of scientists, scholars, and soldiers?"

"The gods would do well to consider gifting him some fields fit for wheat and some cattle free from hoof rot."

Felice gave her a small, stiff smile. "But they did not. We must play the hand they dealt us."

"Will Merlon give him what he wants?"

"Whilst Arion holds Alice, he will want to if he is able; but Merlon cannot feed both kingdoms with the resources available unless he buys more from the western continent. Your husband does not possess the desire or the coin to compensate him."

Petronella's voice dropped lower, and she glanced over her shoulder before whispering. "Why is Alice so important Merlon demands her return?"

Her voice hesitant, Felice frowned, staring unseeing into the flames. "She is Merlon's daughter and the heir to his throne in the coming years, so if trouble is coming, of course he wants her back. Arion can't know how much pressure Oceanis is under for resources themselves. They have always been the grain basket of the North. Arion does not expect that to change. He thinks Merlon is greedy as an Argentian for gold and will yield to pressure to be generous."

"Our army won't fight for long without food or pay. If they are starving and let loose in Oceanis, discipline will vanish. The consequences will be terrible."

Petronella finished her wine and reached for a cloak against the damp chill in the corridors.

"Look after Alice."

"It's dangerous to wander the castle at night. Where are you going?"

"To talk to Arion."

Felice lurched to her feet. "You can't be serious. The man is dangerous."

"I need to change his mind."

"Petronella. Think about what you are doing. He holds no concern for you until you prove you are pregnant with his heir."

Petronella smiled as she reached the door. "He doesn't know whether we succeeded last night. He's a logical man. The odds are he won't kill me."

She managed a reassuring expression for her First Lady as she slipped through the door, but the smile slid from her face as she hastened down the chilly corridors to her husband's suite. Arion became more unpredictable by the day, and his hatred of her grew apace. There was no guarantee of a safe return to her chambers. But for the kingdom's sake. She had to try.

Chapter Five

Retired for the evening to his rooms in the North Wing, with views over the Iron Mountains and the source of Eperan wealth, such as it now was, Arion, King of Swords, reclined in the most comfortable chair in his study. His scarred oak desk supported one long, leather-booted leg, and the other carried the generous weight of Lady Violet de Grym, who snuggled with the grace of a cat in his loose, one-armed embrace. She coiled jewelled fingers into the silken hair of his goatee and gave a little wriggle of happiness. The neckline of her unlaced gown drooped a little lower over her bosom.

Uncomfortable under her weight, he shifted as pins and needles prickled his foot and wondered when the woman would become bored.

They had already enjoyed bed sport. Lady Violet was an enthusiastic proponent of the art of love, as her current state of relative undress revealed. Arion, by contrast, had not bothered stepping out of his clothes. Now, though, he believed it prudent to give the woman the illusion of contentment she sought. Better to keep her happy and compliant. One never knew when a compliant and satisfied woman might be handy, and above all things, Lady Violet was both compliant and handy.

Propping his chin conveniently atop her perfumed blond head, Arion skimmed the contents of the latest dispatches from the troops camped at Goldfern, the river port that thrived at the head of the Great Fall on the border of Oceanis.

According to General Harison's note, all was satisfactory. Tents erected, billets found for the officers, and cannons ready to roll. With a bit more food, *a lot more food*, Arion rephrased mentally as he read, then all would be well. The fertile plains of the Oceanis farmlands stretched before them downstream, unguarded and with the harvest ripening. Wagons and serfs gathered in the rearguard to transport the booty to the windmills of Blade. The troops were spoiling for a scrap and in high spirits despite the dreadful weather, and they awaited orders. He wished his most gracious majesty well, blah blah blah.

Arion crumpled the letter in his fist and tossed it with unerring accuracy into the heart of the fireplace, stifling a wince at the pain flaring through his hand.

His right palm caressed Lady Violet's ample hip, and her soft fingers snaked from his beard, wandering down his neck to lie across his heart. Picking up her hand, he mouthed a kiss on its back while his eyes flickered over the delicate pattern of flames in the hearth as his mind roved over his invasion plans.

He helped his concubine to more wine and had raised the flask for himself when someone knocked on the door. Eyebrows contracting in irritation, he barked the intruder in, uncaring if his men of the bedchamber should lay eyes on Lady Violet. Most did more than look at her, in any case.

Decanter in hand, he froze as his attention locked on the last person he expected. His wife. His casual lover sat up with a shocked gasp, spilling wine on his doublet and catching him hard under the chin with the top of her head, making his teeth click together like a set of castanets.

Arion jerked to his feet, tipping her off his lap to the floor. He did not bother to help her up. Lady Violet staggered upright, clutching her loosened gown to her overwhelmed modesty, and dodged around

Petronella into the antechamber. A rumble of derisive laughter from the gentlemen lounging around the fire and playing cards accompanied the slamming of the outer door. Arion seated himself, his ever-ready anger under tight control.

"Wife."

Petronella's blue eyes narrowed. "Husband."

Arion allowed himself a small smirk. For once, he had got under her marble skin. He should have paraded his paramour around sooner.

"To what do I owe this unexpected pleasure, my dear?" he inquired.

A pause. He schooled his features to passivity as his wife struggled to ignore the situation.

"I would talk to you about your intentions toward the Kingdom of Oceanis." She managed in the end, although her knuckles turned white as she gripped the door handle. She remained on the threshold, unwilling to enter the room. Sensible of her.

"Do sit down."

She drew herself up, reminding him of her height, which he so often forgot. "I prefer to stand."

"As you wish. Some wine?"

He raised his own glass to her in an ironic salute and swilled a fresh mouthful around his palate.

Her court-schooled face didn't change, but he caught the thought as it crossed her mind. *"I would rather drink rat's piss than drink with you."* The start of sadness that blossomed in his chest surprised him as he witnessed her mental response. A sliver of fear lanced through his body, and he gave an inward shudder as he banished the thought. He must be drunk. Perhaps he had imagined her voice in his head. He must have imagined it.

"No, thank you."

Her actual words, quiet and controlled, brushed his ears like dry leaves. Even now, there were times when he genuinely admired her. He had put her through enough misery during their time together.

His dark gaze dropped to her ring, and he stifled a hiss of pain as the matching band on his own forefinger flared to life, digging its claws into him like an angry cat. Gritting his teeth, he fought for serenity as a bolt of icy flame shot up his arm and slashed through his head. He raised the wine to his lips again and cursed himself for stalling. Might as well finish this conversation. She would have to know soon enough.

"About Oceanis, my dear. You heard me correctly in the hall. Princess Alice is now regarded as a hostage. Nothing you can say or do will make me change my mind. The matter is beyond your remit."

His tone should have told her not to interfere, but remarkably, she stood her ground. Her slender chest rose in a deep breath as she marshalled her arguments.

"This is without precedent, Arion. You must understand." She said, forgetting herself and stepping further into the room. "Our relationship with the Court of Waves is based on trust and mutual advantage, not destruction and war."

He sprang out of his chair and slammed the goblet down so hard the crystal shattered into shards of diamonds, scattering rich drops of wine like blood across his desk. His wedding band clawed his flesh again, and his icy temper ignited with the lightning pain in his skull. Why didn't she listen to him? When had she stopped obeying him?

He skewered her with his glare, willing his words into her head so she would understand as she shrunk away.

"Without an heir, our granaries are empty. Our workforce is starving, our output is falling, and our kingdom's income and power are declining. Merlon is the one who reneged on precedent to help his neighbour in times of trouble. He puts his prices up and sends his emissary to me with a revised offer that takes us back to what we paid before the rains came, but we can no longer afford those terms either. I have given him a choice and a chance. If he grants me supplies, there will be no war, and his daughter will continue as our honoured guest under the protection of the Court of Skies. If he refuses, I will punish him through her and lay waste to their lands to get what we need. I mean what I say. Our kingdom must endure. You understand what I must do to ensure this. I will kill her. I will kill you. I am bound to this land, these mountains, this realm. I am King of Epera, and the Royal line of Eagles will prevail."

His normally quiet tones raised to a roar of defiance. A stunned silence replaced the general banter of his men in the anteroom. His wife took a shuddering breath, her hand going to her heart.

"You will murder me?" Her eyes searched his for the truth.

His mouth twisted as he replied in a voice quieter now and rough with suppressed grief. "My father, on his deathbed, informed me of the curse in our land. The royal line must continue for the health of the kingdom. Your role as my queen is to supply an heir. If you cannot give me children, you must die if I am to retrieve the ring that binds you to the land and take another wife. I have given you ten years. You have failed. Time has now run out. I must do what the kingdom demands. Epera is dying."

His words dropped like stones into the well of her disbelief.

"You are talking about old magic." Her voice hushed. To say the word in Epera could lead to death.

Arion's face gave nothing away, but his lips thinned to the width of a dagger blade. "Dark Magic. I will rid our land of its pernicious influence, as my father wished, and heal our kingdom."

"I don't understand what my ring has to do with anything. Please, just take it." She fumbled at her finger, but the jewel clung to her hand, impossible to shift. Arion shook his head as she struggled, his face as bleak as his voice.

"We are cursed, you and me. You cannot remove your diamond any more than I can remove mine. They are bound to us, body and soul. You are the Queen of Epera, so your coronation band is yours to wear until you die."

“I may be pregnant now. Please.” Her words came out in a shaky whisper. She hardly dared look at him.

He stilled and looked at her.He released a long breath. “You have a month to tell me. Or less.”

She took a wary step back, too aware of the broken glass winking in his hand. The temptation to score her flesh the way his wedding band now seared his own almost overwhelmed him. Hurt for hurt. Pain for pain. Endings and beginnings.

“Get out.”

He didn’t raise his voice. His hand raised of its own volition, causing her to back into the outer chamber, her stunned blue eyes never leaving his face. He waited until the door shut behind her and hurled the glass.

The shard flashed across the room like an arrow, burying itself in the door at head level, and he slumped into his chair, clutching his blighted hand to his aching head as he choked back his frustration. His life, her life, and the dying kingdom. Bound together and failing all.

Chapter Six

Petronella twisted the key in the door to the corridor, her heart thudding, knowing a mere lock would not hold back the inevitable. Her eyes darted around the chamber like a frightened animal, searching the shadows for danger.

"My lady, what happened?" At her side in an instant, Felice clasped her hands. "Tell me," she said, when no answer came.

Petronella's hands shook, her fingers like ice. "He's going to have me killed," she whispered.

Matching shock paled Felice's dark cheeks. "That can't be true. Surely, he won't."

Petronella nodded. "He will. He says he has waited long enough for an heir, and he will kill me for my ring. He can take another wife. I never wanted to marry him. Why did she die? Jana should have been the one to wear it."

She glared at her wedding band and tried to yank it off her finger. The more she pulled, wringing tears from her eyes, the more the metal gripped her like a starving python.

"It must come off. It must." Eyes wild, she grabbed her eating dagger from a nearby table and laid her hand flat against the polished wood. Felice gasped and jumped at her, snatching the blade as it flashed down.

"My lady, stop."

"Give it to me. I'll cut my finger off."

"You will do no such thing."

"I am your queen. I command you."

Felice wrapped her in a hug, holding her close to her heart. "You are my queen, my charge, and my friend. We will find a way."

Petronella's chest constricted as she breathed in the familiar scent of earth, flowers and honey her nurse always wore. A wave of grief rushed over her, and she wound her own arms around her friend, a long-dammed well of tears falling to flood her face and soak Felice's gown.

"I'm sorry, so sorry. I have let you all down. Arion, our country. Our people. My family."

"You have never failed me."

She guided Petronella to a seat and laid a fine woollen coverlet over her shivering shoulders. Petronella clutched its warmth. The rush of tears spent, she took an unsteady breath. Felice pressed a goblet into her hand.

"Here. Heartsease Tea. You need your medicine."

Petronella nodded her thanks and sipped. The glass rattled against her teeth.

"We have some time, yes? He won't... do anything now?"

Petronella managed a nod, struggling to collect her flying thoughts. "I have up to a month."

"Of course, he is waiting to see if you bleed. We need to plan in case you do."

Petronella glanced up, one eyebrow raised.

"What are the chances that I won't bleed? After ten years of trying to conceive? Of wishing, hoping, praying and all your medicines for a healthy pregnancy? Don't fool yourself, Felice."

Her nurse acknowledged the riposte with a shrug.

"So, we make a plan for your escape."

"I can barely leave my rooms, let alone the kingdom."

"You will die if you don't."

"I am a Queen of Epera. My duty is to bear an heir to the crown. If Arion requires a new wife, I must be the sacrifice for the land. It is simple."

"Can he not... put you aside? Divorce?"

Petronella brightened as a spark of hope appeared, before slumping into her chair again. "That is not what he said. He says dark magic has cursed us, and he needs my ring. Can he hate me so much as to want me dead? Or is this some sort of arcane law we know nothing about?"

Felice gazed into her own cup, her brow knitted. "I wish I knew more about the workings of a king's mind and your nation's history than I do about brewing medicine. I cannot believe he hates you enough to put you to death. That cannot be the reason. It is a pity Mistress Eglion is not here. She would know more."

"She's been gone for months. Her rooms in Blade are empty. I don't want to die or abandon my land. This is my kingdom. Why can I not bear it a child?"

Felice's face dropped. Her sombre expression did nothing to lift her hopes.

"If we run out of time, you may have to make a terrible choice. Sacrifice yourself or leave."

Despite the soothing nature of the Heartsease tea, Petronella couldn't find sleep once her first lady had left her. Her tired mind looped into knots, considering the problem. During the endless night, and for the first time in years, she hugged her belly and pleaded with the gods she didn't believe in to fill her womb with her hated husband's child.

"If this is what you require to save my kingdom and my life," she said into the thick silence, "please let me bear an heir for Arion, King of Epera."

As ever, the gods gave her no reply. Her light-deprived eyes played tricks on her in the absolute darkness of her bedchamber. Tears leaked down her cheeks. How had it come to this? On her wedding day, despite her anxiety and doubt, she had experienced a moment of pride when Arion bent over her, placing her ring on her finger.

For a few short months, she could forget her role as a replacement bride for her beloved sister. She and Arion had lain together and spent hours planning a kingdom of inventions and learning, had attended masques and hunting parties by the score. The Grayling had soared over fur-wrapped nobles in robes of russet and purple and red and spread his noble wings across an ice blue sky. The sun had shone on snow-clad meadows that sparkled in the winter and grew rich yellow grain in the brief, hot summers.

All gone now. The Grayling confined and lonely in his quarters in the Falconry. Muddy fields, blighted crops, starving people, falling output. Teeth clenched against her despair, she fumbled for the flint beside the bed and lit the candelabra. Dancing shadows rippled against the walls. Seeking distraction, she fumbled under her silk pillow for the smuggled book she had been waiting to read, although what good it would do her now, she couldn't imagine.

Biting her lip and hoping for answers, she turned to the first page. How she longed for Mistress Eglion's patient, ironic eyes on her as she read. They had sat for hours in silent study over the years, surrounded by scrolls and books as they tracked down information and further learning. Mistress Eglion had vanished. She had sent to her teacher's lodging for word of her several weeks ago, but the cowed servant returned with the news that her rooms were empty. No-one had seen her. She had disappeared like mist, leaving only silence and this book behind her. It was possible that the soldiers forced her to work in the mines. Or she was already dead. Huffing a forlorn sigh that sent the flame on her candles dancing, she slanted the book toward the light and put her brain to work with her former tutor's tobacco-stained voice echoing in her head.

"The answers are always in the text, Petronella. Sometimes in the gaps between the words. You only have to look."

No one could call *"Ye Arte of Conceivinge"* an easy read, and on Felice's advice, she had already tried many of the remedies it contained. The candles had burned an inch, and Petronella yawned, turning pages that held nothing new. Why had Mistress Eglion given her this?

Ready for sleep, she started to close the book when something odd about the page caught her eye. Squinting, she peered again at the narrow text. A misprint? Holding it closer to the candlelight, she scanned the dry paragraph again, and this time, spotted the discrepancy. It was almost indistinguishable from the script. Separate letters and numbers inked in at the end of a line. She read them again, frowning, and eventually grasped what they represented. A library reference number.

Chapter Seven

Having spent the night in a clammy tangle of blankets as she tried to sleep, mind whirling at her discovery, Petronella drooped with fatigue in her accustomed seat the next morning. Domita admitted the servants bringing breakfast and crossed the room with a tray of day-old bread and herbal tea for them all, her bright freckled face unusually grave in the dull morning.

"Is this all there is?" Arabella asked, curling her lip at the dismal offering.

Domita scowled at her. "We're eating more than the rest of them."

"That's enough, Arabella. We will make do and be grateful." Petronella nodded to the women to help themselves and wandered over to the window seat with a cup of steaming tea. Her mind tumbled over itself, and she itched to search the forbidden library for the mysterious reference she had discovered in the night.

Outside, serfs hurried across the courtyard through rain and mud to carry out their errands. Horses steamed, heads bowed in the downpour. Taking to horse, officers shouted irritated instructions at perspiring grooms.

Her father and Count Dupliss supervised proceedings from their place in the doorway to the long-disused chapel. Their dark woollen cloaks did little to shield them from the rain. Petronella rubbed at the condensation fogging the window and surveyed them with narrowed eyes as they put their heads together, deep in conversation. Unease stirred in her belly.

Sweating servants loaded barrels of food and water onto a line of carts drawn by skinny horses. Shivering in the rain, bowmen and pikemen mustered on both sides of the huge portcullis that led out of the castle, their collective breath clouding the air.

Domita joined her at the window-seat and handed her a heel of stale bread.

"They are preparing to move against Oceanis. I overheard a footman talking to someone in the gallery."

Petronella leaned her aching head against the heavy glass. "They have started," she murmured. "This is all real. We are going to war with our neighbours."

Domita grimaced. "Not yet, but soon, if Merlon makes no reply."

They stood at the window, each lost in their own thoughts. Petronella jumped when a shrill scream from her maid's room split the air.

Felice lurched to her feet.

"That's Alice."

Petronella glanced around, realising she had yet to set eyes on her youngest maid that morning.

She hurried with the others to the comfortable chamber the two junior maids of honour shared between them. The princess shifted uneasily in her bed by the window. Her hair, escaped from its night-time braid, twisted like seaweed across her pillow. The bedclothes tangled around her bespoke a restless night. Perspiration dotted her forehead. Her eyes darted like fish under her closed lids, and she shouted something unintelligible again, making them all jump.

"How does she sleep through her own screaming?" Arabella said, reaching for the girl first. She slapped her hand hard.

"Alice, wake up, you're scaring the queen."

The princess gave another blood-curdling screech, giving no sign Arabella's words had reached her.

Felice's hand shot out as Arabella aimed another frustrated swat.

"Leave her, you dolt. She's not asleep."

She turned to Domita. "My leather pouch, hanging on the hook by the door in my room."

Domita disappeared, glaring at Arabella as she went, and returned seconds later. She thrust the bag at the first lady and leaned over her friend on the bed.

"Is she alright?"

Extracting a small purple vial from her satchel, Felice nodded her to the other side of the mattress.

Plump fingers deft and practiced, she poured a couple of drops into a bowl. Petronella admired her Chief Lady's expertise from her position at the foot of the bed as Felice whispered a few words over the liquid. Whether a charm or a prayer, she had no way of knowing.

Felice held the dish out to Domita.

"Warm this," she commanded, not bothering to glance at the girl as her worried frown returned to the slim form of the princess, wrapped in dark visions as she mumbled and writhed on her sheets.

Domita bowed her head and, seconds later, steam rose. Petronella blinked as a start of fear leaped to life in her belly. A pungent aroma of burnt flowers filled the room, making her eyes smart. Felice took the bowl back and held it under Alice's nose. The girl inhaled, choked, and startled awake with a small cry.

Petronella shrank back like a cornered cat, with her shoulders clenched to her ears. How had Domita done that? Medicine was easy to understand, but magic? That surely couldn't be. Arabella's face had contracted in sharp, suspicious lines. She looked as if she were sucking a lemon. Domita avoided her narrowed stare and leaned over her friend.

"Alice. Are you back with us now, child?" Felice took one of the girl's hands as she lowered her bulk to the bed. The girl struggled against the tangle of bedclothes to lever herself to a sitting position against her pillows and cast a confused glance at the worried women clustered around her.

"What's the matter? What happened?"

"You don't remember?" Arabella said, unimpressed. "Why, you would wake a corpse with all your screaming".

"Don't you wish," Domita cut in. "She's not yelling her head off on purpose."

"I am sorry, Arabella. I didn't realise." Alice rubbed her face. Dark shadows rimmed her swollen eyes.

"Can you remember anything from last night?" Petronella asked.

Her maid shook her head. "I went to sleep. I had some bad dreams. You were in one of them." She nodded at Arabella, whose pale eyebrows shot up her forehead in surprise at being the subject of a nightmare.

Alice glanced at Petronella. "And you, my lady, but I can't think now. My head aches."

"I will give you some willow bark tea. Rest now." Felice braced her hands against her knees and stood, reaching for her satchel of herbs. "Let's allow her to recover."

They filed out of the room. Felice busied herself over the fire, and Petronella cornered Domita, grabbing her arm as the girl tried to sneak out of the door.

"How did you do that?" She hissed at her. "Dark magic is forbidden. A cursed activity."

Domita glared back. Defiance and caution waged war on her youthful face. Defiance won.

"How did I add heat to a little bowl? Easy. I held it and told it to warm up. That's not magic." The stubborn lift of her chin dared Petronella to argue with her.

Petronella's blood ran cold. "You performed magic at the Court of Skies? Are you mad? What will Arion do to you if he finds out? If he thinks you can do magic, he will kill you, or send you to the Iron Mountains."

The freckles on Domita's brown face stood out like plague spots as the blood drained from her face, but her eyes flashed, and she held her ground with a confidence Petronella envied.

"I cannot help being what my race made me," she said. "I am from Battonia, and we deal in fire. It is only you Eperans who prefer to gather your knowledge from musty books and dead machinery."

"Domita," Felice's voice held an unspoken warning as she glanced between the two women. Domita ignored her, jerking her head at Alice's room.

"She is from the Kingdom of Oceanis. She deals in water. In visions and mysteries and the sea. You can no more take her ability from her than fly to the moon."

Petronella snorted. "That's ridiculous. The stress of the last few days has taken its toll on her. That is all."

She whirled away and froze as Domita's hot fingers clamped around her wrist.

"She is waking up, my lady. Those blessed by the gods come into their power at sixteen. Soon she will remember her visions, but only with the proper training and initiation rites. If she doesn't receive those, the magic will overwhelm her, and she will be unable to control it. That's why her father wants her back."

Petronella's icy glare travelled from Domita's determined face to the scalding grip on her arm and drew herself up to her full height.

"Remember your place, Domita. I am still the queen."

Abashed, Domita let her go. She curtsied.

"I apologise, my lady. I overstepped."

Petronella nodded at her, and the girl backed away to resume the remains of her breakfast in watchful silence. Petronella retrieved her cup of lukewarm tea and regarded her old companions over the rim with narrowed eyes. She trusted Felice's competence as a nurse. But what powered that skill? Knowledge or magic?

And what had Mistress Eglion hidden so carefully in the library? What did she want Petronella to discover? Her gaze drifted beyond the door, to the library she'd once loved. Abandoned. Forgotten.

She needed to go back. Before it was too late.

Chapter Eight

The killing of the servant marked a significant change in mood among the Court of Skies. Skilled huntsmen returned empty-handed from the quiet forests. The granaries housed more rats than grain, and the farmer's fields floated in a sea of liquid mud. Healthy livestock were succumbing to a virulent sickness that killed within days and left the meat tainted and unfit to eat.

The king met anxious faces and hollow eyes everywhere he went. Even the nobility were pulling in their belts. The peasants crept about their tasks, stealthy shadows hugging the walls. Dogs, cats and rats suspiciously absent. Oceanis had not sent a message, and a steady, dulling drizzle saw torches burning day and night to ward off the gloom.

It was for this reason that little ceremony greeted the messenger from the Court of Oak in distant Argentia when he arrived at the Castle of Air ten days later.

Wet and covered in muck, he performed a shaky bow to the King of Epera, but his hands trembled with cold as he offered his roll of parchment, wrapped in oilcloth to keep out the rain. Arion gave him a curt nod of thanks and waved him away into the care of the Chamberlain, who ordered fresh clothes and a tiny meal.

Arion snatched the letter and marched down the corridor to the privacy of his rooms. This latest act of diplomacy had been a last resort, and his heart thumped with unusual anticipation as he slid the parchment out of its protective covering.

He broke the pentagram seal of the King of Argentia with a sharp fingernail and took the letter to the window where grey light spilled across the page. Rain cascaded down outside as he scanned the ornate script and courtly language with irritated haste. Reaching the end of the missive, he crumpled the heavy parchment with a grimace of rage and ripped the document into pieces, wincing as the pain tore through his injured hand.

"Curse all the gods. That gold mongering, avaricious swine!"

Marching to the door, he threw it open and leaned out.

"Page. Get me Dupliss, Lord Falconridge and the Lord Chamberlain. Now."

"Sire." A faint scuffle of running feet, then silence. Arion poured himself a glass of wine, pacing the room as his mind raced through the options. The ring on his finger sent a warning jab of pain through his arm to his skull, and he shook his head, rubbing his brow.

The door opened, and he glanced up as his two chief councillors entered. Dupliss, wearing his customary dark robes, trickled in with his usual oily grace. Lord Falconridge, his father-in-law, tall, powerful and swathed in ermine against the cold, strode behind him. Seconds later, Colman puffed through the door, his round cheeks red with exertion.

"That bastard in the East refused our request for aid," Arion announced as soon as the door closed. He nodded for them to help themselves to wine, and the four men took chairs around the fireplace.

"I am not at all surprised." Falconridge said, sampling his drink with relish. His moustache came away from the glass with its greying ends stained red. "Daron is always more concerned with matters inside his own kingdom. They are far away. It is not worth their while to trade grain when wine is more profitable."

"We now have no choice but to go to war with Oceanis to feed our people."

Dupliss turned his glass. A narrow smile split his thin lips at the prospect of bloodshed.

"Excellent. The troops are ready and waiting to join Harison's force at Goldfern, Sire. We have transferred as much food as possible to provision them, and the kitchens and granaries of Oceanis will feed them when we take Sunira. That is our first target, as we discussed."

Arion stood again and strode to the window. He'd performed the same action for days, hoping to see the emissary bearing a conciliatory note and a few tonnes of grain from the King of Oceanis. To date, he had been disappointed. Astonishing was the speed at which these kings forgot their daughters as soon as they left home.

"How long before they can be in position?"

"Once we give the order, sire, they should reach the port of Goldfern in seven days on foot, or two by boat."

"How long before our other preparations are complete, Lord Falconridge?"

Falconridge's dark eyes glinted with satisfaction. His fingers toyed with a black stone set in silver that dominated the forefinger of his right hand. "The engineers say they will break through within the week."

"Lord Colman, what is the state of our remaining food resources?"

The chief steward sat back in his chair; his feet stretched to the blaze. "Well now," he began, "I've been thinking about this. It will last us three months if we are careful."

"When you say 'us'," Falconridge said, wiping his moustache, "do you mean the Court of Skies, or the entire kingdom?"

"The Court of Skies, of course. The city stores cannot feed the peasantry as well."

"Place a permanent guard around the granaries," the king ordered, his attention still directed out of the window. "Make sure we feed the guards and their families. Place the Court on quarter rations. My orders. No more banquets. No more feasts in private households, either. A double watch is to be placed in the castle."

"I've had another thought," the Lord Chamberlain said. "We could commandeer the food held in the granaries of our nobles across the land. It could buy us a few more weeks."

Falconridge shook his head. "We cannot spare the troops. Staying on good terms with the nobility is important. They are not used to going hungry."

"Agreed," Arion said. "That will be the last resort. I hope it won't be necessary."

A long pause ensued. The three servants of the Crown exchanged practiced, nudging glances as they debated without words whose turn it was to place their head in the lion's mouth. Falconridge lost.

"The Princess Alice...?" he questioned, with the utmost delicacy of a man dangling over a pit to extract a sovereign from a basket of poisonous snakes.

Arion turned from the window, a calculating smile lighting his thin face. "I have plans for the Princess Alice. Perhaps I still have a way to encourage her father to part with his grain."

Deciding, he nodded to his generals.

"I have waited long enough to hear from the Court of Waves. You march tomorrow. You may leave the girl to me."

Chapter Nine

Petronella found the sight of her youngest lady standing at the window overlooking the courtyard waiting for word from her father, the King of Oceanis, both touching and irritating in equal measure.

Alice had woken them every night screaming about blood and diamonds. Arabella wanted to complain to the king. Felice needed more sedating herbs. They all required more to eat.

Her nerves on a knife edge as she waited for her moon time, Petronella snapped at her ladies, and only Domita, the least patient of them all, brought some comfort to the terrified princess. Alice had lost weight. Black circles ringed her eyes, and she had nibbled her nails down to stubs. Her lute languished in its wooden case, and their chambers no longer echoed with the blithe melodies of the western seaboard.

Arion's temper alternated between glacial and volcanic these days, and his ever-ready blade rarely left his hand. His eyes, cold, piercing and appraising, raked through Petronella's elaborate courtly attire at every meagre evening meal, but she dared not make her excuses and beg off.

He had taken to wearing gloves, rubbing his forefinger and brow more often as the days wore on and the scent of decay billowing around him deepened. Petronella wasn't far from fainting in his company herself. She needed all her court training to pretend serenity.

Prescribed by her first lady to calm her racing heart and mind, Petronella consumed Heartsease tea by the bucketload but still found sleep scarce. Felice watched her closely for changes in her condition, her attention matched only by the king.

On the evening of the tenth day after Arion's latest attempt to conceive an heir, Petronella couldn't rest. Her head pounded and her thoughts churned, trying to find an answer to her ever-present dilemma.

Fumbling for a flint to light a candle, she gathered the woollen folds of her most practical dressing robe around her and peered around the darkened room. Shadows swayed in serpentine form around the stone walls as she held the flame up and squinted around. If she wanted more information, she would have to brave the cold corridors herself.

She shoved her feet into a pair of embroidered slippers and slid Mistress Eglion's useless book into her dressing gown pocket as a precaution in case anyone challenged her. Her rooms were warm and quiet. Stifling her breath with an effort, she cracked open the door to the corridor and peeped out. For once, the corridor was empty.

All her senses on high alert, she approached the library with caution. She was prepared to explain her presence outside her chambers as a nocturnal visit to the king's quarters should anyone ask, but this eve it appeared the sentries had found better targets to guard.

Blessing her luck, Petronella put her shoulder against the ornate, red wood door and creaked it open, shivering as the ice-cold air kissed her exposed skin. Vast fireplaces unlit, the cathedral-like space lay colder than a tomb. She inhaled, relaxed by the comforting scent of parchment and old leather. Her lone candle did little to light her way as she crept forward, squinting into the dark. Massive columns supported the vaulted ceiling that stretched above her head for another two floors. Shelves lined the walls and made dividers along the length, pointing like polished fingers to the central aisle. These barriers created small, intimate rooms on both sides, and in the first years of her marriage, Petronella had spent many pleasant hours here in the company of the nation's most celebrated scholars and her old tutor, Mistress Eglion. Education and learning were all halted now. The enormous room and its famed resources were barely touched.

She stood for a few seconds, dreaming of seeing the library used as it should be, remembering her days of study and the small successes when her own gift for language widened her ability to read the works of people from other countries and other eras.

In recent times, her fellow scholars and former tutors had been studying in the silence of their musty rooms and in small, dedicated groups, the crown funding sustaining them cut off as the treasury dwindled.

Petronella tried to ignore the twist of guilt that ran through her.

Her arguments against the library closure had fallen on stony ground last year, and the icy look on both her husband's and her father's faces when she persisted had sent her scurrying like a mouse back to the sanctuary of her apartments. Once again, she had achieved nothing. Useless.

Squaring her shoulders against the memory, she held her candle higher and picked her way down the stacks to the section she had been looking for, trying to ignore Mistress Eglion's brusque warning of a decade previously.

"Never a naked candle in here, Petronella. There are too many irreplaceable titles to risk a fire."

The shelves stretched away from her in the gloom, and she shuddered. In the daytime, and with the anticipation of scholarly research churning through her, the narrow space between the racks gave her no pause. Now, with the dark pressing and standing in a silence only broken by the odd scratch of a mouse, her spirit flailed, her skin prickled with sweat and the hand holding the forbidden candle shook.

She bit her lip and forced the fear of darkness and enclosure away. Nevertheless, her shoulders hunched as she took the first steps into the inky black and squinted at the titles etched in fading gold on the cracked spines. Part of her mind noted the signs of decay and neglect in the volumes as her light dipped and fluttered.

Her hands numbed in the frigid atmosphere, and goose bumps prickled across her body as her breath clouded the surrounding air. Stopping to collect her bearings by the enormous, unlit fireplace, she gasped as a swirl of icy air billowed from the chimney and snuffed her candle. A whimper of alarm started from her mouth before she could prevent it, and she stiffened, every nerve end tingling as she fought the urge to turn tail and run.

"Come on, Petronella," she whispered. "It's only the library. What's the matter with you?" Her heart thudded as she forced herself to wait to see if her eyes would pick up any type of light. After what seemed like hours, she noticed the slightly brighter rectangular patches that spread down the walls to her left. Windows. At least they were a map of sorts. Swallowing heavily, she picked her way forward with as much haste as she could manage, swearing as her bony hip collided at regular intervals with the heavy desks spaced along the floor. Her icy fingers crawled like a blind man's over the shelf numbers nailed to each stack as she passed.

"Seventy-Six." She uttered a heartfelt sigh of relief and leaned her thumping head against the edge of the history section. It seemed hardly probable that the narrow gap between the shelves could be darker than the rest of the library, but that was indeed the case. She sighed, stifling another shiver, and took her first uncertain step. The shelf was easy enough to find. At least she could reach it, but as her unwilling fingers brushed unseen along the dusty wood, hope collapsed like dead ashes in a cold hearth. It was empty. Disbelieving, she took a few more steps, confusion and anger replacing her fear of the dark. Switching her spent candle to her other hand, she searched the opposite shelf only to find the same space. All the books that should be here had apparently vanished. She dumped the useless candlestick to one side and strode the length of the stack, annoyed beyond reason, both hands sweeping fruitlessly over the ancient redwood. Nothing other than dust. She was stuck. She'd have to risk coming back in the daytime. But search for what? She had no title, just the shelf reference.

"It has to be here. Mistress Eglion led me here. Where is it?"

Turning, she retraced her steps. A sudden pulse of pain through her head sent sparks across her vision, and she swayed where she stood, squinting against the pressure, fumbling for support. Off balance in the darkness, she stumbled to her knees and wrapped her head in her arms for comfort, swallowing against nausea until the icy spasm of energy dissipated. Swiping a hand across her clammy brow, she clambered to her feet, ready to admit defeat. This was a ridiculous quest. Better to return to the silent tomb of her chamber than scurry about like a starving mouse in the dust and damp. Heaving a sigh, she took a few steps out of the stack, trailing her fingers across the gritty shelves for orientation. Her skin crawled, and she jumped when her careless fingers collided with the solid binding of a heavy book.

"What? How could I have missed that?" She patted the adjacent row. As before, it was empty. Her fingers crept back to the volume, and she shook her aching head. She must have missed it somehow. This had to be it.

Hauling it from the shelf, she almost dropped it, surprised by its solid weight. Her nose caught a waft of earth and damp, and her fingers tingled with a surge of energy for which she had no explanation. Thoroughly spooked at the dark silence, she clutched it like a child against her chest and fled through an uneasy darkness crowded with the restless ghosts of scholars' past.

She was nearing the junction of the corridor to her chambers when the sound of marching feet caused her to jerk to a halt and look for somewhere to hide. There was no place for her behind the suit of armour standing vacant guard in a nearby alcove, but a swift kick banished the book underneath its metal plinth.

Too late to avoid the guards as the patrol rounded the corner, she clutched her robe around her and tightened her jaw, heart pounding. Swallowing, drawn up to her full height, she turned around with her fists clenched, hoping her fear did not show on her face.

Four men wearing steel breastplates decorated with Arion's eagle device and blue plumes on their bird-styled helmets marched up the stone floor. The sound of their boots rang in her ears. Two of them carried long, lethal-looking pikes, topped with tempered iron. Sharp, serviceable swords hung in the scabbards worn by the other two. They, however, were the very least of her worries. The tall, overbearing figure of her father in the centre of the group disturbed her peace of mind far more. His thick frame, clothed as always in the dark furs he favoured, dominated the space. Spare glints of silver adorned the collar of a shirt embellished with Arabella of Wessendean's finest black work. His long fingers toyed with a small, thick book bound in black leather and tied shut with a blue ribbon. An inexplicable shiver crept across her shoulders at the sight of it. Frowning, she clutched her robe around her. Her father's sardonic, dismissive gaze met hers with the force of a fist.

The group came to a halt in front of her. The guards did not salute.

"Your Majesty."

Implacable, the highest-ranked guard waited for a response. He stood squarely at attention. The awkward silence built.

"Good evening," she replied, tightening her lips against the tremor in her jaw.

"Out for a little nighttime reading, daughter?"

Her father stepped forward, a twisted smile on his once handsome face. The guards parted for him.

"Were you not told to stay within your quarters after you retire?"

He loomed closer, and Petronella cursed herself for the automatic step back. She shoved her hands in her pockets and tried to ignore the book hidden in the shadows. The tarnished gilt of its binding tantalised her from where she stood, and her jaw tightened. After everything she had just experienced, she'd be damned if she'd let him find it. Her sweating fingers closed on 'Ye Arte of Conceivinge'. Raising her chin, she withdrew it from her pocket and passed it to him. Better this than the prize it had led her to.

Her father's dark eyes scanned the title, and he gave the contents a cursory flick.

"Edifying." He handed it back to her with some force. "At least you are trying, although it's hard to understand how you hope to succeed after all this time."

The thought of what failure could mean made her bladder twist. Pride clamped her knees together and, from somewhere long unused, she dragged a portion of courage.

"Indeed, I am still trying." Her tone carried a ring of ice. She lifted her eyes to him. "Hope has yet to be forbidden, I believe?"

She held his stare for a lifetime before his head jerked. "Escort her back to her chambers."

His disapproving tone allowed no room for argument. He waved her forward like a disobedient child, and the troops closed in formation around her. She inclined her chin and walked the short way back to her rooms, flanked by a rigid circle of iron and steel. Glancing behind her, she frowned as he entered the library and the door slammed shut behind him.

She waited for the guards to withdraw before picking up the skirt of her dressing gown and dashing back to the suit of armour. Flinging herself to her knees, she scrabbled underneath it. The door to the library remained closed, and she flew back to her sanctuary on slippered, silent feet with her trophy clutched to her chest. She locked the door the second it shut and placed her back against it. Safe for the moment, she stomped across the room to her desk, eyebrows twisted with irritation at her constant restraint. They might as well lock her in a dungeon and throw away the key. A mouse had more freedom to move than she did.

Lighting more candles to aid her, Petronella thumped the book down on her mahogany desk, releasing a cloud of mildew, and drew up her chair.

"Of ye House of ye Eagle in ye Kyngdom of Epera"

The history of the king's line, back to antiquity. Somewhere in here, Mistress Eglion had found information to help her. It was a large volume, comprised at random and added to over time, judging by the damage to its spine.

Her fingers shook with anticipation as she lifted the cracked leather cover. Settling in her chair, with a blanket around her shoulders, Petronella hefted the book across her desk, wrinkling her nose at the scent of mould, and turned to the first page.

Chapter Ten

The candles had burned down to puddles in their stands. She awoke in the dim morning light to her ladies knocking at the door begging admittance. Back stiff and her feet like ice, she sat up slowly, peeling her cheek from the clammy vellum and rubbing her eyes. The fire had died back to a heap of sullen ashes long ago. Shivering, she levered the heavy book shut to tackle later, after breakfast. Unlocking the door to her ladies, she avoided their curious gazes as they curtsied and spread out to their morning tasks.

Domita disappeared to the kitchen in search of food and to scare up a servant to clear out the fireplaces, Alice picked up her neglected lute that required tuning, and Felice riffled through her satchel for herbs to mix up another batch of sedative.

Arabella rummaged in her coffers for suitable attire and Petronella accepted her help in gowning herself appropriately to meet the day before seating herself at her dressing table.

"Why did you lock your door?" Arabella picked up a silver-backed brush and smoothed her hair.

Petronella managed a distracted smile at Arabella's reflection in the mirror, pushing her dishevelled hair off her face.

"I fell asleep over a book of fables," she said.

Only half a lie. Her tired mind, scrambled with the effort of mental translation, had succumbed to fatigue forty pages into the ancient text. Apparently, all was well in the Kingdom; a continual line of succession, sunlit, snow-capped mountains, happy, healthy peasants and a roaring mining trade all combined to make the country strong and prosperous. The twin rings traditionally worn by the reigning monarchs of Epera were ancient and powerful in a way that appeared mere superstition to her logical mind. Her coronation band had a name. The Ring of Mercy. Legend accorded it magical properties.

Arabella ran the brush through her hair, and Petronella regarded the jewel where it lay on her finger like a boulder pinning her down. The stone gleamed sluggish and dull this morning in the grey light. She tried to remove it again, but today it wouldn't twist around, let alone leave her hand. Instead, it clung, stubborn as a cancer or an unborn child. The face of the enormous diamond looking back at her was blank. No message of hope twinkled at her from its heart. Petronella's lip curled.

If you can do magic, she demanded of it in her mind, *why can't you make me pregnant? I don't want to die for you. Kingdom be damned.*

She waited, aware of the blasphemy. Surely if this inanimate object held any power, it would react to such mental abuse. But nothing. Just as she thought.

"Magic. Huh," she said, settling her shoulders with an irritated huff of breath.

"My lady?" Arabella paused in her brushing, running her hand down the length of Petronella's hair before she reached for a comb and pins.

"Nothing, just a passing thought. My silver headdress today, please, Arabella."

She caught the sneer on Arabella's pale face as the older woman turned with sinuous grace to her wardrobes. Her own brow narrowed. A snake. She wondered why the woman desired to serve in her rooms and made a mental note to be cautious. The game had shifted in recent days, and Arabella had already borne the king two children. She had to view the woman as a likely candidate for her position.

Petronella met her own gaze in the mirror. Like Alice, her eyes were gathering circles underneath them, and suspicion lived in their azure depths. She eyed Arabella in the mirror as the woman crossed the room, holding a dainty silver headdress in one hand. Her grey eyes, hard, unsmiling and pale as the diamond on Petronella's finger, clashed in reflection with hers.

Petronella winced as Arabella clattered the delicate ornament onto the dressing table and ordered her hair. The woman wore a veneer of liking thinner than the gilt on a cheap necklace, and her thoughts were easy to read. Her thin mouth compressed in a sour twist as she concentrated on taming the heavy mass of silken black into a manageable style. An imp of mischief, long abandoned, gave her an inward pinch of glee. Time to wipe away that smirk.

"Arabella, please request the court physician to attend me later this morning." She had the pleasure of watching shock and rage flash across Arabella's face before she schooled her expression to neutrality.

"Of course, my lady."

Petronella caught Felice's eye in the mirror as she sat up from her position over her kettle in the fireplace. The woman raised her eyebrows and turned back to her work with a shake of her head, whilst Alice glanced up from her lute, confused. Arabella rushed through her hairstyling and flounced out of the room to fetch the physician, and Petronella gave in to hysterical laughter.

"Do you need a doctor, my lady?" Felice asked, one eyebrow raised in sceptical fashion as she poured her potion carefully into a series of earthenware flasks lined up on the hearth.

"No," Petronella admitted. "But the look on Arabella's face was priceless."

Chapter Eleven

Out of breath and rosy with exertion, Petronella and Domita had just finished practicing their knife skills in her outer chamber when the court physician, Heldred Farron, recently employed by Arion to minister to the needs of the Court, tapped on the door.

Felice admitted him to the queen's chambers with a disdainful sniff. Her dark eyes bored an alarm to Petronella when Lord Falconridge swept past her in the physician's wake. Petronella flinched, and her nails dug half-moons into her hands as she nodded to him, her throat suddenly dry. Her gaze snagged on Arabella seated by the fire in the solar. The woman lowered her eyes, but her mouth bore a secretive and satisfied smirk as she pretended interest in her work. Her own eyes narrowed.

"Your pardon, my lady, I was unavoidably detained."

Herron straightened from his bow, battered satchel clutched to his chest, and Petronella's nose wrinkled at the familiar, musky floral scent clinging to his fur-lined robes. Evidently, Lady Violet had taken ill during the night.

Or not.

She managed a spare smile, still wondering about the look on Arabella's face, and preceded the two men into her inner bedchamber, beckoning Felice to accompany them.

"Do you have something you wish to tell us?" Falconridge said.

He helped himself to a glass of wine from the decanter on her table. She swallowed as his formidable silhouette crossed the light from the window. The chamber closed in around her, and she forced herself to take a breath.

"I need a remedy for headaches," Petronella said.

Her father lifted a sceptical eyebrow and took a disbelieving swig of wine as his speculative gaze swept over Felice before turning his dark gaze to the mist-covered view from the window. The atmosphere developed a pre-storm intensity that raised the hair on the back of her neck.

Oblivious, Heldred bent over his own satchel. "I believe an infusion of willow bark would be of help, my lady."

Petronella thanked him as he pressed a fold of dried herbs into Felice's hands, and she allowed time for small talk before he made his leave. Her father paced the carpet until the physician bustled out, and he jerked his head at Felice as well.

"You may go."

Her companion's mouth clamped in a mutinous line, and she stood her ground until Petronella shook her head with a weak shrug. There was no point. Her father would have his say, as he always did.

The door had barely whispered shut before Lord Falconridge slammed his glass down and closed the distance between them. His height and bulk loomed before her, closing off her vision. She took a step backwards, every sense flaring danger.

"I ask you again, Daughter, do you have something you wish to tell me? Because you realise this is your last chance, do you not?"

"And what will you do, Father, with both your brood mares dead? How will you keep your power and influence with the King? Because I do not imagine he is bluffing. Your concern isn't for me, the kingdom or the Falcons. Is it?"

Darius took a step back, one eyebrow shooting up at her tone, and turned his most scathing look on her. She bit her cheek until blood flowed across her tongue, struggling to keep her composure against the wash of fear as it cascaded through her and caused her fingers to shake. She hid them in the folds of her gown as he spat his next words.

"You dare to defy me? Thanks to the curse of magic on this land and your complete failure, our kingdom is dying without a legitimate heir."

Knees trembling, she forced herself to keep her head up.

"I am aware of my duty, sir."

"I will stand by the wishes of the king should you be unsuccessful again."

Petronella's heart contracted in her chest. She lowered her chin.

"Of course you will. You always do. I am sure you will endeavour to replace me with another, more fertile queen and thus keep your position as favoured adviser once they mop my blood from the throne room floor."

She started as he crossed the thick carpet to loom over her. His bunched fist snatched a handful of her casual chamber robe, and she stifled a gasp as he yanked her forward and pulled her up to his face. Rage flamed in his cheeks. His eyes narrowed with hate. She braced both hands against his broad chest and struggled to twist away with a grimace, part fear, part anger.

"Take your hands off me."

"You will be careful of your words, Daughter, if you value what is left of your miserable life. Your role here is to bear a child for the kingdom. No more and certainly no less. Your failure is killing the people. They won't forget even if you do. I will not. Petronella of the Falcons. The Barren Queen, whose people starved."

He gave her a savage shake before he released her and kept his dark eyes on her as he tossed back the rest of her wine and handed her the empty glass. She took it with hands that shook at the humiliation. His dismissive gaze scoured her with his disdain.

"You always were the weak one. Fit for nothing but your precious books. I will break the curse of magic in this land," he said. "I will succeed where you have not."

She stood back, trembling, as he made his leave and slumped to her bed with relief, her head in her hands. The door banged shut behind him, and she willed herself to take deep breaths. The door opened once more, making her start, before Felice's rich, honey-warm scent announced her presence. She took the glass the woman held out to her. Felice took a seat beside her on the bed and patted her shoulder as the Heartsease tea took effect and her headache eased.

"Perhaps playing a trick on Arabella was not my best idea," she said, attempting a smile that wobbled at the edges.

The older woman sighed as she retrieved the goblet and stood.

"Arabella plays her own games, as you should know. Are you well?"

Petronella sighed. "As much as I will ever be." Chewing her lip, she smoothed the gown over her concave belly.

Felice noted her action. "We will know in four days."

"Four days. Then I must decide."

She gained her feet and accepted the comfort of Felice's sturdy arm through hers.

Arabella's head jerked up as they re-entered her antechamber.

"Is all well, my lady?" she asked politely enough, although her avid eyes belied the mildness of her tone.

"Yes, thank you for your concern."

Petronella gave her a secretive, aggravating smile and returned to the book she had retrieved from the library. If the volume held any secrets, she had not found them. The ancient ink faded to illegibility combined with the archaic text challenged her translation skills. Willow bark tea would be the least of her needs at this rate. She turned another page, struggling with the heaviness in her heart. The knowledge that the king could order her execution for dereliction of duty and that her own father would stand by and watch nagged at her, sending her pulse beating with fear.

Only four days to go before she would know whether this month's conjugal relations had borne fruit. And then... what? The sound of marching feet stopping at her chamber door. The forbidding faces and solid phalanx of axe and pike that would surely accompany the raiding party. Arion's grim face. The lifted sword. The block. Her ring falling from her lifeless finger and snatched from her blood. By whom? Arabella?

Mind clouding as her doubts grew, her hand shook as she turned another page. Keep reading. Hide the fear. There had to be a way out. There had to be.

Chapter Twelve

Four days had never passed as slowly, with no further knowledge gleaned. The ancient text had nothing to trumpet but good news and fruitful loins, an unbroken transfer of power down the eons of kings and their queens. Petronella noted grimly the familiar signs of her approaching courses. A tightening in her breasts, cramping in her womb and, sure enough, the dreaded, familiar sight of fresh blood staining her sheets when she woke in the morning.

She pulled her knees up to her chin and wept frightened tears into her bedclothes, and that was how Felice found her at dawn when she slipped in before the others to start her duties for the day.

"My lady," she whispered, approaching the bed, and casting a worried, furtive glance behind her. "We need more time. No-one must know of this yet."

Her matter-of-fact voice broke Petronella out of the well of distress she had fallen into since she awoke and discovered evidence of failure once again. Choking off another dry sob, she slid from the covers. Between them, they stripped the sheets, laying replacements from the chest at the foot of her bed. While Felice brought her the accessories, Petronella splashed icy water on her tear-swollen face, determined to brazen it out to the other ladies if she had to. Felice left the room with the stained sheets and laundered them herself, leaving them to dry in the airing room.

Arabella was in a particularly good mood when she eventually joined them.

"Pardon me, my lady, my children detained me in the nursery. It is their birthday today."

"Of course. And are they in good health?"

"Exceptionally strong." Arabella folded herself into her usual chair in a flurry of pale blue silk and reached for her embroidery hoop with a self-satisfied air that made Petronella want to slap her.

"I may have to return to our quarters later to join the birthday celebration. Would that be permissible?"

Petronella nodded. "Of course."

Arabella allowed her a small smile and settled over her work. In the corner, Petronella noticed Alice wilting over her lute. "Would you like to play for us, Alice?" She asked.

The girl lifted her head. Shadows clung beneath her eyes. It was clear she was the victim of sleepless nights waiting to hear from her father or to be dragged away by Arion's guard. Petronella's heart bled for her. They were in much the same situation, unwilling pawns in a game of kings. She crossed the room and took a seat beside Alice, her gaze steady.

"Is there no news, my lady?" Alice's lip trembled, and Petronella took one of her hands, warming it as best she could between her own. Outside, the rain still dripped out of a dismal sky, and a brisk wind sprang up, lifting the sodden banners that capped the battlements at the portcullis. The blue eagles flapped their futile wings in the wind, chained to their flag posts like The Grayling in the falconry. She avoided looking at his empty perch. The sight of it just added to her pain.

"I'm so sorry, Alice. Our forces left for the northern border of your kingdom."

Alice's tired gaze drifted out of the window to the south.

"I want to go home, my lady." Her voice was a fading whisper that Petronella could only just hear. "I have such terrible dreams. I want my father, but the crucible bears flames and iron, not water, and the streets of Sunira are running with blood."

Her voice had taken on a monotone. Petronella watched as Alice continued to talk. She didn't blink once. Petronella ceased to listen, watching the girl in the grips of her 'magic' sent pricks of apprehension across her shoulders. Witnessing what she called one of Alice's 'turns' felt like an invasion of her lady-in-waiting's privacy, never mind her fear for the girl's sanity.

"We will get you home, Alice." She whispered it to the girl, barely noticing as Arabella put down her embroidery and left the room. Alice turned to her suddenly, her face white, her eyes blank and staring.

"Did you see? Did you see it? Danger here," she said, digging her nails into Petronella's hands so hard that Petronella snatched them away, rubbing the crescent-shaped rings they left in her palms.

"Alice, wake up now. Come on." Her own voice was taut and high with fright.

Alice's eyes returned to the courtyard, unseeing, and remote as a statue.

"Felice, do we have any more of that potion?" Petronella called over her shoulder.

Felice grunted up from her favourite position by the fire to administer the potion, and Alice came to with a start, wiping perspiration from her face.

"There. You are back with us again now," Felice declared, returning the precious potion to her stores, and giving Alice a reassuring pat on the shoulder as she handed her a second concoction.

"I wish I didn't keep doing that," Alice grumbled. "It gives me dreadful headaches."

Petronella rolled her eyes. "It gives me the shivers," she declared. "Honestly, Alice, are you certain you don't remember what you see?"

Alice shook her blonde head, eyes fluttering closed as the calming potion took hold.

"Domita, help Alice to bed," Petronella commanded. "She needs to sleep."

Domita slid a powerful arm around her friend and helped her out, murmuring reassurance.

Felice stood up. "I'm going to see if those sheets are dry."

Petronella nodded her permission. Turning back to her desk, she made another concerted attack on the book as her only diversion. Her chambers were quiet, except for the tap of rain driven against the windows and the crackle of the fire. She took her seat and forced her tired eyes to focus. Tension gripped her shoulders as she sat. Waiting for marching feet, ears pricked like a hare hiding in the last patch of corn to be cut at the end of the harvest.

Chapter Thirteen

In the king's wing, Arabella, Countess of Wessendean took the stairs from the drying room in the laundry at a hasty trot, brushing past servants as she hurried along corridors punctuated by thick groups of gossiping courtiers and grumbling yeomen waiting for an audience with the king. Many of them scattered before her like dry leaves in a gale. Those slow to move caught a brutal shoulder in the ribs as she cut her way through the throng.

At the last door, she squared her shoulders and faced the king's guard with ruthless determination.

"Rupert. I demand to see the King. It is urgent."

Rupert, a towering block with a face of granite to match his brutal fists, and a sharp iron pike, stood his ground to the left of the entrance. He noted her tapping foot and the hands on her hips. He lowered his pike across the door in front of her.

"No-one in. King's orders."

"It will anger him that you are keeping me out. This is important." She hissed, refusing to back down.

Rupert stared into the space above her head. "No-one in. King's orders."

Arabella glared up at him, aware of the interest the altercation was attracting from the crowd behind her. "I will have your head for this."

The guard remained unimpressed. On the other side of the door, his fellow guard, Valence, examined his nails in an insulting display of indifference. "The King is engaged in court business."

Ready to argue, Arabella whirled to him, clenching her fists. She gasped as the door in question opened and Lady Violet blundered out, weeping, her thick blonde hair halfway down her back and her mulberry gown unlaced.

Arabella blinked after her but recovered quickly enough to duck into the room under the pikes and elbows of the surprised men. She slammed the door behind her with a vindictive smirk. So much for guards.

Crushing silence awaited her inside the king's personal office. She glanced around the empty room. A fire blazed in the grate, and there was the usual flagon of argent wine and two thick crystal goblets on his knife-pocked desk. Untidy piles of papers littered the surface, and a quill lay discarded on some sort of official document, dripping thick black ink across the surface. A chessboard waited in front of the fire, leaving a game half played.

A frown creasing her brow, Arabella glanced at the adjoining door. That one led to the king's own suite. His inner chamber. It was a place she had known well once, but now she was uncertain whether it was the best place to be when she shared her news. She stared at the door and jumped when it opened and the king marched in, fastening his shirt with quick, jerky motions of his fingers, his usually swarthy face parchment pale with rage.

Arabella swallowed and took a couple of quick steps backwards, dropping into a court curtsy before he could accuse her of invading his privacy.

"Sire."

Arion stopped before his desk and glared at her as he poured a glass of wine. Swirling it once around the goblet, he tilted his head back and drank half in two smooth swallows. Rubbing the back of his hand over his mouth, he replaced the glass and stared down at her in silence. Time stretched out, and Arabella remained where she was in deep obeisance, head lowered, waiting either for his command to stand or the cold stab of death as he flicked a casual knife in her direction. Coal shifted in the grate, seeming to break him out of his daze, and the deadly atmosphere in the room lightened a small degree.

"You may rise."

Arabella did as she was told, knees trembling with fear and exertion. Slowly, she dared to meet his steely gaze. He seated himself on the edge of his desk, picking up his dagger, and carved idle patterns into the ancient wood.

"You wished to see me?"

Arabella nodded, uncertain now how to begin. Words crowded behind her teeth, begging to be spoken.

"Well?"

She jumped at the snap in his tone. A warning sounded deep within her brain, but Arabella ignored it. She took a deep breath, catching hold of her skirts in case she had to either duck or flee.

"The Queen..."

That got his attention. His head jerked up, the entreaty in his dark eyes so marked Arabella almost regretted what she had to say next. She bowed her head.

"The Queen is not in a childbearing state."

Silence. Arabella waited, hardly daring to breathe. She glanced up at him under her lashes, trying to judge his mood. His jaw clenched, and his hand went to his brow. In grief or anger, it was hard to tell. When he spoke, his voice was as hard as nails. Ruthlessly under control. Each word bitten off and spat out like bitter pills.

"The woman who just left here tells me she is pregnant with my child. You have borne me two children. And my legally wedded wife is barren."

His cynical gaze met hers at last. "You are quick to run here with the sad news, Arabella. Do you have a solution in mind?"

He raised an eyebrow at her. Deep cynicism etched new lines onto his swarthy face.

Arabella swallowed, her mouth dry. Skirts rustling, she moved closer and looked up at him. He smelled of rich wine, cinnamon, and something else less pleasant, which she always ignored. Her hand raised of its own volition to hover in a place over his velvet-clad heart. She didn't dare to touch him.

"I could give you rightful children." Her harsh whisper dropped into the silence between them. Ready to skip away at any sudden movement, she searched his face for his true feelings. He stared down at her, his mouth a thin line, and gradually he smiled. She waited, suddenly breathless with anticipation, as he lowered his face. Anticipating a kiss, she closed her eyes, leaning closer, and jerked when his words came out in a hiss by her left ear.

"I have a fancy for much younger game. My next bride will be Alice. Princess of Cups."

She stumbled back, her hand going to her mouth. He smirked and raised his glass to her. A casual toast that did nothing for her shattered self-esteem. His sardonic gaze flicked over her, leaving raw anger behind.

"I thank you for your information. Go. Before I kill you."

Hand clutched to her trembling heart, face red with rage and embarrassment, Arabella left. She ignored the staring faces of the crowd and marched through them in much the same manner as she had entered, intent on finding Lord Falconridge.

Chapter Fourteen

With Alice asleep and Arabella absent, Petronella gave up on the book she had stolen from the library. Closing the cover with a petulant thud, she dropped it into the trunk and turned the key.

Domita glanced around at the noise. The girl stood sentry by the window, one hand on the velvet drapes, the other pressed against the small panes of rippled glass. Petronella grieved for her. Domita revelled in action and adventure, happiest hunting or helping with the horses. How she must hate being trapped in these rooms.

"Domita, Felice. I have something to tell you."

The urgency in her tone brought the others to her side, and Petronella gestured to them to take seats at the table where they usually took their meals. She chewed her lip as she seated herself, dreading what she had to say. A tense silence developed, punctuated by the crackle of the fire.

"My lady?" Domita exchanged a questioning glance with Felice, who shrugged.

Petronella reached across the table, and Domita extended her hands. Petronella kept her eyes on the freckled skin of her maid's strong fingers as she drew an unsteady breath, taking comfort in the warmth of the young woman's grip.

"The king has told me that my life is forfeit. My time is up. He needs my ring to crown the next queen and get an heir for the kingdom."

She winced as Domita's palms heated with the strength of her response.

"So, no prizes for guessing who thinks she is in line for the throne." The girl snatched an eating knife from its repose on the table and aimed it at Arabella's vacated stool, still scattered with the detritus of her needlework. The tip pierced Arabella's embroidery hoop and quivered there with as much outrage as Domita herself.

Felice nodded. "I thought as much. She has changed in recent weeks and, of course, she has already borne two children to him. She must think she has a chance."

The two women looked at Petronella, who met their gaze with sadness.

"I have decided."

Felice and Domita exchanged glances, and the atmosphere tightened like a noose.

Petronella took a deep breath. "I have decided to give up my life for the good of my country." Her words clattered like a bucket of stones onto the table between them.

Domita swallowed. Felice waited, her copper cheeks blanched.

"How do you know your death will result in a good outcome?" Domita asked into the tense silence.

Petronella sighed. "I don't, but I have failed to provide an heir, and the kingdom is dying. The penalty for my failure is death. My father will not lift a finger to prevent it."

"And the book told you nothing?"

They had grown used to the sight of the Queen pouring over the ancient script in recent days, burning through candle after candle.

Petronella shook her head. "There is nothing there. It is no help at all. Not once has this situation ever arisen." Her voice shook with frustration. "I was certain that the answer I was seeking would be in this book. Mistress Eglion must have thought so, too. Why would she direct me to it otherwise?"

She shoved herself away from the table and paced the room. Felice watched her, a heavy frown creasing her normally placid features.

"It can't be right." Felice said, twisting her hands together so that her golden rings glinted in the candlelight. "It doesn't sit well with me, my lady. There must be another answer. I've said this before, I know." Her dark eyes met Petronella's, trying to dissuade her.

Domita was silent, chewing her lip, her face thoughtful as she considered the problem. She glanced up, her eyes sparking with a new idea.

"I could get you out."

Petronella frowned at her. "There is no point. Arion needs to take a new wife, and soon. I cannot run away and leave my kingdom to starve."

Domita shrugged and shook her head. "I agree with Felice. I don't think this is right. You owe it to yourself to leave while you can. Create more time. Find some help, perhaps. Besides, I cannot believe Epera would benefit with Arabella as its queen, children or not."

Petronella stared out the window. Gloom shrouded the courtyard, the torches struggling to keep alight in the sodden atmosphere.

"I can get you out," Domita repeated. Eyes alight, she joined Petronella and took her hand. The warmth from her palm was comforting. "I have a friend in the stables. We can get you there, disguise you, and Dominic can escort you, at least out of the castle grounds."

"And go where?" Felice asked. "Who will she go to for help? Who would ever dare to shelter the Queen of Epera once word gets out she has forsaken her kingdom? Arion will put a price on her. His men will hunt her down at every turn."

"My father." Alice's soft voice made them all jump.

The three stared at the reed-slim form of Alice, who swayed where she stood, supporting herself against the wall. Dark shadows haunted her face, and her eyes were remote and far-seeing.

"The answers you seek are to the west. The Kingdom of Oceanis will take you in."

CHAPTER FIFTEEN

Later the same morning, Domita sauntered to the servant's stores and appropriated three plain, woollen cloaks and matching pairs of sturdy boots. She scurried through the rain to the stables and hid her booty in an old harness chest, throwing in a few candles and her own flint. Straightening from her task, she snared the gaze of Old Harold, the head coachman. Arms folded, a dark silhouette against the ever-grey sky, he stood in silence in the doorway of the coach house. A strong aroma of horse dung, tobacco, and gum disease drifted from him.

"And what do you be about, missy?" he enquired, shifting a wad of tobacco from one side of his mouth to the other as he cocked a grizzled brow at her from under his sodden hat. Water dripped from his hair onto the flags, and his eyes glinted, malicious silver slits in a nest of wrinkles. It was impossible to tell whether he was smiling. The silence stretched. Domita clenched her fists, feeling her palms warm as she conjured a defensive hidden flame, ready to throw it if she had to.

"I was searching for my lady's saddle blanket," she said. "She wishes to go a-hawking."

Old Harold raised a cynical eyebrow. "In this weather? There are grooms for that work. You wouldn't want to soil your hands and that pretty gown in this mucky yard." He nodded at her. "You take yourself off now, missy. Leave that to me and my lads down here."

Domita held her ground, affronted. In the hot southern land from which she came, she'd spent a lifetime in the stables, shoulder-to-shoulder with grooms of both sexes. No-one knew horses better. The flame she held grew hotter.

"I think you are forgetting to whom you are speaking," she said. "I am Lady Domita Lombard, of Battonia, Third Lady to the Queen of Epera. I carry out her wishes, not yours."

"Titles and such cut no ice with me," Old Harold replied. "So far as I'm concerned, I takes my orders from the king. You are in the king's yard, which makes it my yard, and I will have no one interfering with me work. Get you gone." He strode forward, his speed and agility belying what she knew was a great age.

Blood boiling, Domita took a defensive stance. She looked deep into the man's eyes and extended her palm. A small flame revolved in the centre of her hand, and she watched with satisfaction as his mouth fell open, displaying worn and blackened teeth. A sticky wad of half-chewed tobacco tumbled to the floor, and he took a wary step back.

"Fire Witch." It was a hoarse whisper.

Domita allowed him a spare smile. "If you don't want me to let go of this fire and torch the whole of your gods damned stables, you will leave me alone. My business here today is none of your concern. If I hear you have told anyone about seeing me here, I will come after you and light your tobacco whilst it is still in your mouth. Understand?" The flame grew stronger and made a darting lick at his face.

All sense of self-importance dissolved. Old Harold jammed his hat further onto his head and backed away.

"As you say, as you say," he muttered.

Keeping her in his line of sight as long as possible, he turned and made swift progress across the huge stable yard to his quarters. Domita relaxed and closed her fist to extinguish the fire, casting another wary eye around the harness room. Her full lips thinned. She had no illusions that the man would stay silent.

"Ha, well done, that was."

She jumped again as a skinny urchin crawled out of a space between two near-empty grain bins in a darkened corner. Light flashed from her hands once more and bounced off the vivid blue eyes of the boy as he gazed up at her in awe, swiping muddy hands down his ragged britches. A huge cobweb decorated his dirty blond hair.

"How'd you do that? Is it magic?" he demanded. "Show me how you do it."

Domita's mouth twitched.

"Hello, Dominic." She smiled down at him and closed her flame, hands on hips.

He grinned up at her. "It were a treat to see you do that to the old man. He'ms a scary one alright. Ne'er 'appy whatever ye do. 'Ave you got any grub?" His blue eyes swivelled to the harness trunk and back to her again.

Domita shook her head. "Sorry, Dominic, no food."

He heaved a sigh, narrow shoulders slumped. "We don't gets nothin'." He told her. "I had a crust last morn. I could eat these 'ere steeds. They has more'n we do."

Domita's mind was working overtime. She swept a practiced gaze over the boy. Something in his brash cockiness always reminded her of Nino, her younger brother.

"I might be able to get you some food. But I need you to help me do something really important. Without saying a word to a living soul. If you do, they would have you tortured and killed, and they would hang you on the castle walls and the crows would peck out your dead eyes."

Dominic's eyes, huge in his thin face, widened as he processed these grizzly ideas. "It might be worth it if I had some food." He grinned again. "Leastwise I'd go to me death with me belly not stickin' to me back bone. What do ye want me to do?"

Chapter Sixteen

Petronella glanced round, shoulders relaxing with relief as the door to her chambers swung open and Domita rushed in like a spring gale, bringing the scent of rain and stable with her.

"I've found our helper," she announced, shaking drops of water off her cloak and hanging it up to dry. "Also, Dupliss has posted soldiers everywhere." She lowered her voice and moved closer. Petronella nudged a mug of warmed spiced ale at her.

"How many guards?"

Domita grimaced as she raised the drink to her mouth. "Too many. We must do this quickly, my lady. I overheard Sargent Connington tell Bertram and Arnold to take first watch on your door. They will be here soon."

"I can deal with soldiers," Felice said, displaying a large bottle of the sleeping potion. "Pour this into a flagon of wine. Domita can offer it to them if it becomes necessary. She's good at flirting."

"We must be careful what we say in front of Arabella. I don't trust her," Petronella said, taking a small sip of ale and savouring the tang of warm apples and cinnamon over her tongue.

Alice glanced up from the settee at the fireplace where she had been nursing her drink, gazing into the flames.

"Where is Arabella?" She asked. "She's been gone since this morning."

"She went to attend her children's birthday celebrations." Petronella said, turning a page to discover an old map of Epera tucked inside.

She traced a finger across the ancient parchment. It would be useful up to where the border of Epera met Oceanis. There was a blank space after that. Someone had marked the paper with one simple word. Cups. They would need a guide.

"Arabella's children do not have a birthday today. 'Tis not for two more moons." Alice said.

The other women's heads snapped around. "What?" Petronella said.

They exchanged glances as the immediate implication of this struck home and scattered like startled mice into action. Petronella rolled up her map with shaking fingers, and Domita dumped the small bag of collected supplies into the trunk and pocketed the key. They raced to their accustomed places and were settling in position when Arabella's shrill tones lambasting the newly arrived guards met their alarmed ears.

"Let me in," Arabella demanded. "My duty is to the queen."

The male voices were a mumble as they exchanged views on this. The door flung open, and Arabella marched in, her usually pale face flushed.

"The cheek of the guards this morning," she said, executing a brief curtsy to Petronella and taking her place at her embroidery stand.

"More than usual?" Petronella asked, keeping her tone conversational. She glanced over a book at Arabella, who drew a needle case out of a pocket in her gown, selected one and threaded it with ruby silk.

"They must have doubled the guard when I was with my children."

"Ah, yes. I trust the celebrations passed as planned?"

"Excellently so. Guildford is happy with his new sword, and my daughter, Felicia, well pleased with her hound puppy."

Felice's eyebrows raised nearly to her hairline, and she buried her face in her mug of ale to hide her incredulity. Petronella's eyes narrowed, but she kept her expression civil.

"Indeed, those were generous gifts."

Arabella bent over her embroidery, and Petronella's mind raced in the ensuing silence as the women continued their tasks. She hardly dared to breathe. Guards outside her chamber door after weeks of no protection. Arabella lying about where she had been that morning. It must be both she and Alice were now considered hostages.

She glanced across at the girl as she sat in her accustomed place on the window seat. Her lute lay across her lap, and she caressed the ribbons bound around its neck with delicate fingers, weaving her hands through the silk in waves of blue and green. Her absent gaze scanned the dull sky as she hummed one of her folk tunes under her breath.

The rain eased off for once, and Petronella crossed to the casement, blinking almost in fear as the clouds parted like curtains in a playhouse and a dazzling ray of sunshine spilled golden light into the courtyard, turning every puddle and drop of water into a million liquid diamonds.

The few people who were working outside snatched off hoods and hats, delight and surprise showing in equal measure on pinched faces as they pointed at the sky.

Domita raced to the window, her brown eyes sparkling in the glare that bounced from the pale stone and turned the moss-clad walls emerald. The air sharpened to a crisp, clear blue, and the view towards World's Peak, the tallest mountain in Arcanis, snapped into sharp relief. A rising wind snapped the banners on the flagpoles to attention. Petronella drank in the sight with giddy delight. Her companions crowded the window. She creaked open the casement and a fresh breeze swept in, as exciting as the embrace of a new lover.

"Incredible," Felice said, her ample bosom swelling as she inhaled the crisp air. "Six months since we've seen the sun."

Alice continued to hum her absent tune, eyes still fixed on the view to the west, full of yearning for home. Domita leaned out of the window, bracing her arms against the stone sill. Petronella grabbed the back of her skirt in case she toppled out as she waved to a young boy in the courtyard. He flapped his hood at her, a grin splitting his grimy face. Other people, servants and nobility alike, spilled into grounds to claim their glimpse of sunshine.

Arabella crowded behind them and admired the view, raising her hand over Petronella's shoulder to draw her attention to the twists and turns of a flock of starlings. They had taken wing in the afternoon sun, and their graceful flight traced delicate, shifting patterns on the pure blue sky.

"Ouch," Alice blinked and dropped her instrument with a shiver of discord. "Arabella, you stabbed me." She rubbed her shoulder. Arabella frowned, startled.

"I'm so sorry. I still had my needle in my hand. Are you well?"

"Yes, no thanks to you." The princess picked up her lute and marched across the room, still rubbing her arm.

The women gave a collective groan as the clouds closed back in. Familiar gloom enclosed their quarters. Petronella's heart sank as she shut the casement. It was easy to forget such things as warmth and sunshine existed. The brief reminder underlined how important it was for the kingdom she bear a child and underlined just how much she had failed.

By mid-afternoon, their nerves had stretched thin.

The guard changed outside the door and Alice continued to rub her shoulder and cast dark glances across the room at Arabella who, having offered her apology and a glass of wine from her own store as a peace offering, now acted as though nothing had happened.

Petronella invented a task for Arabella to undertake, and she was quick to leave, arguing with the guards as she passed.

Petronella gathered the rest of her household in a circle around her at the window seat.

"We have to go tonight," she said in a whisper. "Directly after dinner. If we wait, we won't be able to sneak away now we have a guard."

"What if the guard escorts us to the hall and back to your chambers?" Felice said.

"We need some excuse to leave the meal, so they don't escort us."

They exchanged glances, seeking inspiration. Alice gave a whimper and clutched at her stomach.

"I feel sick," she whispered.

Petronella turned to her. The girl's face was pale as milk, her lips turning blue.

"By the gods!" Petronella steered her into the nearest chair, and Felice plumped down beside her, checking her eyes, her breath, her temperature. The princess groaned and bent over, gasping. They lurched away as she vomited pale red wine all over her blue skirt.

Felice's nose wrinkled at the stench. "This is poison," she said. "Why would anyone want to hurt Alice?"

Petronella's gaze landed on the goblet and flagon by the Princess's chair. She retrieved the items and gave them to Felice, who inhaled the aroma with a grimace of distaste. She nodded, her face hard.

"She drank little of it, thank all the gods. Domita, fetch me my satchel. Hurry. We may already be too late."

"When you come back, find Arabella." Petronella's voice held a ring of steel. "Bring her here. Do not take no for an answer."

Felice snatched the bag when it arrived, her normally deft fingers shaking as she sorted through the contents.

"What else do you need? What can I do?" Petronella waited for instructions and glanced at Domita, who stared, dumbstruck, at Alice's pale face.

"Domita. Find Arabella."

Her third lady jumped, clearly unwilling to leave. "Will she die?"

"We will look after her. Find me Arabella. Quick!"

Domita raced away to do her bidding, her mouth set in a thin and unwavering line.

Petronella stroked Alice's hair and bathed her twisted face as Felice scurried through the contents of her medicine pouch with anxious fingers.

"I can treat symptoms. Milk thistle and turmeric to cleanse the liver, dandelion for the kidneys," she muttered. "I need to know what she used. The bitch."

Shaking her head, Petronella watched helplessly as the old nurse flung herbs and spices into a pot of water and swung it over the fire to steep. Alice's colour worsened by the minute. Her eyes had shut, her breathing came in shallow pants as her arms clutched her belly against the writhing in her bowels.

"Don't let her go to sleep." Felice warned as she stirred, stopping every few seconds to test the strength of her potion. "Keep talking to her." Petronella leaned over her and murmured reassurance, Alice's breath hot against her face.

"This can only mean one thing," she said over her shoulder. Her fingers shook as pressed a damp cloth to bathe the feverish forehead. "Arabella wants Alice gone. So it looks as though her bid for my throne has been unsuccessful, and Arion wants Alice as his queen instead."

Felice poured her potion into a cup and diluted it with cool wine. Petronella helped her lift their patient into a more comfortable position.

"It certainly looks that way," the old nurse said, tilting the small bowl to Alice's dry lips.

Petronella gritted her teeth, biting down on her fury.

"I do not care what he does with me, but I will not let him unleash his cruelty on her. She must travel with us."

Alice gagged as the two women encouraged her to drink. Felice massaged her throat, helping her swallow.

"This will do nothing immediately. Where is Domita?"

"Here."

They glanced around as Domita entered, Arabella clamped close to her side, arm-in-arm. Rage paled the blonde woman's face. Her lips pinched shut, and her grey eyes promised murder.

Domita threw the woman into the nearest chair and leaned over like a lighthouse. She thrust her hand in front of Arabella's face. Her flame flickered like a beacon, turning her own brown eyes lamp red. She thrust her hand close enough to raise a flush on the older woman's marble skin. Arabella flinched away, scowling.

Petronella blanched at this most obvious use of magic in her presence, but her own anger ignited along with the flame in her maid's slim hand.

"You tell me what you've given to her, or I will happily burn your sallow old face down to the bone," Domita said. "And don't think anyone here will stop me."

"I've done nothing."

Arabella cut scornful eyes at Petronella, who stood and faced her with her blood thumping in her veins. Her tongue struggled to find words through the trembling in her body and the sudden pounding pain in her head.

"You traitorous bitch," she said. "You already have two children to the king, but now you want me and Alice killed so you can claim yourself a crown. What have you given her? Tell me."

Arabella stared at her; contempt twisted her features. Her eyes narrowed into slits against the flame. A stray strand from her elaborate hairstyle drifted into the space between her and Domita and sizzled alight, leaving a sickening stench behind.

"You. Useless Queen. Know-nothing and worthless. What makes you think I'm the only one who wants her gone?"

Petronella nodded at Domita, who moved her hand closer. Arabella hissed like a snake and huddled on the velvet couch to avoid the heat. Behind them, Felice waited, eyes narrowed, hands braced on her ample hips.

"Information. Bitch," Domita said, moving the fire in her palm in a slow circle around Arabella's face. The woman's grey eyes followed, pupils huge.

"Burn her." Petronella's rage had climbed to icy heights. She hardly recognised the iron command in her own voice. A wrench of pain sprung to life in her ring finger and arced like lightning into her skull. She grimaced, one hand going to her head as Domita's fire crept forward. Arabella gasped.

"Stop. I'll tell you."

Domita paused. They waited. Arabella writhed against the cushions. Her fragile skin reddened with sickening speed as the flame licked closer.

"Devil's breath and coltsfoot bane," she whispered.

Felice snapped into action as Alice moaned once more. Petronella stared at Arabella, hatred kindling within her like a brand on her soul.

"I want to know who else you are working with."

The woman's gaze locked on the flame dancing before her eyes, but she still managed a sneer.

"You would never believe me if I told you. Useless failure. You are anything but loved."

Petronella fought for patience as Alice writhed in her seat. Domita waited, flames ready, for further instruction. Making up her mind, Petronella shook her head.

"Domita, I want you to take Arabella somewhere extremely underpopulated. Shut her up. Lock her up. Tell no-one and come back here."

"Arabella," Petronella leaned over her former lady of the chamber, her jaw as stiff as granite. Each word she uttered shivered like shards of ice into the space between them. "No matter what you think of me, I am still the Queen of Epera. I command here, not you."

She nodded to Domita, who extinguished her flame and extended her hand. Arabella scowled and knocked the hand away. She levered herself from her seat and stood without aid.

"You understand Domita can kill you, do you not?"

"She's a witch. I know that much. Wait until I tell the king and your father you are harbouring a Fire Witch in your chambers. They will end her themselves."

Petronella allowed herself a small smile. "There is only one witch here, and her name is not Domita. I am also not entirely sure Arion wouldn't execute you for your part in this, so think yourself lucky I am not telling him." She stood back, clearing the way. "I do not want to see this person again," she said.

"My lady."

Domita marched Arabella out, exchanging pleasantries with the guards as they went. Petronella had to hope the heat in her body as they left, supposedly as friends, would keep a warning well behind Arabella's treacherous lips.

Satisfied Domita could contain Arabella, Petronella whirled back to where the first lady was administering medicine. Alice slumped against the cushions; her skin waxen in the wan light trickling through the window as the sun dropped. Felice crouched beside her, two fingers on the girl's pulse. A pale green trickle of potion dripped down her chin where the nurse had been forceful in her administration. Sweat drenched Alice's forehead as she panted out each breath. Felice heaved herself up from an ungainly crouch and surveyed her patient with worried, dark eyes.

"What do you think? Will she live?" Petronella asked, her voice a hoarse whisper.

"We will know in half an hour. Gods rot Arabella. I hope Domita throws her down the nearest well."

"If Alice lives, she will have to come with us. We have no choice now."

The older woman's eyes widened.

"My lady, I will not be going with you. Someone needs to stay here to give you time to leave."

Petronella's heart twisted. "No, you must come. How can I leave you here? We must all go."

Felice turned, her face set. Petronella grasped for her hands.

"I will not leave without you."

She scanned her old friend's face, looking for agreement, but found only sorrow.

"My lady, this is the only choice. I can say that you and the others are ill. They will trust me. By the time they find out you have gone, you will be away and can lose yourselves in the crowd. The soldiers will look for three nobles. People don't look twice at peasants."

"And when they find out you lied? "

Felice ploughed on, ignoring her. "I will also slow you down, my lady. I am not young, not fit, not slender. Also, my face is well-known in the city, especially in the markets where I buy herbs and medicines. I will lead them to you as sure as the sun rises in the sky."

"You will die." Petronella's voice rose, and unbidden tears stung her eyes. She shook her head. "I cannot let you do this. I will not let you sacrifice yourself for me."

Felice raised her greying head. The light caught the gold embroidery of her elaborate headdress and the warmth in her eyes. She took a deep breath as squeezed Petronella's icy hands. "I have led a blessed life, my lady. I have known love, plenty, and comfort. And I also know you must live. The Earth itself tells me this is so. Watch."

She let go and stepped back, smiling.

Petronella blinked, half hypnotised. The First Lady cupped her hands and opened both palms. A soft gold light surrounded her, a liquid, honey-like hue reminiscent of honeysuckle and roses and warm, rich soil. Petronella shook her head with the realisation that the expensive perfume Felice always wore was her living, magical essence. She breathed it in.

"Show me Petronella, Queen of Epera," Felice said.

A tiny tendril of green formed in Felice's hands. Mouth open, Petronella marvelled as the plant rooted itself between her fingers and grew. A slender shoot rose from its human bed and twisted upwards, seeking light. The stem thickened, the leaves broadened, and Petronella gasped in awe as a single flower blossomed and bloomed into a delicate glory of snow-white petals, tipped with azure blue. A shimmering aura flickered around it, like the glow of a candle or the ice shine around a full moon. It almost belonged to another world.

"How?"

Felice cradled the fragile bloom with such tender love in her expression, Petronella's heart clenched in her chest and tears pricked her eyes.

Her old nurse finally met her blurred gaze.

"This flower could not grow if you did not have a place in this world." She stepped forward and offered the bloom to her. "Take it," she said, when Petronella stared at her. "This is you. What you should be. What you should become."

Petronella took a nervous step away, her hands behind her back. "I can't take that. 'It's..."

"Magic," Felice said.

She waited. Petronella's chest contracted, torn between relief and dismay as the flower faded.

Felice relaxed her stance, her shoulders slumped. The glow surrounding her dimmed and died, and the flower turned to dust as she lowered her hands.

"I have offered, and you have refused," she said, almost to herself. "I can do no more. You must learn for yourself."

She gave Petronella a smile frayed at the edges and leaned once more over her patient.

Petronella blinked, speechless. Domita with her secret flames. Felice with her gift of earth and herbs. Her gaze wandered down to Alice, still tossing and turning on the couch. She wondered what ability the Princess had locked up inside her. Her troubled gaze drifted to her heavy ring, and she twisted the jewel on her finger. The Ring of Mercy. She'd scoured the book but found no reference to magic in the Kingdom of Epera. It made no sense. Why not?

"I don't understand, Felice. What happened? Does Epera have magic? What is it?"

Felice helped Alice to another few sips of potion. The girl murmured, twisting away from the sour liquid, and the nurse allowed the first glimmer of a smile for her charge.

"I have little knowledge of the magic of Epera, my lady. It has long been banished and denied in your land, but I believe this is your task. To find it once again. Perhaps in this way, you will aid yourself."

Bewildered, Petronella turned to the window. The sky dimmed as the hazy, unseen sun dipped below the western mountains, and she wrapped her arms around herself in the twilight darkness, leaning her aching head against the cool glass.

The rustle of Alice's gown as she twisted and turned and the conversation outside her door as the guards changed shift were the only sounds that punctuated the heavy silence of her chamber.

Downstairs, the servants would be preparing a meagre dinner. Locked in a distant and cobweb-filled room, Arabella would be angry and shivering. Domita would be swinging down the corridor, greeting courtiers and guards with her usual cheer. Arion would be servicing Lady Violet perhaps, or meeting with her father and plotting war with their neighbours. Or planning her death.

Her eyes pierced the window and travelled around the courtyard as the serfs lit the torches. Their flames sent ashy sparks to the sullen sky like messages to another world. Beyond the castle walls, tumbling down the steep mountainside, lay the mysterious factories and homes of the citizens of Blade. She would have to traverse those foreign streets, picking her way like a rat amongst rubbish, hugging the shadows. No longer a queen but a fugitive. She shivered as she closed the heavy curtains. Behind her, Alice gave a huge, shuddering sigh and sat up.

Chapter Seventeen

Feathers bobbing on helmeted heads, a contingent of king's guards escorted Petronella and Domita as they left the sanctuary of the queen's wing to attend the evening meal.

Felice had stayed to nurse Alice, who was making a gradual recovery. Lines of worry and sorrow creased the old nurse's face as she watched them prepare for supper. She seemed to have aged twenty years in one afternoon. She nodded gravely to Petronella as they parted company.

"Gods be with you, my lady."

Petronella carried the memory of her sombre expression down the endless corridors. Domita marched as steady as a soldier behind her, skirts rustling, a loyal and welcome presence.

The barrage of noise, colour and the combined tang of perfume and cooked food assaulted her senses as they entered the Great Hall, and the guards took their stations around the room. Knots of courtiers gathered in groups, exchanging idle gossip. Speculative gazes swept her body, looking for indications of pregnancy. They parted for her in a casual fashion as the herald announced her. A few of the most loyal sketched their bows and curtsies. Petronella nodded left and right as she approached the top table where husband and father waited, wondering which courtier hated her the most.

Dinner was no feast tonight. Servants were laying trenchers of black bread and some sort of stew at the lower tables. At the King's table, the offering was mutton, aged beef, and the bread was white and stale.

Bowls of pottage lined the board. The torchlight glinted off the silver dishes.

All her senses acutely aware, Petronella made an obeisance to the King and slid into her seat. Domita took a vacant place next to her. Arion jerked his head in acknowledgment of them and nodded to the company, who took their places and set about the food. Tankards lifted, and the conversation crept up a notch, but the atmosphere was more subdued than before.

Petronella made a valiant attempt at chewing her meat. Aware of their imminent departure, the details of which were still hazy, some sort of adequate meal was in order. Domita ate all presented to her and Petronella did her best to match her enthusiasm. The beef was chewy, covered in a spiced sauce to disguise its age. She forced it down with the help of large mouthfuls of rich Argentish. On her left, Arion devoured his meat and gestured to a page to refill his goblet.

"Where are the Princess Alice and your other ladies tonight, Madam?" he asked.

Petronella willed herself to remain calm while her heart thudded in her chest. "The Princess and the Countess are indisposed, my Lord," she answered. "Lady Felice is administering to their needs."

"Ah, what malady do they suffer that makes them miss their food?"

"A pigeon from the kitchens hung too long, I believe," Petronella said. "They are as sick as cats. 'Tis not a pleasant topic at a dinner table, but Lady Felice will do her best to make them well."

"Indeed, although the Countess of Wessendean did not appear ill to me when I conversed with her this morning."

Petronella frowned, toying with her meal. He was baiting her. "Neither did the Princess," she said. "They both succumbed this afternoon."

She glanced up at him from under her eyelashes. He scowled and returned to his plate, his gaze remote. "You will report their progress to me."

"Indeed." She inclined her head.

Dinner continued in stilted silence. She forced herself to eat, gaining a little energy in doing so. The court kept their heads down, taking their tone from the royal table.

Girdred's songs this evening featured lovelorn maidens and a sacrifice to a mystical dragon from some gods' forsaken island. The plaintive melodies matched her mood. Petronella noted Lady Violet had the grace not to meet her icy glare.

Her mind roamed, going over their plans for their escape. Felice had promised she would have Alice up and moving in time. The girl's face was ghastly green as they left. Luckily, she had been too weak to protest when the first lady took a pair of scissors to her glorious mane of honey-gold hair. Few peasants in Epera had the luxury of wearing their hair long for fear of vermin or lice. The same fate also awaited her when the time came.

Time dragged.

The court grew merrier, while the king grew sourer with each goblet of wine, and Petronella prayed for release. A slow trickle of nervous perspiration made its way between her breasts. Anything was better than sitting here pretending everything was normal. Beside her, Domita sat up, clapping both hands to her mouth. Petronella lurched sideways as Domita retched. Arion removed his brooding gaze from the bottom of his goblet and peered around.

"Another one?" he asked, one dark eyebrow rising.

"We beg your leave to retire, sire."

Petronella placed an arm around Domita, who surprised her by vomiting her meal over the table. Her neighbour, the young Earl of Wessendean, recoiled with disgust, his round cheeks paling.

"Papa, she is being sick all over me," he said, scraping his chair from the table and mopping his sky-blue sleeves on a napkin.

Arion glowered at them. "You may indeed retire, Madam. See her to her chamber. Poisoned pigeons. That is all we need."

He glared at the courtiers, who were craning their necks to see what was happening. "Anybody else eaten bad pigeon?"

The court buried their heads in the trenchers. Arion waved Petronella away.

"Out of my sight. You, page, clear that up."

The young servant bowed over the table, and Petronella made a hasty, undignified exit, with Domita still retching into her hands. The nobility stared after them, and a ripple of laughter and conversation floated in their wake like flotsam on a tide.

Once out of the Great Hall, Domita lifted her head and gave her a twisted grin.

"I'm sorry, my lady. 'It's not the poison, just a purgative. We couldn't tell you before, or it wouldn't have worked so well." She drew a kerchief out of her sleeve and used it to blot perspiration from her freckled brow and wipe her hands and face.

"My gods," Petronella breathed. "That you would dare be sick all over the king's table."

"I tried to wait until he was drunk enough not to send the guard with us. Quick now. We have to meet Felice."

The two women hastened down the corridors, the torchlight sending their shadows scurrying like rats ahead of them. The east wing was almost empty and colder than a tomb.

At the fourth door, down a deserted corridor on the second floor, Domita stopped and tapped a quiet tattoo. The door cracked open amid a subtle perfume of mothballs and dust, and her nurse poked a cautious head out.

"Quick, in here."

The small bedchamber was barely lit. A single bed hugged the white-washed wall; a narrow, many-paned window creaked in the wind. Alice, almost unrecognisable with her cropped hair and dressed in a serf's homespun tunic and hose, staggered to her feet from the straw mattress. Petronella steadied her and turned a worried frown to her nurse.

"Will she be well enough to travel?"

Felice set her mouth in a rare grim line. "She has little choice. Your turn."

She indicated a stool, and Petronella sat. Felice went to work on her headdress and her hair tumbled down her back to her waist.

"I'm sorry, my lady, but I must cut it."

Petronella shrugged. "'Tis only hair. Do it."

She waited as Felice plied her shears. Ebony locks cascaded to the floor to be swept up by Domita. She caught them as they fell, marvelling as the weight left her head. The icy breeze from the ill-fitting casement raised goose pimples on her newly bare neck.

"That will do." Her first lady put down the shears and fluffed the rest.

Petronella put her hand to her head. Vanity was requesting a mirror. Logic urged haste.

"The clothes?"

Domita helped her out of the costly court gown. Felice folded it up as small as she could and stashed it in a disused coffer covered with a dust sheet. Skin prickling with goosebumps in the freezing chamber, Petronella clambered into her new identity.

The hose made her legs itch, and the rough homespun tunic was huge. She pulled it in at the waist with a wide leather belt. Sturdy shoes weighed heavily on feet more used to velvet, and a thick woollen hood, serviceable and warm, replaced her delicate veil. Felice regarded her with a critical eye and handed her a pair of wool mittens.

"Keep the gloves on to hide your ring. You are serfs now, not nobles. If we meet anyone, I am in charge."

Domita collected the small sack of provisions they had accumulated and handed it to Petronella, who hoisted it over her shoulder.

"Names," Domita said. "We have to decide what to call you."

Petronella blinked. Changing her name had never occurred to her.

"I'll be Joan." Alice said, her voice soft in the shadows.

"Then I'll be Cecilia." Her new identity felt as alien to her as the moon.

Domita nodded, her brown eyes serious as she regarded them.

"I think they will pass. Hand me the scissors."

Felice passed the shears over and Domita shrugged her hair free of its normal coil. The russet mass cascaded over her shoulders like a wave of autumn bracken. Petronella grabbed the tool before she could cut it.

"No."

"What?"

"You are not coming with us."

Domita stared at her; the beginnings of a scowl pasted on her forehead.

"But of course I am. You need me."

Petronella faced her down. "Felice will need you more."

"My lady..." Felice began.

"No. I command it. Domita can protect you, and you can come to us in Oceanis. I will not leave you here alone and defenceless. You will need every advantage once they find Arabella."

Domita's eyes glittered with hurt and an undercurrent of simmering rage. Petronella clenched her fists, trying to keep her feelings under control. She could not give in to her headstrong maid of honour.

"Domita, I ask you to guard and protect Felice as you would myself. Please give me your word you will do so."

A myriad of warring emotions flickered across Domita's face. Petronella battled for equanimity. She could be condemning them both to a premature death, and the knowledge tore at her. Tears pricked her eyes, and she raised her chin, forcing them back.

She waited. The spiteful wind blew through the chamber, and their breath fogged in the damp air. Petronella continued to hold her maid's defiant gaze, willing her to comply.

Seconds ticked by like hours before Domita's shoulders slumped, and she bowed her head.

"Yea, madam. As you will."

Petronella shook her head at the remote, formal tone. She could almost feel Domita's fierce, resentful gaze boring holes in her back as they collected their meagre supplies and slipped into the corridor. Spirit sinking, she wondered if she had just lost a friend.

They had travelled half-way to the kitchens before meeting the first set of guards. Petronella's heart leaped in her chest. Alice let out a small, alarmed whimper.

Felice stepped in front of Petronella and grabbed her arm, while Domita did the same for the princess, earning a startled yelp from the girl.

Petronella winced. Felice's grip was talon-sharp, and she had to quell all her instincts to snap away. She turned her gaze to the floor and cringed. It was only partway an act. Chosen for their impressive northern height and build, the guards towered over the small group of women, a threatening, belligerent presence. A pungency of leather and sweat accompanied them.

"Where are you heading tonight?"

The guard asking the questions loomed closer, hand on sword. The plumes in his helmet waved in the dim light from the nearest torch, and his ale-soaked breath enveloped them as he closed the distance. Petronella lowered her eyes. She cowered away, casting her face further into the shadow of her hood.

"Do not interfere, man. I am on the Queen's duty. These two," Felice punctuated her words with a vicious shake, "have managed to half kill her ladies with their maggoty offerings, and I am on my way to the kitchens to see them chastised as they deserve."

"Is help needed? This one looks shifty to me."

The guard raised his hand toward Petronella's hood; whether to strike her or to take a better look, she couldn't be sure. Domita took a small step forward, ready to intervene.

"Leave these pestilent idiots be, you fool. Dare you step between the Queen and her justice?" Felice demanded, barging past.

The guard huffed a sarcastic laugh and stepped back. "Queen's justice?" He snorted. "First I've heard of it. What does that pale bitch do while we sweat and starve?"

"She ensures people get their just desserts when they pedal offal into her chambers. Unless you want her to speak with Lord Falconridge, get out of my way."

Felice elbowed him aside, and the guards parted around them, guffawing amongst themselves.

"They could have stuck something in her wine as well," one of them sneered at their departing backs. "Then the King could get an heir, and we wouldn't all be starving to death." Felice kept her back to the men and swept down the corridor.

Petronella stumbled along in a daze, her heart torn in two. Until this moment, the possibility her subjects might hate her had been an abstract concept. Wrapped up in her velvet and with heat in her rooms and food in her belly, she had been unaware of it for years. The lack of respect from the courtiers was normal now, but the knowledge their disregard was general, and travelled across and through the ranks of the populace, was dreadful and embarrassing in equal measure. Her cheeks burned.

Further down the corridor, Felice glanced around and caught sight of her stricken face. "No matter, my lady," she said, under her breath. "Pay no mind to them. They will eat their words when you return and make an heir."

They rounded a corner and started down a corkscrewing flight of stairs. Petronella pressed close against the wall, making room for another group of servants on their way up, carrying buckets of water and clean linen.

Felice marched them at dizzying speed through the kitchens. Petronella had a confused sensation of blasting heat from the two vast fireplaces hung with skinny offerings on spits turned by dispirited sprites dressed in rags. Serfs, cooks and scullions crowded the room, taking advantage of the warmth, if not the scraps, from the top table. Coal was in plentiful supply. It was food that was lacking.

Servants in disgrace being so commonplace an occurrence as to raise no eyebrows, no-one marked their progress. Felice propelled them at a near run across the soaking, puddle-strewn, wind-swept courtyard to the yeasty warmth of the stables. Alice kept up a tiny, continual moan of pain but offered no other word of protest. Domita said nothing, directing them to the furthest stable block and into the tack room.

Petronella blinked in the dim light, wiping water from her face and looking around her as she shivered. The candlelit windows of her own chambers glowed with warmth and comfort from here. A horse snorted nearby, making her jump. Their breath fogged the chill air, and the icy breeze crept under her sleeves to stroke her bare arms like the touch of Arion's knife. She shuddered. Out here or in there made no difference. Either way, her life was in permanent danger.

"Here." Domita opened the chest and tossed out two of the rough wool cloaks she had hidden earlier and two pairs of boots. "You will need these. Get them on quickly."

Petronella shrugged the folds of her cloak around her quivering body, grateful for the added warmth. Alice let Felice drape the warm cloth around her and clung to the older woman, shoulders shaking. A cart lumbered to a halt by the door. Heart in mouth, Petronella retreated to the darkest shadows, but Domita smiled as a young boy ducked inside. He fell to his knees, snatched off his grubby hood, and gawked at her in awed silence. His pale eyes shone like smoked crystal in a thin, grimy face.

"Here's your ride."

Petronella stared at the boy, hardly strong enough to lift a bale of straw, let alone escape a castle.

"You can stand," she said, with a spare smile. "Kneeling is rather giving the game away, don't you think?"

"Yes, Your Majesty." The boy scrambled to his feet.

"This is Dominic," Domita said. "He's going to take you away. Did you get it?" she asked, turning to the boy.

The lad nodded. "Everything like you said. Dead horse, maggots and rotting meat in a basket. It stinks."

Petronella recoiled. "What?"

Domita gave a short laugh. "It's not possible to ride out of here in the state carriage, my lady."

"So how?"

Domita gave her a grin.

"People rarely bother with the knacker's cart," she said. "Especially one as disgusting as this. "

Dominic caught sight of her appalled expression and gave her a nervous smile.

"It won't be that terrible, Your Majesty," he said. "The nag is only dead this morn. I got some rotten meat in a basket, an' I'll be nearer to it 'n you."

Petronella tried to quell her rising trepidation. The dreaded tramp of booted feet on cobblestones in the distance decided her.

"As you say," she said.

Turning, she snatched Felice to her in a crushing embrace. Her nurse returned the hug and then pushed her away.

"Go now," she said, her voice rough with unshed tears.

She met Domita's gaze but couldn't reach out to her. Domita nodded, her face sombre and determined, her arms wrapped around herself.

Struggling to avoid the alien body of the dead horse, the runaways clambered into the wagon bed. Dominic lowered a tarpaulin over them, leaving a small gap for air. Petronella closed her mouth as her stomach heaved, trying not to inhale. The stench of rotting meat filled the narrow space under the wagon cover with a life all its own. She tucked her head into her chest and breathed through the cloth of her cloak, filtering each lungful.

Beside her, Alice's body was overly warm, her breath coming in shallow gasps. Domita passed their slim supplies into the hollow remaining and stepped back. Petronella's last view of her ladies before the closing tarp plunged her into darkness was of their worried faces highlighted in the flickering glow of the rushlight. Domita grim. Felice trying to smile through her tears.

Blackness. A lurch as Dominic swung himself up into the driving seat and clicked his horse into action and the shake and roll of the cart as it lumbered over the courtyard to the portcullis and the guards.

Her world narrowed to the maggot-infested meat, the dim flicker of rush light as they passed under each torch, the shallow, gasping breath of the terrified girl next to her, who shook from head to toe. Rain pattered down on the tarpaulin.

"Ho."

The cart lumbered to a halt. Petronella curled up as still as possible, one stealthy hand reaching for Alice to comfort and to warn. Her own heartbeat faster than ever before. Every possibility flickered before her. Had their young driver done this run before? Was he friends with the guard? How well could he keep his head and his nerve?

"Name? Destination?" The guard's voice was hoarse and ended in a croak and a cough.

"It's me, Tim. Dominic."

The close darkness under the tarp lightened in a swoop as the guard's torch swept over it.

"Where you goin' this time o' night?"

"Down to Blade with this dead nag." Dominic's treble voice sounded a long way away. "It's a ripe 'n. Coachman wants it gone before it spreads the sickness."

Petronella held still as a corpse as the boy reached back and lifted the tarp enough to reveal the head of the horse, tongue lolling. She stifled a smile at the guard's involuntary reaction as the reek of rotting meat bloomed under his nose. Taking a lungful of fresher air, she willed herself still, small, and dark. The guard choked and stepped back.

"Garn. Get that loathsome thing out of here."

"Aye, Tim."

Dominic dropped the tarpaulin, and the cart moved off across the drawbridge and turned onto the rutted road leading down the steep and slippery hillside that led to the town of Blade.

Heart still beating faster than pistons, Petronella breathed a little more freely with every turn of the wheels. She longed to throw off the cloth and sit on the driver's seat with Dominic but made herself keep still. Alice was motionless beside her. She wondered whether the girl had fainted with fright.

Dominic's voice was hushed as they clattered further away from the castle.

"You alright, Your Maj?"

"So far, Dominic. What about you?"

He chuckled. "Worth it for the food, I reckon. That Domita, she stole me a whole roast chicken. And a pot of stew."

Surprised to feel hot tears scalding her cheeks, Petronella rolled her eyes in the darkness. Domita, she thought, picturing the events that would unfold like fate in the castle over the next few hours. I am so sorry.

Chapter Eighteen

The rain eased as the cart lumbered away from the palace. Petronella shivered and moved closer to Alice. Runnels of icy water from the edge of the tarpaulin splashed her cheeks, washing away her tears.

The steady clop of hooves on the slippery cobblestones, the occasional slide and dip as the horse fought for purchase and Dominic cursing under his breath as he guided them around the largest potholes were the only sounds punctuating the silence.

Despite the thin layer of straw, the warped planks of the cart dug holes into her narrow hips and the fetid air was making her feel distinctly sick.

Alice was so still it was impossible to know if she was alive or dead and Petronella dared not risk using her voice to ask a question. She fumbled for Alice's hand and gave it a squeeze. The princess returned the gesture, but her grip was weak. Petronella made a mental note to get a draft of Felice's potion down her as soon as they stopped.

Distant sounds filtered through the tarpaulin. The drumming thud of heavy machinery, a rhythmic counterpoint beat of hammers on metal, the rumble of cartwheels and the iron clop of hooves, and voices in the distance creeping closer. The chink of coin exchanging hands as Dominic dropped his toll into the outstretched hands of the Gate Wardens and they passed through without stopping into the capital city of Epera.

The nightlife of Blade pierced the tarpaulin.

They had entered through the North Gate and so far, were travelling in a straight line to the centre where the markets, merchants and bankers held court during the daytime. Voices were louder now.

Dominic steered the cart through the throng. The world was a jostle of metalled wheels clanging, horses snorting and harnesses jingling. The stench of mud and dung from the slick wet streets and smoke from the eternal chimneys crept in under the musty cover.

Shouting and swearing and the sound of raucous laughter billowed outwards in hop-scented waves from the taverns they passed. The noise echoed from the neighbouring buildings and rang down the cramped central thoroughfare.

Petronella longed to sit up and see it all.

Ten years previously, draped with flags and banners, Blade had basked in sunshine to greet her arrival. Her world had since shrunk to the relative luxury of the castle and the woods and fields surrounding it when the weather had allowed her to go a-hawking. Even these small freedoms had dwindled without her noticing, like a body boiling alive in a pot when the temperature creeps up so slowly it doesn't register.

She reached her hand out, touching the rough side of the cart through her glove, drinking in the sounds of the city. Of life.

Their progress slowed in a tangle of carts at the crossroads near the centre.

Even at night, Blade never slept. Its furnaces and factories continued to churn out manufactured goods for the continent of Arcanis.

They supplied arms and armour, pots and pans, knives and fence palings, bottles and glasses, coal and stone, copper, tin and iron ore. Tools, utensils, jewellery, and metal items too countless to mention made the bulk of the Eperan wealth from the bounty of the Iron Mountains that raised their peaks to the sky in the highlands behind the Castle of Air.

The cart made an abrupt turn right, then left, and the overwhelming clamour of the busy street dimmed a little.

Dominic drew the cart to a halt and reached a dirty hand back to pull the tarpaulin from their tired faces.

"It's alright, we can get out here," he said, hopping down from his perch and stamping his feet to get the blood circulating.

The weary horse put its head down and wheezed. Dominic gave him a pat and removed his harness enough to allow the beast to dip his head to the nearest water trough and drink, before skipping around to give the women a hand down.

Petronella rubbed life back into her limbs and turned to Alice. The girl's face appeared green in the wan glow percolating through the gloom from a single rushlight on the rough stone wall. Their combined breaths rose in the frosty air. Dominic had brought them to the courtyard of a tanner's yard. The reek of piss and stale beer met her outraged nostrils, and she started as a starved-looking feline appeared out of the gloom to rub around her ankles. Dominic bent down to stroke it.

"He likes you, I reckon. Come on." Picking up the cat and resting it over his shoulder, he retrieved his own small bag of belongings and led them over to the nearest door, set squat and solid against the gloom of the night.

"Where are we going?" Petronella asked, unwilling to enter a room with a potentially locked door.

"This is me home. I'm taking you to meet me ma and pa. We'll decide what to do next. Don't worry," he added, catching sight of Petronella's face, "they don't like the king."

Petronella nodded her acceptance and quirked an eyebrow at him.

"How do they feel about the queen?"

Dominic shrugged, avoiding her gaze.

"My folks feel right sorry for ye, locked up in the castle with 'im and not allowed out. And besides," he nodded at Alice, who was swaying on her feet, barely strong enough to stand. "That'n needs a rest. She's more for the knackers than the nag in't cart."

He banged his knuckles against the door and opened it, standing back to usher them in. Inside, dark stonework closed around her like a fist, squashing her down. Accustomed to the soaring ceilings and ornate fixtures of a much more privileged life, she gazed around, curious.

The door led straight into a well-swept room of grey stone. A small, banked hearth flanked by cooking implements and an oven set into the chimney breast gave out a welcome heat. A couple of stools stood before the fire, and a small table rested against the far wall. Bare and unadorned, only a hollow carved into a wood panel on the opposite side of the fireplace added a touch of decoration. A single candle lit the niche and shed flickering light on a symbol etched in the wood behind it. The figure resembled the number eight lying on its side.

Dominic dropped the cat to the floor, where it picked out the warmest spot on the faded hearth rug and washed its ears. He put the bag on a tall shelf. Bending to the fire, he added a couple of coals and jerked his head to them, self-conscious.

"This is where I grew up. It ain't much. I'll fetch me mam and pa."

He followed Petronella's perplexed stare to the rough wall. A rosy blush swept his boyish cheeks.

"We'm's traditional believers here, my lady. I hopes that is sound with thee."

Petronella frowned. It was the first symbol in the book from the library, and she had seen it many times as she turned its ancient pages, but it hadn't occurred to her to wonder what it meant. She crossed the room and traced her fingers over the indentation.

"I thought it was a decoration. Traditional believers? What does that mean?" she queried, trying not to cause offense.

"The sign of the Mage, my lady. The guardian of Epera. He looks after us all. Leastwise, that's what we likes to think,"

"Oh, I see." Petronella frowned as she peered at the symbol. It was familiar to her. It formed the decorative carving of doors and windows and lay embedded amongst the clouds and swords of the Throne Room floor. It even featured on the posts of her four-poster bed. Why had she never known what it represented before?

"Are there many believers like you?" she asked.

Dominic shrugged, shuffling his feet.

"The guards don't like it, ma'am. They take people who worship the Mage. They make them work in the mines all day and night. They took my uncle."

His voice rose in distress, and Petronella shushed him, fighting an unexpected maternal urge to hug the boy and soothe away his hurts. He wouldn't thank her for it, a child doing the job of a man.

"Dominic, whatever you believe, I am grateful for your service."

She stooped to him, encouraging the boy to meet her gaze.

"You have saved our lives tonight. I will not forget."

The boy gave her a small, shy smile and squirmed away through the narrow doorway into a further chamber. Petronella could hear the murmur of sleepy and surprised voices through the walls.

Turning to Alice, she urged the girl to sit near the fire. The princess slumped onto the rug with a groan. Dark shadows under her eyes told their own tale of exhaustion. Petronella reached for their small sack of belongings and frowned as her searching fingers encountered some unfamiliar objects. The blasted book, for one. *That will weigh us down*, she thought, hefting it to one side. She found the bottle Felice had included and poured a small amount into a clay bowl.

"Here, drink this."

Alice took the draft from her and drank.

"I'm sorry, my lady," she said, her voice a bare whisper. "I am not myself."

Petronella smiled and patted her hand.

"We are safe for now. No-one will look for us yet."

Alice took her turn to look around the room, running a finger around the bowl for the last of the potion. "I'm thirsty," she said.

"Yes, me too. We can get water from somewhere. Do you know what that sign is?"

She pointed at the carving. The princess gave it only a cursory glance.

"Oh yes, of course."

Petronella rolled her eyes.

"Why am I the only individual in the Kingdom who knows nothing about these things?" she said.

Alice summoned the strength needed for a small smile.

"They have kept that knowledge from you, my lady," she said, holding out her fingers to the fire. "Your husband and his father before him have been doing away with followers of the old beliefs for years. The king is terrified of the old magic. It is common knowledge at the Court of Waves and across Arcanis. I find it hard to believe no-one warned you."

"We have never spoken of it. In all my lessons growing up, my tutors never mentioned it."

Petronella reached for the old book and drew it across the floor.

"I found this book in the library, on the directions of Mistress Eglion. I had never seen it before, but look, on the first page."

She turned the volume and indicated the symbol at the beginning of the archaic text. The long-dead author had inked the sign in bold with a flourish of confidence. The girl shrugged.

"'Tis an ancient work, my lady. How many weeks since you last saw Mistress Eglion?"

Realisation was dawning.

"They think she is a believer and have taken her to the mines. She must have left this for me to find, but I can't think why. It is of no use at all. Nothing about the old ways, or magic, or what I must do to get a child. Just stories from the past."

"The scribes stripped the library of references to the old ways years ago, before you arrived in court. No-one mentions the old beliefs in the King's presence, nor his father's when he still lived. The servants say 'tis death to talk of it. My mother also told me never to discuss the old religion or use magic whilst I was here."

Petronella turned her gaze to the flames, resting her cheek on her rough, hose-clad knees.

"What would have caused them to turn away from the gods?" she asked.

"I don't know."

They jumped at a tentative rap of knuckles on the door from the inner chamber. Petronella scrambled to her feet, helping Alice up.

"Please don't knock on the doors of your own home," she said, managing a smile for the couple who lingered in the doorway, their son having dragged them out of bed.

Dominic prodded his reluctant parents into the room. He could have been driving cattle to market. The man was tall and spare, his once golden hair thinning and sprinkled with grey, peeked from under his much-patched night cap. Hands reddened with work hung like spades from thin, finely muscled arms. His wife crept forward under his arm, a tiny woman with a shy smile and the nervous air of a sparrow snatching crumbs from under the paws of a sleeping cat.

"My Ma and Pa," Dominic said, "Ellen and Mattias Skinner. Say something, Pa."

Master Skinner lowered his gaze to the boy. His crumpled face wore a complex mixture of affection and warning.

"Your Majesty," he began, "you are welcome in our home."

His voice was harsh as the croak of crows, bleached out over years of leaning over the noisome vats of piss and bark that made up his work.

Petronella shook her head. "We are more than grateful for your help, Master Skinner. You have a son to be proud of."

The tanner ruffled his boy's tousled head. "Aye, he's a rum 'n all right."

Dominic ducked away and reached for his satchel of goods.

"Look what I brought ye" he said, lowering the bag with care to the narrow table of crudely joined planks. He dug into the worn leather folds and levered out a wooden platter covered with a clean cloth and a sturdy pot.

"Supper," he said, whisking off the coverings like a street magician and displaying a huge roast chicken, a fresh loaf and a large serving of vegetable pottage to his bewildered parents. The two elders gasped. Petronella's mouth filled with saliva as the rich aroma met her quivering nostrils. Her stomach rumbled.

"Where did you get that? You never stole it, child?" His mother stared at the food as though it were a vision and might disappear in an instant.

"I never did. Tis a reward. What her lady," he nodded to Petronella, "gave me for seein' them safe away,"

Mister Skinner's frank blue eyes met her gaze.

"Then a finer feast we ne'er did see, Your Majesty," he said. "Come, let's eat. Mother, a pot, let's warm this stew. Dom, fetch water, and there's a jug of ale in the scullery. Stir up the fire. Quick now."

His family scurried to do his bidding, and, within a few minutes, the unlikely group were sitting at the table, scraping up gravy with hunks of bread torn from the loaf bound for the King's table that Domita must have stolen from the kitchen bakeries on her way to the stables.

The small chamber was lit by the glow of the fire, and a couple of rush lamps illuminated cheeks glistening with fat from the chicken skin. They talked as they chewed, discussing the situation. Petronella's habitually tight stomach relaxed enough for her to enjoy her meal for the first time in months. Door barred against intruders, belly full, she was rapidly succumbing to slumber. Alice, too, having eaten sparingly and taken some more potion, lolled in her seat at the table.

"Now, my lady, we can sleep out here by the fire and you may have our bed. Dom will sleep with us, or in the stable as he wills," Master Skinner said when the plates were empty. "The night is nearly over, in any case."

Petronella shook her head.

"We wouldn't dream of turning you out of your own bed. Alice and I will do perfectly well here by the fire. We will be on our way at first light. We have no desire to bring trouble to your door."

Master Skinner allowed a weary grin to pass over his worn features. He yawned and scrubbed both his hands over his face, dislodging his nightcap.

"I am owed a favour or two by the landlord at the Sign of the Falcon," he said. "We shall see what may be done. Dominic, your second task of the morning, after you have delivered that cart to the knackers, mind you bag the hide for us o' course, is to get word to the tavern we have a couple of hides ready for transport. Think you can do that?"

"Aye, Pa." Dominic's eyes sparkled in the firelight as he sketched a small bow to his queen. The food had brought a glow to his pale cheeks.

"You tell Domita she's a good 'n' kind lady, won't ya?" he said, covering a yawn with a greasy paw.

Petronella smiled at him again. "I will, as soon as I see her."

The boy hefted the bar from across the door and disappeared into the courtyard. The sound of the horse being unharnessed and led away met her ears, and she curled up in front of the fire with Alice, wrapping her cloak around her against the chill of the floor.

Placing the plank on the door again, the Skinners showed them a chamber pot placed discreetly in a corner, bade them a quiet night, and retreated to their small bedroom. The cat leapt onto the table and lapped up spills of gravy before curling up with Petronella. She drifted asleep in front of the fire with a contented purr vibrating through her chest.

Chapter Nineteen

"Find them!" Arion's roar of rage battered the ears of his father-in-law, Lord Falconridge, and forced Arabella backwards to the door of his study. She clutched the handle behind her, grey eyes dark with fear, as she exchanged glances with Darius, who stood his ground with his back to the fireplace, furs in place, bearded chin raised, ready to defend himself.

Arion turned on his father-in-law, clawing for his dagger with his uninjured hand as he lunged for the man, fury bursting from every pore.

"You let them go?"

Darius parried the flailing blade easily, knocking Arion's arm aside, and landed a blow on his injured hand that was enough to send a start of agony through his skull and drag him away from his anger.

"We were not to know the queen would take matters into her own hands," he said, eyes blazing with his own thinly disguised anger.

Arion glared at Arabella. "And you. You were supposed to report her movements to me. And now they are both gone. The queen and her intended replacement."

Arabella swallowed a gasp of terror as he strode towards her.

"I am sorry, sire. I thought her resigned to her fate."

Arion paced in a small circle, throwing his dagger onto the cluttered desk and reaching for wine instead.

"They can't have gone far. Send troops after them. Do whatever it takes. Find them. Get them back. Talk to De Winter. She'll know."

"And Domita." Arabella cut in.

Arion glared at her, daring her to open her mouth again. "You will mind your place, madam. You have failed me in more ways than you know."

Chastened, Arabella bowed her head. "Sire."

Arion jerked his head toward the door. "Get out of my sight. Both of you."

He waited, standing erect and unyielding as they bowed their way out. Door shut, he slumped to the floor in front of the fire, cradling his injured hand and stifled the scream of frustration and panic that clawed fingernails down his back.

She was gone. Out of his control. His ring dug agony into his hand, skewering deep to the bone. He hugged it to himself and took another slug of wine, waiting for the agony to pass along with the shock of betrayal and the heartache of loss.

Gone. She had left him. Deserted her kingdom. Failed him.

His jaw clenched. He would find her. And she would die.

Chapter Twenty

Petronella woke to find that Dominic had left in the sulky afterlight of dawn to alert the tavern keeper. Mistress Skinner followed him a short while later, basket over her arm as she set off for the market. Her husband bustled about his business, gifting them a grim smile. He nodded as he bent his height through the low door.

"Keep it shut, now. 'T'won't be long 'ere they'll be looking for 'ee."

It was nearing midday before a quick knock on the door and a word from the master of the house indicated the beginning of their journey. Dominic crowded in behind him, breathless from his run across town.

"They are expecting you at the tavern," the tanner said, "'t'is better you travel in the daytime. You will attract less attention in the crowd. Make yourselves known to Jacklyn Sommerton when you arrive. He's the innkeeper. He keeps a pleasant house, does Jack, but not everyone is favourable to our cause, so keep things quiet."

The two women nodded. Petronella's pulse raced. Part of her wished not to leave the cosy little house in the Tanner's Yard. Even the acrid scent of the vats was becoming familiar.

Mistress Skinner entered with her basket over her arm as he finished speaking, her eyes round with fear.

"There's a rumour flying around town that soldiers are coming down from the castle," she said, gripping her husband's elbow in her two tiny hands and looking at him with such trust and desperation, Petronella turned away, unable to bear it.

"We will have to leave now," she said. "Where is the tavern?"

"The sign of the Falcon. 'T'is on the Southern Way, up close to the city walls on the south side across from the Cryfell."

"I can go with 'em, Pa," Dominic said.

"You had better not," his father advised him. "Them soldiers know your face, and they know you should be up working in the castle, not down here escorting strangers about."

"But Pa, I can get them straight there."

"No, lad. You've done enough." Petronella cut in. She gripped his narrow shoulders. "Truly, we can get to the tavern by ourselves as long as we know the way."

The boy's mouth turned down. "I want to help ye."

"You already have, and I shall reward you for it."

She reached into her satchel of goods and took some coins from a leather pouch, handing them to Master Skinner. "Here. Use this to buy yourselves some more food, or for anything else you need."

The man stepped away, hands clasped behind his back.

"Nay, your ladyship. We're not taking your money. Though I thank ye for the thought. You need that to bide you by on your journey. 'T'is a way to the land of Oceanis. You'll maybe have to pay for food, rides and bribes and such."

Petronella took a breath. "You have my blessing for the kindness you have shown us," she said. "I am going to seek a reason and a cure for my childless state and to ensure the princess travels safely to her father. I have every intention of returning to do my duty to our kingdom. I will not forget your kindness today. You have my word as queen."

"I believe thee, my lady."

The man nodded his head, and his wife stepped forward, holding out her basket. "I found some things I thought might be useful, Your Majesty," she said.

The wicker container housed a twist of salt, a water skin sealed with wax, two sharp daggers with bone handles, a couple of flat loaves of bread and a spare hunk of cheese the tiny woman had probably had to fight for, judging by the disarray of her hood and a tear in her cloak that hadn't been apparent when she left.

"Mistress Skinner, we thank you."

The woman blushed. "'T'were little enough, my lady, for such as yourself."

There was an awkward pause. The time had come for departure.

"When you leave the courtyard," Master Skinner said, "turn right and head downhill. You'll want to go left at the sign of the Black Eagle. Don't go in, no matter what. It's the soldier's hostelry and a nest of informers and spies. Go through the market, cross the Cryfell at the Silver Bridge, and get yourselves on Southgate. The Falcon is the last tavern, hard by the city walls. Blend in. Don't speak unless you must. "Your accent gives you away."

He bowed. Petronella held out her hand for him to shake, but he raised it to his thin lips and kissed her ring through her dirty glove.

"The gods go with thee, my lady, and the Mage's blessings too. And you too, my dear," he added, turning to Alice, who gave him a smile that completely transformed her face, filled her eyes with sunshine and caused young Dominic to blush scarlet.

They tucked the daggers into their belts underneath their cloaks and placed the bread and cheese, carefully wrapped in a clean cloth, into their bag. Petronella levered the book out, regarding it doubtfully. It was bulky and, so far, held nothing of interest. She was about to drop it onto the table when Alice gave a slight gasp by her side.

"Better to keep it for now," the girl said.

Her stare was blank, her voice monotone. Petronella's heat sank. She'd been hoping the stress of palace life was the major cause of Alice's turns, but apparently not.

"Alice?" she probed, trying to be gentle. The girl snapped to.

"T'is alright, my lady," she assured her. "I know when they are coming now. It's a little easier to control. What did I say?"

"That I had better keep the book. Do I have to? It's heavy."

Alice quirked an eyebrow. "Do you trust the gods yet?"

"No." Petronella sighed and shoved it to the bottom of the sack with the rest of their provisions on top. She heaved the bag over her shoulder, where it rewarded her with a hard slap on the rump.

They took their leave of the Skinners and sloped away through the yard with their shoulders hunched. The working serfs paid them little heed. Attracted by the reek of bloody hides and the huge vats of urine and excrement dotting the space, flies buzzed in droves around their heads.

The two fugitives swatted them away as they passed under the archway leading to the courtyard and, as directed, turned right.

Although they had explicit instructions to blend in and be unnoticed, both women were hard-pressed not to raise their eyes and stare around them as they left the relative peace of the Tanner's quarter and joined the noisy throng in the city proper.

The streets were narrow and dirty, cramped by the clutter of manufactured goods that spilled from the narrow doorways of huddled shops. The women avoided barrels and crates, squinting in the gloom cast by the overhanging upper floors.

Refuse and mud crowded the gutters, and a noxious stench of rot and decay billowed upwards, released by their shuffling feet.

"'Ware b'low."

They skittered sideways to avoid the contents of a chamber pot tossed from a whore's window. Rats scurried between piles of rags and rubbish. Petronella swallowed bile as a grime-crusted street seller trod on a scaly tail and retrieved a squealing specimen from a mound of offal. Eyes darting, it wriggled in his grasp. A quick stamp of his boot and the man's dark eyes twinkled as he met their startled gazes.

"Agh. Supper," he said, baring teeth green with mould. He brandished his trophy at them.

"Tuppence?" he asked.

Alice retched and shrank away. "I hate rats."

The ratcatcher shrugged and dropped the limp corpse into a pocket hanging from his belt. His eyes narrowed. "Starve then, damn ye," he said.

"Come on." Petronella grabbed her elbow and urged her on.

Beggars aplenty huddled in doorways. A man playing a melody on a tin whistle was attracting a small crowd, and Petronella's sharp eyes caught the stealthy dip of a pickpocket's fingers as he circled the spectators like a lazy fly. His hands, light and darting as fish, dipped into unwary pockets, secreting fine linen handkerchiefs and a dagger before he drifted away. Forewarned, she dragged the heavy bag around her shoulders until it dangled in front of her. Cumbersome as it was, it contained everything they had of value, and to lose it now would be a disaster.

They continued along slimy streets, dodging their determined way through the crowd, keeping their heads down and hoping to pass unnoticed. Snatches of conversation drifted around them, punctuated by the constant crash of clanking machinery.

"There's bread at Numkin's stall."

"Nay, tis all gone. The ratter's caught some fine' uns this morn, tanner for three."

"There's King's soldiers on the way from the castle."

"Nah, that's a porker."

"'T'is true I tell thee. Queen's gone missing."

A snort of laughter.

"Done away with more like, and about time, too."

Petronella trembled away from the speakers, shoulders hunched, dodging around them into the narrow street. Alice caught her up as they rounded a bend and stopped, the human traffic flowing around them with curses abounding and bouncing around their ears like heavy blows.

The Tavern of the Black Eagle was huge. Standing proudly on a corner of the thoroughfare, the building dominated the entry to the market further down the way. It wrapped the street for sixty feet in two directions, with entrances giving onto both roads. Narrow windows abounded, paned with cross-hatched glass. Black half-timbering crawled up the walls and supported the upper chambers where a bevy of harlots hung from the casements, taking the air. Their breasts dangled, unclad and free to the chill breeze as they called to passers-by.

The sign of the Black Eagle swung from gold chains above both entrances. The doors opened to disgorge a small squad of the city's finest, well gone in drink and struggling with the laces of their tunics, reaching for their helmets and swords. A raucous chorus and the shrill sound of a piper bellied out around them, along with a cloud of pipe smoke and the reek of spilled ale.

"Orders," one of them shouted. "Kingz Orders. Odures. Somethin'."

He belched and lumbered into his fellows, who propped him up and scanned the street with bleary eyes.

"Where are they then? Them Castle Johnnies?" the drunk demanded, thick fingers fumbling as he tried to do up his buttons.

"Coming." This came from their captain, who exited behind them. He fastened the top button of his tunic with a business-like air. "Sort yourselves out."

The men grumbled but complied, fastening their laces and buckles and forming ranks of formidable blue serge. The crowd parted around them, keeping their eyes down. They carried the disease of authority and sharp swords. No-one was immune from attention.

Petronella nudged Alice. "Come on," she said. "We're better off well away from here." They backed away, heading for the marketplace.

In happier times, Blade Market had been a wonder of the manufacturing world. This was the place to come to if you sought the latest machinery and gadgetry, expensive jewellery from the most talented artisans in Arcanis, or fine and well-balanced swords and daggers.

Stalls stretched far down the street and spread out in the windswept city square. The tallest buildings Blade could boast hemmed the edges. Banks and civic services had their homes here. The Town Hall and Civic offices dominated the western side, the Merchants' Guild, the east. Here was the beating heart of Epera and the financial powerhouse of the kingdom. A formidable, splendid, self-important expanse of granite and grandeur.

Now, it was a shadow of its former self. Petronella halted at the entrance and gaped around.

"By the gods, how much it has changed," she whispered, hardly believing the evidence of her own eyes.

The first and last time she had seen this place was on her sixteenth birthday.

She remembered these counters piled high with goods and foodstuffs from across the continent. Cheeses, spicy sausages and salami from the Argent. Warm and smoky spices in barrels from Battonia. Fish from Oceanis, carefully packed in ice and straw and transported with haste by boat up the Cryfell and up the Fool's Road from the port of Goldfern. Beer and wine from the rich vineyards of the Argent even now supplied the Court of Skies.

Ten years ago, the authorities had draped it in the blues and greys of the House of the Falcon in honour of her arrival. Cheering people lined the streets. Joyous faces were lit with expectation. They held their children up to see her. Banged their pots, hammers, and swords together to make a Blade market welcome loud enough to reach the castle itself. Arion at her side, she'd trotted on a fine white mare at the head of a long train of attendants dressed in royal blue velvet and silver. Her reluctant, ringless hand trembled on his arm. A page in her house livery strode just behind, carrying her beloved Peregrine Falcon, symbol of her house. A betrothal gift from Arion. The Grayling, though hooded, had bated and stretched his wings, eager to fly. The sun beamed on the procession. She remembered her terrible fear at the speculation in the eager faces and the enormous responsibility that lay before her.

The banners and flags of that long ago day flapped only in her memory. A decade on, her reign a failure, tears stung her eyes at the desperation laid bare before her. It was a dispirited place now. Wary-eyed traders armed with cudgels surveyed the crowds from behind their depleted tables. Rubbish blew across the space like fluff under a deserted bed in the damp breeze. Shoving, quarrelling groups of people desperate for sustenance surrounded those stalls with anything for sale.

"Oh, Alice, how I have failed them."

Her gaze roamed the empty stalls. The market was a quarter of its former size. City guards shoved through the restless crowd, eyes and blades flashing. They at least appeared fed. Serfs cowered away from them. Hungry children cried, and servants with hollow eyes from the greater houses haunted the streets. The rotting stench of hanging bodies dangled a warning from the city gibbets on Castle Street and added a pungent twist of despair. The bread stalls stood locked, anything they had to sell, long gone.

By her side, Alice was silent, staring around with tears in her eyes. All around them, the life of the Blade went on. Hammers beat out their incessant tattoo on iron and steel. Bilious smoke still rose from innumerable chimneys, staining the stone and choking the air. Blade was still producing its weapons and manufactured goods, still trying to sell to its neighbours.

The vintners and the ale merchants were doing a brisk trade with the more well-to-do classes. The peasants, with little coin to buy, were making do with water from the city wells and fountains. In recent years, water was one commodity that suffered no shortage. The tiny amount of grain arriving was coming from the Argent. She knew from Arion the prices were sky high, but now Oceanis had declined to trade, this was the only source of ingredients for bread.

Looking at the empty faces, bereft of all hope and driven beyond endurance, Petronella's spirit shrank with matching despair. At that moment, Arion's obsessive desperation to provide for their people made utter sense. She peered at the sullen sky and then down at her barren belly.

"This is my fault," she murmured to herself. "They are dying because of me. I must do something." Her nails dug into her palms, her skin hot with self-hatred, her heart heavy with guilt.

They had lingered too long. Tramping feet behind and a quick shove to her shoulder sent her stumbling forward into the mire. She fell heavily, sprawling on her hands and knees, into an icy puddle that drenched her woollen hose. A loud laugh followed, and Petronella took her time gaining her feet, wiping sticky muck from her forehead.

"You're in the way, peasant. Move."

Petronella darted a quick glance at Alice, surrounded by a troop from the tavern they had just passed. Like every soldier in Epera, the men towered over her, lust in their eyes. As a group, they stank of old sweat and rancid ale. Petronella's heart sank. A quick glance around the vacated space in their immediate vicinity told her all she needed to know about the possibility of help from the citizens of Blade. Heart pounding, palms sweating under the heavy gloves, her fingers crept to her belt where the gifted dagger hid.

The princess dared to do nothing but stare at the ground with both fists clenched and the rumble of male comments grew louder. Unlike herself, Alice's body was a study in curves, and the soldiers were appreciating her in the crudest of language.

One man snaked out a lecherous hand to test the ripeness of her breast. Shaking with fear, Alice twisted away, wrapping her arms around herself in a vain attempt at protection. Petronella raised her gaze, and her voice snapped like a whip before she could stop herself.

"Leave her alone."

Her assailant took another glance, and his eyes widened.

"Oh ho," he said, "You're a girl as well. Wouldn't have thought it. Hey, lads," he called over his shoulder. "This is a comely 'un too. We could take 'em both."

Petronella's eyes narrowed. "I said, leave her alone."

"Ha, not a chance. Who do you think you are, eh?"

He reached a meaty fist forward and grabbed her arm, jerking her against him. Her hood fell backward, exposing her short black hair and delicate features. The man whooped, his embrace tightening. Petronella stopped thinking. The lessons Mistress Eglion had forced her to learn in her teenage years, practicing until her legs trembled and her hands dripped with sweat, were called into instant use. She had her dagger out in under a second and flicked it upwards, scoring a long gash up his thigh and stopping shy of his balls. Mistress Skinner knew a well-crafted knife when she found one. It went through her assailant's skin as easily as filleting a fish.

The man gave a hiss of pain and let her go, one hand going to the slash in his garments already freshening with dark red blood. She ducked under a blow from his other fist.

"I suggest you let me go," she said. "I'm handy with a blade."

He glared down at her. "You'll be coming with us. Assaulting the City Guard." His voice rose, alerting his mates, and his hand clamped down like an anvil on her shoulder, holding her away from him. He made to wrest the knife away from her with the other, but she twisted and slashed at his hands, skipping backward as he let go, swearing, and jammed his fingers in his mouth.

His companions left off tormenting Alice, and the group turned towards her with one accord, their mouths set in determined lines, fists clenched. There was an ominous sound of slithering steel as the injured giant, cursing obscenities, pulled his sword from its scabbard.

"Run."

She had the foresight not to use Alice's name in public. The girl stared at her in shock, then took off like a minnow into the market, darting through the crowd like quicksilver. Petronella followed a few steps behind, the bag cradled in her arms to hold it still.

Heavy, booted feet and shouts of alarm spread out behind them as the men gave chase, but a shout of warning went up off to the left as an abandoned stall lit the leaden sky with flames.

Petronella glanced back as the soldiers wheeled around, eyes sparking with alarm. A billow and stench of smoke drifted across the stalls, and the fire leapt easily to the next table and the next. People clamoured in panic, scrambling backwards. A few of the most enterprising took advantage of the confusion to snatch at the few goods left unattended in the chaos, and the guard turned their attention to dealing with the mayhem. Stifling a grin, Petronella sprinted after Alice. The ragged peasants parted for the two women as they dashed, breathless, through the market. Ranks of sullen citizenry closed around them with mule-like determination as they passed. Apparently, the peasantry had no love for the City Guard.

Reaching the edge of the market and realising no-one was chasing them, the two women collapsed against a vacant stall and gasped for breath. Alice stifled a hysterical giggle, clutching a stitch in her side. Petronella wiped the knife clean on her cloak and slid it back in her belt, scanning the crowd for any attention, but most people had deserted this end of the market to watch the City Guard do some proper work for a change.

"That was too close for comfort," she said, checking the bag to make sure everything was still the right way up.

"Yes, that's what I thought."

The ragged curtain of the stall against which they were leaning parted, and Domita appeared, a light flush staining her freckled cheeks from her run through the crowd. She leaned against the table and grinned at them, arms folded, although something in her expression bespoke her grief at leaving Felice behind and trepidation at her reception. Her glorious russet hair was gone, replaced by the hasty hacking of a less than expert barber. It was clear she had done the shearing herself, without the aid of a mirror, but nothing could dim the sparkle of adventure in her eyes.

"Domita," Alice started forward.

"By the gods, what are you doing here? Where is Felice?" Petronella demanded. Furious at Domita's disobedience, she planted her fists against her hips, though her treacherous heart lightened at the sight of the girl.

"She told me to come after you, my... Cecilia," Domita said. "And just as well I did, too." Brown eyes shining, she lifted her chin, and splayed her hands, stretching her fingers. "Best fun I've had for ages. Excellent work with the knife, though."

"But Domita, the King... What did you do with Arabella?"

Domita pushed herself away from the table.

"We'd better talk and walk. The King's Guard is out looking for you."

They set off for the river. Petronella kept glancing over her shoulder, sure they were being followed, but she could see no-one who stood out from the crowd.

"I had to let Arabella out," Domita explained in an undertone as they quickened their pace. "She had no water, and I couldn't leave her to die of thirst. I did it quietly when I thought she might be asleep to buy you more time. Felice told me to go straight after you. She said the worst the King would do was put her in prison. She is the King of Argentia's cousin. He won't want to kill her and risk the wrath of the Argent as well as Oceanis."

Petronella raised a sceptical eyebrow. "I hope you are right."

"So, of course, Arabella must have gone straight to the King. I heard the rumours around town as I arrived. They are not far behind us. Closer than I wanted. I don't know what happened to Felice. I hope she's safe."

"You should have stayed." Petronella hitched her satchel more firmly to her shoulder, her jaw clenched.

"Felice herself told me to follow you. She said you need me more than you think."

Petronella shook her head in resignation, and Domita grinned. Petronella risked a glance sideways. Domita winked and loped along beside her like a stubborn wolf, unrepentant.

They had to stop when they reached the river. The Cryfell started in the northern mountains and tumbled in a series of spectacular waterfalls down the mountainside. It provided water to the castle and turned the wheels of the many mills and factories lining its banks as it raced in shallow loops north to south through the city of Blade.

The icy waters sent their goods down to the waterfall port of Goldfern, where sweating dockworkers transferred them to wagons to continue their journey. The Oceanians had the arduous job of pushing against the water to make their trade journeys upstream. In recent years, as the rains continued and the roaring river grew in strength and width, Oceanis goods had arrived by road. It was less effort.

Counting houses, warehouses, jetties, and wharves built of wood crowded its banks next to waters that were continually rising. The City authorities had replaced them three times in the last seven years, since the rains started and the river grew, claiming more territory day by day.

The Cryfell was dangerous; a wild water, rich in fish. Trading vessels flying the Eperan banner bobbed at anchor against the jetties, but little commerce was taking place on the river or the road. Demand for Eperan goods may be high, but Petronella had now seen first-hand the state of the citizenry and she realised their production must have slowed, as Arion had stated.

In place of trade, soldiers and horses crowded the jetty downstream on the opposite side of the water. Black-clad soldiers and ragged serfs combined their efforts to hoist crates stacked to overload with weaponry and barrels of food aboard the waiting vessels. No wonder the civilian population was starving.

A boat cast off from the jetty as they stood there. Soldiers lined the decks, and the overladen craft put up its sail and tacked its way across the rolling current to the middle of the river, where the turbulent water ran deep, swift, and icy cold.

"They are travelling down the Cryfell to Goldfern. We must keep going," Petronella said, heading for the bridge that cast its graceful lines across the watercourse and divided the north of the city from the south.

Almost as old as Blade itself, Silver Bridge soared across the turbulent water in a smooth arch like the curved wing of a bird. It dominated the view downstream and acted as the major crossing point. The bridge had grown over the years, as the river spread its arms ever wider. Now, it was the home of the Silversmiths, and ornate buildings lined its single paved street with quarters that combined living space above and shops below.

The best and most imaginative artificers lived here, and their designs decorated their windows and drew the eye with colour. Earrings, torques, necklaces and bracelets, belts and buckles, pins for hair, hats, and cloaks. Pommels for swords and daggers, embossing for shields and harnesses. All jostled for attention and begged to be bought. There were more of the well-heeled here than anywhere else. Small, exclusive taverns and tailors dotted the bridge at intervals and catered to the wealthiest clients. Even the brothels on Silver Street were magnificent. Petronella raised a cynical eyebrow as she recognised the slim, neat figure of Count Dupliss as he stopped at the exit to the grandest of these to light his pipe. He inhaled with the air of a man with little on his mind. She stifled a smile as they hurried past, unnoticed.

CHAPTER TWENTY-ONE

Wealthy lords and ladies seeking passage away from Blade to their country estates crowded the straw strewn courtyard at the Sign of the Falcon. Serfs looked on with envious eyes as their masters and mistresses boarded carriages gilded with gold and coats of arms, deserting the beleaguered city before the food ran out. A well-bred scrum was taking place for the last seats on a departing coach. Its surly driver hunched in his seat, ready to roll, and took no part in the proceedings. Voices, fists and eventually swords clashed to decide the lucky occupants.

The grubby band of women dodged the melee and the puddles as they made their way to the main door, skirting trunks and bags piled up in drifts on the sodden pavements and guarded by servants who looked down their noses as they trudged past. In the portico flanking the main entrance, Petronella stopped and took a supporting breath, using the moment to scan the activity for anyone who looked more than ordinarily suspicious. She glanced at her companions. Domita's gaze was excited and alert, already in love with the adventure. Alice was hanging on with grim determination. Judging by the shadows that were creeping underneath her eyes and the dispirited droop of her narrow shoulders, it was clear that the sprint through the market and the long walk had taken her strength.

The door opened, and a wealthy couple shoved them aside as they emerged, turning up their collars against the biting breeze. A bellow of rich laughter followed in their wake. They had little choice now but to step over the threshold if they wished to avoid attention.

Taking a deep breath, Petronella squared her shoulders and entered. She immediately wished she hadn't.

This was clearly the wrong door.

As one, the carousing, velvet-clad inhabitants raised their heads from their slim meals and more generous tankards and sneered. Petronella's skin prickled with embarrassment as a wave of scarlet swept up her chest to her cheeks.

Dark northern oak panels lined the walls, and expensive wax candles provided the light. The patrons were enjoying the same meal that Domita had stolen for Dominic. It was a step down from what they would normally order in more prosperous times, but the appetising smell of roast meat that met her nostrils started her stomach rumbling.

One gentleman, clad in dark forest green and seated nearest the door, glared and flapped his hand at them as if he was shooing chickens across a farmyard.

"Be off with you, peasants. This room is not for the likes of you."

His iron-grey gaze was stony and uninterested, but not to be argued with. Petronella's eyes drifted to his jewel-encrusted sword. His hand hovered over it, the threat clear. Behind her, she felt the others back away and, against all her instincts, she lowered her head. She didn't have it in her to apologise. Gritting her teeth, she backed out of the door and joined the others in the portico. Domita was frowning, already scanning the building for an entrance more suited to their attire. Alice's ashen face crumpled as hot tears dripped down her face.

"I'm sorry, Alice," Petronella said.

Alice shook her head like an angry horse shrugging off flies and brushed a rough homespun sleeve across her damp cheeks. "'Tis nothing. I am tired, that's all."

"We might need to go around there."

Domita pointed at a smaller door huddled like an afterthought at the end of the long building, and they bundled their way towards it. Petronella passed a hand under Alice's elbow. The girl was wilting and in danger of collapse.

The door at this end of the building gave onto an unadorned great room. No decorations brightened these dark stone walls. A roaring fire in the grate was doubling as the kitchen here, and barrels of beer and cheap wine lined the walls behind the bar. Spills of gravy stained the bare board tables, and the floor needed a good sweep. A tattered serving wench was doubling duty both as a kitchen maid and tapstress. Her dark hair straggled in greasy tails down her sweating face from under her hood as she made her way to her next patron. A brace of tankards in one hand and a heavy wooden tray balanced against her thin bosom on the other, she hurried between the hungry customers. By the fire, a skeletal child of indeterminate sex chopped wilting vegetables and ladled them into a second pot.

The patrons at this end of the inn were of the middling to poor sort. They huddled around tables, exchanging gossip, eating and drinking as well as they could. Pipe smoke curled in a blue haze around anxious faces. Petronella cast her gaze around until she found a recently vacated table in the corner by the fireplace, and they seated themselves on the benches. Domita ordered ale from the wench on her way back from serving the last table.

The woman nodded and scurried off. Alice scrubbed her hands over her face and yawned.

Petronella avoided leaning elbows on the sticky boards and scanned the crowded room, searching for someone who could be the owner of the inn, this Jacklyn Sommerton. The present company comprised some more well-to-do serfs like themselves and a wealth of artisans, craftsmen and sales folk from all parts of Arcanis.

The room was heavy with tobacco smoke and the acrid smell of damp wool and old sweat. Eager spoons scraped wooden bowls of pottage. On the opposite wall, seated uneasily at a small table nearest the door, another group of strangers, subtly different from the rest, snared her attention. Neither artisan nor craftsmen, it was a group of four men, too large for the space they were occupying. Their cloaks were travel-stained but superior quality and made for heavy wear. Petronella noted the tooled leather on feet and hands. Each of them sported a long, finely made, expensive sword, but no jewels adorned the hilts. These were weapons of war, made for killing, not decoration. They wore no uniform, so they weren't soldiers. A subtle air of menace radiated from them. Skilled at judging faces and postures from all her years at court, Petronella could sense that they were outsiders here and that the patrons were as aware of them as a herd of deer stalked by hungry wolves. There was an empty border around them, a subtle space promising violence if crossed. Their faces were down at present, obviously in close conversation with each other.

She nudged Domita with her foot and indicated the group with a subtle glance. Domita's gaze flicked around the bar, ostensibly for the serving wench who was crossing the room, analysing the men in a split second.

"Smugglers?" she suggested in an undertone, "but their clothes are too fine."

One man glanced around. His thoughtful gaze clashed with her own. She was aware of a flash of aqua blue from a pair of penetrating eyes. Petronella dropped her head. It wouldn't do to be singled out now. Her forehead contracted with an unexpected stab of pain that struck her right between the eyes. She put up a hand and rubbed the spot, a frown on her face.

The serving woman wormed in-between them and put the tankards down. Petronella thanked her.

"Where can I find Jacklyn Sommerton?" she murmured, pulling a coin out of her pouch, and putting it in the woman's work-worn hand.

The woman's eyes widened as she glanced at the coin, and her sticky fingers convulsed around it. Petronella had no notion of how much three mugs of ale in a tavern cost, but it was probably much less than what she had just given over. The coin disappeared in the blink of an eye into the woman's tattered bodice. Perhaps she'd thought it a bribe.

"He'll be serving in the Oak Room. Are you wanting food? We've pottage and black bread."

"Yes, please. I need to speak to Master Sommerton. I'm a friend of Master Skinner."

These appeared to be the magic words. The girl's eyes sharpened. "I'll get a message to 'im."

Satisfied, Petronella sat back and took a welcome pull of ale. Accustomed to rich wine, it tasted thin and bland, but it slipped down her parched throat just the same, and for that she was grateful. The warmth of the fire penetrating her thick clothing made her long to push back her hood, but she dared not risk it. A low-grade headache dawned behind her eyes, and she massaged her forehead, stifling a yawn. She glanced at the serving maid, who was nudging her ragged assistant into action. The child disappeared like a rat through the back door, and the serving wench returned to them with steaming bowls of pottage on a tray.

They thanked her and dipped bread into the stew. There was no meat here, but the well-seasoned vegetables and potatoes filled their empty stomachs. Alice was the first to finish and put down her wooden spoon with a clatter.

"Better," she declared.

"I should think so. You hardly ate anything last night," Petronella remarked. "Domita, I have to thank you on behalf of Dominic and his family. The meal you stole for him was utterly delicious."

Domita chuckled. "It was the last chicken in the kitchen, and what he deserved. He's a character, that boy."

"He thinks you are good and kind. There. That's exactly what he asked me to say." Petronella smiled, glad that she had passed Dominic's words on so soon. Domita's answering grin eased her aching heart just a little. She hadn't realised how much she relied on her third lady's cheerful presence until it suddenly vanished, and with it the woman's trust and friendship. Apparently, Domita had forgiven her, and she could unpack that small, additional burden of guilt and lay it down.

They finished the meal, swiped their bread around the empty bowls and nursed their drinks. Other customers came and went, but the group of potential smugglers in the corner sat on, calling for more ale. Despite the food, her headache worsened. Petronella drummed her fingers on the table.

After what seemed like several hours, the back door opened and the owner of the inn strode in, rubbing his hands together. The serving wench nodded her untidy head at their group, and he advanced with a purposeful, limping stride that favoured his left leg. Dark eyes in a rumpled face that looked as if it had once been fuller. Long black hair tied in a haphazard fashion at the nape. Subdued, good quality clothing and a grubby white apron, marked with gravy stains, wrapped his narrow waist. He stopped at the table and nodded.

"You be looking for me?" he asked, in a voice that struggled not to shout.

"We were told to ask for you by Master Skinner. There are some hides to transport."

"I was told just the two."

"Change of plan. There are three. Is that a problem?"

"I don't like surprises and sudden changes. Makes me jumpy." He rubbed his chin, looking at the three women. "But I shouldn't think so. Come with me."

He preceded them out of the back door. Glancing back once into the main room, Petronella's gaze clashed with that of the same man who had glanced at her earlier. His hood shadowed his face, and she could see little of his features. The corner of his mouth raised in the slightest smile as he scanned her. She shuddered as the door closed behind them, her headache worsening with the rising tension in her shoulders. Something about him was familiar.

Jacklyn Sommerton led them through a maze of passages and then upstairs into a small room on the first floor. He closed the door as Petronella came through it and bolted it behind them.

"Now then," he said, crossing to the window and glancing out, "which one of you's the Queen?"

Petronella looked at Domita. She could see the fear in her eyes. Domita gave the smallest of shrugs. Petronella swallowed. "I am." She put back her hood. Sommerton's gaze widened as he took in the shorn hair.

"Well, I'll be blowed. Dominic said it was so, and so it be." He sketched her a bow and then lumbered to a stool. "If 'tis all right with thee, I'll sit awhile, lady," he said, easing a hand over his knee and rubbing it hard, through the fabric of his breeches. He caught Petronella's gaze and laughed. "'Tis all still there, my lady. But I took an arrow in my last battle, and part of the head is still in there. They say I'm lucky to still have the leg, but it hurts a bit. Not fit for the army anymore, so I put me savings to work instead."

They waited until he tested his leg again and stood up, leaning on the mantel over the small fireplace.

"Now then. I've got to get you out of here, Dominic tells me. And I'm hearing already that the King's Guard is here searching the city for ye. They'll likely start at the top and work down, but we need to move ye, and fast. We'll be getting you out on a boat down the Cryfell as far as The Fall at the port of Goldfern. That's the border 'atwixt the Swords and the Tides. It'll cost ye a fair bit. The Captain'll offload thee, but after that you'll be on your own. You'll have to find your way down through Goldfern and down to Oceanis by yourselves. There'll be no guide for ye and if they pick you up on this side, it'll be over, no question. The land down there has plenty of Swords soldiers. It's where they are hoping to cross into Oceanis since they can't go all the way there by boat. I'm guessing the captain'll drop you as close as he dares, but twill still be dangerous right enough." His tired gaze scanned their small group, and his trepidation showed clearly on his face. "Are you armed?"

Petronella indicated the blades she and Alice wore on their belts. Domita grinned. "They've got me." She splayed her hands, and the innkeeper's face softened as he watched the flames dance on her palms. "Aye, that's a welcome sight. Blessed by your gods, you are, lass," he said. "Was that you, settin' fire to the market this afternoon?"

"Fraid so. Sorry." Domita said, closing her fists. "I've got my bow as well. We're not completely defenceless."

Jacklyn heaved a sigh. "Right enough. I'll have to trust the gods'll look after ye. Even so, I'd be happier if you had a guide."

"Tis my land," Alice reminded him, her voice soft. "I know the way."

A sharp blow to the door made them all jump.

"They're here, Jack." A woman's voice, high with fright, hissed a warning through the planks.

Eyes narrowed, Jacklyn sprang into action. Shoving them aside, he heaved the door open and beckoned them through, limping before them down the corridor, one hand steadying himself against the rough wall. They descended a flight of stairs and Jacklyn herded them into a room on the ground floor, turning a heavy brass key to lock the sturdy door. Shouting voices, the overturn of tables and the ring of steel on steel told their own tale of mayhem taking place in the tavern. The tavern master's face was white under his beard as he heaved a heavy desk aside and bent to roll back the carpet. He shoved a couple of candles at Domita.

"You take these, lass, you're going to need 'em." Domita grasped his offering, and he bent to a section of the floor, running his fingers expertly across the oak planking. Brief pressure at a certain point led to a loud click, and a portion of the floor rose in front of them.

The three women exchanged glances.

"Get in."

The bellowing voices were moving closer. Down the corridor, a woman shrieked, a plunging note that ended in a moan. Petronella winced and Domita took the steep, narrow stairs in front of them, using her flame to light a candle.

"Come on," she hissed. "'Tis alright."

Petronella pushed Alice forward, and the girl joined Domita in the narrow space under the trapdoor.

She raised her troubled gaze to Jacklyn, who was white to the ears and attuned to every sound as the soldiers systematically ransacked his tavern. The anger and grief in his eyes as the smell of smoke took hold told its own story. He took her arm, pushing her to the passage.

"Go, my lady," he whispered, his voice taut with tension. "Follow the passage. It'll take thee to the waterfront. You need the captain of the Dove. Terrill Corn. He'll take thee downstream. Hurry now. Beware the rats. There's plenty down there."

"We are indebted to you," Petronella said, as his grip became more urgent. The sword fighting had reached the corridor. She wondered who was defending the inn. There was a thud and a groan as a body backed into the door.

"Gods be with thee." The door shook as it took a blow from a determined shoulder.

"Open up in the name of the King."

Chapter Twenty-Two

Jacklyn gave her a push and Petronella skidded down the narrow stairway as he closed the trapdoor over their heads, plunging them into darkness. They waited, breathless, as he dragged the carpet and heavy desk into position. The thump of a brawny fist on aged oak and footsteps overhead followed.

Jacklyn's muffled voice remonstrated with the soldiers, pleading his innocence as he limped to the door. Petronella waited, her pulse pounding.

"Let him go. Let him go." The thoughts screamed through her aching head. Derisive laughter, an agonised groan and another thud as a heavy body hit the floor over their heads. Her heart broke for the man.

At her side, Domita handed her a candle and urged her to move, her grip urgent and hot through her sleeve. Alice was whimpering under her breath. Soul torn, her eyes stinging, Petronella had little choice but to follow Domita's lead. The girl lit her own light and held it aloft.

Barrels stamped with the Argent mark, filled with potatoes, vegetables and wine, lined the corridor that led into the dark distance, narrowing the further it went from the inn.

Their shadows danced before them, and Domita lengthened her stride until they were jogging, clothes catching on dimly seen protrusions of rock on the damp walls. Scraping her elbows on the unforgiving stone, Petronella was soon panting to keep up, her heart knocking against her chest. She forced herself to keep breathing, struggling against the closeness and confinement of the narrow passage. She fixed her gaze on her candle and tried to ignore the dark. Alice was clutching a stitch in her side.

Behind them, the sounds of fighting dwindled until all that remained was the sound of their collective breath in the heavy, damp air. The tunnel sloped downwards. Water dripped stealthily over their heads and puddled at their feet. They passed entrances to other tunnels running off at wild angles on both sides. Their candles picked out the translucent glow of dark eyes and the tinny click of tiny claws, as barely seen companions rippled away from their light. The walls and floor grew wet with slime. Algae slicked their fingers. A faster pace was impossible.

"We must be under the river," Domita said. "At least they didn't follow."

"They'll be waiting at the wharf," Alice said as the ground levelled out and they picked up speed again. "They know that's where we are going. What is that noise? What's following us?"

"Rats. We'll deal with that when we must." Petronella stamped on the embers of guilt spreading through her as her mind returned to the sight of Jacklyn's gaunt face. She hoped the Skinners had avoided the atrocities undoubtedly taking place as the King's Guard tore Blade apart in their search.

Alice skidded to a halt.

"Rats?"

Petronella glanced around, irritated, as the girl spun in a circle with her candle. Furry bodies skittered away from her light.

"Alice, come on."

"I hate rats. I hate them." Her voice trembled with revulsion.

"Better get going again, yes?" Petronella stretched back a hand and gave the girl a sharp tug that broke her out of her terror. Alice gave a startled yelp and picked up her pace as a lone rodent leapt over her boot.

Under their anxious feet, the rock path gave way to scree mixed with sand and grew wider as they ascended on the southern bank of the Cryfell. The tunnel at the furthest range of their candlelight was still blacker than ink. Petronella shielded her flame from a stray draft, and they waited, pressed against the damp earth walls, trying to sense the surrounding conditions. The odd thump as something heavy dropped, the rumble of cartwheels and a blur of low-voiced conversation filtered to them, over their heads, muffled by distance. Petronella crept forward in the blackness, stealthy as a riverside rat, ready to dart back to shelter if she had to.

Her quiet passage led to a subterranean room with no exit. Claustrophobia jumped to claim her. She licked her dry lips as she held her candle higher, looking for the way out.

Domita crept up behind her, and together they shone their candles around the perimeter. Sandstone formed the walls. Their flickering lights illuminated an array of carefully stacked barrels and boxes. A warm and somehow comforting aroma of wine and cinnamon hung in the air. Rubbing her stomach, Alice sank down on a sack of pungent cloves and squinted around in the gloom, keeping an eye out for inquisitive intruders.

"This is a storeroom, but there's no door," Domita said.

A loud thud on the roof triggered a cascade of dust that drifted in the candlelight like golden snowflakes. Their heads jerked up. Dim light outlined a trapdoor half hidden in the shadows cast by the thick timbers supporting the ceiling above.

"We'd better go back to the tunnel," Domita whispered. "Anyone could be storing things in here or transporting them on to the Tavern."

Petronella shook her head. "The fire at the inn may have alerted them. If this is Jacklyn's black market supply chain, they won't be coming down here for a while. We'll have to wait until it's quiet and take our chances."

They jumped as another heavy object crashed down on the floor above their heads. A light cascade of tiny pebbles stung Petronella's face as she squinted at the source of the noise. Her tongue flicked out, tasting the dust that followed. She frowned.

"Grain," she said. "They are unloading sacks of illegal grain up there."

A tumult of squeaks grew in the darkness of the tunnel behind them. Alice sprang from her seat, scrambled onto it, and pulled her cloak around her with a squeal of fear as a wave of rodents washed into the room. They swept like a wave of dark water over Petronella's feet, darting and hurdling each other for the slim pickings on the floor.

Domita held her hands out in front of her, spiralling defensive flames as she urged Petronella behind her. The rats ignored her, more concerned with the impromptu supper fallen from above. More of them entered behind. They emitted a sour, sewer-like stench, their fur greasy. The rodents fell onto their meal. Once they had devoured every grain, they turned and eyed the human intruders with steady curiosity. A rippling river of tiny claws and teeth, eyes red in the flame light, they advanced.

Setting her jaw, Domita threw her fire forward, and the disgusting scent of scorched fur met their outraged nostrils as she drove the rodent army back to the entrance of the chamber.

Petronella gripped the bone handle of her knife as she eyed their pursuers from a perch she had taken up on a handy barrel. Alice was shaking, her hands trembling as she brought out her dagger.

Domita strode forward as she drove the rats back to the tunnel. They feared her flames. They backed away, leaving the incinerated bodies of their comrades as evidence of their retreat. Petronella used the intervening period to glance up at the trapdoor. All was quiet now.

Domita cursed as the lurid heat from her hands flickered and died. She retreated to the storeroom.

"What happened?" Alice's voice was thin with fright.

"My flames don't work for long without light." As she spoke, the army of rodents made a cautious foray in groups of ones and twos, passing Domita to infiltrate the beleaguered group of humans. The Princess stifled a panicked gasp.

"We've got to find a way out. Quick, Domita, help me stack up these boxes."

Petronella dropped to the floor, and they dragged crates and barrels together to form a ramshackle platform under the exit. Petronella grabbed for a handhold and climbed upwards, her determined gaze on the ceiling. She reached up and pressed her cheek to the damp wood, trying to concentrate on what lay on the other side, and heard only silence. Below her, Domita was holding out her hand to Alice, who scrambled up behind Petronella. The barrels rocked with the uneven load.

Petronella took a deep breath, braced both hands against the trapdoor and gave a small, preliminary push. It didn't budge. The furtive scurrying of hundreds of small bodies was growing louder. The rats were completely silent, but their malevolent, determined presence dominated the small space.

"You'd better hurry," Domita said, barely contained panic in her voice from her place on the floor. She kicked out, and there was a scuffle as she flipped an adventurous rat back into the pack with a flick of her foot.

Gritting her teeth, Petronella applied more pressure. The trapdoor moved a fraction, allowing another cascade of dust and spilled grain into the space. The rats swooped. Alice whimpered an indistinct distress call as she shuddered on the makeshift platform they had created.

"Do that again," Domita said. "It's distracting them."

Grunting, Petronella shoved once more. “It’s the sacks,” she said. “They’ve left one over the entrance. Alice. Can you go down? Let Domita up here.”

“I’m afraid of rats. Don’t make me, please.”

Petronella bit down on her tongue. “I need one of you to shove and hold the trapdoor long enough for me to slide a knife in and slit the sack of grain. Can you do that in your current condition?”

“No.”

Petronella had yet to hear a sulkier teenage voice. “So do what I say and start kicking if you want to survive,” she snapped.

Domita was still striking out with concentrated fury as she reached an arm up to the supremely reluctant Princess.

Petronella turned her attention once more to the underside of the trapdoor. Sliding out her slim dagger and balancing herself as best she could as the barrels teetered underneath her, she inserted the point in the narrow gap where a thin dust of chaff was still spilling on her upturned face. She blinked, eyes watering, forcing the weapon upwards. The blade met the resistance of the sack, and she pushed with all her strength. She grimaced as the knife slid home. It felt sickeningly like sinking a dagger into a human body. An increased cascade of chaff and grain rewarded her effort, but it was nowhere near enough to be effective.

Alice was down at the lowest level of the platform, gasping with fright with each feeble kick of her small, booted foot. The rats advanced in a steady stream, encouraged by the advent of more food. A scuffle, the barrels lurched, and Domita joined her at the top of the pile.

“They are climbing up me. They are in my hair,” Alice screamed, terrified. “Hurry!”

Petronella closed her ears to the girl’s panic. “I need you to push at this side. I’m going to slash the sack, and then I’ll help you hold the door open. Ready?”

"Always."

Domita climbed as far as she could and crouched under the trapdoor. Bracing herself with her legs as Alice screamed a warning below, she took a breath, bent her back and heaved with all her force.

The platform wobbled, and Petronella thrust her knife into the narrow gap. Grabbing the weapon with two desperate hands, she plunged it deep into the sack and ripped the blade towards her. The bag split, and the two choked on dry mouthfuls of raw wheat as it disgorged its contents in a steady waterfall of dust.

Down below, the rats went into a frenzy of feeding, leaping after the grain, tumbling off the platform and into the mess of bodies. Petronella added her weight to Domita's, forcing the trapdoor to remain ajar. Spitting, eyes half closed, she tried to ignore the wheat as it cascaded over her face, into her nose, up her sleeves and down her tunic. The two women gritted their teeth and held on as the load lightened and they could rock the door open. Dim daylight penetrated the gloom. Delighted rodents fought for their meal. Alice spat chaff from dry lips, her blue eyes sparkling in the dim light illuminating their brief internment.

Uncaring now what might lie on the other side and nearing the end of her strength, her muscles burning from the unaccustomed effort, Petronella stood and heaved the door all the way open. The board banged down, raising another cloud of dust as she hauled herself to the filthy floor of a derelict and deserted warehouse.

Balancing on the makeshift ladder, Domita reached a hand toward the traumatised princess. Pure terror propelled her eager flight through the exit. Domita boosted herself out, a grin splitting her dirty face as she let the trapdoor shut behind them. Petronella coughed, spitting dust, her eyes still streaming. Domita beat chaff from her clothes and gestured for Petronella to hand her their sack of supplies, still strung over her shoulder. Shaking out the remains of the canvas, she fashioned a makeshift bag, scooped some grain into it and knotted it closed.

"Can't waste good cereal," she said in answer to her companions' questioning stares. "You never know when it may come in handy."

Domita rummaged in the satchel for a skin of water and handed it to Alice. Petronella slunk to the gap in the wall serving as a window and squinted into the lowering afternoon.

Rain was slashing down, and the wharf was all but deserted. The last group of soldiers were taking ship, shoulders hunched against the deluge. The river raced like a tempest. Even as she watched, raging water boiled over the jetty, washing a couple of empty carts before it. Several boats tethered to the stone walls dotted the mooring and rose with the flood. Along the dock, looking upriver, a small knot of men standing ankle-deep in the deluge were scanning the rows of warehouses. Petronella's blood ran cold. Had the King's men found them already?

Domita joined her at the window and handed her the waterskin. Petronella took a greedy gulp. The water was tepid and slightly stale, but it helped wash the dust out of her throat. Both women gasped as river water rushed in under the door, soaking their boots.

"Time to leave," Petronella said, handing the container back to Domita and reaching for the bag.

"Alice?"

The Princess slumped on one of the remaining sacks of wheat, shivering with the remains of her fear. The water curled around her dainty feet. Petronella wasn't sure if she imagined it flicking out watery tongues of froth to stroke the girl's flesh. She shuddered, turning away.

"Alice. Come on, we must go."

They shoved the door open and sidled out, hugging the walls stretching away from the knot of men at the other end of the wharf. Rain swept down, driven by a rising gale.

Petronella winced as icy water soaked her feet. She hurried her pace, forcing her legs through the current, and scanned the names of the riverboats as they bobbed like tethered birds on their ropes. None boasted the name of the Dove. Drawing a blank downstream, Petronella glanced at her companions and then at the group of men still standing in the distance. They had no choice. If their promised transport was still here, it had to lie in the other direction. The water was up to her knees now and soaked her cloak. Her teeth were knocking together as the wind pierced her sodden garments.

Domita swore as the river rose another inch. Petronella glanced at Alice. The girl was gazing at the raging torrent like a long-lost lover, her blue eyes alight. Her eyes narrowed as the princess scooped her hands through the water. Far from trickling through her fingers, the water formed an almost solid bubble between her small palms. The girl tossed it from hand to hand, like a child's toy, and she raised the liquid globe to her ear, head cocked as if it was talking to her.

Petronella swallowed, her throat dry. She wondered at the extent of the young girl's power. Turning her back with an effort, her shoulder blades prickling with unease as her companion played, she set her sights on the boats upriver.

The river wanted to bowl them over.

Gritting her teeth, Petronella toiled upstream, bracing herself against the wooden buildings as the flood rushed in up to her thighs now. The men in the group had spotted them. Petronella's heart sank as their leader peeled off and strode towards them through the deluge. She reached for her dagger and glanced back at Domita, who was balling her fists, ready to let out her flames if required. Alice kept her head down. She was giggling under her breath, playing games with the icy waves as they swirled around her. She didn't appear to feel the cold at all.

Petronella's eyes widened as the man drew closer. He swept his hood back, and she gasped as she recognised him. The stranger from the tavern, whose piercing stare she had encountered before the raid, was the same man who had appeared as an emissary from King Merlon. He gave her the briefest of acknowledgments, the barest nod. His aquamarine eyes fixed on her youngest maid, still toying with the water and humming to herself.

"Alice, Princess of Cups," he said. His voice was determined. It wasn't a question.

The girl startled and the ball of water she had been playing with dissolved in her hands.

Petronella swept her knife up. Domita's flames roared into life behind her. She could feel its welcoming warmth on her back. The man ignored them, locking eyes with the princess.

He sketched a bow, his cloak swirling around his knees and clinging to his boots.

"Your father sent me for you. You know me." He held out his hand and gestured to the boat, now struggling in its bonds against the quay. "I am Lord Joran Weir. These are my men. One of them is Captain Terrill Corn, owner of the Dove. You have been looking for him."

Alice straightened, eyes narrowed. She scooped up a handful of water and held it easily in her palms, where it froze into an icicle aimed straight at his heart. The playful kitten had turned into a tiger. Claws bared.

"Show me my father's token as proof," she said.

Lord Weir inclined his head and took his hand from his sword. He extended his palm to her.

"By the High Priestess," he said.

Petronella blanched as a crescent moon tattooed on the flat of his hand blazed blue. Alice relaxed her stance and the ice crystals melted into the water once again. Domita doused her flames. Only Petronella still gripped her knife in shaking hands. The man cocked a sarcastic eyebrow at her and held his arm out to the young princess.

"Shall we go, Your Highness, before company arrives?"

He started forward, and Alice took a step. Behind them, Terrill Corn was gesticulating to his friends, who were guarding the gangplank. The Dove rocked on her line. A bird eager to be gone.

"Joran. They're coming!"

A shout from the tallest of his men standing on the gangplank, steadying it with one enormous foot as he squinted into the gloom. Petronella dragged her attention from the princess and turned to look at the road.

Swords drawn, the King's Guard marched in formation down the slippery street. Behind them, a rank of archers slung their bows, faces grim under their plumed helmets. Petronella's spirit quailed at the force they represented. A group of townspeople watched from the shelter of shop doorways, muttering amongst themselves, but none dared to come forward. The soldiers ploughed onward, their boots pounding through puddles that were expanding to floods. Water sloshed around their feet as they drew up at the edge of the river. The archers strung their bows and waited for the command to fire.

Joran grasped Alice's arm and pulled her to the boat.

"Princess, we must go. My orders are to take you to your father." Joran's tone was urgent.

"Not without the queen." Alice twisted in his grasp.

"We cannot take an enemy of Oceanis across our borders."

Spirits sinking, Petronella stared at the approaching cohort. She took a reluctant step towards the bank. "Go, Alice," she said.

Domita's heartfelt sigh beside her said more than words. The girl raised her hands, ready to send flames in their defence. Petronella stopped her with a hand on her arm. "No, Domita. Go with Alice. Keep her safe."

Domita shrugged her off, bracing her legs in the freezing water. She raised her arms again, her full lips a stubborn line. "You go, my lady. I will hold them off."

Joran's tone was implacable. "My orders..."

Chin raised, Petronella glared at Joran. "If your orders are so important, just know that Domita is not an enemy of Oceanis. Take them both. I will stay." The water swirled around her hips, tugging at her, urging her to the bank. Joran's eyes narrowed, and she jammed a hand to her forehead, stumbling to her knees in the flood as pain flooded her head. Alice's eyes widened, and she yanked her arm from Joran's iron grip.

"What are you doing? Leave her alone!"

Eyes closed against the crushing grip on her head, Petronella breathed more deeply as the pressure lifted. She staggered to her feet, stifling the urge to be sick. She raised her eyes to meet Joran's icy stare, but the pressure in her mind did not return.

On the bank, the archers raised their bows. On the gangplank, the tallest of the men notched his own weapon with casual ease.

"Stop, in the name of the King," the Captain of the King's Guard put all his parade-ground force into his voice, but still struggled to be heard over the roaring of the river.

Joran turned away, presenting her with a dismissive view of his broad back. "Princess. Come with me now." He took hold of Alice's arm again, more forcefully this time.

Alice shrugged him off, her chin raised in the defiant way she had when she wished to make a point. "You are leaving the Queen of Epera to die. Was that your order?"

"Aim." On the bank, the captain of the King's Guard gave his command, his voice drifting in the wind.

Joran's eyes snapped back to Alice, and then returned, almost reluctantly, to Petronella. Her forehead stabbed once, and she lifted her ring hand to rub it. Joran's gaze sharpened at her reaction and the battle taking place behind his eyes finally ended.

"As you wish, Princess."

"Fire!"

Brown eyes sparking with fury, Domita faced the onslaught and flung her arms to the sky. Her palms lit like beacons, and her flames raced out with a roar like a caged dragon to meet the avalanche of arrows. Petronella watched with her mouth open as the projectiles disintegrated to smoking ash against the sullen clouds. The archers on the bank watched, fear and anger written across their faces as they sent up another barrage. Domita, laughing like a demon, waved another casual cascade of fire to incinerate them. Cloak swirling, Alice bent to the river, ushering water towards her like a shepherd herding a flock of liquid sheep. She scooped her hands through it in the bank's direction and seconds later, a triumphant wave of water boiled up and out to the troop of men, rolling them like driftwood across the street. Alice lowered her hands with a smirk. The two young women watched the outcome of their joint power with their hands on their hips as the King's guard scattered in disarray. Alice giggled.

Joran rolled his eyes. His mouth twisting, he performed an exaggerated bow to Petronella, who scowled at him. Domita sent another arc of flame into the air for the hell of it.

Alice stood back, letting Petronella in front of her.

"After you, my lady," she said.

Chapter Twenty-Three

Petronella took a proffered hand and forced her weary legs to step onto the gangplank of the Dove.

The tallest of Joran's men, a rangy Northerner with a complicated runic tattoo running down the side of his left cheek, gave her a small bow, keeping one wary eye on the frantic activity taking place at the edge of the river.

Petronella stumbled aboard, fighting for balance as the man offered his hand to Alice. Domita scrambled up herself, wearing a grin like a fox. On the bank, the King's men picked themselves out of the shallows and wrung out their tunics, searching desperately in the clinging weeds for dropped weaponry. A lot of shouting was going on. Joran stifled a smile as he followed them aboard.

"Come on, let's get going before they re-group."

Terrill Corn, the 'boat master' as he styled himself, settled the fugitives in a rough shelter in the stern, which stank of rancid oil and ancient fish.

Petronella shivered in her wet clothes. Domita, warm as usual, was already steaming herself dry. Alice's face was alight with enthusiasm. She flung a hand into the open and played with the raindrops, waiting for the journey to start. The small craft rocked as the crew cast off. A shouted command from Terrill and the crew oared the boat into the raging current. Petronella's stomach lurched. Out of the rain, in the dim light of their crude shelter, she hugged herself, trying to stifle the shudders trembling her thin frame. Her warrior maid held out her hands.

"Here, put your hands over mine. I'll warm you."

Biting her lip, Petronella extended her arms. Domita smiled, nestling herself against the side of the lean-to and crossed her long legs. Her palms gave out a steady light. Petronella marvelled at the sensation as Domita's flames radiated life into her clammy hands.

"It's so strange," she said. "Like holding your hands over an actual fire."

Domita smirked. "We Battonians have our uses. If you take your cloak off, I can dry it for you."

The Dove moved out into the channel, and the men hauled the patched square sail aloft. A ferocious current took hold of them as the wind bellied the sail and the old boat swept downstream, bourne on the flood like a bird of prey, leaving the city of Blade and the distant shouting of the King's Guard behind. Petronella pressed the back of her head into the stained boards, eyebrows contracting at the sharp headache that had dawned once more. She swallowed against nausea, unsure if it was the rolling of the old craft, or a nervous reaction. Domita's hands continued to cast warmth, but it did little to stop her shoulders cramping with tension. She breathed a little easier as the last of the city settlements dwindled and kept her eyes on the distant hillsides and forests that claimed the landscape, still expecting to see soldiers, but here all was still and quiet. A wild solace of water and mountains and greenery populated with birds and fish.

Joran ducked in, his broad shoulders blocking the dim afternoon light. Unaccountably uncomfortable at his silhouette against the grey sky, Petronella made more room for him, pulling her feet under her. Domita extinguished her flames. He nodded barely.

"Are you well, princess?" he asked. His voice was rich and melodious.

Alice was sitting further back in the flimsy shelter, humming one of her melodies. Her gaze was remote, and she didn't respond to him. Raindrops chased each other in random patterns around her hands.

Petronella gazed up at him from under her hood.

He was tall, like her husband, but his hair, tangled back and tied with a length of slim leather, was honey brown. Seen up close, he possessed a firmly chiselled face, tanned with exposure to the elements. His eyes, whose piercing gaze she remembered from the tavern, were a peculiar mixture of green and blue. A wet, woollen cloak clung around him, outlining a trim and muscular physique. His legs were long, hard, and well-muscled. His boots were supple leather, soaking wet like everything around them, but he didn't appear to feel the cold.

Petronella shivered as drops of slimy water cascaded off his clothes and onto her face. If he realised it, he took no notice. Was it her, or did he give the cloak a brief twitch as he stood there, releasing more freezing water in her direction? Piqued, she backed off as much as she could. Domita chuckled under her breath as she scooted over, making room for Petronella to prop herself against the creaking timbers.

"Princess?" Joran's tone was more urgent.

Alice glanced up. Her shorn hair lay dark gold and otter-sleek against her head. Her eyes were as white and blank as river stones. Petronella gasped and shrank away. Joran cast her a disdainful look as he crouched next to the girl.

"Can you hear me?"

Alice's eerie gaze snapped to his and held. Petronella bit her lip as she fought for composure. She reached for her precious bag of goods and fumbled inside for the flask containing Felice's potion. She offered it to him, cursing herself for the hands that trembled with fear and cold.

"Here."

Again, that bright, disdainful stare. He glanced across at her holding the flagon.

"That won't be necessary, Your Highness." He gave her the title through gritted teeth.

Rebuffed, Petronella shoved the potion back in her bag and glared at the back of his head.

Joran reached for Alice's tiny hand, smoothing it between his much larger, rougher ones.

"Tell us what you see, princess," he whispered.

They lingered in expectant silence. The boat plunged along, propelled by the current and the skill of its captain and crew. Rain cascaded off the roof of the shelter. Outside, the afternoon was drawing in. Petronella ran a tongue over dry lips.

Joran waited with infinite patience as Alice's melody wound on in the dim day. Petronella was almost drifting off to sleep, soothed by the warmth of Domita's shoulder, when the girl gasped.

"Light and Dark," she said. Her gentle voice raised the hair on Petronella's neck. "So dark. Just the night and the cold. Always cold. He used what lies asleep beneath the stone heart of Epera."

"Who used it, princess?"

Alice lowered her head until it was in her lap. Her entire body shook. "They are coming. Coming in the darkness. Under. Under."

Petronella frowned. "She's talking nonsense again."

She stood up, dismayed at the way her legs were trembling, and shoved her way past Joran. He winced as she stumbled over him on the way out. Behind her, Alice was still muttering as she strode the length of the small craft. Her soft voice snaked after her, mocking her retreat.

"Francis knew. He did. He knew what there was. He told him where to look. Where to dig. And he made it. He made it all."

"What did he make?"

Another long pause. Petronella reached the rail at the bow and leaned on it, gazing into the mirk at the receding city, her knuckles white with tension. Alice's voice, when it came, was as cold and ancient as the Iron Mountains.

"The end of days," she said.

Petronella shivered at the words. She huddled in the folds of her damp cloak with her shoulders jammed to her ears and pulled the hood up, trying to ignore the trickle of unease Alice's nonsensical gabble had brought on. She could feel her heart beating its erratic rhythm, and her hand reached automatically for the satchel of supplies. Uncorking the bottle of Heartsease, she took a shallow swallow, thankful Felice had thought to include it. She replaced the flask and resumed her position, wiping her mouth on the back of her sleeve. The grey water writhed like serpents underneath them.

Alice's voice murmured on, but Petronella ceased to listen. They had left the outlying districts of Blade long behind. Petronella squinted at the countryside as they flew past. The river in spate was a mile across, and they shared the space with branches and logs torn out of the ground by the flood, all heading for Goldfern Falls. She hoped the captain knew exactly where they were. An unwelcome image of the lot of them being swept over the three-hundred-foot drop marking the border between Epera and Oceanis made the soles of her feet tingle.

She cast a look back over her shoulder at the small crew responsible for their rescue.

Terrill huddled at the rudder, his dark eyes slits against the rain as he steered their passage. The youngest of the group, a slim young man with the merest whisper of a beard on his chin, hung off the rail, keeping an eye out for obstacles. The other two men had abandoned the oars and hunched over a game of dice, tarpaulins making a makeshift cover as they smoked their pipes and conversed in quiet voices.

Joran backed out of the more permanent shelter at the stern, straightening his tall form and massaging the back of his neck, his face grim. Whatever nonsense Alice had garbled was obviously enough to cause him concern. More fool him for taking it seriously. Her chin lifted.

As though he sensed her wayward thought, his thoughtful gaze snared hers. One eyebrow slashed upwards in a quizzical expression that made roses of her cheeks. She turned away, facing forward again. Damn the man and his impudence.

He chuckled as he strode across the deck to his men. Folding her arms around herself, she made a hesitant way back to the crowded, makeshift cabin in the stern, determined to put him out of her mind. Domita grinned up at her. Alice had curled up with her head in her lap.

"She's better now. We have food left. Do you want some?"

Petronella slumped beside her and heaved the bag onto her knees. She unwrapped the remains of the food Mistress Skinner had given them that morning, carving hunks of it and handing them to Domita.

The bread was already stale, the cheese a rich, creamy variety from the Argent. The gods only knew what the Tanner's wife had had to go through to secure it for them. She devoured it in seconds and stared regretfully at the rest before wrapping it up again and leaving it for Alice. She settled against the boards. They had nothing to do but wait.

Rocked by the river, the two women dozed until a loud thunk, like a massive hammer blow, smacked against the hull. The boat dipped, and Petronella was shocked awake as her head cracked against the timbers. She clutched the side of the shelter for support and exchanged a panicked look with Domita. Outside, Terrill cursed young Fabian for a fool. The craft steadied, then listed to starboard. Another alarmed shout raised the hair on the back of her neck. Joran ducked his head back inside, taking in the small group with a glance.

"Trouble," he said. "We've hit a snag. Better get out on deck."

"Get the sail down, man the oars," Terrill shouted at the dice players, who were already rushing into action, scattering their tokens.

Gritting her teeth, Petronella scrambled to her feet. Domita nudged Alice awake. Her eyes were as clear as the ocean now, no worse for her excursion into her vision. She stood with youthful agility, joining Joran on the deck in the gathering gloom.

Uncertain, Petronella stayed where she was. Domita packed up their few belongings and slung her bow over her shoulder, her face grim. She handed Petronella her bag and eyed the water. Petronella's mouth thinned in sympathy. Fire and water would certainly not mix. She could almost read the woman's mind as the Battonian scanned the distance between the tilting boat and the scrubby bank off to port. With sinking dread, Petronella realised whilst Domita could shoot flames into the sky, take out a squirrel's eye at fifty paces and master the most recalcitrant of stallions, she did not know how to swim.

The Dove rocked again, and the women ducked to avoid the sail as it slumped to the deck. The Northerner and the younger boy had already taken their places at the oars, fighting to control the vessel in the terrible current. Joran's eyes met hers as he bent to join them.

"What are you waiting for? Bail."

She nodded and grabbed for a pair of wooden buckets. She shoved one at Alice, who gave her a look that told her she was an idiot, and leaned over the bilge where their small craft was taking on water at an alarming rate.

Her own bucket dangled uselessly in her fist as the princess lifted her hands over the icy green water lying in the boat and ushered it over the side. Her actions were calm and deliberate. The water obeyed her, but as fast as Alice bailed, more water flooded in.

Alice glanced up at her. "You'll have to help. I don't have as much control over this as you think. Not yet."

Petronella dropped to her knees and helped, her arms straining with the weight of the water and the wooden bucket as she heaved it up and over the side.

"By all the bloody gods on the Peak."

The further burst of swearing from Terrill from his position high on the stern, jolted her attention up. The man's eyes creased in concentration, muscles bulging under his tunic as he fought to hold on to the heavy rudder. At midships, Fabian and the Northerner strained at the oars to keep them steady and pointing forward. Petronella followed Terrill's stare and her heart hit her sopping boots. Another river craft was riding the centre of the current and closing fast. It was bigger than the battered old Dove by far and flew the King's colours. His eagle triumphant flapped black wings from the mast.

Grim-faced, Domita drew her bow, bracing herself somehow against timbers shaking with the weight of the water. Petronella swept her terrified gaze around the deck for something to block the leak in the ancient hull. Nothing useful came to mind. Terrill shouted a warning as he heaved on the rudder and swore as it caught on something else unseen in the deluge. The whine and creak of tortured wood turned his whiskered cheeks white with dread. He stumbled as the rudder split.

The boat spun, and the tiny crew strained with everything they had to keep the craft in a straight line. Petronella met Joran's eyes. His face was tight with concentration, his arms and back coiled with tension as he lent his strength to the oars. Terrill shoved himself to his feet and snatched for a bow.

Alice continued to bail with one hand and then caught her gaze, her eyes feral. Icy green water swept across the tilting deck as the Dove listed sideways. Petronella's feet skidded, and she grabbed the tarpaulin-covered shelter for balance. Domita, her eyes fixed on the pursuing boat, yelled and slid, one hand clinging to her bow. Petronella grabbed her other hand with numb fingers. Domita's hand was slick with water. She gritted her teeth and held on. Domita's boots skidded for purchase on the listing deck, and Petronella braced herself to support the girl's weight, aware of the wrench in her own shoulder. The black water of the river yawned behind her friend, waiting to swallow her. Domita gasped, her face a mask of terror as Petronella clung to her.

"Don't let go."

"I won't."

Alice glanced up at them and stopped bailing. Her small jaw clenched, and she gained her feet, bracing herself against the rail. Her blue-green eyes were wilder than the ocean as she made a wind-milling gesture with both arms.

Petronella's eyes widened as Alice gathered the surrounding river into a grim wall of iron-grey water thirty feet tall. Soldiers on the pursuing vessel gazed horror-struck, some standing stock still as the wave loomed over them, others diving overboard and swimming for their lives before the monster could break. Still others ran to the back of their vessel, pushing and shoving each other to get away. Alice grunted with effort, her face creased with anger, and the wall of water, crested with foam, grew. And grew.

"Alice, stop."

The wild thunder of the harnessed river drowned Petronella's frantic shout.

Sweat glistened on Alice's brow, and her eyebrows creased in concentration as she fought to control the spirit of the Cryfell. The Dove lurched, almost grounded, as the surrounding water gathered into a mountain and left them beached on a patch of weed strewn riverbed that had suddenly lost its purpose.

Domita screamed. Petronella glanced round. Terrill's small crew gazed at each other in desperation. The tall Northerner gaped at Alice and bent his knee to the tilted deck. He extended his palm towards the princess and bowed his head.

"'Tis the Goddess herself come amongst us," he said, swiping off his cap.

The youngest boy, Fabian, shook from head to foot, sparsely bearded chin quivering, eyes black with terror. Terrill still stood four-square at the helm, ready to rescue his boat if he could. His cheeks under his beard were completely white.

Joran stood, reaching out to the princess, his hands beseeching.

"Alice, don't."

The girl gave him a despairing look and shook her head, her slim arms shaking with the magical weight of the water they held. Then she faced the king's boat and *pushed*.

The wild wave slammed into the opposing craft with the force of an avalanche.

The men on board had no chance. The enraged water engulfed the boat with a boom of vengeful intent, swallowing it whole. Men, animals, goods, and weapons vanished in the blink of an eye along with the craft itself. The mast snapped like kindling, sails torn apart, decks smashed to splinters.

The rest of the river, no longer contained by Alice's magic, crashed in from both sides to fill the void she had created. Domita screamed again as the Dove rose on the crest of a dual wave and smacked back down with a crack that sent them all tumbling into the furious water.

Petronella had a fraction of a second to heave a breath and clamp her mouth closed as she pitched overboard. She fought the urge to gasp as the cold, unrelenting water filled her ears with a muffled roar. Her fingers scrabbled blindly for something to hold on to as she sank, weighed down by the weight of her woollen cloak. Frantic hands shook with effort as she worked the fastening free.

She risked opening her eyes and kicked her legs as hard as she could, chasing the air bubbles to the surface where she broached, gazing around her in panic as the doomed Dove tipped and disappeared beneath the waves.

The nearest bank seemed impossibly far away. A muffled shout to her left snapped her head around. She was in time to see young Fabian take a breath before he duck-dived into the darkness. There was no sign of Domita or Alice. Her heart sank as she took in the broken, floating body of one of the king's men, turning like flotsam in the flood.

A jolt in the back of her head stunned her, leaving flashes of white light across her vision. Spitting water, she paddled with legs like weeds. Her arms flailed for the bobbing branch that had crashed into her. She hooked an arm into a tangle of branches and leaves and after that. Nothing.

Chapter Twenty-Four

Cold. So cold.

The gritty imprint of tangled twigs and weeds dug furrows in Petronella's cheek. A reek of rotting vegetation filled her nostrils. The water sucked at her ankles, trying to pull her back into its sly, murderous embrace. She couldn't feel her toes. Her right hand lay twisted in a branch that moored her to the bank, and her body ached all over. She moved, and her shoulder screamed in pain. Her breath came in shallow gasps, barely raising her chest. Lifting her aching head, she squinted at the riverbank. Rain-sodden trees crowded together over her head and blocked the filthy grey light of the waning afternoon.

Uncaring, the river roared on its way to Goldfern Falls. Behind her, the forest was dark and silent. Her head dropped to her bloodless arms. She was alive. Alone. Half drowned.

Her heart shuddered as she remembered Domita and her white, terrified face before the impact cast her like a stone into the river. A small, unbidden portion of her soul recalled Alice's wild gaze as she raised her hands. The implacable, deadly force she unleashed that had wreaked such havoc without consideration for the consequences. Magic. This was what magic could do. It could kill people. It was dangerous. Arion was right to stamp it out. Losing strength, she slumped back into the mud.

It took an act of will to raise her head again. A rising wind glued her soaking tunic to her body, and she gritted her teeth against the desire to put her head down and sleep, never to wake again.

Grimacing, she stifled sobs as she untangled her sleeve from the branch holding her and commanded her body to move. She made it to her elbows, arms shaking, and waited for the world to stop twisting in circles around her. The pain in her shoulder eased as she moved her arm to a more natural position. A pulse of pressure in time with the heartbeat thumping in her left temple reminded her of the blow to her head that had knocked her out. Concussion. The thought had barely crossed her brain before her body convulsed like a landed fish, and she threw up a lungful of river.

Eyes streaming, her breathing eased as the dirty water cleared her lungs and Petronella struggled to her knees. She used the log to pull herself to her feet and staggered as her hide boots sank in the mud. Blinking waterweed from her eyes, she squinted around.

The Dove and its crew had vanished. The river raced on, unheeding, as she scanned the banks, desperate for a sight of her friends. A rotting jetty, clothed in weed, hugged the loop of the bank. A single abandoned rowboat, scabbed with fading blue paint, bobbed at its mooring. Stagnant water pooled the reeds in scum. The mud reeked of rotting fish and vegetation. Trees crowded the banks, their branches dipped in mud. Birds cried harshly from the forests. She had no way of knowing how far the current had carried her or where it had belched her out. A scudding breeze cut through her, chilling her to the marrow as she rocked with fatigue, trying to gather her scattered senses. She scanned the swirling waves one last time before a piercing wind sliced through her sodden garments to alert her to her situation. She would have to leave the exposed riverbank and find shelter, at least.

Shuddering with cold, she stumbled into the gloom, tripping on brambles unseen in the darkness. The forest closed around her. She slithered and slid on the ever-present mud, her head pounding on every step. Far enough away that the voice of the river faded to a hushed whisper, she checked its direction as it hurtled onwards to the south. Darkness was falling as she turned right and followed its course downstream to Goldfern. It was the only destination she could think of.

The wan light from the distant sun had dropped below the horizon when Petronella's last strength gave out. Slipping once again in the darkness, the weight of the satchel she still somehow carried over her shoulder was enough to drag her over, and she rolled like a felled log downhill.

She smothered a scream as her body pounded over rough terrain. Something in her bag broke with an audible snap. Her arms flailed, trying to protect her head from further damage. She crashed through bushes and dead leaves and eventually fetched up in a muddy heap at the base of a ravine.

Gasping for breath, Petronella waited once more for the world to come to rights around her. Grasping a hand around her middle where a new dull ache bloomed, she stumbled to her feet and peered through the mirk with wild eyes. Trees crowded her in every direction, blocking out the grey twilight. Rotting leaves shifted under her feet. A branch snapped under her foot.

Somewhere in the darkness between the trees, something was watching her. Waiting.

All her senses on red alert, her hand locked on the small dagger still strapped securely at her waist, and she backed up, shivering, against the nearest tree. Wolves made their homes in these forests. Wild boar. Bears. The trunk at her back comforted her by a small degree, and she glanced up, wondering if she had the strength to climb, but the closest branch was ten feet above her head.

Leaves swished to her left as she stood with her shoulders crushed against the bark, her eyes struggling to pierce the gloom. She sniffed. A familiar warm, smoky scent crept up her nose. One she hadn't experienced for months. Pipe smoke. The smell tickled her nostrils, invoking memories of days spent in study and sunshine. Of a worn wooden desk and acres of parchment. Of books and ink and quills and a pair of icy blue eyes swathed in wrinkles and long white hair. She half gasped a name, spilling it out into the chilly night air, and clamped her hand over her mouth. Mistress Eglion, tutor, librarian, and scholar, was surely not the only person in Epera who favoured Argent Gold in her pipe.

The stench of rotting vegetation grew as the stranger moved closer, disturbing the long untrodden mat of undergrowth. Petronella tried to hold in a whimper of panic, her dagger clutched so tightly in her fist her nails dug into her palm through her thick glove. Icy sweat dotted her brow, and her stomach clenched as her eyes continued to probe the inky dark.

The footsteps stopped five feet away. Petronella swallowed, clenching down on her terror, raising her chin. Gods help her, she would go down fighting if she had to.

"Who's there? Show yourself." Her voice came out weak. Thin as small ale.

A chuckle reached her from the shadows. An amused, familiar voice from her past. Rough as bark, smoky as a pipe. As welcome as slippers and a warm, warm fire. "Petronella, Queen of Epera. What a night for a stroll down the river."

Petronella slumped against the tree. Her knees gave way, made boneless with relief.

The figure stepped closer, and a lantern appeared out of the blackness from beneath a shielding cloak. Mistress Eglion raised it and peered at Petronella as she shaded her eyes from the light, feeble as it was. The old woman had been tall once. Now, she stooped over a gnarled stick twisted with vines and carved with symbols Petronella couldn't make out in the darkness. A loose robe of faded purple shrouded her thin frame. Her hair was white, a mess of tangles. A long black cloak dangled from her shoulders, and her eyes were shrewd and knowing in their nest of wrinkles.

Her former tutor's tone was wry as she gripped Petronella's arm with surprising strength for one so old. "I believe you may have had enough of stumbling in the darkness," she said. "I have been waiting for you. Come this way, my dear. 'Tis not far."

"What are you doing here?"

Questions crowded her mind as Petronella limped after her. Mistress Eglion's head twisted stiffly on her wrinkled neck as she glanced back.

"All in good time, my dear. We need to get you somewhere warm and safe."

The woman led her through the tangled wood with a sure step that bespoke long acquaintance with the narrow paths. A white owl followed them, its hooping call leading them from tree to tree until the forest gave way to a wide clearing.

The beech standing at its centre was huge. It commanded the ground and sky around it. Its branches spread like protective wings over the tussocked grass and dry leaves. Petronella stumbled to a halt as she took in its breadth and height, silhouetted against scudding clouds and lit by a scrambled moon. Lantern light sparked in Mistress Eglion's blue eyes, and she stopped as well.

"Breathtaking, is it not?" she said. "I have read this is the oldest tree in Epera. It has stood for eons and all trees in the land owe allegiance to it."

She strode ahead, stick thumping. Despite the icy breeze, the branches hardly moved. The owl accompanying them swooped to the lowest branch. Petronella's shoulders hunched under his watchful stare as he judged her. She dropped her gaze to the ground and concentrated on her footing. Ancient roots lifted the surrounding earth into warped hollows and hillocks. The air was pungent with damp soil and fallen leaves. Mistress Eglion picked her way with unerring ease over the rough terrain and stopped, waiting for Petronella to scramble over the divots to reach her.

A dark hollow made a deeper shadow at the base of the vast trunk. Mistress Eglion scanned their surroundings before she gestured at Petronella to follow. "Come, quickly now."

She turned and entered the heart of the tree. Swallowing her trepidation, Petronella followed her.

The passage in front of them wound down like a corkscrew into the loamy ground. The air was damp and musty here, and Petronella was aware of a creaking, whispering noise which coursed up, down and within her like a voice in her bones. Perhaps it was the voice of the tree itself. One hand traced the ridged bark as she followed Mistress Eglion along the cramped passage. Her shoulders clenched as claustrophobia claimed her, and she had to crouch to avoid collision with the lowering roof.

The light bloomed into something wider as they ducked through a narrow opening and into a circular space. Petronella's eyes widened as she noted the carvings on the interior.

Mistress Eglion stepped back and ushered her in.

"Welcome to the Temple of the Mage. You are safe, here."

The sign of the Mage, carved deep in the polished wood, decorated every bare surface on the inside of the trunk, along with other symbols she thought she should know and yet which glided away from her knowledge even as she grasped for it. The entire room pulsed with power. Each beat matched the pulse that thudded in her wounded head. Her vision swam. She leaned against the nearest wall for support.

Mistress Eglion shuffled over to a heap of blankets covering a low pallet carved out of the tree's interior. She waved the lamp and beckoned to Petronella, who shivered as she massaged her aching skull.

"Hold this, child."

Petronella did as she was told. Entranced, her gaze roamed across the carvings on the walls, worn smooth with time, and she found her mind wandering. The scored lines appeared to move and undulate, a liquid language etched in auburn with a life of their own. She had the strange sensation of conversation but without hearing actual voices. Her skin crawled, and she shook her head to dislodge the sensation with little success. The unheard voices buzzed around her skull. Questioning, searching. Mistress Eglion glanced at her from her position over the bench as Petronella let out a whimper of panic.

"Relax, girl. Nothing here will harm you. Look around. Concentrate on the familiar. It will help."

Swallowing, Petronella took her advice and dragged her attention away from the undulating walls. The space was a peculiar mix of both sacred and mundane. The inside of the trunk housed platforms loaded with woollen blankets, and shelves crowded with flasks and bottles and baskets of provisions. Buckets of water lined one section of the wall. A couple of crudely carved stools flanked a low table. Books and scrolls crowded the rest of the space. They overflowed from the narrow shelves onto the floor, stacked into neat columns. Her bemused eyes caught obscure titles etched in gold or silver on ancient threadbare linings. "Of Movinge and Beinge", "Ye Mercye of ye Godes". She shook her head, struggling to comprehend.

Mistress Eglion reached for a wooden beaker and dipped it into a pail of water. She bent over the makeshift pallet, and Petronella took an instinctive step backwards as the mound of blankets shifted and the unseen occupant coughed.

"More light, girl. Help me see here."

Her hand shook as she raised the lantern higher. Mistress Eglion passed a sure arm under a sturdy pair of shoulders and supported the patient enough so he could sip some water. His head lolled against her shoulder, and he muttered something unintelligible.

Petronella backed up a pace, her heart hammering. Fever flushed his cheeks and his frame shuddered with cold, but for now, at least, she was not the only passenger of the doomed Dove to have survived. Lord Joran Weir had somehow made it through as well.

"What is he doing here?" She managed, her tongue tripping over her questions. "Was there anyone else? What about Domita? Alice?"

Mistress Eglion settled Joran to a more comfortable position and offered the beaker of water to Petronella, who gulped it.

The old woman shook her head, her eyes sympathetic. "You and he are the only souls the river flushed out at my doorstep this time," she said. "Sit down. I will get you some food."

She nudged Petronella to a crude wooden stool and hefted a rough wool blanket over her shoulders. Petronella huddled into it, hating her wet clothes and longing for a steaming hot bath. Her fingers traced the egg-shaped lump on the side of her skull, and she winced. Both fascinated and repelled, her reluctant gaze turned to the carved wall again. Her thoughts drifted as her eyes followed the serpentine curls and delicate patterns around the walls. She welcomed the distraction. Anything to avoid thoughts of Domita and Alice and the hungry, snarling water.

She drank in the sight of her erstwhile tutor with hungry eyes, comforted by the familiar bent profile of her stooped back in silhouette as she crossed the path of the light. New lines etched the old face along with a slight tremor in her arthritic hands, blue veined and still stained from a lifetime of holding quills and making notes on parchment.

It seemed so unlikely to find her teacher here, surrounded by the arcane and forbidden symbols of a discredited religion, instead of the books and scrolls of her regimented childhood. She shook her head, blinking away tears.

Mistress Eglion turned to a small iron contraption huddled at the base of the far wall and reached for a wooden spill. Within minutes the small stove burned hot and bright, and the old woman swung a pot of water and another of pottage over the fire to heat. The old woman was as slim as a bird, but something about the figure crouched over the flames brought Felice to mind. She swallowed another dry sob, laying her aching head on her huddled knees.

"You'd better get out of those wet things, dear. The blanket will do for now, and we will dry you out at least. Don't want you getting River Fever, like his lordship, here." Mistress Eglion said over her shoulder. She dipped a spoon into the stew and gave the mixture a stir. Petronella gave an appreciative sniff as the smell enveloped her, and her empty stomach growled. Joran moaned on his makeshift mattress, one arm flopping out of the rough blanket. Sweat dappled his forehead.

"Will he be alright?" she asked.

Mistress Eglion cocked a grizzled brow at her. "It will take a few more hours before he wakes, and he will be weak for a while longer, but I have given him some Feverfew. He's strong, that one. Made it here without my help, though only the gods know how. He was burning up already."

Petronella's eyebrows raised. "He knew you were here?"

Her mentor chuckled. "Joran and I are old friends. He and his men got me out weeks ago. Same way as you, through the Tavern of the Falcon and on to a boat. Lucky for us, the king's guard weren't after us at that point. Merlon sent him to rescue Alice. I told him to bring you, if he could. He wasn't happy with the idea. He has no great love for Epera." She broke off as Petronella shivered and jerked her chin at her damp garments. "Do as I say. Get out of those."

She was warmer without her soaked clothing. She helped Mistress Eglion hang her rough tunic and hose on a makeshift rack near the stove, and the stew warmed her more from the inside out. Mistress Eglion ate little, and Joran, not at all. His hunched form shook with fever. Her tutor tucked more blankets around him. He muttered something and flung out a long, well-muscled arm again. Petronella caught herself staring. Fascinated by his aquiline profile, she forced herself to turn away.

"How long have you been here? We thought you were ill, or taken to the mines like so many others," she asked, once they had scoured the bowls and placed them away.

The old woman lit her pipe and lowered herself to a narrow stool, elbows on her knees.

The pose was so reminiscent of the days of their past Petronella's lips curved into a reluctant smile as she sat and waited for the story, as she had at the age of eight, when she had first made Mistress Eglion's acquaintance at the family manor in the remote northern hills of Falconridge.

"Thanks to the captain and his crew, I've been here waiting for you, young miss. For several weeks now."

"Waiting for me? How could you have known I would come? I didn't know it myself until a day or so ago."

Mistress Eglion chuckled around her pipe as she surveyed Petronella through the blue smoke. "Joran's task was to bring Alice to her father. He's been in Blade for weeks, looking for a way into the castle. I asked him to bring you here to me as well, if he would. The Dove was supposed to meet me at the old jetty, but of course, it never arrived. I have been watching for it for days now. Joran arrived by himself, already full of fever a few hours ago. That was the first I knew about what happened. I've been scouring the banks up and down ever since, hoping the Cryfell might have done what that old boat could not. I must admit to relief that you did indeed survive the water. The Cryfell does not deal well with those who make its acquaintance."

"The river brought me here?" Petronella scoffed, "That is utterly ridiculous. How can a river do that?"

Her old tutor's eyebrows raised. "I would judge less quickly, were I you."

"There are so many things I don't understand. Why can't I bear a child? Why does Arion hate me so much he wants me dead? Why are we going to war with our neighbours?"

Petronella's voice broke on a sob as she blurted her doubts and questions to the old woman, who sat and smoked, listening as she always had.

"There are many things Arion himself does not understand. Perhaps he never will. His family's history is ancient and in recent times, more twisted than I think even the gods could have foretold."

Petronella's gaze was accusing as she met Mistress Eglion's through the smoke.

"You have never told me about the Eperan magic. You have tutored me in statecraft, languages, logic, law, trade, economics, but never, ever magic. Not once. And yet here you are, surrounded by the sign of the Mage, and all these books." She gestured angrily at the walls. "Why was I not told? And why is Arion so set against magic he kills and tortures anyone who still follows the old ways? He believes we are both cursed with dark magic. Why is that?"

The old woman sucked at her pipe. "Thanks to the command of his father, Arion only understands a world without magic. He knows nothing at all about it, and his tutor taught him to fear it. These books are all that remain of the magical knowledge of Epera. As chief librarian, I removed them from the library before old King Francis ordered them destroyed." Mistress Eglion inclined her head with a small smile and pointed her long clay pipe at the bag containing what remained of Petronella's possessions. "I left you one of them."

Petronella snorted. "That dratted book has been nothing but trouble from start to finish. There's nothing there that can help me. I've scoured it from cover-to-cover."

"Really?" Mistress Eglion said, taking another luxurious drag of tobacco. "I'd take another look if I were you."

"What, now?"

"Why not now? Do you have something more pressing to do?"

Huffing under her breath, Petronella levered herself off her stool, wincing at the pain in her stomach.

"The water will have ruined it," she said.

The buckles holding the bag shut had stiffened in the warmth, and she tugged them open. Potion bottles rattled in the musty depths, and she held one up to the dim light, squinting at the contents.

"Here." She handed it to Mistress Eglion. "Felice made this up before we left. She wanted Alice to have it as a strengthening draft. We could give it to Joran?"

"Thank you." The old woman took the slim flask and placed it on a shelf before her wise, expectant gaze returned to settle on her former pupil.

"The book?" she prompted.

Petronella scowled. "If you knew how much I hate this thing, you wouldn't ask me to look again. It's nothing but happy days and folk-tales."

Mistress Eglion raised her wiry eyebrows and waited. Smoke wreathed her head. Her deep-set blue eyes were remote, and her head cocked, listening to something faint in the distance.

Petronella jammed her hands into the bag and dragged the book onto her lap. She was right. It oozed damp. Water had swollen the paper, and the binding had burst, exposing the spine and loosening the ancient pages.

"This is disgusting," she said, as her fingers worked at the sodden, fleshy vellum, trying to pull the pages apart. Her head gave a sudden, violent throb.

She peeled the book open to the page she had last marked and shoved it at her tutor, not bothering to glance down.

"Here. If you want to know so much. You read it."

"No, Petronella," Mistress Eglion's voice rang in her ears. The tone was implacable and to be obeyed. "You read it."

Petronella's skin ran with gooseflesh. Her gaze locked on the old woman, who was still smoking her pipe, but something about her made the short hair on the back of her neck float. That voice. That was not Mistress Eglion's voice. This was deeper. Stronger. Male.

Swallowing, she glanced down at the twisted text, expecting her brain to do the usual knotwork of mental translation. Under her burning eyes, the pages steamed in the warmth, and the ink ran. And changed.

The words... were not the same.

She tilted the page closer to the stove. Steam rolled off it in waves, dampening her face, and she wafted it away, squinting at the lines of text written in an even more ancient dialect than the previous one.

Her eyes widened as she dragged her gaze along the faded script. Mistress Eglion tapped out her pipe and left her stool to check on Joran.

"This is not what I read before," she said, glancing at her tutor.

"The river washes clean."

Rolling her eyes at the enigmatic comment, Petronella read on, frowning as she turned a page, pulling it carefully from its neighbour. Mistress Eglion helped Joran to some strengthening potion. He was surfacing from his delirium, tossing and turning in a fitful half sleep.

Petronella completed the section and sat up, closing the book with a new, thoughtful respect.

"What do you remember about the day your sister died, my dear?"

Mistress Eglion gave a last rough wipe to Joran's sweat dappled forehead and resumed her seat with a sigh. Her eyes were no longer forbidding but had returned to their normal, lively twinkle.

Petronella frowned, crossing her arms around her middle. Contemplating that terrible day, what she could recall of it, sent shivers through her, and an urgent need for the chamber pot.

"I don't know." She shifted on her stool, fighting an almost overwhelming urge to run. "My father said... she fell. We were hunting, and her horse tripped and threw her down the ravine by Raven's Gulch. It was autumn. There were leaves." She jumped to her feet, impatient. "I must go. I have to find the others."

Mistress Eglion nodded. "And what did the book tell you about Eperan magic?"

Her voice was gentle but inexorable. It crept into Petronella's head like a chill winter wind, finding the naked gap between glove and sleeve.

"That it involves the ability to speak mind to mind and to move objects with no need for touch." Petronella's voice was a dull singsong. A child reciting a lesson forced on her against her will.

"That, and much more. Are you yet to be convinced, my dear?" her tutor asked, glancing up at her before throwing another lump of wood into the stove.

"It is impossible." Petronella argued. Her voice rose, and she roved around the small space, seeking a task for her agitated hands as her mind rattled through the events of the last few weeks.

"And yet one of your ladies can summon flames and bend them to her will. Another can command the water to sink an enemy ship."

"Yes. And look where that got us. Magic is dangerous and... and wrong. Arion is right to banish it."

"You cannot blame Princess Alice for her lack of the knowledge of physics, Petronella. She is fifteen years old and a member of the race of Cups. Therefore, she didn't think. She felt. And she acted on her feelings, like all those of her blessed blood."

Petronella's drawn face hardened, but her body was shaking. "She is responsible for the death of her best friend at court. Domita couldn't swim. She couldn't swim and Alice must have realised. And I could n't... couldn't..."

Her memory snared on the image of Domita's terrified face in the last instant before her grip slid away and the grey waters of the Cryfell claimed her.

Mistress Eglion took Petronella's clammy hands in her own worn, dry ones. Her familiar face wore a complicated expression. Half pity, half hope.

"You couldn't save her," she said. "I know."

CHAPTER TWENTY-FIVE

A rush of cold air from the world outside the Mage Tree woke Petronella in the morning. For a moment, she wondered where she was. Mistress Eglion had ushered her to a bunk on the far side of the room the previous evening and Petronella had drifted off into a jumbled sleep that combined equal parts nightmare and exhaustion.

This morning, her aching limbs and the lump on her head were demanding attention. She struggled upwards in the tangle of blankets and scrubbed her hands over her face, flinching at the grittiness on her skin and the rough woollen mittens. A glance across the room told her Joran had left his sickbed. Her eyebrows raised. His own covers were folded, army style, at the foot of his pallet. His sword was nowhere to be seen. Mistress Eglion was also out, perhaps tending to her own needs or to the morning chores.

Petronella climbed from her warm nest with a strong feeling of guilt riding on her shoulders. If Joran could be as sick as he was last night and still get up, what did that make her? Gritting her teeth, she shoved her feet into boots still damp despite a night in front of the stove and pulled her hood over her head with a shudder of distaste.

Outside, it was much earlier than she had thought. The sun crested the trees, shining a rare golden light into the clearing. Above it, the familiar bank of cloud lurked to smother it under another day of gloom. Petronella stretched, wincing at the bruises around her ribs, and glanced around. Birds trilled their good mornings. The air was fresh and clean. She followed the footsteps in the dawn-brushed dew to the gentle ripple of a nearby brook.

Mist wove among the ancient tree trunks. She spotted a couple of deer as they cropped moss with placid calm in a patch of sunshine. Their heads bobbed up at her approach, but they didn't run. Their curious stares followed her; ears twitched in her direction.

She knelt on the stony bank of the brook and steeled herself against the chill of the icy water as she splashed her face.

Cupping some in her hands, she drank, grateful the water was untainted, unlike the river Cryfell itself. She had finished tending to her other needs and was debating the merits of wading into the stream for a strip wash when a heavier set of footsteps behind her sent her blood racing.

She whirled, grabbing for her blade.

Joran stopped and leaned against a nearby oak. A brace of rabbits dangled from his fist. His face was as drawn with fatigue as her own. Several days' worth of stubble peppered his jaw. His hair was a tousled mess. His eyes, under his lowered brow, held shadowed secrets and a cynical, watchful wariness that confused her.

"So this is the Queen of Epera we all have to blame for the current state of affairs, is it?"

Petronella raised one eyebrow in a quelling look. "As you see."

Joran sighed and dropped to his knees. For one absurd moment, Petronella thought he was bowing to her, but he found a narrow blade and gutted one rabbit with quick, practiced movements. At the sight of the flashing knife, Petronella flinched, feeling her gorge rise.

Joran glanced up at her. "Too high to watch where your dinner comes from?" he asked.

"Not at all. I've gutted my share of game in the past," she murmured in return, remembering happier days with her ladies when they still had permission to hunt. Grayling would bring down the prey, and she and Domita would dress a rabbit or a pigeon and roast it where they were, over a campfire. Looking back, those fires had always been easy to light. She bit her lip. The reason was not such a mystery anymore.

Watching Joran and his quick, angry movements, she sensed his frustration. His shoulders hunched, his eyebrows drawn into a frown as he scowled over the task. This was not a man to be won over by words. Only deeds would do to prove she was no threat to him.

Striding to his side, she held out her hand for the second rabbit. He gave her a confused glance before he complied. Kneeling beside him, she copied his movements. The task was soon complete. They buried the skins, heads, and entrails and returned to the temple. Petronella had to step out to match his long stride, wiping her hands off on her tunic.

"Are you recovered from the fever now?" she asked him as they reached the tree. He stood aside to let her enter before him.

"It left me in the night." Joran said. "The potion Mistress Eglion gave me worked well."

Petronella allowed herself a small smile. "'Twas made for Alice by my old nurse, Lady Felice." Her voice trailed off as she wondered how her friend was faring back at the castle. Felice's warmth and reassurance had been a part of her life since before she could remember, and now she had put the woman in harm's way. If anything happened to her, she would never forgive herself.

Her head throbbed, and she winced, rubbing her forehead.

"Lady Felice made her own choice. You should rest awhile; you took quite a blow to the head." Joran said, his voice gruff.

She glanced up at him, shocked he had read her mind, and found his blue eyes focused on her with hawklike intensity. She had the impression the man missed little of what passed in front of him. A flush swept up her cheeks as he continued his perusal, and her thoughts scattered like blown dandelions as his gaze traversed across her face, resting on her mouth.

Up close, he was arrestingly handsome. His face was a study of angles. Long, dark aqua eyes, a thin, straight nose, except for his lips, which were generous and quirked upwards at the corners. It was a face designed for smiling. She had a feeling, for Lord Joran Weir, though, smiles were rare.

He broke his gaze, and she stumbled as she ducked through the low archway into the narrow tunnel.

"I thank you for your concern," she replied over her shoulder. "But I have lingered too long as it is. I must find the others, or at least get word of their whereabouts, and continue to Oceanis. My people are desperate." She dropped the rabbit onto a nearby table, wiping her sticky fingers on her tunic.

Joran gave a derisive snort behind her. "Your people are desperate?" He echoed, hurling his quarry onto the table to join her own. "What about my people? Going about their business in an orderly fashion and about to be attacked by your kingdom and raided for their own produce, their princess, future queen and Seer taken hostage?"

Petronella swallowed, backing away from him in the small space. Unbidden, her hand crept for her knife as his voice raised in temper. Her heart rate picked up.

"It is not Arion's wish," she argued, conscious of the weakness of her voice in the face of his implacable wrath. "'Tis my fault. I am the wrong queen. I cannot bear him children, and I am trying to find a cure. Alice told me I would find answers in the west, and I have my own reasons for bringing her back to her father. I hope to beg him for aid, deliver his daughter to him and then the need for war will not exist, and we will have more time. Surely you can understand that?"

Her fists clenched, she stood four-square, chin raised. She'd said it at last— the final desperate throw of the dice that had occurred to her as she risked everything, including the undermining of her husband's strategy, and abandoned her kingdom.

To her utter shock, Joran threw back his head and laughed. "The wrong queen? Yes. It should have been your sister, should it not? And somehow your father made King Francis wait eight years and take you for his son instead, a girl with as much fight in her as a scared rabbit."

Petronella bit her lip, hard. "I had no choice," she hissed. "Do you think I ever wanted to be a queen? Jana died, and my father told me I had to take her place. He said it was my duty to serve the royal line. He betrothed me to Arion when I was nine years old. I have spent my whole life fitting myself for this task. I have learned many things a queen needs to know, but the only thing Arion wants is a broodmare. I have failed at everything. But especially that."

She laughed in her own turn, a bitter and twisted sound that was swallowed by the warm wooden walls and absorbed into the symbols that decorated them.

A forgotten fragment of memory surfaced somewhere in the back of her mind. Something Jana had said once.

"I don't wish to leave here and join with the prince."

And now she knew why. What her sister must have sensed. Something wrong. Something evil and rotten at the core of their kingdom, whittling away its strength. She took a breath, trying to steady her knocking heart, and Joran's gaze softened, disarming her as he took in her angry face.

"No," he said, stepping back and allowing her some breathing room. "I suppose it is not your fault. I loathe what has become of Epera. It's cruelty to those blessed by the gods, but I do not think you are the enemy."

He sighed and continued to hold her gaze, and her headache intensified with crippling force. She screwed her eyes closed.

"Look at me." His voice was soft, but commanding. "I need to see you."

"No, you don't." She turned away; shoulders hunched.

He reached for her, and she flinched, her dagger back in her hand in an instant as he took her shoulder to turn her around.

"Don't touch me."

His eyes widened in surprise at the speed the blade flashed to his throat. He batted her knife hand away with casual ease.

"Impressive. I see you have had some training."

Petronella's chin jutted. "I can defend myself."

Joran's gaze plunged into hers. The headache returned. Petronella found herself unable to move, mesmerised by the beauty of those eyes as they raked through her defences. She staggered against the rough-hewn table as he broke the contact and stared at the two dressed rabbits, trying to make sense of her scattered wits. A long silence. Petronella rubbed her head, swallowing nausea, and the pulsing headache subsided. She glanced at him. A muscle worked in his jaw as he scanned her face. She frowned, noting the conflict in his eyes.

"I will help you find the others if they still live. Taking Alice to her father is my mission, too."

His tone was flat. Her head jerked up, and he nodded to her, turned on his heel and left the temple. Letting out her breath, unsure whether to be grateful or sorry, Petronella sank to her knees and reached for her satchel. Rummaging through it for her potion, her clutching fingers encountered the stab of shattered glass, and she snatched her hand out, sucking blood.

"Gods damn it." She upended the bag in a flurry of hot temper, tipping her battered, water-laden goods to the packed earth floor. Her heart sank. The bottle containing her precious store of Heartsease tea had broken.

She sat back on her heels, aghast, cradling the fragments of green glass in her lap. Her potion. Her lifeline. Gone. She jerked to her feet, squinting at the various bottles and jars lining the wooden shelves making up Mistress Eglion's precious larder. They held a cornucopia of herbal remedies, but nothing she recognised as an ingredient for her tea.

Chest tightening with fear, she slumped to her bunk, staring at her blankets but not seeing them as long memories of Felice's worried face and steady hands holding out her potion filled her mind.

"No need to be so dramatic."

Mistress Eglion's no-nonsense rasp cut through her racing thoughts, and Petronella's head snapped up. The old woman shuffled in and set her basket of mushrooms down, nodding her head in approval at the neatly skinned rabbits. She turned around and surveyed Petronella. Exasperation stiffened every feature of her wrinkled face. Petronella scowled at her, confused.

The old woman shook her head, stirring up the broken remains of the flask on the floor with the tip of her walking stick. She swept them aside with a sniff of disdain.

"Heartsease Tea." She huffed. "I never agreed with Felice and your mother on that one."

"What?" Petronella said, dumbfounded.

Mistress Eglion glanced at her. Was that regret Petronella could see, sparking in her eyes?

Whatever it was, her tutor shrugged it off in her usual impatient manner. "You never required Heartsease tea. Not for your heart. That works perfectly well, at least." She declared.

"If that is a joke, it is poor," Petronella said. "I have a weak heart. I always have."

"There is more than one use for Heartease tea, my dear."

Mistress Eglion sat, laying her stick with exaggerated care beside her chair.

"Yes, it is an aid for those afflicted with conditions of the heart." Her eyes crept up under her wrinkled brow to meet Petronella's accusing gaze. "In your case, they administered it for another, entirely different reason. Two, in fact."

"What reasons?" Petronella jumped up and paced the room. "I am sick of all these half-truths and misinformation. And from you, of all people, I always thought you would tell me the truth, since you so demanded it from everyone else." Rage was bursting from her every pore. "What explanation do you have? And Felice? I thought she loved me. Why would she lie to me and... and drug me all these years? Why?" She towered over her tutor with her arms crossed in front of her chest, eyes flashing.

"If you listen for a minute, I will attempt to explain." Even under duress, the old woman kept her dignity and her iron composure.

"Go ahead if you must." Petronella snarled. She gathered her pitiful supplies together and rammed them into her bag. "And then I will leave, and I will not see you again."

"That is probably true, I fear. There are soldiers in the forest even now, sent out from Goldfern, looking for more survivors from the king's ship. It appears someone escaped Alice's wave of doom and alerted the garrison in Goldfern."

Petronella rolled her eyes and snatched a spare cloak from her bed, where it had acted as an extra layer overnight.

"Tell me now." She whirled to face the old woman, trying to see through her own fury to the familiar features she had always trusted. It was no good. Mistress Eglion, tutor of her youth, suddenly presented in an altogether unfamiliar light. Ancient and malevolent, her grey hair twisted into corkscrew tangles, her eyes gimlets of hidden secrets, her mouth a thin, severe line.

The part of Petronella that still allowed observation through the red blur of her rage noted the old woman's ghastly pallor. The tremble in her arthritic hands. Still, Petronella towered in front of her with her hands jammed to her hips, her cloak draped over her shoulders.

"Well?"

The old woman gave a shuddering sigh. "When your sister died..."

Petronella's jaw jutted. "I don't want to talk about Jana."

"You need to listen before it's too late. We have all left this conversation for far too long."

Mistress Eglion waited until Petronella's stance softened enough to allow her to continue.

"When your sister died," she continued, her voice a hoarse croak, "you were half killed with grief. It broke your heart. You couldn't sleep, and when you did, you had terrible nightmares. You didn't eat. For weeks. You screamed when you saw your father. Felice was terrified for you. Your parents ordered Heartsease tea not for the physical state of your heart but to ease your emotional distress."

The old woman's hands reached up for Petronella's, and she exerted downward pressure until Petronella knelt in front of her and their heads were of equal height.

"You were so young, my dear, and so distraught. No-one could comfort you. We thought you would die or run mad. Your parents and Felice hoped the Heartease tea would make you forget about what happened. To protect you from your nightmares. To help you heal. That was all. "

Petronella scanned her tutor's face, searching for the truth. "But to let me think I have a weak heart for nearly twenty years? How fair was that?"

Mistress Eglion sighed. "There are always trade-offs to every decision. For what it is worth, I didn't agree. I thought you were made of stronger stuff and would heal in time. I thought it would be better to talk about what happened, but your father over-ruled me. He was afraid you would not recover."

"Jana died when I was only eight years old. Now I am twenty and six. Exactly how long was it going to take me to get well?" Bitterness tinged Petronella's ironic tone. "Am I so weak, as a grown woman, that I cannot handle the truth?"

The old woman flinched. "Ah. As to that —"

Joran's voice from the doorway cut her off.

"Soldiers," he snapped. "They are out in the woods and on the way. We must leave. Now."

He swept into the room, dumped one rabbit and half the mushrooms into Petronella's bag, and turned to face Mistress Eglion. The old woman reached for her stick and propped herself up on it, her face grey. Her wrinkled hand trembled as she drew herself to her feet and cast her gaze around the room.

"Go. Go now. It is imperative the Mage's temple remains hidden. Joran..."

He waited. A private taking orders from a respected general. "Guard Petronella with your life. Your kingdom depends on it."

He gave her a grim nod and reached for Petronella's hand. She dug her heels into the ground.

"Wait."

She captured her tutor's thin dry hands, crushing them in a desperate grip as her rage dissipated. "Mistress Eglion, please come with us. Don't let me leave you as well."

The old woman shook off her clinging fingers.

"I will be fine, Petronella. Go. Now. Joran, follow the brook to the lightning-forked tree and then turn south. There is a little-used pathway there that will take you to Goldfern and the Falls. The soldiers are strangers here. They won't know about it. Quick now."

She pulled Petronella towards her and gave her a hard hug that crushed her ribs and reminded her of her bruises. She inhaled. Mistress Eglion's robes held the lingering aroma of pipe smoke and dried herbs and tough love.

"The gods go with you, my dear. Use their blessings wisely. There is still much to learn."

Joran reached for her once more, and this time Petronella allowed herself to be escorted out of the sanctuary of the temple. Her last sight of Mistress Eglion was of the woman leaning on her stick, dwarfed by the majesty of the tree towering above her head. Her other hand lifted to trace the sign of the Mage in the morning air. A cold draft brushed past Petronella, and the clearing sprung alive in a sudden gale that carried the sound of rough voices to them from the trees.

The wind scraped the dew from the grass, and Joran leaped into a sprint that took her by surprise. Petronella dragged a breath into her lungs and hurled herself after him. Branches swayed and creaked as they gained the shelter of the woods. An unkindness of ravens took flight. Their alarm calls flooded the wild air.

Turning at the last second before the forest closed behind her, her brow creased in confusion. Mistress Eglion was nowhere to be seen, and the clearing contained only the peace of the early morning, dominated by the overwhelming presence of the vast tree. Only a snowy owl remained. Watching their flight from his perch on the lowest branch. Of their frantic passage across the wet grass, there was no evidence at all.

Chapter Twenty-Six

After the first, almost silent, rush across the Mage Tree meadow, to the shadowed closeness of the forest, Joran slowed to allow Petronella to catch up. She snatched air into her lungs, regretting the lack of strength in limbs grown slack over the recent, mostly sedentary months. Joran glanced around, uttered a curse, and grabbed her arm.

"Now is not the time to collapse. Keep up, or I leave you."

She returned his glare, shifting her bag higher over her shoulder. "I can keep up."

Joran snorted, resuming his steady march. She clenched her teeth and lengthened her stride, glancing about her at the early morning forest.

A few lonely birds conversed in hushed voices above her head. The ever-present dampness dripped from the branches as they made their way through the trees, keeping to the brambled byways bordering the muddy path. Apart from those chirps and whistles and a faint sighing wind, it was almost preternaturally quiet. The dense forest stretched around them. A sea of fresh greens.

They were both watchful, listening for the sound of pursuit. Joran's hand clamped around the hilt of his sword, ready to draw it at the first hint of danger. Petronella found her own hand closing around the butt of her dagger in sympathy, and she lifted her legs high to clear the tangle of brambles that tore at her boots and threatened to trip her on every other step. Her thigh muscles were soon cramping with the effort to keep her feet on the treacherous mud. Determined not to complain at the pace he set, she held her peace and squelched after him.

At the end of the trail, a tree blasted to a blackened stump, its trunk split long ago, blocked their way. Petronella glanced around as she caught her breath, looking for the route Mistress Eglion had told them. She could see nothing. The forest encircled them, a poisonous emerald peppered with fungi and moss that dangled from boulders and trees alike.

"There's no path here. What did she mean?"

Joran stood for a moment, surveying the territory. He turned in a small circle, his blue eyes narrowed. They exchanged glances of alarm as the rumble of voices grew closer in the distance.

"She wouldn't have put us in harm's way. Would she?"

Joran shrugged off the leather pack he wore over his cloak and hid it under a bush. "Not deliberately, no." He jerked his chin at her dagger. "Is that the only weapon you have?"

Petronella nodded, her lips thinning as she retrieved it from its leather sheath.

"And do you know how to use it?"

"Would it surprise you to know I do?" she asked, biting down on a more sarcastic remark.

He eyed her with frank disbelief.

"A useless, runaway queen? Yes, it would."

Eyes narrowed; Petronella shot out her hand. The dagger whistled past Joran's right ear and buried itself in the tree behind him.

"I trained at Mistress Eglion's insistence, with one of our best knife fighters from the age of eight, until I left my home to become Arion's queen. I have practiced with Domita since."

Eyes blazing, she marched behind him to retrieve her blade.

"I thought the Queen of Epera was supposed to be merely a decorative fitting."

Petronella turned to face him, her jaw set. "Despite appearances, my sister was not the only one who didn't want to become a queen. Especially not a merely decorative one."

Joran nodded, his eyes hard. "We may have to fight."

Petronella inclined her chin. She turned away before the nervous shake in her hands gave her away. Sparring with Trinian, head of the Falcon Guard, or Domita, was one thing. She had never taken a life. The rasp of metal as Joran drew his sword sent a shiver crawling down her spine and made her bowels churn. She glanced at him, eyes wide.

Joran looked her over, his jaw set. "If it comes to it, act and don't think. If you wait, you will die. Allow your training to take control. Do you understand?" he spoke in a low voice, his eyes fixed on Petronella's. She nodded, her heart in her mouth.

The rough, jeering voices in the distance were much louder now as the soldiers crashed their way through the woods, raising alarm calls from the birds.

Joran waved a hand at an ancient oak bordering the pathway. His face was grim.

"Hide behind there. I will wait on the other side. Try not to reveal yourself unless you must. Understand? If they find you, I will have to kill them all. I know that's not what you want."

Petronella swallowed. She nodded and took a few hasty steps away from the path to the dubious protection of an ancient oak.

Drawing her cloak around her and clutching her precious blade in a hand that was slick with sweat inside her glove, she crouched small and still, listening for all she was worth over the thudding of her heart.

There was the faintest rustle of leaves as Joran took shelter on the opposite side of the path. The birds were still whistling their alarm calls as the soldiers drew closer.

Fighting the urge to break and run, Petronella slid a hand over her mouth to muffle her breath as it fogged in front of her face. The voices were much clearer now.

"Blasted forest," one soldier grumbled. "Can't see a bloody thing through all these trees."

The troop halted before the stump, and there was a brief silence. Petronella could imagine them staring around much as she and Joran had done minutes before.

"Waste of time following this path. Told you they wouldn't have gone this way," someone said.

Petronella froze as one member of the group stepped off the pathway in her direction.

"Just taking a slash," he said to his colleagues.

The other members of his party waited. A waft of tobacco tickled her nostrils as one of them lit his pipe. Petronella drew herself to her feet, flattening herself against the trunk. Her hand tightened on the grip of her dagger. The acrid stench of urine filled her nostrils as the man relieved himself with obvious satisfaction against her tree. The man sighed his relief, and there was a rustle as he buttoned himself back up.

Petronella allowed her shoulders to relax as the man stepped away, but the ground shook as he tripped over a bramble and went down on his knees in the mud.

"Shit!"

Petronella's eyes widened in alarm as the man's sword shot out of his hand and landed in front of her. She gripped her dagger tighter and sent up a prayer to whatever gods might be watching.

His companions guffawed as the man struggled to regain his feet, hampered by his breastplate and the weight of his pack. Further laughter split the silence as he slipped again.

"Wassamatter, Bradley? Drowning in your own piss now?" someone said. "Come on, get a move on. It's not a day for playing mud pies. Not when there's ale and wenches in Goldfern. I heard they fished a fire witch out of the river half drowned. Not much heat left in her now, I reckon."

"What, is she dead?" The other man's voice was as harsh as the caw of a crow as he laughed.

"Nah. Not yet. They're building a gibbet in Goldfern Square, but there's a pile of rocks too. Can't wait to see what they have planned for her."

Petronella's blood bubbled with rage, and her lips thinned. She waited, jaw clenched, heart thudding.

Bradley cursed as he wobbled upright and stepped forward. He bent to collect his weapon.

Petronella hardened her mind, blocked everything but the technique she had learned and struck straight, hard, and true. Her dagger pierced his neck at the base of his skull, and she jumped back to avoid the spurt of bright red blood, nearly tripping over herself.

The man collapsed at her feet, shock stamped on his rough-hewn features. She backed away, sobbing.

Joran hurled himself with an ear-splitting cry between the two remaining members of the group with a concentrated fury that left them no time to react. Petronella winced as the blur of his blade bit into the bare neck between helmet and breastplate of the taller of the two. The man fell to his knees, and Joran whirled, graceful even in the treacherous mud, to take the last soldier under the armpit. He jerked his sword free as the man took a final, bubbling breath and slumped to the leaf-strewn floor.

Silence dropped over and between them. The birds stilled their voices. The woods held a waiting hush, broken only by Petronella's harsh breathing. She pressed a hand to her trembling lips. The two men Joran had killed stared sightlessly at the sky, their lifeblood leaking into the mud. Bradley lay at the base of the tree, face down on a patch of virulent green moss.

Petronella bit down like a savage on her bottom lip, determined to still the shaking that swept over her. Her hand loosened on the dagger.

Crimson blood stained the blade, and she abandoned it to the leaf mould at her feet. Her stomach churned, and she swallowed bile.

"You did well," Joran said as he bent over the former soldiers.

Hands to her mouth, she looked at the ground, trying to shake the image of the dead men. Scrubbing her hands over her face, she risked a glance at Joran, shocked at his casual air as he cleaned his sword on the cloak of one soldier and knelt to rifle through his pack.

"What are you doing?" Her voice was as weak as her knees. She leaned against the tree for support.

"Looking for information or supplies."

The contents of the haversack revealed little about the group's orders. Joran nodded to where the corpse of Bradley was already sinking a little deeper into the saturated leaves. "You could check him as well," he grunted.

Petronella shook her head, shaking.

Joran stopped what he was doing and caught her eye. "You've killed him. He won't bite you. See if he has something that might keep us alive."

She ignored his command and shook her head. "I didn't want to kill him."

Joran glanced up from his search of the other man, his blue eyes blazing.

"This is war. He would have ended you. Or me, or both of us. That was his job. That is my job, come to that." He slapped his hand against his breastplate. "Soldier. Spy. Mercenary. I kill people for a living."

Petronella's chin lifted. "It's not the role of a queen."

Joran laughed. His generous mouth twisted in a mystified expression that only added to her sense of unreality.

"Which queen are you talking about? I know of a failed queen who can't bear children and who has abdicated responsibility for her starving kingdom. That one is being hunted so her poor, beleaguered husband can give the honour to someone else who wants it, since she, by her own admission, never wanted to be a queen, anyway."

He closed the distance between them in two quick strides as Petronella's face crumpled and her shoulders slumped in defeat. His calloused hand under her chin was hard as he turned her resisting face towards him. His iron gaze clashed with hers and, once again, the familiar stab of pain pierced her brow. She tried to tear away, but his grip was implacable.

"No, it's not the job of that queen," he said. "That one runs away and leaves suffering behind her and others to act for her. No-one would miss that queen. She deserves to be hunted."

Petronella's heart contracted in her chest at his harsh assessment. Shame and guilt washed through her. She dropped to her knees and pressed her hands to her face. Her shoulders shook as she sobbed.

He sank with her to his knees onto a damp cushion of fallen leaves. His fingers returned to clasp her jaw more gently as he forced her to raise her head to meet his eyes.

"But I have seen a little way into you now, and you are not that person, are you?" he said. "That queen is dead, if she ever existed. They are all wrong about you. You are a woman with more courage than most, who will fight for what she wants. Someone who tries to protect those around her and is not afraid to strike when necessary. A queen who, given the opportunity, could be not just good, but excellent." He paused, thumbing away the tears that burned shame down her face. "Like it or not, you have to be the queen your people need, no matter what it takes."

Petronella twisted away from his iron grip as a flush crept up her cheeks. She shook her head and rubbed at the grime and blood on her face.

"Jana would have been an excellent queen. I need to give my country an heir, that is all. My father and my husband are both clear about that," she said, her voice dull. "If the answers lie outside my kingdom,

I am duty-bound to find them. If I can save lives by doing so, I must do what I can. It is the only way forward."

Chest hollow with guilt and loss, she bent to pick up her dagger and heaved her bag of supplies over her shoulder. Her legs shook with fatigue and shock.

"I cannot face the King of Oceanis without his daughter, so I need to find Alice and Domita. I am going to Goldfern. Are you coming?"

Joran sighed as he stood, brushing leaf mould from his knees. "Showing your face in Goldfern will put your head on the block."

"Then I won't show my face. What do we do about these men?"

Joran shrugged, sheathing his sword. "There's not much we can do. Someone will find them eventually. A search party will come out when they do not return."

"It's wrong to leave them like this." Petronella bit her lip. The former soldiers had had families and friends. People to mourn them. How could she leave them to carrion?

Joran shook his head and scraped his hair from his face. "We have no way to bury them and no place to put them. We must go. Their comrades will come."

He reached an arm to jerk her out of her reverie. Petronella's dagger flashed, stopping short of his chin. Joran snatched back his hand in surprise.

"You don't touch me," she hissed. "I am nobody's plaything anymore."

She whirled on her heel and plunged through the bushes that formed a near-impenetrable thicket on Joran's side of the path. Thorns tore at her tunic and slashed her tear-stained cheeks as she shoved her way through. Part of her welcomed the pain.

"Petronella, where are you going?" Exasperation laced his voice as he pushed his way through behind her.

"Mistress Eglion said to turn south at the stump. This is south," she said.

Chapter Twenty-Seven

Sprawled in haphazard fashion across both sides of the Cryfell, the ancient trading port of Goldfern marked the border with Oceanis with a spectacular view from the head of the magnificent Goldfern Falls. The town itself failed to do it justice. Hacked from the forest that surrounded it in every direction for miles, its buildings were mostly of wood, thatched with reeds or wooden tiles. Taverns and brothels crowded the jetties where Eperan goods waited to be unloaded from river boats before transferring to mule trains for their onward journey south along the Fool's Way to Oceanis. The Fool's Way snaked for miles down the cliffs alongside the majestic waterfall, a steep and scree-ridden pathway walked by only a few hardy souls and their stout-hearted mules. A timber palisade tried to keep the town in check but had failed in that regard. Dwellings hugged the inner walls to the point of pushing it over. Torches blazed on every street corner, and even from here, the revelry of the overcrowded town wafted towards the weary travellers.

Petronella groaned with relief as she collapsed on a pile of damp leaves in the shelter of a nest of boulders high on the cliffs above the town. It had taken them two days, and the going had been rough. Mud weighted her hide boots. Her tunic and cloak were damp with rain and sweat and clinging to her. Brambles and thorns had slashed her cheeks until they stung as they forced a passage through the overgrown, rarely travelled path on the east of the Cryfell. She clutched her hands over her empty belly as it growled and tried not to think about food. The rabbit and mushrooms they had taken with them were already a distant memory, hastily roasted over a tiny fire at the mouth of a cave they had sheltered in the night before.

Joran crouched beside her and offered her water from the flask he carried in his pack. His expression was grim in the fading light as he surveyed the activity in the town.

Arion's army had arrived. River craft of all shapes and sizes crammed the jetties, laden with soldiers, supplies and weaponry in the process of unloading. Blue flags hosting the Black Eagle fluttered from mastheads, and the warehouses and alehouses were a solid mass of activity. Banging drums, pipes and fiddles reached them from where they crouched, and the scent of ale and cooking food drifted to them across the space. Lights from flaring torches and candlelit windows beckoned with the promise of warmth and comfort.

Petronella shivered in her wet clothes. Every part of her ached. She screwed her eyes in the increasing gloom and gestured to the town.

"Where will they be keeping Domita?" she asked.

Joran glanced at her. "You are still determined to do this?"

"I said so. I want to. She would do the same for me. My duty is to the people that helped me."

He sighed. "They will hold her in the Prison House attached to the City Hall in Town Square."

"In the centre of Goldfern?"

"It's the largest flat area. If they are planning to make an exhibition of her, it will be there."

Petronella shuddered. Impossible to think about Domita twisting on the end of a rope, or crushed under a mountain of rocks, all her golden energy and humour snuffed out, along with her flashing grin and her indomitable spirit.

"She won't go without a fight," she said. "And nor will I. We need a plan."

"You could contact her," Joran said. He glanced at her sideways, his tone neutral.

Petronella frowned. "How?"

"The magical power of Epera."

Petronella snorted. "That I do not have. Try to be practical. If we keep to the side roads, I can—"

"You have the power of the Swords." Joran's voice slashed through her words.

"How do you know? How can you know that? Epera has lost its magic. Banished it for years."

"Not entirely."

She turned to meet his gaze, hands splayed across her hips.

He took her hand, smoothing the band hidden under its rough woollen glove. "You wear the Ring of Mercy, and you are the crowned Queen of Epera. You come from a long, long line of the House of the Falcon. The second most renowned family in the land. Your ancestors have reigned here as queens and seers before you."

She snatched her hand away. "I am useless. The wrong queen. I can do nothing. I told you before."

He gripped her shoulders, forcing her to keep looking at him. His blue eyes, more commanding than she had ever seen them, bored into hers. Pain erupted in her forehead, and she wrenched herself away, gagging.

"You are still blocking it." Joran's voice was relentless.

"How do you know?" she gasped, swallowing bile.

"I was trying to get through to you at the Tavern of the Falcon, and before we boarded the Dove. You felt me then. Don't deny it."

"I had a headache. I always have a headache. Sometimes it's worse than others." The hand she had clamped over her mouth muffled her voice. Her head swam, awash with pain that slashed through every nerve end.

"Mistress Eglion was attempting to tell you something back at the Mage Tree." Joran's voice was urgent. "Your parents ordered you to take Heartsease tea for years to stifle your recall of a tragic event. But your mother wanted you to take it for another reason. One your father had nothing to do with and no knowledge about. She ordered it for your own safety. Heartsease tea does not just block memory. It blocks magic. Your mother took it also, every day of her life during her marriage to your father. For her own safety. I wager she had headaches, too. That's your power trying to speak. The drug prevents it."

A shiver of gooseflesh pricked her neck and shoulders in recognition of his words. She shook her head, wordless.

"You are not taking Heartsease tea now. The effect will leave your body in time, as all potions do."

Petronella's face screwed into a scowl. "How do you know this?"

He took her hand. "Two reasons. One, I have known Mistress Eglion for much of my life. She told me some of your family's history. It is she I must thank for finding me a place in Merlon's household guard." He paused, scanning her face for a reaction. Petronella stared at him, struggling to process the information.

"Second reason, because I can access Eperan magic too."

Petronella gaped at him. "But you are from Oceanis. How does someone from Oceanis claim the power of Epera?"

Joran shrugged as his expression darkened. "All I know is the gods bless where they will. There is no great pattern to it. It is the same our world over. Either you are born with magic, or you are not. My father was a soldier from Epera. My mother is from Oceanis. And before you ask, I did not know them. I was brought up in an orphanage in Blade and conscripted into the army to free a bed for some other poor soul as soon as I could lift a wooden sword. Eventually, I became part of the King's Guard."

"Did no-one ever realise you were... blessed by the gods?"

"Like all those blessed, I came into my full power at sixteen. It was a long time before I found out not everyone could hear me when I talked to them without words. Francis had taken against magic long before that, and the authorities had orders to seek the Eperan Blessed and those who sheltered them. It was better not to use my power openly, but it was driving me crazy. I am lucky Mistress Eglion knew the signs. She realised what I could do and arranged for me to leave Epera for Oceanis before I killed someone, or they came for me, anyway. I have worked for Merlon in some capacity for the last twenty years."

Something in his flat tone and his bleak face warned Petronella not to ask any more questions. She regarded him with narrowed eyes, her mind warring with the information he had handed to her. Who was he? Could she trust him?

Joran allowed himself a small smile. "Yes, you can trust me, Petronella."

"By the gods. Can you hear me?"

Joran's mouth quirked. "I can hear you. You can't hear me or speak to me yet. Apparently, it hurts when I try."

Petronella frowned. "So, if you are so adept, why don't you contact Domita?"

He shook his head. "She has no connection to me, by blood, by friendship, or by race. I can't talk to her. You might."

"So, I could speak to Alice? Or Domita? Or Felice?"

He nodded. "In theory, it is possible, perhaps, with long training. If you are the rightful queen, your ring would magnify your power and, with practice, that might allow you to contact others not of Eperan descent. I can talk to some other people of Epera or hear other people who I know as family or friends, but no-one else."

"Oh." She sat down suddenly as her knees gave out beneath her. Joran crouched beside her.

"We need to find something to eat, at least." He said. "Not much rescuing can happen if you are out of your mind with hunger, and we can't light a fire up here. Someone would see it."

Petronella ignored him. "The flaw in your plan is I am not the rightful queen, and I cannot use this power. I do not know how, and even if I did, I am still powerless until the effects of Heartease tea leaves my body. And we don't know how long that will be. Domita has not got the luxury of time; that much we know."

She lurched to her feet, trying to ignore her protesting muscles. "If Domita is alive and can get some access to light, she can use her flames. I have a dagger. You have a sword. That will have to be enough."

CHAPTER TWENTY-EIGHT

After the darkness and peace of the rain swept forest, the noise and light of Goldfern hit them like a fist.

They had stumbled down a narrow path on the east side of the booming river, hardly able to speak over the crash of Goldfern Falls as it gathered itself for the three-hundred-foot drop into the land of Oceanis. Icy spray made the going treacherous. Petronella snatched at ferns and branches as she slid down to the ancient and ill-guarded gates.

The Goldfern gate guards clearly expected little traffic on this side of the town. There was barely a road at all. Nevertheless, Joran made his way further along the worn planks to a spot overgrown heavily with greenery trying to reclaim ownership of the moss-covered palisade. He glanced around in the darkness and ducked under the branches. Petronella scrambled after him.

The rotten timbers surrounding the town were no match for a shove from Joran's shoulder. He crept under a crossbeam blackened with age and nodded for her to do the same. She risked a furtive glance around. They had entered on the oldest side and were facing the backs of narrow, flimsy dwellings built almost against the wall. Nostrils creasing as a waft of human refuse wafted from a ditch, Petronella jumped as a lone rat scurried over her feet. She pulled her hood more closely over her head and sheathed her dagger. Beside her, Joran hitched his pack over his shoulder and nodded at a patch of further shadow that loomed between the nearest two houses. The two fugitives tiptoed into the alley and stopped to listen to the activity surrounding them.

Petronella's sharp ears caught the troubled treble of a baby crying for his supper. A rumble of voices came to her through the paper-thin walls, followed by a woman's nervous laugh. Smoke from a cooking fire crept out of gaps in the slats of wood. She stifled a cough, waiting to see what Joran would do next. He stood for a few more moments, head on one side like a bird, and then jerked his chin at the main street.

"We have to make our way across town, over the Blackthorn Bridge to the west side," he whispered. "Stay close to me, no matter what happens."

She nodded in the dark and followed like a wraith in his footsteps as he made his cautious way down the narrow alley, one hand on his sword.

The noise of the town grew louder as they left the shelter, and she took a deep breath as they turned into the tide of raucous humanity crowding the dirty streets.

It was a smaller, dirtier, more clamorous version of Blade. Where the houses in her capital city were solid and built of stone and tile, the citizens here constructed their buildings with logs and planks hacked from the forest surrounding the town. The streets were muddy and the cobblestones a danger more than a help, unsteady as they were on roads composed mostly of potholes.

The local citizenry was far outnumbered by the number of soldiers who roamed the streets in droves. Some marched in small groups, obviously bound on official tasks. Many others reeled in drunken camaraderie from taverns and brothels and appeared to be under no discipline at all.

Pulling her hood tight, Petronella kept her head low as she hurried after Joran, keeping a wary eye out for danger as they bundled their way through the throng. Conspicuous by his height, he was attracting the attention of many ladies of the night, but brushed past them all, hardly seeing them. She dodged in his wake, muttering apologies when she blundered into someone in the crowd.

There was almost a party air in the streets.

It was some time before she realised the soldiers of Arion's army were happy to be there because there was food and ale aplenty. Every other man had a hunk of bread or a slice of meat in his fist. Grease-slicked lips and cheeks gleamed in the torchlight. Sunken eyes sparkled in dirty faces etched with want. There was backslapping and comradeship never seen in the Castle of Air. Sour sweat, stale wine and rancid oil made up the perfume of the night.

No-one paid them the slightest attention. They chewed on bread and black sausage and downed pale ale hastily purchased at exorbitant prices from a dirty inn. The tide of people heading away from the outskirts of the town to the narrow expanse of Blackthorn Bridge almost carried them with it. Crowded with people eager for more entertainment, the bridge trembled with the weight of numbers and the river rushed underneath it with a hungry roar that made Petronella fear for their lives. Slick, ancient planks shook with the force of water that threatened to lift the whole thing off its moorings.

She halted and stumbled as the people behind crashed into her. They were all in a hurry to get to the other side. That much was plain.

"Come on," Joran urged, one foot on the slippery walkway, the other still on the bank. "Walk like a queen." She met his gaze and swallowed, feeling sick as the bridge rocked. There appeared no help for it. She scanned the Cryfell up and down. There was no other way across. Clenching her teeth, she forced her reluctant feet forward. Joran turned and strode in front of her with a confidence she could only envy.

The boards were slimy with moisture thrown up from the river and down from the saturated atmosphere.

She grabbed for the balustrade and kept her eyes on her feet as she made her cautious way across, trying not to mind as other, more intrepid souls barged past her, swearing at her slow progress. The bridge swayed like a drunk as she neared the centre. Gulping, she risked a glance at the furious water only a couple of feet below her muddy feet. It shone like oil in the darkness, light from the torches at regular intervals on the expanse reflected scarlet and gold on its surface. Half hypnotised, she remembered Mistress Eglion's rough croak.

"The river washes clean."

She shuddered. It didn't look clean. It looked like what it was — an evil, treacherous monster capable of killing people.

Her head jerked up at the sound of her name. Frowning, she squinted across the crowd to where she could see Joran's tall silhouette outlined by torchlight above the heads of the crowd, close to the other side of the bridge. He was not looking in her direction. Nevertheless, his voice was loud in her head. He might be standing at her side.

"Petronella, get a move on. We are running out of time."

Her frown deepened. Surely, he would not risk calling her name in the middle of a mass of people.

Her brow cleared, and she pressed a hand to her mouth. Icy shivers chased down her neck and back as she swayed, whether with the rhythm of the bridge or with complete shock, she couldn't tell. She gasped as someone blundered into her from behind and pushed her up to the edge of the railing. There was a creak, and she screamed as the old wood cracked under their combined weight, then gave way. She staggered to the rotting slats as the bridge tipped, and the person behind her muttered in her ear.

"That's right, my beauty. In you go, and no one the wiser." The hands on her back were terrifyingly strong. She struggled against the pressure. Under her frantic gaze, the evil black water of the Cryfell hurtled past, ready to claim her again.

"Joran."

It was a cry of desperation, straight from her heart. She scrabbled for her dagger, yanked it free and risked a backhanded random blow upwards. A grunt from her assailant told her she had met her target, and the weight lessened, then lifted completely as he jumped away.

Joran's face was furious as he jerked her to her feet by the back of her sodden tunic and turned to look for her attacker, but the assassin had vanished in the crowd.

Frustration marked his features as he squinted across hoods and carts into the distance. Petronella straightened her clothing with shaking hands while around them the crowd still ebbed and flowed, uncaring.

He glanced down at her, aqua eyes blazing with triumph. "Are you alright?"

She nodded. "I shouted for you."

"I know."

He smiled at her, and her eyes widened at the change in his face. Gone was the stern soldier, the mercenary, the skilled killer of men. This new Joran wore a smile to melt hearts much harder than hers. She swallowed, aware of the tug towards him, the newly forged bond they had made in the last few moments. She didn't know what it meant. Somewhere, in the back of her mind, autumn leaves swirled, and the prick of unease deepened.

"Did you see him? He was going to tip me into the river. I stabbed him."

She scanned the surrounding area for some sign of her attacker, as Joran had, but there was nothing to raise suspicion in the gradually thinning crowd.

He shook his head. "He got out of the way quick enough. We must go. There's a reason for this rush across the bridge."

The blood left her cheeks. "Domita?"

"They know she's weaker in the dark."

Fear washed through her. "By the gods."

Excited people packed Goldfern Town Square. Petronella and Joran fought their way through the press of ill-washed bodies and stopped when they met the backs of a stolid rank of soldiers who were keeping a central area free of traffic.

Petronella swallowed. The scaffold commanded the wide-open space in front of them. An ominous loop of black rope hung from it, swaying in the breeze. A huge bonfire was serving as a light source in the darkness. The crackle of flames and the heat from the blaze was welcome in the chilly night. More ominously, it illuminated the heap of rocks of varying sizes piled next to it. A rough wooden plank leaned against the mound.

More soldiers guarded the southern side of the square, lining the route in preparation for the prisoner. The crowd, now they were here, was a muttering, swaying mass of bigotry. Petronella cringed at the comments and the hatred she heard. It appeared Domita would find no sympathy here.

"Cursed Fire Witch. Hang her."

"Nay, hanging's not enough. Press the magic out of her. Drown her."

Blood drained from her cheeks. She glanced up at Joran in appeal. He was scanning the ranks of onlookers, his height making the most of the view across the tops of many heads.

"We'll never get to her this way," he muttered under his breath. "Hope you like climbing."

Turning, he shouldered his way back through the crowd with Petronella clinging to his shadow. They lingered at the back of the throng before Joran led the way through a narrow alleyway serving as a rat run between the dwellings. They picked their way over rubbish and around water butts, keeping as close as they could to the single-storey buildings. The cloistered space reeked of damp wood. Stripes of candlelight from ill-fitting shutters provided a dim light. Petronella lifted her tired legs high over the debris, forcing herself to hurry in Joran's long-legged wake. He stopped at the back of a closed-up shop with a drooping roofline. Water dripped from a broken gutter into a tall barrel standing close by its bulging, log-panelled wall.

"Here. I'll give you a leg up. Get on the thatch and keep low. We need to get to Domita before she reaches the square. We will be quicker and safer up there."

He bent down, and Petronella used his joined hands as a lever to help her clamber up the water butt. She swayed on its thin edge, reaching for the slimy gutter. She could feel Joran's anxious gaze on her back as she scrabbled for a more secure hold.

"Go on. You can do it, Your Majesty." His voice was firm and reassuring. She could hear the ironic smile in his voice. Taking courage, she took a breath and hoisted herself up, shoulder muscles burning. She ground a toe in the rough wall and boosted herself to the roof, where she crawled the rest of the way and slid along the ridge. Joran took a couple of strides back and almost ran up the side. Petronella raised her eyebrows, impressed, despite herself.

"You've done that before?" she asked, as he joined her, not even slightly out of breath.

"A few times," he said with a shrug.

Together, they peered over the edge of the roof into the adjacent thoroughfare. Soldiers facing forward lined the street at intervals. From here, they could hardly hear the shuffling of the restless crowd in the square. Joran nudged her and indicated a taller building at the end of the street with a jerk of his head. She followed his gaze. The City Hall, although still built of wood, was far and away the largest edifice the small town could boast. Candlelight blazed at the windows. A pair of solid double doors stood at the head of a set of impressive carved steps.

The doors opened, and the tall, spare figure of a man appeared silhouetted in the glare of the torches behind him. Petronella frowned at the familiar shape he presented. Something about the width of his shoulders against the light. Once again, the trickle of fear at the base of her mind tugged at her.

Joran had moved to a crouch and prowled the rooftops like a hunting cat above the heads of the unsuspecting guard. Muddy boots slipping on the slimy thatch, pulse thrumming, Petronella followed him.

The man in the doorway strode down the stairs to a waiting carriage. They were still too far away to make out his features. A whirl of ermine and crimson from a swirling cloak, the subtle flicker of candlelight on black hair flecked with grey. His conveyance trundled forward with a jerk, and the soldiers below them saluted as he was driven past.

Somewhere, a rumble of drums started a steady, funereal beat. Heart racing, she halted on the rooftop with Joran as a small, dark doorway big enough for a horse and wagon opened in the wall of a squat building adjoining the City Hall.

Hand to her mouth, Petronella bit her lip to stifle a cry of relief. Domita, face pale under her freckles, swayed with the rhythm of the cart. Her captors had strapped her hands behind her, and she was blinking in the light of the torches. Water dripped from her clothes and russet hair. Her face looked swollen, one eye bruised shut. A phalanx of soldiers guarded her, but her head was up, and she was alert, looking around her. Analysing her chances, Petronella knew.

Beside her, Joran nudged her to get her attention. "Plan A," he said, under his breath. "We jump the cart, take out the driver and get the hell out of there before they know what hit them. You climb in the back with Domita and get her hands free."

"Plan B?" she asked, already knowing the answer.

"There is no Plan B."

He was running as he spoke, launching himself with determined speed to the final rooftop of the terrace of houses. Petronella took off after him. A stiff wind whipped at her face; the torches blurred beneath her as her feet fought for purchase on the treacherous surface. Domita's wagon was nearing the end of the street now. If it entered the road towards them, they would have little chance to turn the horse before the soldiers flanking the route gathered their wits.

The tumbrel drew closer as they sprinted, gathering speed. As Petronella grabbed all her courage and launched herself into space, she swore she could hear her Jana's delighted whoop of laughter echo through her head.

Chapter Twenty-Nine

Her feet struck wood with a thud that knocked the breath out of her and drilled shock waves through her knees. The horse shied, and the driver cursed his last as Joran ran him through and booted his body off the seat into the road. Catching the reins, Joran urged the nag to a crazed gallop that took no notice of the startled foot soldiers. Petronella stumbled into Domita, toppling with her into the base of the cart. Shouts behind them gave way to the sound of running feet and hastily drawn swords. A poorly aimed arrow whizzed over her head.

Petronella snatched out her dagger and sliced through the ropes binding Domita's hands.

The girl gave her a ragged grin as she flexed her wrists. Petronella's heart broke and her anger flared as she took in the bruised and broken skin on the girl's arms where the bonds had bitten into her flesh and the matching bruises on her face. The guards had evidently been free enough with their fists. They had made rags of Domita's clothing. Petronella frowned. She couldn't account for the fact that the girl was dripping wet.

Braced on the driver's seat, Joran yelled at the horse, exciting it into a further spurt of speed as the cart careened down the muddy streets. Townspeople blundered into each other to get out of the way, their faces a blur of panic. Shouts and shaken fists followed by handfuls of rotten vegetables accompanied their manic flight.

Behind them, the guards were struggling to keep up. A warning horn blared. Petronella flinched as another arrow from an unseen assailant hissed through the air. Domita braced herself on the side of the carriage.

Petronella had never thought it would please her to see a person with flames coming out of their hands, but the sight of Domita's palms as they glowed with pulsing, defensive heat, sent relief coursing through her.

Domita grinned like a madwoman as she raised both palms towards their attackers. Fire roared, splitting the damp night air like festival fireworks, incinerating the arrows soaring towards them even before they began their downward arc. Petronella blinked in admiration at her precision and her fierce, elemental grace. Domita's face was a mask of concentration tinged with glee as the cart leaped onwards and she humiliated their attackers. Perspiration dotted her forehead as she tried to keep going, but her flames flickered as they left the torch-lit streets behind and she slumped to the rocking floor, breathing in shallow gasps as her burst of energy died.

A worried frown creased Petronella's forehead as she screwed herself around against the wild rocking of the cart and scanned the deserted road in front of them. Mist rolled beyond the rotting palisade, yellow and red as it bounced back the light from the torches on top of the barricades. She could see nothing through it.

"Joran, where are we going?" she shouted, over the clatter of hooves and the rumble of wheels.

"Through West Gate," he shouted back.

"Won't there be guards?"

"I said we're going through West Gate. Hold on."

Heart pounding, Petronella joined Domita on the floor of the cart as her knees gave way and she covered her head. The wagon gathered speed as it plummeted downhill, and she stifled a scream as Joran took his precious sword like an axe to the traces, cutting the horse free.

Snorting with terror, it took off into the darkness and Joran leaped off the seat and into the well of the cart with them.

There was an ear-splitting crash as they and the tumbrel plunged through the rotten gate and somersaulted into the air. Petronella bit her tongue and tasted blood as the cart disintegrated around them in a welter of spars and splinters. Domita screamed, and Joran gave an involuntary yell as he sailed over her head towards the waterfall.

Petronella landed in a heap of foliage that knocked the breath out of her and rolled over, spitting out dead leaves. Domita had fallen nearby, slumped in a ragged pile with one arm folded underneath her.

"Domita, are you alright?"

Domita didn't reply, or if she did, her response went unheard over the thunderous boom of rushing water as it galloped to freedom over the falls. The mist undulated like sea serpents around them, almost too thick to see through. Petronella licked her lips and found salt on her tongue. Her exposed skin tingled with gooseflesh where the mist stroked it. She wiped her face, her mind itching with the awareness of power nearby.

"Domita?" Still struggling for breath, she crawled over to her friend, feeling her way through the fog. Domita groaned. "Can you move?"

She passed an arm under Domita's shoulders and helped her sit. Domita gave her a weak grin.

"I'm alright. Just winded."

Petronella nodded and squinted into the mist. "Joran?" She yelled over the noise.

"Here."

His voice was a croak coming from below the edge of the road. Petronella shuffled towards it and gaped at her proximity to the crumbling cliff. The black gulf yawned to claim her. Spray blasted her face, and the river thundered into her ears with deafening force. Another six feet and she would be dead.

Joran, however, had not been so lucky. She slid her reluctant body to the precipice and peered over, blinking moisture from her eyes. The surrounding ground shook with the sheer might of water. Joran's face was pale in the gloom. The mist kissed his face like a deceptive lover. He was standing on a narrow, slippery ledge, fingers clutching at slimy tufts of grass with white-knuckled determination. Below him, the falls stretched downwards into the night. Petronella blanched.

"Don't move," she ordered.

"Believe me, I don't want to." Joran returned with a wry grin as he, too, squinted down into the tumbling dark.

She crawled back to a place of relative safety and surveyed the wreckage of the cart. She hoped some part of the harness might still be there, but it had apparently vanished along with the terrified horse.

"Domita, give me your belt." The girl unwound the leather from around her narrow hips and hefted it over.

Petronella linked it together with her own and gave them an experimental tug. The makeshift rope held easily, but whether they could reach Joran with it and help him climb the cliff remained to be seen. She bit her lip, casting a glance over her shoulder at the steep slope upward to the town. Her mind's eye pictured a large phalanx of men, hastily mustered and willing to brave Domita's fire, marching steadily towards them. To stay was certain death, but they had no choice.

"I hope you are feeling strong," she said to Domita, crawling to the cliff edge again.

Domita shuffled over to her, and they both peered over at Joran, who managed a weak grin at the sight of their terrified faces leaning over him.

"We're using our belts to pull you up."

"You aren't strong enough. Even two of you."

"We have to be. Domita, come here."

Domita edged over. "What do you want me to do?"

"We must do this fast. The longer he dangles, the worse it gets. And his weight could drag us all over. On second thoughts, there might be a better way."

"Hurry, Petronella, this ledge is giving out!"

Petronella picked herself up off the ground and raced back to the broken cart where it lay scattered in chunks across the spray-swept grass. She grabbed a sturdy plank and ran back to the cliff, where she wedged the wood behind two boulders clumped together at the edge of the path.

"I'm going to wedge my feet with this," she dashed out, breathless, "you do the same. Put your weight on me and hold on tight."

Domita nodded, and the two women manoeuvred themselves into position. Petronella winced as the top of the plank dug into her ankles above the hide boots. She did not know if the wood would bear their weight or not. Taking the strongest purchase she could on the plaited leather, she dropped the other end to Joran. A grunt of air escaped her as Domita slid over her and took a grip next to hers.

"Can you reach it, Joran?" she called over the thunder of the water.

"Just."

"On three. Domita and I can't hold you long."

She counted down and braced herself, gritting her teeth against the wrenching pain in her shoulders and feet as Joran grabbed the leather and swarmed up it like a monkey. He exploded over the top of the cliff like a geyser and tumbled over, panting, away from the edge.

Domita rolled off her, rubbing her arms, and Petronella gained her feet. Behind them, a shout from the direction of the town alerted them to their situation. "Hold in the King's name!"

"By the gods."

She screwed her head left and right, but there was no shelter here, only the terrible drop on one side, the fog and a steep and slippery road leading to the land of Oceanis hundreds of feet below in the darkness.

Her heart sank to her sodden boots. She raised her eyes to meet Joran's gaze.

"So near."

His mouth twisted as he nodded. Even Joran couldn't take on twenty fully armed soldiers and live to tell the tale. Domita drooped behind them, her strength given out.

Petronella gazed around in despair as a small contingent of guards marched out of the ruined gate and formed a ragged, reluctant line in front of the ancient wooden wall. Their captain eyed them from a position somewhere at the back of the squad as he bellowed the order to form ranks. The soldiers stared at the wreckage of the cart in disbelief before forming lines with swords drawn. The squad of archers behind them waited with bows at the ready. Fog lapped at them, tasting their exposed skin. Their eyes darted every which way, squinting at the mist. One man's sword was visibly trembling as his body shook with fright.

Frowning in confusion at their strange reaction, Petronella stepped forward, ready to offer herself in exchange for her companion's safety.

The ghostly spears that formed in the mist arrived from nowhere. Coalescing from the fog, they froze to lethal shards of ice in less than a breath and screeched across the intervening space with malicious, penetrating force, as if hurled from a giant's invisible hand.

The troop at which they aimed had no time to react. Mouth open in rampant disbelief, she gasped as spears of frozen water harpooned them like fish, tearing through any exposed flesh with savage grace. Those at the front died screaming with pain and fear, whilst the archers turned and rammed themselves back through the broken gate into the town as fast as they could, pushing and shoving at each other in their haste to get through.

She gaped at her companions. Domita wore a grin like a fox.

"What was that? Where did that ice come from?" Petronella asked, dumbfounded.

“That explains why they haven’t attacked yet,” Joran said, one eyebrow raised as he surveyed the battered soldiers.

“Oceanis has closed its borders.”

The soft voice behind her spun her around. Alice stood on the path below them. Light shone around her and made a halo of her short gold hair. Lips thinned with fury, Petronella drew herself up, but the harsh words dissolved on her tongue at the sight of Domita holding out her arms to her young friend. The princess smiled as she stepped forward into the embrace.

“Welcome to Oceanis,” she said.

Chapter Thirty

Oceanis

Joran was quick to close the gap between himself and the fragile girl. Petronella had barely taken a step before he hurled himself forward to inspect her.

"Princess, are you well?"

Alice gave Domita another firm hug before extracting herself.

"I am fine, I thank you." She said, smiling around. "I am so glad to see you escaped from Goldfern."

Petronella strode the few steps down the pathway to her former maid and companion, her lips still compressed in a thin line of disapproval.

"What do you mean by sending us all into the water with your magic? You must know Domita can't swim. People have died because of you."

"My lady," Domita cut in. "You don't know what happened."

Alice stilled, her face serene, and Joran watched her for a second before he turned to Petronella. "Domita was safe. Alice would have made sure of it."

Sadness marked the young princess's face. "I tried, but I could not help everyone. Domita is my friend. I didn't allow the water to take her, but the Cryfell always demands at least one sacrifice for every life saved." She lifted her gaze to Joran, her aqua eyes filled with regret. "I can't be sure how many of your men survived. I am sorry."

Joran's face shifted with his passing emotions. Petronella read hope, despair and resignation in quick succession. He dragged his hands through his hair, and his shoulders drooped before he raised his head with a sigh.

"They are soldiers. If the gods wish them to join the feast at World Peak, then so be it. We are all in their hands."

Petronella blinked. She hadn't realised Joran's devotion to the old religion. She turned her gaze to the walls of Goldfern. No-one had dared to put their heads out into the lethal mist. Goldfern was a city of Epera. People did not use magic here or risk mentioning the gods in public. Warehouses and factories and shops had taken root in deserted temples and shrines. Magic was long gone.

She gazed at Joran, a man of two bloods who was at home in both worlds, and then faced forward into the darkness and an unknown land. Her fists clenched and her head gave a pulsing throb as his gaze lifted to hers. Her companions waited. Domita exchanged a questioning look with the princess, who gave her a 'wait and see' look.

Domita scowled, too impatient to wait. "My lady?" she asked.

Petronella swallowed. The salty mist pricked her skin. Her head still throbbed, her whole body ached for rest and food and drink. "How strong are your defences?"

Alice smiled. "Strong. You are safe at present."

"Good enough."

The tense atmosphere lifted as her companions relaxed. Domita grinned her relief, and stoic Joran allowed the corners of his mouth to quirk upward in a tired smile.

"If you wish it, there is an inn at the bottom of the Falls. We can rest there tonight," Alice offered.

"Food?" Domita asked.

"And drink and warm baths and comfortable beds."

"Lead on."

The mist lifted as they picked their way down the cliffs, with Alice in front.

The temperature rose as they descended, and Petronella shook her hood from her head for the first time in days. A humid breeze caressed her face, and she loosened the neck of her tunic. They had travelled for another hour and made steady progress down a road that was both cobbled and dry. The air was full of the chirrup of cicadas. Beside them, on the edge of the path, the water was a constant roar. Deep forest bordered the flagged pathway on the other side. Hunting owls called. Overhead, the night sky was cloudless, the moon a waxing crescent above them. Stars stretched endlessly into the dark and the perfume of countless flowers scented the balmy night air.

Fatigue and hunger were claiming them as they reached a rough, white-painted wall that bordered a large courtyard. Heavy glass lanterns flanked the gate that stood ajar to welcome weary travellers. The yard was quiet. Looking around, Petronella guessed in more prosperous times it would hum with tradesfolk and merchants, carriages and mule trains preparing to make the long ascent up the Fools Road to Goldfern with their wares.

The inn itself was an inviting expanse of whitewashed stone. It boasted two levels topped by a flat roof. Vines and flowers in reds and pinks, bleached in the pale moonlight, clambered in abandoned fashion over the walls. Bright blue shutters bordered the windows. They stood open and music from some unseen lute player spilled out towards them, along with the green warmth of fragrant herbs, yeasty bread and rich wine. Petronella's empty stomach growled. She was unsure what her battered body craved most.

Alice preceded them through the door. Music and conversation died to be replaced by resounding silence as the patrons of the hostelry halted their revels and took in the bedraggled, weary party standing on the threshold.

The woman playing the lute placed the instrument to one side and hurried to meet them with a worried smile wreathing her plump features. "Welcome to the Wayfare Inn."

The scowls and frowns smeared across the faces of the other patrons made Petronella doubt the sincerity of her statement.

"They must be from Swords. What are they doing here?" One young man growled from across the room. His green eyes scanned them with hatred, his hands clenched in fists of defiance and Petronella raised her chin, ready to defend herself before Alice cut in.

"They have left the kingdom of Epera to seek shelter with my father, King Merlon."

There was a collective gasp. The customers slid as one from their seats, facing Alice with their hands stretched towards her. They bowed their heads and the crescent moon of Oceanis glowed blue on every palm. The princess returned the obeisance with a smile and a complicated gesture of her slim hands. The company placed their hands on their hearts in return.

"The blessing of our goddess," Joran murmured behind her.

Petronella's mouth dropped open. She did not know the respect young Alice commanded in her own kingdom, or her power.

"By the Moon," the proprietress said, overcome. "My lady, you are welcome in my hostelry. Please, sit. We heard the King of Epera held you prisoner at his castle. We must get word to His Majesty, your father."

"No need, I have contacted him," Alice assured her, as the woman showed them to a table in front of the window. An equally flustered middle-aged man, shaped like a barrel, appeared from the kitchen, tray in hand, and handed over fine crystal goblets filled to the brim with sparkling blue wine.

"This is my husband, Perry," the woman said. "I am named Noella. Your presence honours us, Lady." She dipped a curtsy and clapped her hands at her spouse, who was looking at Alice, quite dumbstruck.

"Perry, more wine. And bring our finest dishes for my lady and her guests."

It had been more years than Petronella could remember since she had made merry. As the patrons accepted their presence, someone else claimed Noella's lute and a lively jig broke out in celebration at the princess's return. Voices joined in, followed closely by clapping hands and stamping feet.

More wine appeared to be passed around, and Petronella's mouth watered at the delicacies of fish and seafood as they arrived at the table, garnished with salads of all sorts and bolstered with delicate black rice.

Noella urged them to eat their fill and brought white bread, as soft as clouds, and rich yellow butter to go with it. Conversation was brisk between them as they shared stories of their recent adventures.

"One thing that has been bothering me," Petronella said, taking another sip of wine, and looking at Domita, "is why were you so wet when they put you in that cart?"

Domita chewed her food, eyes harder than diamonds as she swallowed.

"They wanted information," she said. She shrugged as she reached for another plate of rice. "They knew I was likely afraid of water, and they were quick to realise my flames don't work without light, so that's what they did. They tied me up in a barrel of water and snuffed the torches, and then they beat me black and blue."

Her tone was even, but Petronella could see the tension in the youthful face as she remembered her internment. Bruises stood out like smudges of coal on her skin. Her wrists wore bracelets of twisted raw flesh where she had obviously fought to get free. She caught the young woman's hand in her own, and Domita looked at her in surprise.

"Would you recognise those people again?" she asked.

Domita swallowed and turned her head away. "I will never forget them." Her face cleared as she reached for her own wine and washed her food down. Her chin jutted with pride and her brown eyes flashed as they met her concerned stare.

"I didn't tell them anything," she said.

Petronella shook her head, her own lips thinned to slits. "I wouldn't blame you if you had. But if you ever see them again, I want you to tell me. Do you promise?"

Domita grinned. "I promise." She nudged Petronella's arm. "You can relax, my lady. 'Tis done and in the past. We are here. Safe. Have some more wine." She tipped the remains of a bottle into Petronella's glass and winked as they toasted each other. The music swelled.

Beside them, Joran was eating his way steadily through a whole lobster. He met her gaze as he cracked open the second claw and grinned, his eyes alight with pleasure.

"What do you think of the wicked Kingdom of Oceanis now, my lady?" he asked, one brow slanting upwards in a quizzical fashion that made her smile.

"At the present time, as long as we are all safe, warm and fed, I will gladly accept it for what it is," she said. She took another hefty sip of the wine, enjoying the path of good cheer that blazed through her.

She sat back against her seat, cradling the goblet between her gloved hands. Her head was spinning, and she averted her eyes from the dizzying display of dancing one couple had started, to the cheers of the audience.

"Be careful with the wine. It is potent stuff in Oceanis," Joran warned, taking another sip from his own glass.

"I think it's a little too late for that." Petronella struggled upright and gained her feet, leaning against the table for support.

Noella was by her side in an instant. "There are comfortable rooms prepared for you. I have arranged for you all to have a bath and a change of clothes. What you are wearing is too hot and rough for our weather."

Petronella smiled at her earnest expression. “You are very kind. Thank you for your care of us.”

Noella shook her head. “It is nothing. We wish only for your comfort. Would you like to retire now?”

The room swayed, and Petronella managed a dazed nod. Domita clambered to her feet, rocking a little.

“Much as I would love to stay, I need to sleep,” she said.

Alice reached across and squeezed her hand, her eyes sparkling with the wine and the good company. Safe in her own lands, the shadows had already fallen from beneath them.

“Rest well,” she said. “We cannot tarry long. My father is expecting us in Shoreborne as soon as we may travel there.”

Joran laid back in his chair, stretching his long legs as he reached for the bottle to top up his glass.

“I will be up shortly,” he said. His lazy gaze drifted around the room, latching onto a serving maid with blonde hair. She was dodging the arms of the young man who had confronted them when they first entered. She aimed a playful slap at his clutching hands and turned a flirtatious and equally assessing stare in Joran’s direction. Petronella raised her eyebrow as she turned away, unaccountably disappointed.

“Good night then,” she muttered.

Joran saluted her with his glass. “Until tomorrow.”

The rooms Noella led them to were blessedly far away from the riotous taproom. Footsteps dragging with weariness and wine, they followed her bustling form up a narrow stairway and along a whitewashed corridor to the back of the sprawling inn. Domita hugged her at the entrance to her own room and closed the door. Noella pushed open the adjacent door and showed Petronella through.

Petronella stopped on the threshold, and a smile lifted her lips.

Fine muslin curtains in delicate shades of blue and green stirred in the faint, perfumed breeze floating in from the open window. There was a fireplace, but at present, the space glowed with the light of candles placed there to add a gentle ambiance. Scented steam rose from a worn copper tub standing in front of the hearth. Another kettle full of cold water stood next to it. A stool nearby contained folded linen, various soaps, and sea salt in a shallow ceramic dish.

The bed was a delicate four-posted affair of sea-stained driftwood, hung with the same muslin and covered with crisp white cotton sheets. A coverlet of blue, neatly folded, lay at the foot of the bed where a dainty chemise of light linen also rested. A padded armchair enjoyed the view from the window. The floorboards had been lime washed white and carpeted with rush matting at strategic intervals.

"This is marvellous," Petronella said, taking some more steps into the room.

"I am glad you like it. There are clothes in the wardrobe for you, fit for travelling."

"You must tell me how much we owe you for everything."

Noella shook her head. "My lady Alice tells me her father, King Merlon, will settle everything. You need only rest and travel to Shoreborne, our capital city, in the morning." She nodded at a delicate blue cord hanging from the ceiling by the bed. "If you need anything, please ring."

She withdrew, and the door closed behind her with a solid click. Petronella stepped further into the room and slid her heavy bag from her shoulder. It hit the floor with a thud, and she pushed it under the bed with a decisive shove of her mud-caked boot.

She lost little time in shedding the filthy woollen garments and hide boots of mud-slicked Epera. Nose wrinkling, she heaped them in a pile by the door, unsure what to do with them.

The bath was a blissful experience. She added a handful of the salt from the dish and sank with a sigh into its warm, silken embrace. Lutes and a chorus of voices from the taproom trickled through her window as she lolled, head against the edge of the tub, arms dangling over the sides and dripping water on the floor. The salted water did a fine job of relaxing tight muscles.

The water was growing cold as she heaved herself out, having scrubbed the grime of travel from her weary body. She fluffed her hair dry with the towel, running her hands through the across the length of it. A mirror on the wall in front of a white painted set of drawers reflected a face drawn with tiredness and scratched from contact with brambles and branches as they forced their way along. The short style emphasised her eyes and her cheekbones, bony as they were. Her mouth remained generous, her skin Epera pale.

She shrugged at her reflection as she turned down the lamps and climbed into bed, sinking with a sigh of relief into a mattress that promised golden slumber.

The last thought she had as she drifted into an exhausted sleep was the memory of Joran and his speculative, assessing gaze as he perused the options for bed sport.

She tried not to mind he had not chosen her.

Chapter Thirty-One

Exhaustion dropped Petronella like a stone into the river of her dreams. A tide of chaotic impressions rushed through her mind. She caught the blue spark of Joran's eyes as his gaze bored into hers. The rush of pure exhilaration and Jana's laugh as she launched herself from the rooftops in Goldfern, the hard, implacable line of Arion's mouth as he told her she had to die to save the land.

Felice turned to face her, holding out her precious flower. Faceless men loomed behind her once plump form. She caught the glint of firelight on an axe, and her First Lady lifted the fragile bloom higher, into the light of the full moon shining through a foreign window.

"Take it, please take it," the woman begged her. Then Alice's face, her eyes blank and white as seashells, and her muttering voice.

"They are coming. Under, under."

She saw Mistress Eglion as she had last seen her only the day before, standing at the mouth of the tunnel leading to the temple of the Mage. Her old tutor was pointing a stern and implacable finger to the west, and birds sang in the cold air.

A rustle of leaves filled her dreaming ears. All at once, they surrounded her, twisting and turning, chasing her around a small cave.

Her own delighted childhood giggle weaved through her mind as she begged Jana to stop, to stop. Her laughter chilled at the sight of a broad pair of shoulders silhouetted against the entrance. She could not see the man's face, but the force of his anger was unmistakable, and then a rushing, sliding, pushing against her chest that swung her down and out against her will. The clutching of her tiny fingers as they struggled to grasp bushes and branches lining a steep path. The desperate need to get back, to get back to Jana and then, in her mind, the pain in a head bludgeoned into submission by the blunt end of a dagger.

She woke screaming, with sweat drenching her body.

Domita blundered into her room, her face smudged with sleep.

"What's the matter? What is it?"

Petronella fumbled for the girl's clutching hand in the dim light from the star-drenched sky filtering in through her window. She gripped it with her own shaking fingers, taking comfort from the heat.

"I don't know. A nightmare."

Wearing nothing but hastily donned britches, Joran plunged through the open door and skidded to a halt at the foot of her bed.

"What is it? Why did you scream?"

Petronella took a couple of huge breaths and slid her cold feet to the floorboards. She crossed the room to the pitcher of water on the dresser and filled a chased silver goblet with trembling fingers. She raised it in their direction.

"Anyone?"

Her companions shook their heads, and she drank deep. The rush of cold liquid cleared her head a little, and she returned to the bed, huddling under the light cover.

"I had a dream, but more than that. A memory perhaps. Jana was there, and a man came and... and..."

Her voice stumbled over the words, and she shook her head, frustrated.

"I couldn't see. I couldn't do anything. She pushed me away... down a path?" She flexed fingers that still somehow remembered the tear and scratch of brambles and branches as she tried to hold on. Black dirt had lodged itself deep under her shredded fingernails, her palms scored raw. Her hands had taken a long time to heal. She recalled that now.

"I don't understand. They told us Jana had an accident. I was always told she fell... but I know that's not right. I could feel it. Someone killed her. Beat her to death."

Her heart ached with long-forgotten loss as she buried her face in her hands, searching her faraway memories for more clues, but the visions had gone, chased away by her wakefulness. Domita patted her shoulder as though she were a restive horse that required soothing. Joran paced the room.

"You told me once Jana did not wish to become a queen?" he said. His voice was gentle, a rich baritone, restful to her tired mind.

"I think she told me on the day she was..."

"Did the murderer hear her say that?"

Petronella's hands dropped to the sheets. She shook her head, twisting her ring around her finger. It gleamed, reflecting the silver light of the stars in the sky. "I'm sorry, I don't remember."

Joran fell to a knee beside the bed. His eyes reflected starlight back to her as he took her hands.

"The memory will come back in time as your blood clears of the drug. Don't force it."

Petronella's skin tingled at the contact of his warm palm against hers. Her fingers gripped his of their own accord.

"I'm not sure if I want it to," she said, unwilling to acknowledge the acceleration of her heartbeat as she met his concerned gaze. His bare shoulders gleamed silver in the starlight.

He squeezed back and opened his mouth to reply when they were both dazzled by the light blazing from Petronella's ring. It shone like a thousand torches, illuminating the room momentarily with the glare of sunshine.

Petronella winced as the glare sizzled through her hand and up her arm. It seared a path through her brain. Thoughts from another mind torched her own like comets, throwing white sparks in their wake. Joran snatched his hands away, his eyes dark with shock, and she frowned as he scrambled to his feet, his usually calm face a mask of horror. The glow from the diamond dulled at the breaking of the contact, and remote starlight resumed.

"What is it? What caused that?" She knew nothing but confusion. She'd been wearing the jewel, and it had lain dormant on her hand for the past ten years.

Domita backed away from the bed. "The Ring of Mercy," she murmured. She regarded Petronella with a wary look in her eyes, as if a previously trusted pet had shown unexpected fangs.

"Well, yes, I know what it's called." Frustration turned Petronella's voice to ice. "But that is the first time it has ever done more than just weigh a lot."

"You are waking up."

The girl's voice from the doorway was calm and remote. Petronella was less than astonished to see Alice's eyes were once again blank. She rolled her eyes.

"Another prophecy."

"I think you might do well to listen this time," Joran said. Starlight blanched his cheeks. His eyes were dark sockets above cheekbones etched with silver. He fixed his eyes on Alice with complete trust.

The princess shuffled further into the room, and Domita grabbed her elbow out of habit. The princess leaned against her, but her stone-white eyes did not change.

"It is your time. Time to remember all that was and all that is still to be."

"Ever the cryptic," Petronella said, under her breath.

Alice turned her blank gaze towards Petronella, who shivered as a trickle of fear like meltwater ran down her spine. The princess's voice, when it came, was stronger and far older.

"There is a time for knowledge and a time for belief. That time is now."

Alice raised a shaking hand and traced the sign of her goddess under the starlit sky. Petronella's eyes widened and her mouth dropped open. The mark glittered like starlight, decorating the room with a delicate tracery of silver. It lingered, illuminating their tired faces, then dissolved into the warm night like mist.

Domita grunted with the unexpected weight as Alice collapsed against her.

"I'll take her back to her room," she said, wrapping an arm further around her friend.

Petronella watched their shuffling progress into the corridor and turned back to Joran. The atmosphere between them had shifted in the brief span of time since the ring had blazed its way into the space between them.

He watched her, his gaze intent and wary.

"What was that, Joran?" Petronella asked. "Please tell me what you know. I could feel your thoughts. Could you feel mine?"

He bit his lip, his expression tortured as it met her own. He shook his head.

"It's hard to believe what I have seen," he admitted eventually, when she thought she would die of frustration if he didn't speak. "you said yourself Jana was meant to be queen. And you could not conceive. Despite your own magical potential or your family history and bloodline, by rights, the ring itself should remain forever dormant on your hand."

"What does it mean? I am not with child." Her logical mind was still searching for some sort of explanation.

Bewilderment clouded his features, and he shook his head again. "I have absolutely no idea."

Chapter Thirty-Two

Petronella slept badly and woke from a fevered doze as dawn broke across Oceanis and birdsong swelled in the trees outside. Blinking in the unaccustomed brightness, she staggered to the window and threw open the panes, slanting a hand across her aching forehead.

Dewdrops twinkled on every branch and blade of grass as far as she could see. The world stood hushed apart from the avian voices celebrating the new day.

Rolling fields, rich with ripening wheat, folded their arms at a distance around the inn. Nearer to the boundary, cattle grazed, placid tails swishing. Her window looked out over the rear courtyard. A yawning milkmaid fetched buckets from a nearby creamery. A young man stopped her progress and swept her into his arms for a kiss and a cuddle. She laughed and gave him as much back again before continuing on her way. Her beau leaned on his hayfork as she left, hips swinging. A soft-focus grin stretched across his wide mouth.

Craning her neck, Petronella could see the Fools Road winding up the Falls towards Goldfern. The swell of the river was a familiar backdrop by now. Horses stamped impatiently in their stalls, demanding breakfast.

She smiled as Domita crossed the stable yard, a half-chewed hunk of bread in her hand. The bruises on her face were dark against her tanned skin, the abrasions on her wrists stood out clearly below the sleeves of the close-fitting shirt she wore above tan breeches. Petronella's mouth screwed into a grimace as her grip on the fine muslin curtain tightened. Domita did not deserve such injustice.

A soft knock on the door broke her out of her reverie. She crossed the room to admit Noella, who was holding a heavy wooden tray loaded with sustenance against her rounded hip.

"Your breakfast, my lady," Noella said, bustling in and putting the platter down on a table by the window.

"By the gods, that is a lot of food. Surely it is not all for me?" Petronella asked, gazing at the plate of flatbreads, soft cheese and fruit with something akin to wonder. Her stomach growled.

Noella whisked a cloth from a plate heaped with poached eggs and tomatoes. A tall glass of ice-cold milk accompanied the dishes.

"If you don't mind me saying so, my lady, you could all do with some more food."

Petronella's eyebrows raised. Such an innocent remark. This kindly woman could not know the deprivation currently devastating Epera.

"Thank you."

She eyed the overflowing tray, stomach clenching as she recalled the grey, cavernous faces of her own people struggling for scraps in the rain.

"Eat it, Petronella. Stop feeling so guilty. How will you help anyone if you are starving to death yourself?"

Her head flew around, and she flushed at the sight of Joran leaning against the door frame. He showed no signs of a hangover from the previous evening. His honey hair was dark with a recent splashing and the stubble had gone. A stray lock fell over one eye, and she blushed further, dragging her gaze away with difficulty. His mouth widened in the now-familiar grin.

Her eyes travelled over his face. He seemed unconcerned about the event of the night before, or at least happy to put it behind him. She clamped her lips closed on the questions still cluttering her mind and scraped her chair to the table.

"Alice is up and eager to travel. Domita has selected our mounts, and we are awaiting your pleasure, my lady."

Petronella's brow creased in irritation at his banter in the face of her hangover. She helped herself to a plate of food. She couldn't deny how hungry she was.

"Do you want some of this?" she asked, gesturing to the heaped platter that remained. "There is plenty."

Joran sauntered across the room and helped himself to a flatbread smothered with cheese. He ate with relish, standing at the window, and grinned at the activity in the courtyard.

Petronella busied herself with eggs and tomatoes, trying not to notice the width of his shoulders in silhouette, or the sturdy length of his thighs. "What are you smiling at?"

"Domita. We couldn't have chosen a better groom, I don't think. The horses love her."

Petronella smiled in recognition as a wash of affection bloomed in her chest. "Yes. She is never happier than in a stable. Of course, that was not supposed to happen. Her father sent her to me in the hope I would make a proper lady out of her. We spent our days out hunting with my falcon, the Grayling, before they banned us, and when that happened, we sparred with daggers in my dining room instead."

Joran grinned at her. "Another failure to add to your list."

Petronella shook her head as an answering smile quirked her lips. "Indeed, but not one I am sorry about."

She applied herself to her breakfast as Joran took his leave to prepare for their departure. His absence took some glow from the sunlit room.

Having bolted the rest of the food and gathered her possessions, Petronella joined the others in the courtyard, ready for their journey.

Their hosts had supplied practical garments for their guests that included rich linen hose, tunics embroidered with their traditional blues and aquas and wide-brimmed hats to shade them from the sun.

Fine wool cloaks were now loaded across panniers held at the back of each saddle. Long leather boots hugged their legs.

It was a relief to leave the harsh peasant garb behind and experience the warm breeze on her skin. Petronella's ring flashed on her finger for a change, reflecting the sunlight.

Noella and Perry waved from the door, and there was an air of celebration in the small party as they mounted and clattered across the well-swept cobbles to the Fool's Road.

Petronella admired the sight of Domita on the fine-blooded Battonian stallion she had selected from the rich pickings in the Wayfare stables. Girl and horse were a study in chestnut. She stifled a grin as Domita bent forward to whisper in her mount's ear. He gave a couple of half-hearted bucks, and Domita laughed aloud. Glancing around, she rolled her eyes at the slow pace of the rest of them and urged her steed to a gallop on the soft, packed earth. Petronella chuckled. She rode like a warrior, completely in tune with her ride. Alice shaded her eyes against the morning sun with a smile tugging at her lips as they raced into the morning.

"How far is it to Shoreborne?" she called across to the princess, who was laughing as Domita disappeared into the distance.

"Three days good riding through the hills to Sunira, where the water is calmer. We'll take a boat from there to the capital. Another two days. At this precise moment, Domita is going entirely the wrong way. She will end up in the river in a minute."

Alice wheeled her dapple grey about to wave her blessing at their hosts. Harness jingling, he jogged in place, as impatient as his rider to be underway. The princess turned to the west, her blue eyes alight, and urged her mount to a trot.

Petronella waved at Noella, who stood at the doorway to her inn, encircled by the stout arm of her husband. The woman smiled back at her. "Gods speed you," she called after them.

Accustomed to the sharp lines and jagged edges of Eperan scenery, and the equally spiky shape and mood of its citizens, Petronella spent the journey across Oceanis to Sunira battling disbelief and increasing, unaccountable anxiety.

Their passage was an easy one. The inhabitants of this fair land were rosy with good health, and many were as plump and shiny as butter-fed cats.

Oceanis stretched its welcoming embrace over gentle, rolling hills, ripe with wheat and rich with grass. Lakes, both large and small, peppered the landscape. Tiny villages perched on their banks with reeds, water, wild fowl, and fishing nets, their ever-present backdrop. Boats plied their trade across waters placid in the summer sun. Music and laughter spilled from every tavern they passed. There were shouts aplenty too, and some fistfights viewed from a distance. The inhabitants of Oceanis wore their hearts on their sleeves, just as young Alice did, and lived their lives outdoors, under the benevolent eye of a gentle summer sun.

Petronella had difficulty not shouting warnings to them as they trotted by. Her anxiety increased the further they travelled. She had to get to Merlon and make him treat with Arion. The idea of these innocent people slaughtered, their homes and farms decimated and ground into dust, their blood soaking their fertile fields, made her physically sick. And it would be her fault. All of it.

"Eat, Petronella."

They had crossed the Dernian Hills that afternoon, travelling along dusty roads to the forbidding dark entrances of two long-abandoned mines on the steep slopes overlooking Sunira. They had stopped there to rest the horses and to have a small meal. Sunira stretched below them over the plain on both sides of the Cryfell, a small, peaceful city with an air of serenity about it. Petronella's skin prickled as she scanned it, and she shoved away the bread Domita had given her. She had been glad to put distance between themselves and the noisome, dank air that drifted from the black-eyed, watchful tunnels.

By evening they lounged outside Pike Inn on the wharf in Sunira, waiting for a passage down the Cryfell to Shoreborne.

The warm breeze brought with it the savoury smell of fried fish and vinegar, and the constant din of the dock men and women transferring goods to and from the boats crowding the wharf. Wooden wheels and creaking windlasses underpinned the good-natured banter from their fellow customers at other tables. Alice disappeared inside to arrange rooms for the night.

"He's right," Domita said. "You've hardly touched anything since our first night. And you've hardly said a word. What's the matter?"

"I have no words." Petronella's shoulders twitched with irritation. "I have trouble reconciling all this," she waved her hand at the bustle and peaceful industry all around them, "with what we have come from and what we fear is to come. How can these people not be aware of the danger they are in? How can Merlon not treat with Arion to provide food and prevent an atrocity from happening?"

Joran frowned. "We will know his thinking soon enough," he said. "And he might change his mind when his daughter returns to him. He does not have to worry about her after that."

"He thinks our boundary defences will hold," Alice said, joining them at the table and helping herself to a goblet of wine from the jug. "It is the way of the land in times of trouble. The High Priestess set the wards herself. Your husband can hurl anyone he wants at our border and, if they mean harm, she will defend us. You saw it yourself."

"Epera does not use magic. And magic is the only thing that can fight other magic," Joran said. "He cannot cross the border. War will not come here. You have brought Alice back. Merlon will be grateful. Alice is right. There is little to prevent him from coming to terms now. So please, eat."

He shoved the plate at her once more, daring her to reject it. Petronella ignored him and narrowed her gaze at the princess.

"How do you know what your father is thinking?" she said. "You are not home yet, but you are obviously communicating with him."

Alice rolled her eyes. "Through water, of course. We can scry. It's effective when in our own country. All we need is a body of water, a basin, or even a puddle will do at a pinch."

"We contact people through our fires in Battonia," Domita said through a mouthful of fluffy bread. "And in Argentia, they communicate through the roots of the trees or some such. Don't ask me how. I've never been there."

"By the gods," Petronella said. "I can't believe you people and your magic."

Alice laughed as she raised her glass to her lips. "It has worked for us for aeons since the time of the making of the world by the four great Gods. It would work for Epera too, if your king wasn't so set on eradicating it from your people. That is the real question. Why has he turned his back on it?"

"It wasn't him. It was his father, Francis. That's what they told me in the orphanage when I was a boy," Joran said, spearing a mouthful of fish. "It's said it was grief when he lost his first wife and magic could not save her."

Petronella stared at him. "That can't possibly be the entire story," she said. "Our laws allow the killing of people who display the curse of magic. How can one king's terrible loss account for that? Why would he punish his own people for something they cannot help? It makes little sense. The lonely king tortured by grief scenario is just a romantic Oceanis myth."

"There speaks the Queen of Swords, ever logical." Joran's mouth twisted. "Why do you think he turned, then? And if it was Francis who started it, what makes your husband continue?"

Petronella shook her head with a shrug. "I know nothing about Francis. Arion thinks magic is evil. I do not know why. I wish I did." She glanced at her ring, twisting it around her finger. She had tried several times over the last few days to loosen its grip, but even well-applied goose grease at their last stop had failed to move it. Stifling a sigh, aching with tiredness, she picked up her knife and cut up her discarded fish. Her companions relaxed and refilled their glasses, and an unseen fiddler struck up a jig that soon had Domita tapping her feet.

Petronella's gaze wandered up and down the jetty. Everything appeared normal. Life continued. People smiled, argued, worked and loved. Impenetrable magic warded the borders of Oceanis. She should feel safe.

So why was a fingernail of dread scraping its way up her spine?

Chapter Thirty-Three

The capital city of Shoreborne dazzled the eyes even before Petronella set her feet on dry land. Its streets and white, low-lying buildings settled on the hillsides of two low mountain ranges like snow drifts and occupied a crescent-shaped space on the sandy plains in between. The tallest buildings were temples and shrines, open to the sky and crowned with a crescent moon, the sign of the High Priestess. Incense wafted through the humidity, competing with the tang of the ocean and the reek of fish. The huge harbour dominated the city. Ocean-going vessels flying bright pennants bobbed at anchor. Petronella noted the flags of Battonia and Argentia, and of other lands far away from their continent across the Western Sea. Seagulls wheeled and screamed in the breeze following the fishing boats, and the briny atmosphere brought a thin sheen of perspiration to her face. She licked salt from her lips. Alice leaned over the side of the boat as it docked at the riverside jetty, alert for a welcoming party. Behind her, Domita was as awestruck as Petronella. Majestic temples to the gods raised graceful white arches to the sky, two to each hill. A colossal marble statue towered over the harbour. The High Priestess, her gaze fathomless and remote, lifted her left hand in a blessing to the sea, whilst the other was pointing upwards at the sky, encouraging her followers to look up to the heavens for inspiration. Alice nudged Petronella when she noted the direction of her gaze.

"The marble they carved her from comes from the quarries at Stratus," she said.

"Stratus in Epera?"

"The very one."

"It must have taken such a long time."

"Fifty years, so they say," Joran said, joining them at the rail with his travel pack slung over his shoulder and his sword at his side. He scanned the jetty in his turn and then nudged Alice to get her attention. "Is that who you are looking for?"

Alice's gaze swept across the raucous crowd to where he pointed, and Petronella stifled a smile at the flush that bloomed on her olive cheeks.

"Ah. Your father sent Timoro to meet you." The gaggle of young men were standing foursquare on the jetty, squinting at the vessel through eyes shaded with hands against the lowering sun. They waved when they spotted their princess.

Alice tossed her head, ignoring Domita as she giggled. She leaned over the rail to return her greetings, and the small party waited for the boat to bump against its mooring and the gangplank to run out.

The King and Queen of Oceanis had sent two carriages for them. The cobblestones shimmered in the heat. Petronella mopped perspiration from her brow as she accepted the arm of one of Timoro's party who helped her into its shady interior.

Domita jumped in behind her whilst the greeting party ushered Alice and Joran with some ceremony into the first carriage. Petronella smiled at the young man who took a seat opposite her. His answering smile was polite, but his expression wary, and his smile didn't quite meet his sea-green eyes. He opened a footlocker and presented a deep tray holding a lidded silver flagon and a trio of frosted glass goblets.

"Your Majesty, compliments of King Merlon," he said, holding the tray with remarkable steadiness as the team of horses took the strain and the carriage jolted to life across the cobbles.

Petronella thanked him, while Domita managed pouring and tasting the wine for her. It was tangy and fresh against her tongue, filled with honeyed blueberries and fresh herbs.

"My thanks, this is welcome," she said after her first sip.

The man nodded to her. "You are welcome. My name is Brynn. I am to bid you welcome to the city of Shoreborne."

"We are pleased to be here."

Petronella switched her attention to the lively view outside the carriage windows as they left the harbour and began a long ascent up a handsome avenue lined with majestic palm trees.

The more well-to-do here wore soft silks and delicate laces that drifted like sea foam in the warm wind. Fans fluttered like butterflies, and the women wore their hair in cascades of curls, or complicated braids dotted with pearls and ribbons beneath floating transparent headdresses. Their escorts were scarcely less adorned. The men favoured the close-fitting tunics and hose she had first seen on Joran when he visited the Castle of Air, while the working classes made do with sturdy cotton tunics and pale linen hose.

Their horses clattered up the steep slope, and they passed shops and cafes by the score. Street musicians entertained with flutes or guitars. Fountains abounded on street corners, throwing shining liquid curtains over sea nymphs, monsters and mermaids carved in marble. Stairs carved in the material tracing intricate and serpentine curves, lifted the devout to their prayers. Incense perfumed the air from the altars inside the shrines and temples. The devoted were a constant stream in and out, bearing gifts and offerings to the gods.

Those toiling in the streets were fixing banners and flags to the outside of buildings. Intoxicating scents billowed from cafes and restaurants and reminded Petronella once again how long it had been since her last full meal.

Brynn noted her fascination with the world outside their window as they travelled further up the hill.

"We are preparing for the Rite of the Moon," he explained, taking a glass of wine from the tray that now rested on the spare seat beside him and taking a long swallow. Petronella turned a quizzical look at him until he elaborated. "For our lady Princess Alice. She is due to ascend to the rank of Seer at the full moon. 'Tis the first time for a century that a member of the royal blood is also called to the highest spiritual rank of the land."

Petronella exchanged a glance with Domita. That explained why Merlon was so eager to have his daughter back with him.

"Ah. I was not aware."

"No."

Petronella quirked a brow at him. The ironic tone was unmistakable. She took another sip of the excellent wine as her thoughts tumbled. How would Merlon react to her plan? Surely, he could see the sense in it?

Brynn avoided her gaze in his own goblet, and the rest of the journey passed in awkward silence.

Petronella steeled herself for the meeting with Alice's parents as the pair of carriages swept into a courtyard flanked with marble palisades and acres of glistening glass windows.

A fountain of surpassed beauty dominated the courtyard. A massive marble cup threw water with joyous abandon into the air and then collected it into its depths to repeat the process. The shining vapour was a curtain of rainbows. The rushing sound of the water was soothing rather than overwhelming. It snared Petronella's senses, and she almost missed the courteous arm of their escort as he helped her down. Domita stood at her side, eyes wide.

They were both almost bowled over as Alice barrelled past and hurled herself into the arms of a portly middle-aged man who had arrived on the steps in front of them. A tall and graceful woman stood beside him. She had a kind face and an air of serenity about her that Petronella instantly envied. She was less sure about the feelings of her husband, King Merlon. He was shorter than his wife, his bright green tunic fitted closely to a stomach that called food a friend. His face was round, made for merriment. A long, greying beard bound in blue braids swallowed his lips. He held his daughter close to his heart and met her gaze over her bright head. The relief on his face was palpable, but there was a reproof there as well. Easy to read. Petronella forced herself to remain calm, but her heartbeat raced in her chest. Joran came to stand at her side. His solid presence was comforting somehow.

"Don't forget to breathe."

The light mockery triggered instant irritation as it echoed through her head, and she flicked a glare at him.

Merlon released his daughter to the care of her mother, whose greeting was equally heartfelt. Petronella stepped forward to meet him as he strode down the stairway, his legs splayed against his broad frame for balance. He inclined his head almost reluctantly, his shrewd blue eyes scanning her face, and she offered him a tentative curtsy.

"You have my thanks for the return of my daughter," he said. His voice was melodious and surprisingly quiet for a man his size. He indicated the palace with a sweep of his arm. "Come. Rest. We will talk after we have celebrated the safe return of our Princess. We have much to discuss, you and I."

Petronella let out a breath. At least he hadn't ordered her to turn around and head back to Epera or had her thrown into prison. Or killed her.

Joran's voice was laughing as he read her thoughts. "*Oceanis is civilised, you know. We would at least offer you dinner and a comfortable bed before throwing you into the sea and letting the sharks eat you.*"

"Stop laughing at me. This is serious."

"Thank you for your hospitality, my Lord," she said aloud. "I realise my presence here is a cause for concern."

Merlon paused and scanned her from head-to-toe. Petronella flushed uncomfortably under his intense scrutiny, wondering what he was seeing. His shoulders twitched under his robes as if shaking off an unpleasant thought. He looked at Joran, who swept into a courtly bow.

"Welcome, Joran, I thank you also for your service. Meet with me in my chamber at the turn of the hour. I would speak with you."

"As you request, Sire," Joran said.

Merlon preceded Petronella up the stairs to be greeted by Queen Clarys. Her hand clasp was cool and gentle, much like the lady herself. She ushered them into the shade of the palace interior, where smiling servants showed them rooms, offered baths, clothes and explained that a feast was to be held later in the evening at which they were guests of honour.

The door, with its bas-relief of shells and fish, closed behind a smiling maid assigned as her attendant for the duration of her visit, and at last, Petronella allowed her guard to relax. She turned to the tall doors that led to a balcony and found a shady courtyard planted with olive trees and white roses. Their delicate, feminine scent billowed on the breeze into her room, and she gazed around in wonder. The walls displayed circular plaster frames that housed exquisite paintings of ocean and city scenes in tones of aqua and blue. A dressing table topped with an elaborate mirror awaited her pleasure. Colourful glass jars of cremes and cosmetics arrayed with geometric precision decorated its surface. A carved double armoire, panelled in some unfamiliar pale wood, stood against one wall. She wandered across to it and peered in. Rows of delicate, airy gowns hung like coloured mist and rippled softly in the gentle breeze from the open balcony doors. Petronella shook her head, astounded. This must be Alice's doing. She'd communicated with her parents to ensure all was in place to welcome a queen. A tired smile lifted one corner of Petronella's mouth as she closed the wardrobe door. This place was as beautiful as paradise. Safe. Crossing the room, she sank into a silk coverlet embroidered with frolicking mermaids and was asleep in minutes.

Chapter Thirty-Four

The feast for Alice was a riot of noise, laughter, music, and festivity. Petronella lost count of the members of the Oceanis nobility who crammed into the vast courtyard that acted as banqueting room in this summer land. White marble columns adorned with flowers in blues and pinks flanked the space. Musicians and entertainers of every kind occupied both centre stage and remote corners. Song and dance were the chief attractions, accompanied by light, delicious delicacies specially prepared in the palace kitchens to tempt palettes jaded by plenty. Wine flowed as freely as the conversation.

The Court of the Waves adored their princess. The love they held for her was clear in the smiling faces of servants who served her, and the respect given to her by her fellow nobility. Merlon's face was open and relaxed, his kindly eyes often creased in laughter. The still centre around which the activity occurred, Queen Clarys was a graceful and serene presence. Merlon entertained, his gestures broad and his chuckle expansive. He thought nothing of a casual hug, a slap of a shoulder. His short, barking laugh lifted across the music with effortless ease and Clarys strolled at her side, smoothing their entry into Oceanis society with tact and compassion.

Petronella's head was whirling from the wine and the music by the time she slid between the sheets and collapsed into slumber with a groan of relief. She woke with a start the next morning when her maid, Marla, knocked on the door to help her dress.

An hour later, dressed in deep violet silk and with her head thumping from the previous night's uninhibited consumption of Oceanis wine, she mustered courage from somewhere and followed the comfortable curves of Marla, her maid, as the girl led her through the Palace to her audience with the King.

At Merlon's request, Domita's presence had not been required. Domita had shrugged at the news.

"'Tis of no matter," she said. "I am going with Alice to her meeting with the High Priestess at the Temple of the Moon. They are talking about the ceremony, and I am interested in learning more about it. I am sure you will be safe with King Merlon."

Merlon met her in his own antechamber. The small room glowed with sunshine. A startling selection of wine and a collection of the most beautiful and fragile glassware she had ever seen graced marble shelves. The overall impression was of light and glowing colour, ease and delicacy. She lowered herself with care into the chair the king waved her to and took a long breath to calm her nerves as he closed the door to ensure their privacy. He offered her wine, which she refused. Merlon smiled in wry acknowledgement and offered her a glass of diamond clear water instead.

"Our wine is stronger than it looks, indeed," he said, settling himself in his chair and regarding her gravely over a pair of spectacles he had retrieved, shamefacedly, from a drawer in his desk.

At Petronella's smile, he grimaced. "My wife tells me it is pure vanity and that I should, of course, wear these in front of all. However," he shrugged, "my heart can reveal to me the things that my eyes do not always see."

"And what does your heart reveal to you about my presence here, Your Majesty?" Petronella kept her tone as cool and level as she could, while her toes curled in her fragile silk slippers as she waited for his reply.

Merlon scanned her again, sipping his wine with relish. Her heart sank when he shook his head.

"I believe your intentions are honourable, Your Majesty. But your presence here is a cause for grave concern. I am eager to determine your thoughts on the matter."

Petronella took a breath and a sip of her water as she composed her reply. The future of their kingdoms could depend upon it.

"You are, of course, aware that Princess Alice was being held a house prisoner by my husband," she began, picking her words with care. "I hope you know this is not the outcome I would ever have wished for, and I tried to talk to my husband about the matter between our kingdoms. He would not listen to me. It was Alice herself in one of her visions who convinced me that the answers I seek were to the west and that the Kingdom of Oceanis would accept my presence. It was also apparent to me that Arion was planning to marry Alice to beget an heir, without her consent, or yours. I could not conceive. Our land and people are in desperate straits."

Merlon gave her a courteous, although distant, nod. This information was obviously not news to him.

"I understand that Alice's visions can be... persuasive," he said, turning his goblet between his palms. "But your presence in my kingdom has given Arion every reason to continue his harassment at our borders. I have received messages this week demanding your return at the earliest opportunity should you arrive, or he threatens us with invasion. At the present time, I am at a loss how this event could occur as our borders are heavily guarded, as you know?" The raised eyebrow and the question at the end of his sentence left Petronella in no doubt that her veracity in this matter was under some scrutiny.

Petronella nodded. "Yes, we saw evidence of that when we crossed at Goldfern. I was not aware your borders were so well protected. We do not use magic in Epera."

Merlon's head raised from contemplation of his wine, and his gaze stiffened. "Indeed. We know this. It is of great sorrow to the rest of Arcanis that Epera relies on blunt force and cruelty instead."

Petronella shook her head. "I do not condone the cruelty, and up to a few short weeks ago, I would also have discounted the use of magic. However, I have also seen how its absence appears to be harming our cause, rather than helping it. If this journey has taught me anything, is that it is folly to go against the natural order of things. I am afraid that my voice carries little weight with my husband. He holds me in no great esteem. He is a man desperate to feed his kingdom. We need an heir to heal the land. That much is still true and will always be true, no matter how much Arion tries to deny magic, or turn away from it as his father did. My choices in this situation are few. Either I stay in my kingdom and allow Arion to murder me to retrieve my ring and remarry to gain an heir, or I undermine his strategy, steal away his intended bride and beg her father to reconsider our request for food aid, whilst I try to find a cure for my barren condition."

Merlon nodded. "As you say, I believe your intentions are entirely honourable. Part of me would agree with you and consider his threats so much bluster had I not just received this." He retrieved a piece of vellum from his desk and Petronella's heart clenched as she recognised the thick, slanting hand of Arion's penmanship slashed across the page. "Your husband sent a bird, which arrived yesterday. This latest despatch states he is aware of your presence in our kingdom. He now says that unless you return to him, accompanied by a year's worth of grain by the end of the month, he will invade my kingdom. He appears certain about the success of his action. Alice has had several visions confirming his intentions since her arrival. So, I ask you again. How can he achieve this invasion?"

Merlon had not lifted his voice. There were no weapons of war in the chamber, but Petronella's body stiffened as her blood chilled in a sudden wash of ice. She shivered in the warm room and stared in horror as the water in the glass solidified under her eyes. Clamped to her goblet, her fingers turned blue. Unbidden, her mind cried out for Joran.

She shook her head with difficulty, teeth chattering. "I do not know, sir. Arion shares nothing with me."

"You know of no weapons in the air? Nothing that can drop out of the sky?"

"I know of nothing. Truly... but...,"

She took a painful breath against the frozen constriction of her chest. Ice traced delicate patterns over her skin beneath the fragile gown.

"Yes?"

Unable to move her neck, Petronella lifted her eyes to his in desperate entreaty. "Despite the assurances of my companions, I have been full of foreboding since my arrival on your soil. I too, am afraid that he has found a way."

She gasped as the pressure lifted and heat flooded back to her limbs. The ice in her glass melted. Hands shaking, she took a gulp of water.

Merlon refilled her goblet and handed it to her. "I am sorry, my dear. I had to know what you know." Still struggling to recover her composure, Petronella managed a small nod. "You are free to leave. Drink something warm. It will help. I will ask our Chosen warriors to investigate further, but, my dear Madam..." He paused.

Petronella waited for his judgment. He had aged in just a few minutes. She was sure there were lines on his face that had not been there before their meeting. Her heart went out to him.

"We will do our best to make you welcome and keep you safe, but your safety does not come above my need to protect my kingdom or my people. I hope that is clear."

She managed a small smile as she met his weary gaze. Somehow, she rose from her seat with grace. Her ring flashed in the sunlight, a tiny jolt of power that enabled her to stand tall.

"I understand, sir. I would be the same."

Shoulders prickling with tension, Petronella retreated to the privacy of her room and was unsurprised to see Joran lounging outside her door as she gained the first floor.

"You look white. I heard you call. Are you well?" He pushed himself from the wall with one booted foot and opened the door for her to pass through in front of him.

She frowned as she removed the intricate purple headdress she had donned for the meeting with Merlon and tossed it to her dressing table. It floated to a graceful landing, and she shook her head in wonder, lips twisting.

"I find that for all its beauty, the kingdom of Oceanis and its Blessed population could probably kill you without blinking and you would not know where the attack had come from," she said, turning to face him.

Joran grimaced. "I perceive Merlon has introduced you to a power that is a particular strength of his."

"You perceive rightly. I wish I had been better prepared."

Joran shook his head. "It is better that you weren't. The last thing we need is a battle between a king and queen of opposing beliefs and matching strength. This way, Merlon knows you are telling the truth. He would have had no hesitation in handing you back to Arion if you had lied to him. And he would know. Believe me."

Petronella heaved a sigh as her hopeful mood vanished under the familiar avalanche of guilt.

"You may be right. But matching strength? I hardly think so. I have failed. My actions have placed Oceanis in a terrible position. Arion has informed your king he will attack if I am not returned. Did you talk to him?"

Joran nodded. "We met again early this morning. I tried to ask him to send food aid, but he had already received your husband's message and I could have saved my breath. He is worried about our borders.

No-one has ever tried to breach them before now. He has already made further preparations for our defence."

"He doesn't trust his kingdom's own magic?"

"It is more that he doesn't know what your husband has achieved without magic. If our borders are impregnable, how else does he intend to invade?"

Petronella shook her head. "I do not know. I have been full of anxiety since our arrival here. You know that."

She drifted over to the balcony and let the scent of the roses that drifted from the courtyard soothe her mind.

"Joran?" she asked in her mind.

He came to her side. An intoxicating wave of sandalwood and cedar enveloped her. She inhaled. There was something about his solid presence that both excited and calmed her. He stood so close her skin tingled. His breath stirred her hair. Her fingers tightened on the metalwork of the balcony railing.

"Do you know more of the power of Swords apart from our ability to communicate like this?"

A chuckle. *"I believe you may have, shall we say, more abilities I could help you discover.* "

"I need to know how to access them. Will you help me?"

"I am yours to command."

She whirled to face him, a frown creasing her brow. "Do not tease me, Joran."

He didn't move, and she had to look up. His eyes were soft as they travelled over her face, and his lips were very close as he whispered in her head.

"Oh, my Lady. I never tease."

Heart pounding, she drowned in his gaze, lips parting. He lowered his head.

A smart knock on the door broke the moment, and he stepped back abruptly as Domita announced herself. Petronella smoothed her hair and tried to cool her heated cheeks as Joran smiled at her, bowed and left, winking at Domita as he passed her.

"He's pleased with himself," the girl said, joining Petronella on the balcony.

"He has just agreed to help me practise the Sword's magic power." It would do as an excuse to cover the leap of excitement that they had both just experienced.

Domita stared at her, mouth agape.

"You'll catch flies. Stop looking so shocked."

"I am shocked." Domita caught her hands and whirled her round. "Shocked, pleased, delighted and overwhelmed. Alice won't believe it. We thought you would never accept the idea of magic."

"I am not sure if I have to be truthful." Petronella said, rubbing her brow where her habitual headache was forming. "I just have a feeling if I have any of this power you are all so fond of, I am going to need it."

Chapter Thirty-Five

"Gods damn it." Exhausted from another hour of concentrated study and lack of sleep, on the morning of Alice's initiation, Petronella shoved the book to one side and scrubbed her hands through her hair, glaring at the foxed pages. She'd never yet come across a volume so hard to understand. The book seemed to delight in confusing her, and she could swear that the information it yielded was not always the same when she read it again a second time.

Hushed voices from the courtyard drew her across the room, and she leaned over the balcony railing, grateful for the distraction. Over the last few days, she had witnessed many a pair of lovers of all ages and sexes show their love and passion for each other under the light of the waxing moon. As she massaged the tense muscles in her neck, her maid, Marla and her girlfriend, Elta wandered in. Elta reached into the pocket of her apron and, keeping an eye out for the ever-vigilant palace garden staff, snipped a rose for Marla. She offered it with a gallant bow. Marla took it with a giggle and a kiss. Marla glanced up and blushed when she noticed Petronella at the railing. Laughing even harder, she grabbed Elta's hand, and they scurried away. Petronella shook her head and smiled at their receding backs.

The last week had rushed by in a flurry of excited preparation by the city of Shoreborne for the Rite of the Moon. Petronella had endured a week of intense training, encouragement, and ridicule from Joran. Thanks to him, she had mastered the art of snuffing out a candle from across the room and had a better grasp on her telepathic communication ability. These successes seemed a slim reward for the effort involved. Using magic was an arduous process that left her skull pounding and a profound desire for sleep. She'd seen less of Domita, who was either off with Alice somewhere, or down at the stables helping with the horses. Alice, she had hardly seen at all. The princess had spent the last few days in solemn meditation and training with the priestesses at the Temple of the Moon.

The responsibility was huge, Joran had informed her. If Alice survived the initiation and earned acceptance from the Goddess, she would deal with matters of moral integrity in the kingdom. The King would rely on her premonitions to guide his domestic and foreign policies. Alice would have access to the most wondrous of her nation's magic, a fast track to the light and wisdom of their High Priestess.

Petronella's lips quirked in a rueful acknowledgment of her own flimsy abilities by comparison. She glanced at the nearest candelabra and allowed herself a figurative cheer as all three candles flared to life under her mental command.

Joran's mental request for entry heralded his arrival before his knock on the door. She lifted her head to smile at him as he crossed the room. He was holding something behind his back and trying hard not to think about it. She could tell.

"What do you mean by invading my chambers at this time of day, Sir?" she said, stifling the temptation to leave the safety of her seat and risk moving closer.

Joran grinned. "I came to give you a gift. It's traditional on a day like this."

She sat up, bemused. "I have nothing for you."

"Nor should you. This is the Festival of the Moon and the day we consecrate our new Seer. It's a sacred day for all who revere the sacred feminine and acknowledge that part of themselves. Our Goddess it at her most powerful today and therefore it is traditional to present a gift to all who resemble her. I found this for you."

He took the chair beside her and held out a small box decorated in mother-of-pearl gleaming with the softest tones of pink and green. She took it, gazing at it in wonder. It reminded her of the box of blue salt Joran had presented to Arion what seemed like a lifetime ago in the Great Hall in Epera. She thrust the memory away. Now was not the time to be reminded.

"Joran, it's beautiful. Thank you."

He smiled. "Open it. The present is in the box."

Blushing at her own naivety, Petronella lifted the lid. Delight fizzed through her, and her fingers shook as she stroked the contents. He'd commissioned her a jewel. A majestic, swooping peregrine falcon, lovingly rendered in silver and enamelled with her house colours of blue and grey.

"Oh Joran. It's beautiful." She had tears in her eyes as she stared at it.

"I know you miss the Grayling. I can see him in your thoughts."

"I do. So much."

"You can wear it as a brooch, or a necklace, or as a headdress. I had the jeweller make different attachments for it."

She turned it over in her hand, marvelling at the workmanship.

"I had something to ask you."

"Yes?"

"Will you attend the festival with me tonight?"

Her head jerked up. "Me?"

"My lady of the Falcons, Queen of Epera. Will you accompany me to the evening's celebration?"

He restated it formally, with an expectant grin quirking his lips. Petronella hated the blush that scalded her cheeks, but she had no difficulty at all with her reply.

"I will."

Eyes alight, Joran rose and gave her a courtly bow. Petronella marked his progress across the floorboards in bemusement as he sauntered out, whistling. What was happening between them? She was married to Arion. Why did she not even spare him a second thought? She glanced across at the courtyard, with its banks of roses where the full moon would rise in just a few hours, and regarded it with suspicion. A wave of soft laughter arose from her open window, and she shook her head. Was it something they put in the water around here?

Placing the ornate jewellery box gently aside, she heaved a sigh of reluctance as she pulled her book towards her. Festival or no festival, time was ticking on. She was still no nearer to finding a solution to her problems, and try as she might to ignore it, the icy clutch of dread she carried still dragged her screaming every night from dreams of blood and diamonds.

Chapter Thirty-Six

The Rite of the Moon began with a formal ceremony at the magnificent temple on Cator Hill.

Wearing her new necklace and dressed in a silk gown of rose pink, Petronella joined the serried ranks of courtiers, merchants and workers in the stately grounds in front of the palace as they formed a procession, with Alice and her parents at the front.

The priestesses at the Temple of the Moon arrayed Alice in a simple robe of white silk. Her golden hair formed a halo around her head, and in her hands, she held the Oceanis version of Petronella's book and a small, silver cup. A silver diadem in the shape of the triple moon crowned her forehead, and she made the journey barefoot over streets carefully swept and washed that same afternoon. Ranks of solemn priestesses from the major temples of the city followed her and behind them, the secular guests, headed by the King and Queen of Oceanis, walked together.

Domita grinned and nudged Petronella as the procession moved gracefully into order.

"They look all serene and highbrow now," she whispered, "but they have been fighting in the temples for their places in the ceremony, petitions to the king, fisticuffs, sea scorpions in the milk. Everything."

Petronella stifled a giggle.

The expression on the faces of the priestesses was remote. They chanted a soft prayer to their Goddess, asking for her blessing.

Petronella, as visiting royalty, found herself at the front of the line of guests. Joran walked to her right, with Domita on her left.

A hushed, expectant throng of people crowded the streets. Many of them held sticks of incense and cast petals and whole flowers at Alice's small feet as she passed, whispering prayers and blessings. The moon rose, full and strong in a cloudless sky. The air of reverence was palpable.

The rightness of it struck Petronella as she followed along. She gazed around, noting the devout and trusting faces, and wondered how the blessed of Epera might have conducted a similar service before the banishing of their magic. Tears pricked her eyes. Brushing them clear, a familiar face at the edge of the crowd caught her gaze. Craning her neck and standing on her toes, she was sure that she had just glimpsed Mistress Eglion taking an unobtrusive place amongst the citizens. She nudged Joran to gain his attention.

"Mistress Eglion is here," she said, under the chanting.

He flashed her a grin. "I am not surprised. She would hate to miss it."

As vast as the Temple of the Moon was, it could not hold all the people of the city who wished to attend.

Alice moved to her place at the altar in the heart of the Temple of the Moon, her gaze fixed on the statue of her Goddess, who waited to bless her followers. Candles burned in holders shaped like cups in recesses placed around the circumference of the sacred circular space. The temple was open to the sky and dominated by the light of the full moon. The congregation climbed to seats to surround the young princess in a full, unbroken circle. A slow, steady rhythm, beaten out on unseen drums, matched the gentle swell of waves breaking on the shore under a mile away. Outside, the streets filled with more people, waiting their turn to greet the new seer.

A hush descended as the last of the congregation took their seats. The drums still pulsed, quieter now but inexorable as the tides or a beating heart. The High Priestess took her place at the altar and raised graceful arms to the statue. Silence fell.

"O Lady of the quiet water, hear our prayer."

"Hear our prayer," the congregation responded.

"We meet this night to consecrate our child, Alice, into your wisdom and understanding. We ask that you take her and raise her to your right hand, to act for us in all spiritual matters and to bless our kingdom with your guidance and nurture."

"Wisdom and understanding. Guidance and nurture."

Petronella repeated the responses with the rest of the congregation. Beside her, Joran's face was a soft and devout mask. Domita was gazing at Alice with both love and sorrow written across her face. Petronella shook her head. Domita was going to miss Alice once she ascended to her new role. She faced forward once again as the High Priestess continued her evocation.

It was a service of dedication, not unlike a marriage. The High Priestess of the temple asked Alice if she willingly accepted her role, to which she replied in a clear voice. "From my heart with love and my soul with compassion for as long as I live."

There was an out breath from the audience. A sigh of gratitude that went beyond words to touch their hearts. As Alice took her final vows, tears pricked many eyes. Domita sniffed and wiped her nose on her sleeve. Entranced, Alice didn't even blink as the goddess-blessed water marking her brow dripped into her eyes.

The procession moved out of the temple and down to the shore under the statue of the goddess. Many townsfolk were already there. Families had visited the beach that afternoon to place blankets and picnics in readiness. Minstrels and musicians had tuned their guitars and lutes. Stalls dressed in silver, green and blue bunting waited, bursting with goods, ready to sell wine, spirits and food to the hungry festival goers.

Petronella frowned as she joined the throng, Joran marching beside her. He was twirling a daisy between his fingers. Someone had thrust it at him as he left the temple. Domita sloped along beside them, uncharacteristically silent.

"I don't understand," Petronella said. "It was beautiful, but I thought something else would happen, apart from the prayers and the invocations, I mean."

Domita nodded. "The big event is yet to come. That service was the official, civic one. The real High Priestess is out there," she made a sweeping gesture with her hand at the dark ocean. "Alice must undergo her test, and the High Priestess herself will decide if she is worthy to serve as Seer. You will see."

"What if she doesn't find Alice worthy?"

Domita's brown eyes were cavernous. "Then Alice won't come back."

The crowd grew thicker as they gained the beach. Their feet sank into the soft sand, cold now after the heat of the day. The sky was black above them. Stars, too many to count, freckled the sky above. The full moon had risen and hung like a lantern over the ocean. Its light formed a silver pathway across the water. At their backs, the colossal statue of the Goddess who guarded the city, reached her marble arm across the gentle waves.

Her fellow priestesses escorted Alice to the water's edge. The head priestess retrieved the sacred text. Alice gripped her cup in both hands, trembling slightly as the waves rolled in gently, anointing her feet. The crowd gathered, stilled, and once again, the steady drums picked up the rolling beat of the ocean waves as they washed their timeless rhythm against the shore.

Alice drew in three deep breaths, in time with the drums. She saluted the moon with her cup and then waded into the ocean. Her robes floated around her at first, and then gradually, slowly, she disappeared beneath the waves.

The people on the shore began a quiet, insistent medley of prayers.

"O our Lady, we beseech thee. Bless our Seer in the name of the High Priestess."

Petronella swallowed, staring at the oily patch of water that had recently held Alice. Seconds passed. Then minutes. She exchanged a terrified glance with Domita, whose tense face glowed in the moonlight. Joran's face was serene, his lips moving with his prayer, in accord with the priestesses who faced the water, lifting their hands to the moon. Domita started when Petronella clutched her hand.

"Surely this is taking too long," she said under her breath.

"It's her test. We must have faith in the Goddess," Domita said, but her grip on Petronella's hand was scalding. She could sense Domita's intense desire to rush forward and rescue her friend. Only her fear of the water held her back.

The Head Priestess cast her arms to the crowd, then turned to face the vastness of the ocean. Set against the expectant silence across the long beach, her voice was thin, but somehow carried to reach their ears as clearly as a crystal bell.

"Lady of the Water, High Priestess, we beseech thee," she cried out to the water and the sky. "Do you take our child, Alice, as your Priestess and Seer, to serve in your name, with your will and wisdom?"

There was a terrible silence. It stretched and filled the shoreline and cast its quiet over the people who stood there, entranced. Petronella shook her head, but the silence continued, and the pressure in her ears grew until she could hardly bear it. The people of Oceanis gazed at the ocean in perfect trust. They waited.

The Goddess of Oceanis rose out of the water. Her feet glided over the ocean. Her gaze, remote and eternal, fifty feet above, commanded the attention of every soul present. Waves formed her garments. A headdress fashioned in the phases of the moon crowned her head with silver and she carried an ancient scroll in her hand. Stars danced in her fathomless eyes. She floated down the silver pathway and towered above them all. Petronella shivered at the weight of her presence. She could hardly breathe.

Raising their right hands, the crowd sunk to the sand in a rustle of clothing, and on every palm, the blazing symbol of the crescent moon shone its azure light into the starlit eyes of their goddess. The High Priestess scrutinised them all, her gaze at once objective and filled with deep understanding. Petronella found herself observed. A small glow of warmth bloomed in her chest and pulsed in her ring as the eyes of the Goddess of Oceanis swept over her.

The Goddess raised her left hand and, graceful as a dolphin, luminous with magic, Alice burst from the water. The crowd released its indrawn breath. Petronella gripped Domita's hand tighter as the girl let out a muffled sob of relief. Alice waited, her arms trembling as she held her cup up to the beautiful, ageless, terrible figure that towered far above her. The crowd stilled, their sigils glowing.

The High Priestess spent an endless moment examining her new Seer.

Petronella found her nails digging into her palms. Had Alice met the exacting standards of this most exacting of judges? She could see Alice shaking where she stood as the ancient, steady gaze pinned her to her place in the vast ocean. The young princess fell to her knees in the water, arms and cup still reaching in supplication, and finally the goddess nodded. She raised her right hand and traced her symbol on the Oceanis night sky.

Petronella's jaw dropped in wonder as the lines glowed silver and then tumbled downwards like rain to fill Alice's cup. Still shaking, Alice tipped the cup to her lips and drank. The crowd sighed in wonder at the moonlight that illuminated her from within in that first precious moment of communion. Alice drained the vessel and tipped her head back. Her face shone with a fine, silver white light as the goddess' power filled her.

The Goddess nodded once more, and her ancient voice cracked the pressured silence like thunder.

"Use my power well," she said.

She withdrew as quickly as she had arrived, and, released from her spell, the crowd burst into wild cheers.

Drums took up a wild, thudding rhythm, joined by guitars, flutes and fiddles. Fires and torches burst into life as people tumbled into each other's arms, laughing, hugging, and smiling. Dancing began, smoke and flames warmed the night sky. The people opened their strongest wine and toasted each other.

The King and Queen of Oceanis helped their newly Blessed daughter to the shoreline, and she turned with them on either side of her to face the joyous crowd. They stilled long enough for her to trace her own blessing on the balmy night air. The symbol slashed a path like lightning and then faded. The crowd erupted and Alice sank to her knees in the damp sand.

Domita started forward, a huge smile splitting her face, and then stumbled to a halt with a gasp. Petronella followed her gaze and clutched Domita's hand again. Alice knelt in the sand, dripping water. Her eyes were silver stones.

Domita swallowed and stumbled to a halt.

"Perhaps it's better to leave her just now," Petronella suggested. "Shall we have some wine?"

She nodded at Joran, who took the hint and strode off to the nearest stall. Petronella took both Domita's scalding hands in her own. The girl was shaking.

"Was this what you expected?" she asked, trying not to cause offense.

Domita shrugged, her full lips working to suppress a sob. Her eyes darted from Alice to Petronella and back again. Petronella tugged her down to the sand, uncaring that the damp ground quickly soaked her silk gown. She squeezed the girl's hands and accepted the wine that

Joran gave her. Domita ignored the thick glass tumblers Joran had brought with him and drank half the wine out of the bottle, her throat working. Petronella bit her lip in alarm, dumbfounded.

"What do I do?" she asked Joran.

"Give her some time. I think she's only just worked out what Alice's ascension may mean for their friendship."

Domita returned the bottle to Petronella after another good swallow and scrubbed her hand across her mouth. The look on her face was nearly enough to break Petronella's heart.

"She doesn't need me anymore."

"Domita..."

"No. She's a Seer now. She won't need me, or you, or anyone. Her life won't ever be the same. Alice... our Alice... is gone."

Domita scrambled to her feet and gazed around with wild eyes at the enormous party that was taking place in front of them. Music swirled. Drums beating, hands clapping. Campfires warmed the night sky and cast rosy hues and fragrant smoke across the goddess-blessed people.

Petronella frowned as Domita swallowed and her jaw tightened.

The girl glanced back at Alice, whose eyes were still a blank silver, and then, squaring her shoulders, forced a ghastly smile onto her face.

A group of girls nearby were passing a wine bottle backwards and forwards between them as they danced to the rhythm of a guitar. With the saddest shrug Petronella had ever seen, Domita shook herself, tossed her head and sauntered over to the group, throwing an arm around the nearest girl, a beauty with long, golden hair, who passed her the bottle. They started a wild gyration around the nearest fire. Domita was dancing almost within the flames themselves. She leapt over the bonfire to shouts of surprise and encouragement, and took off across the beach, trailing sparks.

"Domita—"

Joran stopped her with a hand on her arm as she made to go after her friend.

"Leave her for now, Petronella. She will be alright when she calms down. Alice won't be communing with the Goddess at all hours. This is just Domita, reacting in her own way."

"Are you sure? She looks like a mountain rolled over her."

"She needs to let off some steam. Let her go for now. You can talk to her later. I'm sure Alice will, once the immediate effect of talking with the goddess has worn off. Seer or not. she's still human and very young. She won't be able to remain in the Goddess' mind for long."

Petronella sighed and took the glasses from him. "You know so much more about this than I do," she said, as she filled them.

Joran sank down into the sand with her and accepted the glass of wine she offered him. He grinned as they touched glasses. "It's not every day you get to see an actual goddess," he said. "We should be celebrating. I think we have finally proved to you that the Gods really do exist."

Chapter Thirty-Seven

Petronella and Joran strolled the length of the long beach, content to dip in and out of the riotous celebration taking place around them as they sipped their fill of wine. The scent of food and the ever-present incense spilled in copious quantities over innumerable fires filled the night with aromatic incense that heightened senses and lowered inhibitions.

Music of all kinds spread across the shoreline.

Holding hands, they danced to the wildest of jigs played by a man possessed as he cavorted with his fiddle around a fire and sighed at the most plaintive of melodies whispered by a blind woman and a wooden flute. Couples wandered off together into the night. Some people made love openly under the light of the maternal moon, their bodies twisting gracefully, like fish, as they moved around and into each other.

Wrapped in accord, conversing out loud and mentally, Petronella and Joran strolled on, around the headland and away from the crowds. Their hands brushed, and then held. His palm was an anchor. Warm, firm, rooting her to the world, while her imagination took flight and her heart thrummed with anticipation and yearning. For what, she could not be sure. Their banter and laughter changed by degrees to the tingle and awareness of desire. He stroked his thumb across hers and her breath caught. Her mouth dried.

The music faded to a gentle background noise, drifting in on the wind as it rustled the sea grass dotting the dunes. The ocean hushed its timeless song across the sand and eventually, with an inevitability that had been building since they first laid eyes on each other, they sank together amid the privacy of the dunes.

"Petronella."

His voice in her head was a husky whisper, even as his lips found hers. They traced a gentle path along the line of her jaw to her throat before returning to her mouth. His breath was warm with wine, his body warmer against the coolness of the sand.

Petronella had no more thought than a bird taking flight as she nestled against him. Her fingers tangled in the silky thickness of his hair as she brought his mouth to hers with a ferocity and yearning that needed no interpretation.

The moonlight bathed and blessed them in equal measure. Joran worshiped her breasts with his hands and his mouth. Kissed each pale scar on her flat belly and healed it with soft murmurs of sympathy that pricked her eyes with tears. She traced the battle scars he had collected and hidden over the years. Her greedy hands roamed with abandon over his warrior's arms, his chest, his buttocks.

As his mouth moved lower, her eyes burned midnight blue and when he entered her at last, her head tipped back, and she sighed her bliss into the starlit sky.

The ring on her hand blazed into life to melt with the moon. There was no pain, just the perfect blending of Joran's mind and body with hers. A fusion and healing and heated release that she had never known in her life before. Their fused mindscapes were starlit. Eternal and endless as the night sky, full of potential and possibility, blazing with the icy heat of remote suns on undiscovered planets.

Afterwards, they held each other. Later, they made love again, and when the dawn broke, they tidied their clothing and drifted back to the palace. Neither of them said anything. There was nothing they needed to say.

Apart from a few bleary-eyed guards, the palace appeared almost deserted as they wound their way through the convoluted corridors to the guest wing. Joran escorted her to her door and kissed her knuckles with courtly grace. His eyes, dark in the night, scanned her face. She shook her head, wordless, and leaned into him. His lips grazed her hair. He stood back, a crooked smile on his lips.

"Thank you for this night," he said.

She managed a wan smile in return, cupping his face with her hand. Soft stubble grazed her stroking fingers. His warmth and vitality leached into her skin. Her ring gave a gentle tug at her senses. She found herself reluctant to let him go. Unwilling to return to the real world. She pulled herself away with an effort.

Dawn was filling the sky, and the stars winked out as she clambered into bed. A smile curved her lips, and she sank into slumber, one hand reaching to the vacant space beside her, as the morning sun banished the night. And for once, she had no dreams.

Chapter Thirty-Eight

Far from sleep in the Castle of Air, Arion had risen before the dank dawn to pace his chamber. A swipe of pain in his hand and head around midnight had been savage enough to claw him from sleep and propel him out of bed to the chamber pot where he retched up his supper. Groaning, he leaned over the porcelain and forced his eyes to remain open.

As soon as they closed, he could see his wife, dressed in white and holding out a long, graceful hand on which the Ring of Mercy shone so brightly it dazzled his eyes. Something had happened. Something terrible. He knew it.

As dawn broke, and in the absence of his councillors, he made his reluctant way to the bowels of the castle to interrogate the former head of the Queen's household, Lady Felice de Winter.

Felice showed no sign of surprise to see his tall shadow at her cell door. She gave him a distant and dignified nod from her seat on a low stool as the door clanged open. The room was small, dank and dirty and the doorway so low Arion had to stoop to enter. A pair of grim-faced guards flanked the entrance, swords held ready.

Arion's skin crawled as Felice raised her disdainful dark gaze to his. The knob of a candle guttered in a battered pewter holder on a rough-hewn table. An earthenware jug and a wooden tankard stood next to it. Felice hugged a warm cloak close to her body. Her face was paler than he remembered. Smudges of grime marked her cheeks, and she appeared smaller without the gold headdresses and voluminous skirts she usually favoured. The abundant warmth of an unexplained perfume dominated the underlying reek of piss, old blood and fear that normally permeated the castle dungeons.

She quirked one greying eyebrow at him and waited for him to explain the nature of his visit.

Arion scowled. "Petronella is in Oceanis."

Felice shrugged. "It is possible."

"Why?"

"I believe she is trying to do her duty as Queen of Epera, as she always has."

"I sent Merlon a message to return her to Epera should she arrive, or his kingdom will suffer the consequences. Her duty is here, by my side, in her own kingdom."

"I believe she thinks otherwise."

The old woman turned her gaze away into her cupped palms. His skin crawled as he saw what she was holding. A delicate white flower crowned with azure blue. His breath clogged in his throat and his palm clamped around his dagger.

"Where did you get that?"

Felice turned her palms towards him. Arion cursed himself for taking a step back. She regarded the delicate plant as fondly as a mother beholds her child and then placed her hands over her heart, where it promptly disappeared.

"In here," she said.

"Earth Witch." His voice was hoarse.

"Believe what you will, my lord." Resignation tinged her voice. "You live in fear and want, in the shadow of the actions of your late father. 'Tis not my destiny to change that."

Her face was infinitely sad as she turned her palms towards him once more. He stared in horror at a circlet of tangled brambles and shards of flint that lay there, black as death. His dagger flashed as he raised his hand. He turned its icy edge towards Felice's throat.

"Explain yourself."

Felice regarded the weapon with a question in her eyes. She raised her gaze from it to his face. He steeled himself as the vicious plants writhed to life in her hands. The glass tore at her unflinching skin. Blood oozed around her fingers and dripped to the floor, and the ring on his tortured finger burned like ice.

"Your father abandoned his covenant with the land before you were born. This is the result."

"My father was a worthy king who rid our nation of witchcraft and led our country to greatness."

"If that is what you believe, there is no persuading you." Her voice was flat, almost disinterested. Dark blood pooled in her hands, mixing with the slimy blackness of the twisted weeds. She held her hands out to him once more. "This is the crown your father left for you to wear, my Lord. Are you satisfied?"

Arion swallowed, forcing his words out in a roar over the clutch of dread that roiled through his stomach and sent pain flooding through his hand and head. "I will have no more of witchcraft and magic. If she lives, my wife will return to meet her fate, and those who harbour her will know the depth of my displeasure. Oceanis will not deny me, and they will regret the day they turned their backs on us. As for you..." He loomed before her and his shadow cast in the light of the single candle shrouded her features in darkness. "Felice de Winter, I hereby sentence you to death for witchcraft."

Felice parted her hands, and the brambles tumbled to the floor where they disintegrated to join the detritus of filthy rushes at her feet. She wiped her hands off on her soiled skirt with a grimace of distaste. Her eyes filled with a mixture of pity and cool disdain. Arion glanced away, unable to hold her gaze. Deep in his heart, he felt something break. He couldn't have named his emotion as Felice lifted her shoulders on a sigh of resignation. She didn't cry. Or beg, or break. Instead, a simple, dignified sentence.

"As you wish, my Lord."

He left her with her hands clasped loosely in her lap. That accursed flower bloomed once more between her fingers.

Shivering, he left her, grateful for the sound of the key grating in the lock.

The Grayling, blind beneath his hood, beat his sturdy wings in anticipation of action when Arion strode through the falconry with a hastily scrawled message to Lord Darius of Falconridge clutched in his fist.

Arion avoided its vicious, flashing beak and booted the unfortunate Master of the Falcons awake. The man struggled from his thin pallet with his hood awry. At least a week's worth of stubble peppered his cursing jaw. His eyes widened in alarm when he realised at whom he was swearing.

Arion waited, impatient, for the man to stammer out an apology and rub the sleep from his eyes. "I need this sent to Lord Darius in Goldfern at once. Use your fastest bird," he commanded, thrusting his order to attack with some force into the man's greasy palm.

"At once, Your Majesty." The man bowed Arion out.

Dawn had broken on a day of slashing rain as Arion splashed across puddles to the warmth of his rooms. Reaching for the ever-handy flagon, he poured himself a hefty draft of wine and gulped it down. It did little to banish the crushing sense of guilt and fear that had taken a grip on his mind. The warmth went some way in diluting the pain that roared constantly now from his hand to his head. His face twisted as he eased the glove from his swollen fingers and allowed his reluctant gaze to take in what the pain signified. The puffy flesh of his forefinger buried the Ring of Justice in a constant, twisting noose. From his fingernails to his wrist, his hand was entirely black.

Chapter Thirty-Nine

Petronella awoke with a jerk as the mid-morning sunlight warmed her pillow. She stretched a crick in her neck and rubbed her eyes. A pleasant lassitude lingered that made her long to stretch and go back to sleep, preferably with Joran's arms around her. Her cheeks warmed and her body tingled as her mind roamed through the events of the night before.

It had been... wonderful.

One servant must have already braved their hangover to prepare a bath for her. The tub steamed, inviting her presence, and she crossed the room naked to slide into the silken water, reaching for the soap. Birds sang in the olive trees outside her window and laughing voices chattered in the courtyard. She ducked her head under the water, blotting them out, and then surfaced, blowing bubbles. The curtains at her window billowed. She blinked. She was not alone.

The stranger stood at the entrance to the balcony. Clothed in stark black, his sudden presence against the crisp white of her curtains was like staring into the dark mouth of an empty grave. Thick set. Tall. Long, tangled blond hair. A raw scar disfigured his face. It ran from the corner of his right eye and carved a ragged, oozing path across his tattooed cheekbone to the corner of his mouth. Her eyes flashed to the sword at his side, the knife in his fist. Her memory offered the vision of a dark night on a crowded bridge, dangerous water sliding past her terrified eyes, and the desperate, random swing of her blade.

She gasped, sliding backwards in the bath and scrabbled for a weapon. Her hand found her bar of soap, but there was nothing else there to aid her. Her dagger was still in its scabbard under the bed where she had kicked it days ago. She cursed herself for not being more wary. The man waited. He appeared to enjoy watching her panic. His eyes held the deadly certainty of a striking hawk.

"Who are you?" she ground out, still scanning the room for something to aid her.

The man gave her a painful, lopsided smile that didn't meet his eyes.

"I am here to collect your ring," he said, taking a step forward into the room. He raised his knife.

Her diamond pulsed once on her finger, and her panic left her. Cat-like, he glided towards her. Each footfall brought him closer, and her gaze locked on his dusty boots. She seemed to have all the time she required to bring her arm up and toss the wet soap with unerring accuracy into the path of his next step. She was out of the tub and sprinting for her dagger before his thick body thudded to the floor.

Grabbing the scabbard, she whirled, knife in hand, as he regained his feet, face twisting in rage. She didn't wait for him to close in. Eyes narrowed, she fired the blade at him with all the force she could muster. It pierced his left eye, and he gave a shriek of shock and fear before his body collapsed underneath him.

She sank to the bed, her hands reaching for a robe. Fastening it around her body, she crossed to the corpse. His blank, one eyed gaze stared up at her. Her knife protruded from his skull. She swallowed against a wave of nausea as time snapped back to normal speed.

"Joran."

She had a fleeting mental image of him snatching up his sword, and then his feet pounded down the corridor outside her room and the door slammed open. He stumbled to a shocked halt at the sight of the body and turned to her, face ashen. His hair was standing on end, a mess of tangled honey, his jaw stubbled. He scraped his hands through his hair.

"I don't believe it."

"Do you know who this is?"

"He is… was… a paid assassin. His name is Bastien. He is notorious. Never misses a kill. How did you manage it? You should be dead by now."

"I was in the bath. He surprised me, and I thought he had me and then… something happened. My ring pulsed and… it was like time slowed down."

Joran's eyebrows raised to his hairline. "Or perhaps you sped up?"

She shrugged. "Whatever happened, he's here, which means I was right. Your borders are not safe."

"Unless he was here before they closed."

"Someone tried to kill me on the bridge at Goldfern. I stabbed him, remember? If this is him, the borders were already closed." She swallowed and reached for a daygown. "We must tell Merlon. I knew I was right to be worried. Arion's forces have found another way in."

Hurrying down the corridor to Merlon's quarters, they bumped into a phalanx of the Palace Guard, faces creased with sleep and anxiety running the other way. Their captain saluted, relief clear on his plain face.

"We received word from the Seer that the Queen of Epera was in danger."

"Alice. Where is she?"

"The princess is at the Temple of the Moon, Your Majesty. She sent a message to her father a few minutes ago."

Petronella indicated her room with a backward jerk of her head. "There is a dead man in my chamber. We need an urgent audience with King Merlon. Will you escort us?"

The officer dispatched half his detachment to investigate Petronella's room and accompanied them to Merlon's antechamber, where they found him in deep communion with the interior of a black crystal bowl. Exchanging glances, they waited. Sunlight blazed from the rainbow of coloured glassware and painted prisms on the porcelain tiles. Dust motes floated in the golden air. Merlon blinked through his spectacles at them and wiped droplets of water from his beard.

"Madam. You are well? Thank all the gods, my daughter has been trying to send me a message all night, but of course, like everyone else, we were..."

Petronella raised one eyebrow. The man was blushing.

"I am well, sir, I thank you, although the man sent to kill me has met an unfortunate end. I believe it is as we feared. Arion has penetrated your defences."

Merlon blanched. He leaned over the bowl again, listening intently.

She exchanged glances with Joran. He was regarding the older man with a fond exasperation that bespoke a long acquaintance.

"He looks like a man with a hangover being sick, but he is communicating with Alice."

"You sound fond of him."

Joran smiled. *"He rescued me. I was a lost soul, magically gifted, with no knowledge of how to control anything. I was a fierce fighter. Dangerous to others and myself. He taught me himself, and Mistress Eglion is a wise woman as well. I owe them a lot, and I have worked for them both ever since."*

She chuckled. *"I understand perfectly regarding Mistress Eglion. Have you seen anything of Domita?"*

"My deadly love, I was sleeping the sleep of the just until your call awakened me. I should have been with you. I am sorry I left." Her cheeks warmed. His fingers brushed the back of her hand, a gentle caress that touched her heart more than it should have.

Merlon finished his conversation and lifted his head. Water dripped from his blue-ribboned beard.

"My daughter wished to know you were unharmed. I am happy to tell her you are here and hearty. We still do not know how this man gained access to our land."

"He has followed us somehow. There was an attempt on my life in Goldfern. I believe this was the same man."

"My daughter is receiving the impression of darkness and enclosure. I do not understand what it could mean."

Petronella stared at him. Her mind tumbled backwards to the day of the sinking and Alice's voice. "They are coming under, under." And then the next thing she said about the end of days. Her stomach clenched.

"In Epera, we do not allow the use of magic," she began, conscious that her words were about to bring about the end of peace in Oceanis. "But we are a nation skilled in science, machinery... and mining. Arion and my father have been transporting those with magical ability to the mines in the Iron Mountains as punishment for years. What if they have not just been mining... but tunnelling?"

The older man's face contracted. "That is surely not possible. It would take years to tunnel from Epera to Oceanis. And why? Why would he want to? We are no threat to him."

"Oceanis has something that he wants. He needs grain and a quicker way of transporting it other than trudging up the Fools Road and up the river to Blade. He also wants Petronella to return." Joran's words tumbled over each other as he made the connections. "They know magic wards the borders and that they can't penetrate them. So they are using a different way. One that is not an acknowledged border and does not have magical protection."

Merlon's face screwed into irritated confusion. "But where? It could be anywhere."

"The hills above Sunira. The disused mines there. We passed them on the way here. It is the obvious target if they need to fill their granaries quickly."

The king shook his head. "It still makes little sense. We would have negotiated fairly. That is not a good enough reason. There must be something else he wants to go to such trouble for so long."

"Perhaps he wouldn't have needed to go to much extra trouble. Arion's father, King Francis, ordered tunnels to be dug around Epera for years."

They wheeled at the fresh voice in the small room.

"Mistress Eglion, after all this time," Merlon bent over his desk to greet her.

Mistress Eglion leaned on her stick. Her ancient face was pale in the morning light and creased with wrinkles, her eyes smudged with fatigue. She offered him a perfunctory bow.

"Arion is doing what he feels he must to save his kingdom. However, it comes with an element of revenge. Magic has caused him nothing but pain," she said.

"Revenge on Oceanis? What have we done to deserve this? We have negotiated fairly at every turn."

Merlon's voice rose to a roar that raised dust and caused the glasses on their shelves to dance in sympathy.

The old woman limped further into the room and slumped into a seat. "Apparently, that is no longer enough, and he has no more time to wait. He has simply invaded Oceanis to take what he needs for Epera."

Merlon blinked. His face momentarily frozen.

Petronella glanced at Joran. His jaw flexed as his face settled into grim lines and she followed the tangle of his thoughts as his mind danced down a path of memory to a well of loss that lay at the core of his being. She swallowed and pulled her attention away before she invaded his privacy.

She poured water for Mistress Eglion and handed it to her with a hand that shook. The old woman took it and drank. Merlon scried a message to his daughter before crossing the room to send for Queen Clarys. He walked like an automaton, his knees stiff with shock, and avoided her anxious gaze. Closing the door against intrusion, he turned to Joran.

"You will lead our fight?" It was a question, not a demand.

"I will."

"We will wait until Alice and Queen Clarys arrive to plan our strategy. Mistress Eglion, as the Seer of Epera, I have to ask you to tell us whatever you know."

"The Seer of Epera?" Petronella's voice was taut with disbelief. "Not just a tutor and librarian?"

Mistress Eglion settled herself more comfortably in her chair and rolled her eyes.

"My dear child, I informed you that the Mage Tree was a temple and I hold the remains of Epera's magical knowledge. I am disappointed that you did not perform the slight shift to enlightenment that would have led you to the logical conclusion."

Petronella narrowed her eyes. "As you have seen fit to keep so many secrets from me over the years, it should not be a surprise to learn that you have been most successful in ensuring my knowledge of magic is approximately zero."

Mistress Eglion glared back. "For your own good, my dear."

The arrival of Queen Clarys interrupted their budding argument. She swept into the room on an olfactory wave of saltwater and bergamot. Regal in ocean blue silk, her thick honey gold hair coiled with delicate ribbons of silver, she nodded to the company and took the King's hand in her own. Her blue, fathomless gaze washed over them, and Petronella dropped boneless into the nearest chair as the angry words she had been about to speak dissolved on her tongue.

"Peace be with you. If we are to work together, we must be friends, must we not? Merlon, shall we offer our company some wine? We will discuss deeper matters when Alice arrives."

Petronella blinked as Merlon did as his wife suggested. She took the crystal goblet he offered her and drank. She did not know what to say. If the situation had been reversed, Arion would have clapped the opposition in irons at the least by now.

"I believe you passed the test Merlon set you. He does not view you as a dangerous enemy." Relief tinged Joran's voice in her head.

"No, but he could regard me as spoils of war, could he not? Or a bargaining chip. Is that what he has in mind?"

"He and Queen Clarys will listen to all of us, including you, before we decide. It is the way of Oceanis."

Unbidden, Petronella remembered Alice's words from weeks ago. 'We all have a voice."

The newly made Seer had been speaking nothing but the truth.

CHAPTER FORTY

When Alice arrived, it was in company with Domita. The two young women were deep in conversation and apparently still the best of friends. Petronella breathed a sigh of relief. Merlon quirked his brow at the sight of Domita, but Alice cut off his query with a quick wave of her hand.

"'Tis important that Domita attend, Father. We cannot waste her abilities."

Merlon grunted and waved her to another seat. Domita bowed to her hosts and sank into it with long-legged grace. She appeared no worse for wear for her wild night and accepted the wine with thanks.

The King lowered his bulk into his seat and nodded to Mistress Eglion. "Let us start with what we know."

"It is what I have feared for years since the death of Queen Gwyneth. Arion is now desperate enough to ignore centuries old agreements to feed his people. Recent events have merely conspired to propel his plans forward and given him an excuse."

Merlon shook his head with a sigh that ruffled his beard. Queen Clarys bit her lip, her normally placid expression reflective as she remembered.

"The death of my sister caused so much suffering." She glanced around at the group and acknowledged Petronella's confused expression.

"Francis was much older than Gwyneth, but deeply in love. My sister died in childbed, her child with her. Francis was distraught. We were told he tried everything he could to save her, both medicine and magic, but nothing worked. He turned against magic from that moment on. It altered him. He became a different person. He remarried, took another wife, Ariana of Wessendean. She birthed Arion, but she and Francis were never happy. Ariana returned to her estate after that and died in the year before your wedding."

Petronella frowned. "We had this conversation before, as we journeyed here. I still do not understand why a man would blame magic for the death of his wife and cause our entire nation to suffer for decades afterwards."

"We are all at a loss for that. What we know is that your country itself is dying and the people with it. Arion is still clinging to the belief that magic is to blame for this, rather than the way forward."

Petronella grimaced. "He believes that evil magic has cursed us. That is the entire reason for my journey. I could not conceive, and now my husband threatens your country with war. It is my fault." She jumped to her feet, unable to bear her guilt, and shook off the restraining hand Mistress Eglion placed over her arm.

"Tarry a while, my dear. I have further information to share. It will do you no good to run off without hearing it."

Petronella regained her seat, ready to bounce to her feet at any moment. Her stomach churned as her old guilt snaked through her.

Mistress Eglion sought the eyes of her audience and waited until she had their full attention before she began.

"You have been told that Francis lost his wife in childbed and shunned magic when it could not save her life. This is not entirely true."

Alice's eyes widened at this, but other than that, she remained immobile, her face calm. Petronella glanced at Clarys. She retained her usual dignity, but one slender hand crept to her heart. Her fingers toyed with a locket containing the portrait of a young woman that hung there. Merlon glowered behind his desk as he reached once more for his wife's hand. Joran shifted uncomfortably in his chair next to her, but no-one interrupted Mistress Eglion as she continued her tale.

"It is true that Francis was deeply in love with Gwyneth, despite the difference in their ages. They married and she had just given birth when she died. What is not true is the nature of her death."

Petronella bit her lip. She could see the thoughts in the old woman's mind as she formulated them. Not as strong as the connection she could share with Joran, but the form and shape of them were easily read. Her heart sank.

"There was a rumour flying around the Court of Skies at the time that Gwyneth had taken a lover and that the child was not the king's. Most people were careful to keep the information from Francis, however word of it came to his attention on the day she gave birth. He visited her rooms. Word reached us she was extremely ill. That the birth had weakened her. Francis was strong in his magic then. He could have flown in the mind of an eagle if he chose. He sent the physicians away and stayed with her. The same day, she was dead. Francis emerged from her rooms a changed man with a babe in his arms. I thought at the time the child must have died too. Francis carried it out of the castle. No-one dared challenge him. When he returned, his arms were empty."

Mistress Eglion paused and took a large sip of wine to moisten her throat. Her gaze was distant and thoughtful as she perused the contents of her glass.

"I believe the decline of Epera began then. It was hardly noticeable at first. Francis recovered, took another wife, Arion's mother. Arion was born. All was well. But small things changed. Francis aged. His health deteriorated. I stopped hearing his voice in my head. His focus shifted to science, industry. People vanished, especially those who displayed the strongest magical abilities. The temples and shrines closed.

People stopped mentioning magic. Some people left court voluntarily only to be hunted down. The country itself prospered. We grew rich with the expansion of our industries to manufactured goods and the export of raw minerals. Arion was barely three years old when I left court myself. I had seen enough by then to confirm my suspicions."

"Which were...?" Petronella prompted.

Mistress Eglion sighed, and her shoulders slumped in resignation. "I believe Francis murdered his beautiful young wife in a fit of jealous rage. I believe that terrible injustice sundered his contract with the Mage and in that moment, he lost the right to wield his power. He did not know that would happen, and he could tell no-one. He had to go on pretending all was well, but he had set the land on the path to destruction. We are living with the result."

"But surely the magic would revive upon his death when Arion ascended to the throne?" Petronella asked.

The old woman sat back in her chair and shook her head. "I do not know, my dear. It has never happened before. Have you ever seen Arion perform an act of magic to your knowledge?"

Petronella shook her head in her turn, biting her lip. "Never, that I have seen. He hates and fears the thought of it. Arion has been told all his life that magic is evil, and he believes it has cursed him. There has been no-one there to teach him otherwise. He was told by his father of his bond to the land only when his father was about to die."

Her old tutor turned her staff in her hand. "Then it is possible the magic of Epera died forever in the Eagle's line when Francis turned it unjustly on his wife and child. I think Francis spent a long time looking for the source of Epera's magic, searching for a way to restore his power, but he was unsuccessful. He ordered tunnels dug deep in the heart of the mountains across Epera endlessly. Obsessively. In the end, he simply gave up on the search and forbade the use of magic to keep himself and his heir safe on the throne. He changed his world to suit what he became. A man without magic. That is power too, of a sort."

Merlon gave a hiss of disbelief. Domita shook her head in disgust.

"Arion knows nothing of magic. How he must fear us," she said.

"That is your answer." Joran said, with a grimace. "He is a man living in fear. Fear of his own end, fear of magic. Fear of failure. It is inbred in him and has been since birth. He will destroy us to rid himself of it."

"We cannot allow it." Merlon drained his cup and pinned them with his gaze. "Alice, what say you?"

Alice raised her head from where it had slumped to her chest during the meeting. Petronella expected to see her blank gaze again, but the new Seer showed no sign of it. Her eyes were clear aqua, transparent as the ocean.

"The Goddess tells me that Arion is taking advantage of something that was already there. He does not wish to destroy us totally. Punish us, perhaps. Reduce our magical ability, certainly. He believes he can use our resources in place of his own and feed his country in that manner. He requires the return of his wife. There is something else, though." Her eyes clouded as she gazed around at them.

"Please speak of it, my dear," Clarys urged as she noted Alice's hesitation.

"I think there is someone other than Arion. Someone who truly wishes the ultimate banishment of natural magic from all of Arcanis."

Amid the expressions of shock and disbelief from her companions, Petronella's mind jumped back to their disastrous voyage and Alice's vague mutterings at the time as she had turned her back and walked away.

"Do you remember your vision on board the Dove? You said something about someone wanting what lay in the stone heart of Epera? That Francis had found it and had been told where to dig. Something about the end of days?"

Alice grimaced, her face clouding. "I remember nothing of the visions I had before the Goddess blessed me with the ability to remember and make sense of them," she said.

"But perhaps that is it. The miners have not spent years digging tunnels and searching under Arion's orders."

"Then whose?"

She shook her head, bewildered. "Francis, I imagine. After that, I don't know."

There was a pause. Mistress Eglion cleared her throat.

"I am afraid I do."

The company stared at her in disbelief, and the old woman's brow contracted in irritation. She settled her fragile shoulders with a jerk and glared around at them all, blue eyes bright under her hooded lids.

"In my early years at court, my official title was Chief Librarian. I know who was studying and what they were studying."

"And?" Petronella prompted.

Mistress Eglion huffed a sigh that disturbed the golden dust motes dancing in the air. Her eyes slid to her former charge.

"Your father, Darius, my dear," she said.

"No."

"Yes. He withdrew book after book on engineering, mining, even what we had on surviving underground. In the time before they ordered the library shut, he must have read every single book, scroll, and scholarly paper on those subjects we had. Some more than once."

Petronella flinched as all eyes turned to her. Her cheeks flushed as shame drilled into her. She shook her head, closing her hands over her ears.

"No. It can't be."

"Oh, I believe he thought he was helping, initially, at least." Mistress Eglion said. "Always keen to stay in with King Francis, was your father. Or so it would seem. Very ambitious, even as a young man. There is something else, however."

She took another sip of wine. The glass rattled against her teeth.

"I took it upon myself to remove the kingdom's magical collection, before Francis could get his hands on it, but I could never find one title. A very ancient book. In the wrong hands, very dangerous. With close study, it could reveal a way to claim the power of the Shadow Mage. The Shadow God of Epera. I am sorry to say that I believe that volume is in the possession of Darius, Lord Falconridge. Petronella's father."

Petronella sat like a stone as every drop of blood drained from her cheeks. That small, heavy black book. The one her father carried with him like a sacred relic. Was that it?

"But Francis never reclaimed his magic. He renounced it all. Even if my father has the book, it means nothing..." her voice trailed off as she met Domita's anxious eyes. "Alice's vision on board the Dove."

Domita nodded, her face infinitely sad.

"He found it. On Francis' orders, perhaps, but he found it."

Joran stood, a tall, forbidding presence.

"The question is, did he learn how to use it?"

Her gaze shot to him. The sadness and distrust that lingered there sliced her heart into pieces. She raised a hand to him. Her ring sent rainbow shards of light dancing into the room.

"Joran, you must believe me. I did not know."

She felt him withdraw from her, even though he didn't move. His eyes hardened. His mouth thinned. Tears stung her eyes.

Merlon stood with a jolt that rocked his desk. His thick shoulders rose with his voice, his anger filled the small space, and he paced in front of them, running his hands through his thinning hair.

"Arion or Darius, or both, whatever or whoever we are facing, makes no difference. We must defend ourselves in whatever way is possible. Our ancient borders are impenetrable to enemy forces, blessed be the Goddess. We must send our defenders to Sunira and prepare for an imminent attack from the direction of the mines. Joran, you will travel there with all speed. Take our Water Warriors and any others blessed by the High Priestess, if you can find any willing. We will need their skills."

"I will send messages to our sisters and brothers blessed by the Goddess in Sunira," Alice offered. "Although it grieves me beyond measure to tell them such a terrible thing."

"I will go with you, Joran," Domita said. "I can do significant amounts of damage."

"Thank you, Domita."

"I will go with you as well, if you will allow me," Petronella said. She left her chair. Her heart was a stone in her chest, her thoughts churning in confusion as she took a deep breath. "I have achieved nothing and brought this upon you all by coming here. I will return, as Arion wishes. If I can, I will try to stop whatever it is my father has planned."

"We cannot know what we face," Joran said. "Until then, all we can do is defend ourselves in the best way we can."

Mistress Eglion used her walking stick to lever herself from her chair. Petronella reached an arm to her. The woman seemed to have aged twenty years during the meeting. Mistress Eglion patted her arm away and gained her feet without further aid.

"I will go with you, then. I must return to Epera." She raised her gaze to Petronella. "You will not travel alone, my dear," she said. Petronella managed a tremulous smile for her erstwhile tutor.

Merlon helped his wife to her feet and kept a tight hold of her hand. Their gazes were sombre as they surveyed the small group.

"Petronella, Queen of Epera, it is my sad duty to inform you that our two nations are now at war." His voice was gruff and remote, laced with regret. "As I mentioned in our previous meeting, if you choose to remain in my country, you will be my guest and I will do what I can to protect you. However, I cannot guarantee your continued safety on our soil. As you wish to return to your own land, as per the wishes of your sovereign lord, I will do nothing to hinder you. I will send a message to your husband regarding your wish to return at once."

Petronella raised her chin, although her fingers sought the comfort of her ring as she twisted it.

"I had thought to beg aid from you. It appears that Arion has run out of patience."

Merlon's face was an impassive mask as he drew himself up to his full height. The affable monarch of earlier meetings retreated. She was utterly afraid of him in that moment as the temperature in the room and her blood took a rapid, chilling dip.

"As have I, madam, as have I."

She curtsied as he and Queen Clarys made their stately way to the door, arm in arm, heads together.

An awkward silence floated in the vacant space behind them. Domita bounced to her feet and paced the room like a restive horse. A trickle of fire traced her outline as her brow contracted in fury.

Deep in concentration, Alice used Merlon's scrying dish to send urgent information to her colleagues in Sunira. She pushed the bowl away once the communication was complete and remained seated at Merlon's desk for a while longer as her searching, formidable gaze found each of them.

Petronella shrank from the accusation she found there. She stifled an urge to cast herself to her knees in front of the girl as she would if the Goddess herself were to appear in front of her. This was Alice. How could she be afraid of Alice?

Her gaze clashed with Joran's. His expression was as bleak as a winter snowdrift as he looked towards her. Her eyes pricked with tears as his back straightened, his jaw tightened, and he closed his mind to hers. An ache of sadness pooled somewhere near her heart and lodged there, shortening her breath. He bowed to Alice.

"I must be about the wishes of the King. I will inform you when we are ready to travel." He jerked his chin at Petronella, nodded at

Domita, and marched from the room. Petronella flinched as the door slammed.

The four women remaining stared at each other. Petronella reached out to them, testing Joran's belief that she should be able to speak to them without words.

Alice's mind was as fathomless as an ocean. The Goddess ruled there almost totally, expect for the tiniest speck of emotion that was still Alice. Petronella shuddered as the Seer's gaze sharpened at the intrusion. She withdrew and tested Domita instead. A tangled morass of grief, anger, and confusion radiated out from her in waves. Domita's agitated pacing increased. She seemed unaware of Petronella's mind reaching for hers. By contrast, Mistress Eglion's mind-space reflected the peace of sunlight on snow. It was a crisp, invigorating expanse where knowledge and the power of pure thought held sway.

Mistress Eglion's eyes brightened. *"Good morning, Petronella. You have remembered this power, at least."*

"This outcome was never my intention."

"The road to hells, my dear. War has been inevitable since the death of Queen Gwyneth."

"Is it true? About my father?"

Mistress Eglion's eyes dulled with sadness.

"I do not wish to think so, but yes, I fear it is so. He is a formidable scholar, Petronella, and he hates our natural magic. Who do you think tutored Arion so thoroughly against it in his youth?"

"I still cannot believe it."

"I wish I did not."

Petronella frowned when Mistress Eglion broke the mental connection and shuffled to the door, head bowed with the weight of her thoughts. As the women parted company to prepare for their departure, more questions tumbled through her mind, but chief amongst these were those that lived at the very heart of her. Joran. The severing of their mental connection bore all the impact of a slamming door.

Staring at the blank space in her head where Joran's voice had lived, her heart contracted at the loss. She returned to her bright room with footsteps that dragged as if already bound with the weight of shackles and chains.

Merlon's guard had removed the corpse of the dead assassin and cleansed the room in her absence. Not even a smear of soap remained as a reminder of the violence that had taken place just a short while ago. She bit her lip hard against the familiar tug of failure and guilt as she pulled her battered satchel from its resting place under her bed and prepared to leave.

Chapter Forty-One

Darius, Lord of Falconridge, had ordered the placement a rudimentary camp at the mouth of the mine known locally as Travi's Tunnel. The rank and file of his army stretched back in the chilly darkness of the mine itself, huddled into dugouts, sullen with hunger and crowded together for warmth. Darius had set up his personal base just inside the entrance, in a shallow cave. A rough curtain cordoned off the surrounding space. His camp-bed rested against one rocky wall, a makeshift desk and sturdy chair waited for him next to the entrance. Satisfied with his quarters, he pushed the curtain aside and stretched in the welcome heat of Oceanian sunlight. A warm, herb-scented breeze ruffled his beard and lifted his hair as he scanned the rocky hillside with the light of malice in his dark eyes.

The town of Sunira sprawled on the sheltered plain below. Sunlight glinted off the mighty Cryfell as it rolled along through the fertile plains to Shoreborne. Boats bobbed at anchor at the jetty. Grain was being harvested from the fields, the workers scattered in regular ant-like rows as they toiled to collect it. The town itself was undefended as far as he could see, although in this land, that meant nothing. There was no stone wall or wooden palisade, no moat or defensive earthwork. The buildings were white, remote and graceful. A faint aroma of incense from the temples crept up his nostrils, which creased with distaste as he inhaled. Distant bells from these same temples began to ring. Was it his imagination, or had those bells signalled a flurry of activity in the distant fields?

He gestured for a spyglass and swept it in an arc from left to right, his brow creasing as he scanned the scene. The citizens of Sunira were deserting their labours. Drivers hauled carts half full of grain from the fields to the dusty roads. The peasants urged their carthorses and oxen to greater effort as other workers rushed for the dubious safety of the town. Darius grunted with satisfaction and closed his spy glass as a young soldier rushed towards him, his pale face pink and sweating in the heat.

"This just received by pigeon from his Majesty, my Lord." He panted, thrusting the note into Darius's broad palm.

Darius read the note with greedy satisfaction and turned to General Harison, who arrived at his side, sweating in the heat.

"We attack at dawn," he said. "Ready the men."

General Harison saluted, his swarthy face grim, and issued another order to his second in command, who bolted into the darkness of the tunnel to organise the troops.

"There is nothing to stop us," he said, resuming his own observation of the territory. "They are such easy targets."

"Nothing that you can see. That does not mean they cannot defend themselves."

General Harison's thin cheeks paled. "Magic, you mean?"

Darius stifled his impatience with the man with difficulty, although the general's attitude was hardly surprising. The latest generation regarded the Old Ways as the curse of a bygone age, fully surpassed by the advantages of knowledge and science. A small, select band of troops trained by himself were quick to root out any who displayed evidence of magic ability. Those unfortunates found themselves wrenched from their families into the mines, there to work in service to their great nation.

Or at least, that was the official version.

"The citizens of Oceanis are unusually skilled in the Forbidden Art," he said. "Whether there are sufficient numbers of them to overcome our forces remains to be seen."

The General turned his own bleak, assessing gaze to the quiet city below them. The fields were empty now, dotted with abandoned carts, sweet ripe grain blowing in the summer wind.

"We will feed our people at last," he said. "No matter what."

Darius smiled an acknowledgment, but his dark eyes were as cold as dead coals as he strode back to the tunnel.

Arion's army - his army - stretched backward into the mines. The infantry were the possessors of sharpened steel, cannon, brute determination, and a desperate need for food, but they were useless against defensive magic. For that, and for other, even less legitimate reasons, Darius needed a magical force of his own.

Twisting the black diamond ring around on his finger, he swept aside the rough serge curtain that separated his quarters from those of his men and poured himself a drink. The army went about their clamorous business beyond his nook as he took a seat and thumbed through the papers cluttering his makeshift desk. The jumble of letters blurred in front of him, and he pushed them aside. He couldn't concentrate on them. Not when he was so close to proving his control over the former Blessed of Epera and claiming the throne.

Alert for prying eyes, he glanced around the small room before reaching into a pocket of his robes and withdrawing a small, leather-bound black book tied with a blue ribbon. His hands trembled slightly as he fumbled with the fastening.

Contained within its pages was everything he had studied to harness the power of the Shadow Mage over the years. Incantations, diagrams and instructions that enabled him to connect to a side of the Great God those self-satisfied, natural magic bearers both feared and overlooked. The so-called Blessed of Epera had no requirement or reverence for this Shadow God. Darius was his sole and most dedicated acolyte.

He would never own the power. Not in his blood, like those blessed by the Gods at birth. But he had paid his dues to the Shadow Mage and put the dark jewel he'd discovered to work. It was hard to close his mind to the memory of his courageous, determined, defiant oldest daughter and her screams as he pummelled her into oblivion and shut those snapping grey eyes forever, but he had closed his mind to them at the time and in every nightmare since. He could hardly bear the sight of his youngest daughter and her white, tortured face and huge blue eyes. She was a constant reminder of the price he had paid for magical power.

Darius's broad chest swelled with pride as he squinted through the entrance of his quarters into the darkness of the mines at the columns of the army stretching back for a mile or more beyond his sight. Francis had never realised what he was giving up when he refused the price to regain his power.

A hundred ragged and dispossessed people now mingled with his men. Individually, they could be mistaken for miners, serfs and slaves. Collectively, they were the remnants of the most magically gifted people Epera could produce, and now his chance had arrived to test their power properly for the first time.

Casting another furtive gaze behind him, he peeled the book open, and reminded himself again of "The Way of the Dark". He mouthed the words to himself, comforted by their familiar, twisted shape in his mind and against his tongue. Power snaked from his ring and his skin crawled as it trickled through the mine, black as treacle, hugging the dirt-packed floor, twisting between the dirty, unsuspecting boots of the foot soldiers, to his own people. Enslaved. Harnessed and controlled. The skin on his arms pimpled with goosebumps as he felt them stir. His to command. His to use in fulfilment of the ultimate revenge.

Beyond the thin privacy his curtained quarters provided, the rank and file muttered, shouted and rattled their way to prepare for invasion. No-one heard him as he took a quick swig of wine, squared his shoulders, and uttered his first command.

Chapter Forty-Two

The river boat called Swordfish, the fastest of Merlon's extensive fleet, travelled in convoy with several similar craft hastily convened by Joran at Merlon's command. Flags flying, their bright green sails billowed in the breeze off the river as the oarsmen and the ship's crew combined their skills against the current. God's blessed Oceanians worked with the water to hasten their progress upstream.

Joran and Domita spent long hours discussing possible tactics and strategies with Merlon's finest Water Warriors, and Petronella spent long hours in the company of Mistress Eglion at the prow of their boat, watching the passing scenery and the increasing number of river boats travelling the other way, downstream to Shoreborne.

The gulf between herself and Joran had widened and solidified in the last two days. She found it hard to deal with the space in her heart and his absence of expression when he had to speak to her. As ever, she retreated into the dignity of a queen, albeit a disgraced one.

"It is not your fault, Petronella."

Mistress Eglion had not let this argument rest during their journey. Now, settled in a sheltered space between barrels of water and cases of medical supplies, the two women used the slim time remaining before they docked to practise their mind-to-mind communication.

"Of course it is," Petronella argued back. *"I was so sure that Merlon would see the sense of my argument and agree to supply Epera."*

"If I had not told him the truth, it might have worked. I am now asking my own questions as to the wisdom of that. However, just as her goddess rules Alice, so am I instructed by the Mage. And it is not within our gift to argue with them when they choose to share their visions or their knowledge."

"How did you become my tutor, Mistress Eglion? I have often wondered over the years. You were not at our estates in the time before Jana... died, were you?"

"I arrived shortly before that dreadful episode. The Mage informed me your family needed my service. Also, your mother sent me a message and asked me to come. She held powerful magic in her own right that she never dared to use in front of her husband. She took heartsease tea for years to block it so he would not know of her ability, but she grew more afraid with every passing year."

"My mother was one of the Blessed?"

Mistress Eglion paused before she answered, tapping out her pipe. When she spoke, her mental voice trembled with sadness.

"Briana possessed the power of illusion and concealment. It is a rare gift known to only a very few of the Eperan Blessed. She bound it. Gave up its use for the rest of her life to keep you safe. She was one of the bravest people I ever knew. It is a pity you never knew her as she truly was. She could have taught you so much."

Petronella grimaced. *"I wish she had. To me, she always felt so distant, as if she couldn't bear to be close, and she became even more remote when Jana died. Did she ask you to teach me when she could not?"*

"More to guard you until you came of age, and of course, to prepare you for your role as a future queen. I was entirely prepared to instruct you in using your magic as well until your mother begged me not to, and I realised how dangerous that might become. Your father's hatred of magic became clear when he negotiated your betrothal to Prince Arion. What to tell you became a constant argument between Felice and me.

Your mother sided with Felice. She was terrified of Darius by then. Of his violence and his rages. So unpredictable."

"I know he was always adamant we adhere to the king's decrees. He insisted our family's first duty was to the Crown. And I suppose I knew on some level Mother was afraid of him. I barely remember her. Just her white face and her voice. So quiet, as if she did not want to be heard."

"His beliefs about magic were very clear when I arrived as your tutor. It has taken me many years to understand why."

Petronella dropped out of the mental communication, exhausted. She was still too new to it to support the connection for long.

"Will you explain what you know to me?" she asked. "We have time for this now. And I am not as resistant as I was to the idea of magic."

"Willingly, my dear, although what I must reveal to you is going to cause you much pain. I hope you are ready."

Mistress Eglion took her hands. Petronella was conscious of the smooth warmth of her gnarled fingers as they closed over the Ring of Mercy. A bolt of power chased light across her vision and left her dizzy. Petronella's heart raced under her tunic. Swallowing, she forced her fear down.

"I think I can guess what you are going to show me. I will try to be ready."

"Then open your inner eyes, Petronella. Now."

Chapter Forty-Three

"*Jana, wait for me,*" I call out to my sister in my head and receive her musical laughter in response as she urges her Battonian mare, Glory, into a canter through the trees that lead to our secret place in the hills. I know the path well. It connects our well-favoured manor to the distant, flower-filled meadows on the lower slopes of the hills called Falconridge. We are ringed to the north by a tall mountain range called The Reach. I have never crossed it, but Trinian, captain of the Falcon guard, once told me that there is an ocean on the other side, bleaker than winter and crossed only by a few. Our family has owned this land forever. It is the source of our name and our lineage. It is as familiar to me as the lines on my grubby, ink-stained palm.

"*Keep up, Petronella,*" she says. "*You're such a coward.*"

Swallowing my trepidation at moving much faster than the sedate walk Lady Felice de Winter allows, I urge gentle Misty to a trot. My bony knees knock at her round flanks, my tiny feet bounce inexpertly in the stirrups.

I cast a worried glance backwards at the manor walls we have put behind us. The low autumn sun gilds the grey stone and wraps the turrets and towers in a gentle glow of comfort. There are a few servants toiling in the stable yard we have just left, but Felice and my mother are working together in the herb gardens on the other side of the building. Mistress Eglion, our tutor, will be enjoying her pipe at this time of day, catching the last of the sunlight on the pages of yet another book, her greying head wreathed in a golden, fragrant halo of smoke. There are no dissenting voices or commands to return.

Up ahead, the way narrows, and the fine oaks and beeches of our father's well-tended estate give way to plantations of pine and spruce as the path ascends the steep hillside. The air is full of crisp, cold sunshine, mould and autumn leaves, and I stifle a shiver as a cloud crosses the sun. Foraging squirrels dart across the path, preparing for the onset of winter.

Jana and Glory have all but disappeared. The subtle drum beat of Glory's hooves kicking up clumps of soil and mud from the bridleway and the gentle trickle of the brook as it cascades down to the moat fills my ears. Misty's small hooves move a beat behind, but Jana is projecting to me. I know where she is going. What she is seeing. I can feel her excitement, her joyful self-confidence. She is leading me. Not that it matters. I know where we are going. Where we always go, to our cave, half hidden by overgrown bracken in the hillside above the manor.

I am breathless when we arrive. Laughing, I slide off Misty's back and lead her through the narrow crevice between damp rocks into the cave itself. It is much colder in here. Our breath fogs the chilled air. I huddle in the folds of my cloak as Misty picks at stray leaves and hay left from an earlier excursion.

Jana has dismounted and is stirring a patch of soil with the sole of her boot. She stares out of the entrance at the spectacular view, but she is not seeing it. Her expression is suddenly pensive, her arms hug herself. I step across to her and raise my eyes to hers and place my hand on her arm.

"What?" I ask, mentally. *"It's your name day tomorrow. Your formal betrothal. Are you not excited?"*

She sighs and turns away from the view, and we sit on the damp stone. She takes my hand, turning it over and staring at my soft ink-stained palm and my short, nibbled nails as if she can read my future there, but of course that is Forbidden.

"'Tis just that I have no wish to leave here and join with the prince," she says in her normal voice.

I stare at her.

"Not wish to join with the prince. Not wish to be Queen of Epera when the old king dies?" I ask, bewildered. "But you will travel all over the kingdom and wear beautiful clothes and see everything there is to see, and your firstborn son will be king in his turn. How could you not wish for that?"

Jana smiles, but her smile is not happy. Her full pink mouth has stretched into a hard line like the stripes you see on rock. For a moment, her expression is as dark and hard as the mountains that interrupt the enticing peace of our hidden valleys and produce our nation's wealth. She shakes her head, and her voice drops to a whisper.

"We won't be together. And we can never, ever use magic. It is forbidden, remember?" She says, her breath so close to my ear it tickles.

"Mother says I can visit." I remind her, trying to cheer her up.

To my mind, Jana would be the best queen in the world. I truly could not wait to see her in her wedding robes, riding into Blade on Glory next to Arion, the Crown Prince. I went to bed some nights trembling in anticipation and counting down the days, now numbering two, till the servants handed us into our carriages to begin the journey south to the Castle of Air. Our Lady Mother, our nurse, Felice, and Mistress Eglion had been planning and packing for weeks, and the castle was in an uproar of merriment, drinking and dressmaking only the Steward, Master Ash, and my father appeared able to quell.

"Jana?" I ask, in my head again. *"We can still be together like this, in our minds. No one will know."*

She smiles at that. A genuine smile this time, and I catch my breath. Jana is the most beautiful person I have ever seen, but especially so when she smiles, and her ice-grey eyes shine like mountain crystal. I take her hand in mine and press it to my chest bone, where my heart beats swift and sure. "We are always together in here."

"There's something else."

Her smile shifts as she shakes off her gloom. Now it is mysterious, teasing. The big sister smile I know so well.

"What, oh what? Show me."

I jump up from the ground, questions already crowding my mind. Jana's abilities have been growing over the last few months. We have progressed from hearing each other on odd occasions, to having full-blown conversations despite time or distance. This is exciting enough for me. I cannot imagine what else she might have uncovered.

Jana grins, nods at a pile of leaves lying dormant on the stone floor of our cave, and closes her eyes. To my delight and excitement, the leaves swirl off the floor in a burst of whirlwind energy and dance around our stone hideout.

Jana opens her eyes, and her expression turns mischievous. With another jerk of her head, the leaves burst into life like a flock of russet gold butterflies and turn towards me. I gasp as they sweep forward and chase me around the cave. Giggling, I skip away, hopping and jumping, hoping to evade them, but everywhere I go, Jana sends her dusty soldiers to blanket my hair and tickle my cheeks. The horses startle from the cave, snorting with disgust, and I am soon out of breath and weak with laughter.

"Enough," I cry, holding out my hands. "Pax."

"Indeed, stop," says a hard voice, totally unexpected, from the mouth of the cave. It is our father.

Jana jumps and whirls around. The leaves whisper to the ground. Her eyes meet mine, and her voice in my mind fairly shouts at me.

"Say nothing. Nothing!"

I flinch and put my hands over my ears, though her voice rings in my head and is nowhere near my ears.

Our father ducks under the low mouth of the cave and, once inside, straightens to his full, forbidding height. His head brushes the ceiling, and his shoulders swallow the light. I gulp and back away from him, darting a glance at Jana, whose truculent expression does not bode well.

Our father is unpredictable in temperament. Mild-mannered and charming when he wants something, but swift to anger. I saw him beat a groom almost to death once when the man dared to challenge him. My silent, white-faced mother never does. Only Jana, his undoubted favourite, has ever dared.

My father is rarely in residence. His duties at court ever take him from us. When he returns, our family spends hours together grouped by the fire, swapping news and stories, especially when the winter wind freezes birds out of the sky and the snowdrifts stand ten feet high.

This is a different father, wearing a strange and twisted expression I have never seen. There is something about him that sends a spiral of panic into my heart and belly. My bladder twitches, and I clamp my knees together, already feeling the switch of his belt.

This has rarely happened, and never to me. But I know what we are doing is forbidden. There will be a punishment. I step closer to Jana, whether to receive or offer protection, I don't know. She stands tall, her head high. Whatever happens now, an apology is far from her mind.

"Papa," she says, her voice cold but high with tension.

"What do you think you are doing?" he hisses, taking another step forward, then another. His anger is almost a palpable thing, advancing before him like a gale before the storm, creasing his eyes into slits. His mouth tightens white with rage whilst his cheeks flush, suffused with crimson like Mother's roses in the arbour below her bedroom window.

"What is a daughter of mine, bound to the Crown Prince of this realm, its future Queen, doing playing with forbidden magic like a common...."

"Common witch?" Jana finishes for him, her voice as hard and flat and angry as his. "Are you going to order my death, as you did Mistress Whitehorn last week, because King Francis says so?"

"Jana," I whimper a warning at her, because the air is full of hate and mistrust. I have never seen my father's fury aimed at us like this. Never. She flicks a glance at me, and her voice, in my head, is full of raw command.

"Leave. Now. Run."

I watch as she folds her hands behind her back, and there is a flash of silver as her small eating knife appears in a clenched fist.

Our father advances, closing the space between them with two swift strides. I forget to breathe as his hands lunge at her throat. His fingers make claws like trees in winter. She slashes with her hidden blade, and he gasps, jumping back. He fixes his gaze on her. As focused as a snake about to strike.

"There will be an end to magic in Epera. I have seen to that," he says. "For the time being, you are bound to be Queen of this realm. You will obey its laws. Our entire family, our history and fortune, and my plans for this kingdom will end in ruin if you do not."

Jana raises her chin. "I will not be a queen in a land without magic."

A shadow crosses his face at her statement. He shakes his head, and for a second, his shoulders seem to slump in defeat.

"Then you will be the price I pay."

Confused by his words, and the sadness in his expression, I frown, but I have no time to dwell on what it means. He sets his jaw. His hand lashes out, backhanding her across the face, and her head snaps back with a dull thud against the sharp stone wall. I feel the pain in my head. My hand reaches up to rub it. Jana's eyes turn to mine, and she has a second, no more, to beg me to leave before his hand closes like a vice around her throat and he uses his strength to lift her from her feet. Her eyes slam shut.

My legs jerk involuntarily to life. She is using her new skill to push me away, out of the cave, down the hillside. My new riding boots slide ineffectually along the path, scrabbling for purchase as I struggle to get back to her.

Crying out, fighting her strength, I resist. Brambles, branches and jagged stones slash my palms. Dirt digs deep beneath my nails as I battle to stay, to struggle back to her against her iron will, but my father has her now, grunting with fury like a wild beast. I am still within her mind. I cannot, will not, leave her. My head rocks from side-to-side in time with the thud of his fist and my skull throbs with pressure. Her throat is a mass of raw, crushed pain. I gasp for breath. A warm trickle, then a flood of blood, bursts from her nose, spewing into her mouth. Two sharper, devastating blows to the left temple. He strikes with the butt of his knife, with all his warrior strength and anger behind. Experiencing it all with her, I whimper at the devastation and the pain.

"Petronella, run, run, run..." Her voice is a fading whisper. I know she's leaving me when I stop sliding down the path and sag to my knees in the dirt as my bladder finally lets go.

But I cannot run. My heart cracks open with a twist of grief so painful it shatters. An iron fist reaches in and wrenches the wreckage from my chest. Exposed. A shameful and broken thing with a hole at my centre in the shape of the world. I am a dirty mess of piss and fear, tears and guilt and then Jana's world goes dark, and so does mine.

Chapter Forty-Four

Mistress Eglion's hands left Petronella's as the memory faded and died. Petronella's head dipped to her lap at the force of grief that shook her and turned her inside out. The pain in her heart was still unhealed and unendurable, even eighteen years later. Tears drenched her cheeks. Mistress Eglion patted her shaking shoulder with one un-practiced hand while the other reached for her pipe.

"My father. I don't believe it. My father?" Sobs muffled her voice.

"I am sorry, my dear." Mistress Eglion sat up to light her pipe. Petronella inhaled the familiar, comforting warmth of Argent Gold and smudged her hands across her eyes. Her head lifted heavier than a cannon ball, and she gazed, unseeing, at the view across the river. Her arms crept around her own waist. A sorry attempt at comfort.

"It is him behind all this, isn't it? I was hoping you were mistaken."

Mistress Eglion huffed out a fragrant sigh. "I am afraid so. Many things are falling into place."

"He hates magic and those who can use it. Truly hates it. And what did he mean, he had 'seen to it' magic would disappear?"

"You know he has always had Arion's ear, do you not?"

"There you go again, asking questions."

"Tis the Mage's way, my dear. He always wants us to think for ourselves."

"So what if he had the king's ear? The Falcons are the second family in the land. It is well-known and expected he would advise the king."

"As a younger man, a charming, helpful, persuasive adviser, he also had the ear of King Francis."

Petronella gasped. "You think it was him? Who told King Francis his beloved queen was bearing a bastard child?"

"You know how quickly gossip races around the Court of Skies. He may not have said so in person, but he made him believe it. I am sure of it, Petronella. Darius was in love with her. She wouldn't have anything to do with him. A woman so kind, so gentle. Her magic was in her love. Her compassion. King Francis never believed she loved him. Your father tried to seduce her. He failed. She rejected him - oh, so gently, and he turned on her. With terrible, fateful results. The thing is...."

Mistress Eglion took another breath of tobacco., her eyes squinting in their wrinkled nest against the smoke. "I know Darius of old. Your father is the most un-magical being I have ever had the misfortune to meet. He hates our natural magic because he wants it. He does not have it. The Mage's gift has passed him by completely. So, he is jealous and fearful of all who wield it. He relies on his intellect and charm instead. He broke Francis' power by his manipulation and in his turn, your husband is breaking your land. But never forget, they are dancing to Darius's tune."

Petronella climbed slowly to her feet and leant over the bow. Nausea churned deep in her belly. She stared at the passing river banks, hardly noting the beauty in her surroundings.

"What do you know of this Shadow Mage?"

The Seer tapped her pipe out on the deck. "More than I would like and less than is useful. It would have taken Darius years to harness even a small amount of its power, especially as he has no magical blood of his own." She swallowed heavily and glanced across at Petronella before turning her face to the fertile banks as the boat moved onward. Her voice dropped to a reluctant whisper.

"He would have had to use your sister's blood, perhaps more, to access it."

Petronella flinched, clapping her hand to her mouth at the sudden surge of nausea that claimed her. She retched, shoulders heaving.

"Don't tell me anymore."

"I am sorry, my dear."

Her tutor waited for Petronella to regain her composure, rocking herself gently. Her staff lay across her lap. Petronella stared at it, taking in the intricate pattern of owls and ivy that curled around it. Something about it tugged at her memory and vanished before she could retrieve it.

"What would happen after he accessed the power?" She forced herself to ask the question. Her nails dug indents into her clammy palms as she waited for the reply.

Mistress Eglion shook her head. "That, I cannot answer. I do not know what he would do next. He has no power of his own. Perhaps we are just surmising. Perhaps there is nothing other than a normal army to worry about."

Petronella focused her attention on her tutor's mindscape. Bursts of white energy cast snowflakes in huge swirls across the pristine blue sky. Black clouds formed on the horizon of the old woman's thoughts, sending questions like storm waves through her habitual peace.

"But you don't believe that."

Mistress Eglion's gnarled knuckles tightened on her staff. Her mouth tightened. "No, I don't."

Chapter Forty-Five

Acrid smoke and gunpowder polluted the summer breeze as the boat bumped against a jetty crowded with panicked, shouting citizens seeking transport away from the ravaged city. Petronella waited with Mistress Eglion as the passengers of the Swordfish disembarked. The water warriors formed a guard across the bottom of the ramp to prevent the craft being swamped by the terrified Sunirans, who pleaded with them in desperation for permission to board. The industrious calm and bustle that had welcomed their small party only days ago had vanished in an instant, replaced with chaos and fear, but the port still reeked with the oily scent of fish, overlain with sweat.

The captain of the vessel conversed briefly with Joran, who swept the crowd with his gaze and then nodded, face grim.

"Hold fast now." The captain yelled over the din. "Once our passengers are disembarked, we will take all the women and children we can to Shoreborne and return for more."

A clamour of pleading greeted his words, and he nodded to one of the senior crew members, who began the arduous task of gaining order in a voice more used to shouting orders against a rising gale.

Joran and Domita sprang into action, barely taking time to make their farewells as they pounded down the gangway and waited for the band of the Chosen, who had left the capital to fight with them.

"Hold, now." The captain of the Swordfish shouted again. "We will return, and with more ships. You men, take shelter in the inns and arm yourselves. We will return."

Bowing to the inevitable, the wrench of separation twisted through the heartbroken crowd and, grim-faced, the men hugged their families and stood back. Cries and sobs of anguish echoed off the sunlit buildings as the families broke apart and prepared for departure. Petronella dropped her eyes to the travel-stained deck and choked back her own tears. Mistress Eglion muttered something and twisted her stick into the deck, her dismay palpable.

The captain waited until Petronella descended the gangplank with Mistress Eglion at her side before he waved groups of Sunirans aboard. Joran collected the water warriors around him to receive last-minute instruction and his bleak, distant gaze caught her hers one final time before he headed them away from the jetty to the centre of the action at the north of the city, where the grain fields and granaries were situated. The pounding of cannon competed with the agitated bells clanging an alarm in every temple.

Heart in her mouth, ears already tortured by the sound of distant screams, Petronella made her way at a more sedate pace, matching her stride for the slower one of her tutor.

Terrified townsfolk buffeted and jostled their way past as they picked their way across a wharf littered with the dismal detritus of mass evacuation to the broad paved street leading to the city centre. A wail went up behind them as the late arrivals reached the wharf to find the last of the vessels had set sail. Petronella's heart pinched with pity for them, but there was nothing she could do.

Ahead, on the rise, a dark trail of loaded carts ascended the hillside to the caves, guarded by dark-clothed Eperan soldiers. The copper tang of blood and roasted flesh turned Petronella's stomach as they rounded a bend in the road and stumbled across the broken bodies of a family too slow to leave their burning home. She backed away, horrified. Mistress Eglion's face tightened into a grim mask. Her ancient hand clenched around her staff, and she set her stooping shoulders in determination as they toiled up the hill in the heat to the centre of town.

Black-clad soldiers spread like plague everywhere, and with little purpose to their actions Petronella could immediately discern. Her former worries about the attack were apparently correct.

The Eperan troops were starving, and there was little true discipline in this first, furious rush. Soldiers appeared from wrecked houses, waving triumphant loaves of bread and chunks of cold bacon in their grimy hands. Whole families had died defending their homes and food stores from callous men who marauded and swarmed like gutter rats. Her heart ached at the sight of broken and twisted bodies, and her hands itched with the need to blast the intruders away. Only Mistress Eglion's steady presence kept her focused as they pressed forward against the tide.

She had thought her husband's army was only interested in food, but the Oceanians were intent on guarding their temples, as well as their granaries, warehouses, and people. Bands of priests and priestesses in small groups, distinctive in their white robes, warded the entrances to their precious shrines and strategic buildings with protective, water-based magic. Localised fog and mist featured most times, disorienting the Eperans who did not know the territory and missed the walls of icicles that appeared out of the mist like walls of crystal spears to hook and fillet them like fish as they advanced, unknowing, into the fog.

One group of Joran's troops acted together to conjure a spinning vortex of turquoise water that deflected the advance of a group of Swords soldiers. Like everything in Oceanis, the conjured shield was as beautiful as it was effective as it stole the swords from the soldiers' unsuspecting hands and spun them away. The time it bought afforded a chance for the people they guarded to avoid massacre.

The townsfolk were running for their lives, clutching those minor items that meant the most to them. Bags bursting with food and skins of water slung across their shoulders, whole families helped each other carry their elderly and their young and their beloved pets.

The wail of terrified children punctuated the general shouting along with the frantic barking of dogs as the attack from the north of the town gained ground and more soldiers appeared, their faces dark with smoke and sweat. They leered and loomed, stabbed and killed like demons conjured from a ghoulish nightmare. Still, the Blessed fought back. The air shimmered with power as they worked in small groups to cast their energy around their city and give their people time to retreat.

Many of the goddess-blessed had already perished, their magic with them. Their bodies lay in tangles, their shrines put to the torch. Blood ran in the cobbled streets, and Petronella's anger, already white-hot within her, flared anew at the total waste laid bare before her despairing eyes.

At the city square, Petronella dragged her tutor into the shelter of a doorway as a fresh cohort of soldiers swept in from the adjoining street, closely pursued by a determined band of Oceanians who were wielding both a wall of water and literal harpoons to stop them progressing further. She swallowed, her mouth dry as the Eperan soldiers regrouped and attacked.

The Oceanians not wielding magic had little choice but to give way when they met solid steel. Her hands shook as her husband's troops cut down men and women with ruthless efficiency. The air rang with screams of pain and rage. The streets were slick with the blood of the fallen, a brutal reminder of Alice's visions so many weeks ago.

The few members of the Blessed who remained in the group were trying to cast a protective wall of ice around the citizens, but there were too few of them. A young woman turned her frowning attention from their efforts and screamed as she pointed up the nearest street where another group of Eperans were approaching from the hillside. The shield of ice collapsed, and the Blessed gazed at each other in complete despair.

"They cannot fight," Petronella yelled in Mistress Eglion's ear over the din of crashing steel.

"Cups' magic is defensive." Mistress Eglion informed her. Despite her habitual calm, her wrinkled knuckles were white as she took a firmer hold on her staff.

"What is Swords' magic?" Petronella could feel her ring pulsing with energy as her anger grew.

"Offensive. That is why Joran is so good as their leader. He can use his own power and God's blessed speed to attack as well as defend."

Jaw clenched so hard the muscles in her neck hurt, Petronella left the shelter of the doorway, her hand raised toward her own forces. She yelped as Mistress Eglion used her staff to strike her arm down.

"Remember the nature of the power you bear. It is the Ring of Mercy. You use it in anger at your peril."

"You are the Seer of Epera. Can you do nothing? Why will the High Priestess of Oceanis not act to prevent this?" Petronella's eyes were wild as she fought her desire to see the invaders punished. Power rippled around her, feeding off her anger, barely contained by her will.

Her tutor stamped her staff once on the paving stones and the noise of the battle faded, as if she witnessed it through a closed window. Her voice was quiet as she continued to observe the action.

"The Gods have ever placed mere humans like pawns on a chess-board and watched as we destroyed each other. The faithless amongst us consider the Gods toy with us. We are below their lofty gaze and our actions mean nothing to them other than entertainment."

The old woman's expression clouded as the soldiers advanced with cutting precision. The Oceanians fell before them like ripe wheat in a field sewn with blood. Mistress Eglion's nails tightened their grip on her bruised arm as Petronella lunged to their defence again and bounced off the protective shield.

Thwarted, Petronella fixed her with her a despairing glare.

"What do you believe, Mistress Eglion? What should any of us believe?"

"I believe the Gods want us to decide for ourselves how we conduct our lives, and they give us choices in all matters, large and small. The lives we live are the total of our choices. All those we make and all those we do not. The Gods do not make our choices, although they may set up the circumstances that make those choices necessary. That is how they give us the opportunity to learn from our mistakes."

She leaned her staff against her shoulder and took both Petronella's hands in her own old, gnarled ones. Petronella gasped at the surge of power blowing through her. The old woman's eyes were deep blue, nested in wrinkles, and they twinkled into hers like the ageless hope of stars.

"As humans, we have free will. As wise humans, we acknowledge this and take personal responsibility for our actions. The Gods bless us with knowledge and power, my dear, and as Seers, we are supposed to be impartial. However, they do not make our choices for us. We are still human enough for that."

She caught Petronella to her in a crushing hug over far too soon.

"I can no longer stand by. There is a greater force coming, and you need to continue. This is only the beginning, Petronella. Not the end. Never think you have won." She stood back and traced the huge diamond sparkling on Petronella's finger, a rueful smile tugging at her lips. "The Gods will bless you. Goodbye, my dear. Guard my temple."

"What? No!"

The Seer left the shelter of the doorway before Petronella could stop her. A tiny, fragile old lady, she strode to the middle of the square and raised her staff toward the soldiers. A simple gesture of her arms scattered them like winter leaves and slammed them against the solid walls of the surrounding buildings to slide, broken, to the flags.

"Look," a terrified young priestess raised a shaking finger to where the new group of people had gathered at the head of the street.

Petronella's eyes widened as she followed the woman's deer-eyed gaze. The air surrounding the new group pulsed with malice. She sent her mind towards it, but her feeble attempt bounced back as if it had met a wall. She tried again but could not penetrate it.

White faced, the few remaining Oceanians fled, their eyes stark and dark with terror from this new offensive. Petronella's eyes widened as she marked their determined, implacable progress. This was no normal army.

They were of all ages, men, women and even some children. All ghostly pale, dressed in black robes little more than rags. Her brow wrinkling with bewilderment, she thought she recognised a few of them through the dirt and grime on their skeletal faces. Barefoot, they advanced until they surrounded Mistress Eglion. Their faces twisted in pain as if they were being tortured and moved against their will. Dark power rippled around them. Amulets of some dark stone on a silver chain enclosed their necks. The chains had meshed with their filthy, sore-encrusted skin.

"Mistress Eglion," she screamed an alarm and launched herself at the old woman.

Her ring pulsed with wild energy, but Mistress Eglion blocked her forward progress with a wave of her hand. It was like facing the force of a hurricane, although not a hair on her head moved.

"Your task is not here, Petronella. You know what you must do. I will hold them here for a while to buy you time, but you must go on. Do not fail me."

Mistress Eglion was ringed by the tattered army now. Three of them turned their heads slowly toward Petronella. She swallowed a wave of nausea as she caught the twisted thought as it was flung into her mental landscape from their direction. It was a promise of dark pain.

"You next."

Around them, the sounds of fighting and the screams of the dying continued, but here, in the square, the air was still and silent as the eye of a storm. Power sparked around the circle of the attackers as they raised their hands together. They conjured a tornado of malicious black energy that sucked power from a source far away on the hillside and gathered itself to attack. The Seer of Epera raised her staff and summoned her own whirlwind of pure white energy. The two forces clashed in the centre and fought for precedence, equally matched.

Black clouds and white collected and swirled against the hot blue sky. Birds wheeled and screamed above them. Petronella clapped her hands to her ears, her heart bleeding as she registered their turmoil and distress. A flash of the Grayling on his lonely perch in the Castle of Air blazed to the forefront of her mental vision. He was bating, wings a blur, his avian mind awash with fear.

Mistress Eglion waited. The sizzling, sparking energy gathered in the circle, jolting from one skeletal body to the next as the power built. At the last, the old woman lowered her staff. She would not fight her own. Her patient, steady gaze sought Petronella's.

"Every end is a beginning, my dear. Do not blame these people. These are the Blessed of Epera, and the Shadow Mage has turned them into slaves. Find your companions, *and may the Mage always bless and protect you. You are my granddaughter, last of the line of Owls, born to be Queen and the Seer of Epera. I freely give you my power. Go now, I beg you."*

She had time to trace the sign of the Mage in the charged air before the energy in the circle burst in a flash of dark light that pulsed with triumphant force.

Mistress Eglion opened her arms and her mouth in a cry that never came. Petronella's scream rent the air instead, sending the birds spiralling into the storm-shocked sky. Lightening blazed where her grandmother stood, a star-shaped silhouette against the dazzling light.

Petronella staggered against the rough stone wall behind her as her grandmother's power poured through the space between them to torch her mind and light every nerve end with raw energy.

Her ring burned on her finger, and she thrust her hands towards the space where Mistress Eglion had been. Grief and rage tore at the roots of her, and power flickered at her fingertips, ready to unleash her fury. A stab of pain in her bruised arm and her grandmother's warning were only just enough to hold her racing anger. She clenched her arms around her stomach, forcing her rage back down to a place where it could harm no-one as her heart cracked open with fresh grief.

The dark army surveyed the empty pavement where their target had stood seconds before. Their confusion and sorrow as they turned to where Petronella crouched in the doorway was easy to read in their pale faces. The grief in their eyes was hard to bear. Some of them were crying, but they had no choice but to turn their tortured faces towards her.

With Mistress Eglion gone, the protective shield she had conjured disappeared as well. The vast noise and confusion of the battle scattered her senses and scraped on her nerves. Awash with fear, Petronella swallowed once before adrenalin claimed her, and she sprinted for the nearest exit. Her ring flared to bat away the closest members of the dark forces as she concentrated on putting distance between herself and them. Her heart thudded with loss and anger at every fall of her foot. Above her head, the birds coalesced into one swirling, darting mass. They followed her as she raced to the heart of the battle.

She reached for Joran's mind with little concern for his disdain and tore at his mental barrier until it fell before her. His mental landscape was a bleak, dark place. He was fighting. His sword arm tiring as he cut down soldier after soldier. He was trying to protect the main granaries, barking orders at the Oceanians, who were putting up their own barriers. She was aware of the dark army behind her turning to the Sunirans now, using their swirling vortex of air-based power to smash and smother the defences flung up in desperation by gentle people with only compassion in their hearts. Gritting her teeth, tears flooding her cheeks, feet skidding on the blood-slick cobbles, she ran on.

Gasping for breath, she skidded to a halt near the marble entry of the granary complex, clutching her side where a stitch had developed.

Fire arcing across the sky a few streets away must be Domita, using her own form of combat to protect the city. Backed up at the doorway of the largest storehouse, Joran parried the attacks of one soldier after another. Blood and dirt spattered his face. His clothes were filthy, and she could feel the weariness in his body and soul as he gritted his teeth and fought on. His mind had closed almost entirely. Pockets of resistance from the townsfolk remained, but it was clear Arion's troops had the upper hand. She dared not distract Joran by calling his name, either out loud or mentally, but there must have been something between them.

His gaze jerked to meet hers, and his concentration wavered. She screamed a warning at him as his opponent pressed his attack and then, with a sickening, tearing sound she experienced in her own body, the soldier gave a yell of triumph as he found an opening and pressed his attack home. Joran slumped to the ground. Petronella staggered in pain as Arion's forces flocked the building and kicked his limp body out of the way to gain access to the rich stores of grain within.

With their attention diverted, she dashed in a crouch across the open space and fell to her knees at his side.

"No, no. Joran. Please, please wake up. Joran!" She grabbed his shoulders and shook him. His head lolled. His skin under the grime was deathly pale.

The blade had entered his left side. Blood oozed in a steady stream from the wound, filling her nostrils with the grim smell of salt and iron. Gritting her teeth against panic, she ripped strips off her clothing to effect a makeshift bandage soon soaked with blood. She did not know whether it did any good or if he was alive or dead. Her hand clamped like a claw around the ragged wound, her mind reached out to him again and again, but there was no reply, just a blank space.

Her frantic gaze swept him; her ring pulsed with savage energy, but there was no outlet for it. Nowhere she could allow it to go without breaking her own covenant with the Mage. The granary courtyard was full of her husband's army intent on taking the last of the grain. They took no notice of her, another grieving citizen. There was no-one to help them.

Behind her, the soldiers formed a chain, and a line of sacks marked with the wheatsheaf crest of Sunira passed from the warehouse into the courtyard.

The cries of the wounded and dying drifted across the city, along with the smoke and the smell of blood. The soldiers laughed as they loaded sacks of grain onto the nearest carts and started them on their journey back up the hill. Granaries empty, the troops withdrew as the battle horns wailed from the entrance to the caves on the hillside. She remained on her knees next to Joran, still clamping his wound with a hand that refused to let go as the clash and the dismal tolling of the remaining temple bells replaced the din of battle. She was still there, rocking out her grief and her tears, when a comforting hand on her shoulder helped to ease the tight muscles on her back.

"Domita."

Domita crouched next to her and cast her own gaze over Joran's still form. She pressed her cheek close to his face and sat back on her heels. Petronella lifted her eyes to Domita's. The girl was filthy, covered in grime, and she smelt like a bonfire. Her eyes were red. Tiredness and grief marked her features.

"He still lives, I think. But for how long, I don't know. His soul is already seeking release."

Petronella clamped down on her anguish at the gentle statement. Blood soaked the cloth of his tunic and caked her hands. She could feel it drying and flaking on her fingers the longer she knelt there, still clutching his side. Her voice was a mere whisper as she said. "Mistress Eglion is dead. She was my grandmother, you know."

Domita bit her lip. Her brown eyes clouded. "I am so sorry."

Tears made streams of the dirt and blood on Domita's freckled cheeks as she surveyed the aftermath of battle. The dead sprawled across the space, both Oceanians and Eperans twisted together in the last moments as their lives ran out. Smoke drifted in the air.

The sobs of the wounded nearby and the wails of the homeless marked the end of the battle in industrious Sunira. The last of the carts rumbled away from them, back towards the mines and Epera.

Her heart like a lead weight in her chest, Petronella clambered to her feet.

"Will you stay with him? I have to go."

Domita's brow furrowed. "Go? Go where?"

Petronella turned her gaze to the mines. Their twin dark entrances reminded her of Arion's bleak eyes.

"To fulfil my vow to Merlon. I will do as Arion wants. This is my fault. If I hadn't come here, none of this would have been necessary."

"After all this, you will go back? He will kill you, Petronella."

"I know. He may as well. He has taken everything he wanted."

"I will go with you."

Petronella shook her head. Tiredness overwhelmed her, and she fought to get her words out.

"Stay here. See to Joran. Go to Alice. Tell Merlon I am deeply sorry. I never meant for any of this to happen."

Domita protested, but Petronella stopped her by putting a shaking hand over her mouth.

"As my friend, Domita. Please, look after yourself and those others we care about."

There was a long pause. Domita stared into her eyes before enveloping her in a hug as warm as a blanket in front of a fire. Petronella blinked as a spark of warmth swept through her to heat her chilled blood and calm her shattered nerves.

"The Gods go with you, Queen of Swords," Domita said.

"And with you, my friend. Always."

She squeezed Domita back and knelt once more to place a gentle kiss on Joran's grimy forehead.

"Goodbye, my love. I am so sorry."

She waited, stretching her mental senses to their limit for any sign of him, but there was nothing. Just a blank and endless silence. The sun was setting behind her as she faced the mines and began the long ascent up the hill in the wake of the grain carts.

Chapter Forty-Six

It was full dark by the time Petronella reached the outcrop of boulders marking the boundary of the Eperan Camp. A waft of stew cooking on campfires greeted her nostrils as she forced her weary legs up the last bend. A low murmur of conversation crept to her on the wind, punctuated by the distant laughter of the victorious. Carts and crates of goods cluttered the stony flat ground around the mines. Canvas sacks full of pilfered grain heaved into piles still waited to be added to the transport. Making her way with difficulty on the rocky pathway at the top of rise, sliding on the scree, and dodging around the stolen spoils, she lifted her gaze to meet the narrowed glare of a sentry who materialised out of the darkness and poked his sword at her chest.

"You can put your sword away," she said, before he could speak. "I am the Queen of Epera. I wish to see your General, and I am unarmed." This last was a lie. She had hidden her knife in her battered satchel and changed into her Eperan clothing on her way up the hillside, despising the hot, heavy cloth and gloves even as she donned them.

"Don't look much like any type of queen to me," the guard muttered, giving her another tentative prod.

"Nevertheless, that is who I am. You can accompany me if you wish. I am sure your commanding officer will be pleased to see me."

The guard's brow creased into a bemused frown, but he ordered her to walk in front of him and escorted her under arms into the presence of General Harison. The man had opened the top button of his tunic and was regarding his stained stockings in the light of the campfire in front of his tent, glass of wine in hand, as the guard poked her forward. Harison's eyes narrowed in irritation.

"What is this?" he said, shooting a steely glare to his subordinate, who snapped to attention, eyes front, as his superior lurched to his feet and reached for his dusty boots.

"Says she's the Queen of Epera, Sir. Sorry to disturb, sir." Her escort mumbled, face flushed with embarrassment.

"The Queen of Epera?" General Harison peered at her, cynicism smeared across his fleshy face, and Petronella snatched her hood from her head.

"Satisfied?" she said, when his eyes widened, and he took a step back.

"Fetch my Lord Falconridge," Harison snapped.

She clenched her fists in her gloves as her father strode into the light of the campfire. He still wore his customary furs, despite the heat, and she swallowed hard as he loomed over her, blocking out the light. His face was alight with triumph. Her bladder tightened as her blood fizzed with rage. She fought hard to keep from using her own nails to tear the smugness from his cheeks.

"Petronella, what a pleasant surprise."

She screwed her eyes closed. Somewhere inside her, her mind revolted against his delight in toying with her and anger flared higher, but the other constant beat of sorrow that took precedence in her heart drowned it out. Jaron. Mistress Eglion. Jana. Oceanis. She was almost too tired to feel afraid. Almost.

"You have been looking for me. Here I am."

His tone changed, and his eyes narrowed. "You have led me a merry dance." He walked in a slow circle around her. "I assume you have realised the futility of running away from your duty to our kingdom?"

Petronella sighed. "If only you had another daughter, Father. You could try again."

He stepped closer and thrust his bearded face at her. "And what do you mean by that?"

"Nothing other than what I said. I am here to negotiate a truce. Withdraw the army from Oceanis, and I will return to Epera and submit to Arion's will. He can kill me to take another wife, if that is what it will take to heal the land."

Her father chuckled. "You are here already. At sword point." He waved a broad hand at the circle of soldiers who had surrounded the campfire. "You are hardly in a position to negotiate. I could kill you now, and take your ring, station my forces in Oceanis."

She raised her chin. "You could. But you won't. Arion is at least honourable. And he is still your king. He has his grain, and I am returning to the Castle of Air. Those were the terms of his demands. They are now fulfilled. His forces will withdraw. If you want to remain his trusted servant, you will comply."

She forced herself to meet his gaze with her own. It was taking all her effort to remain on her feet. She had no way of knowing what his plans were, but he would have something hatching in that fertile brain of his, augmented by the power of the Dark Mage, and she had to stay alive long enough to find out what it was.

Her father's eyebrows contracted at that. His chilling glare pierced her through like a winter gale.

"I have my own reasons for returning that you know nothing about. I should at least thank you for saving me the time of searching for you further."

He gestured to the ring of soldiers. "Take her to a covered wagon, chain her and place a guard on her. I want eyes on her at all times."

The soldiers marched into the firelight, their faces implacable under their helmets. Petronella flinched as one meaty fist closed on her arm, and they jerked her away.

"By the way." Her father's tone was at once jovial and perfectly modulated to score a direct hit as he called after her. "You might like to know that Arion has condemned Lady Felice de Winter as a witch. She will die at the king's pleasure for her part in all this."

Petronella jerked to a halt, causing the soldier leading her to lose his grip.

Hidden inside her glove, her ring flared, and she put a hand up to her forehead as a warning pulse of energy shot through her. She bit down on the pain his words had caused, determined not to give him the pleasure of seeing it, although she stared hard ahead into the darkness of the mines with eyes awash.

"Then I hope you are both prepared for the wrath of her cousin, the King of Argentia," she said, over her shoulder.

They chained her in a wagon with barred sides. A battered tarpaulin stretched over the roof, offering dubious protection from the elements. It was none too clean.

Petronella kicked at the soiled straw lining the bottom. It spilled over the side of the cart, and she slumped to the wooden floor with her back against the driver's box, relieved she had reduced the squalor by some small degree. Curious eyes bored into her from all sides as the soldiers went about their business. She buried her head in her knees and ignored them until sheer exhaustion overcame her and she drifted into sleep.

Someone thrusting a loaf of bread and a charred sausage through the bars was enough to wake her. A slim skin of some sort of liquid followed. Rubbing the crick in her neck, she raised her head from her bent knees enough to glean who had spared her this small kindness and blinked in surprise as her weary gaze clashed with that of young Dominic Skinner. His blue eyes widened with alarm as she spoke, and she lowered her voice to a whisper with an effort.

"By all the gods, what are you doing here?"

"Joined the army, your Maj."

"Why?"

He grinned at her, stirring his foot in the soiled straw under her cart. "Army still needs some'un to help with the nags. An' they promised us food."

She narrowed her eyes. "You followed us, didn't you?"

His cheeks pinked under the grime as he shuffled his feet.

"I was worried. Thought it best. Where's Domita?"

She grimaced. "Safe, I hope. I told her to go back to Shoreborne. If I am lucky, she obeyed me, but you know Domita. There are no guarantees."

"An' the lady Alice?"

"She has joined the ranks of the Seers. The highest in Oceanis. I saw the High Priestess myself on the night of her ascension."

His in drawn breath and shining eyes told her what he thought about this. "So, are you one of us now, your Maj?"

She managed the briefest of smiles for him and waggled her eyebrows in warning as an older soldier approached with suspicion written across his face, one hand on his sword. Dominic melted into the shadows with the ease of one experienced in the art of vanishing without a trace.

Petronella glared at the guard until he backed down. The wine was thin and sour, the sausage burnt and the bread stale, but all were welcome when offered with simple kindness. Her simple supper done with, she put her head back on her knees, blotting out the sight and sounds of the surrounding army with her thick woollen hood. And then, unseen by anyone, she allowed her tears to flow.

Commanding officers booted the army awake in the soft light of pre-dawn before the birds had clamoured their good mornings.

Petronella had spent the night huddled in the depths of her tunic with her hood pulled up over her head for warmth. She had slept little but must have managed something of unconsciousness when she struggled upright to find a thin, army issue blanket carefully pushed through the slats of her cage, so it covered her. Clutching it to her, she managed a tremulous smile. Dominic again. She hoped he had not gone cold to ensure her comfort. At least the men were packing up, which she prayed meant her father had taken her words to heart. She quirked an eyebrow at the thought he would follow her advice now, as a prisoner, rather than when she was a queen in a castle. Something about that did not ring true.

Breakfast bolted down, the soldiers prepared to move. The wounded received aid ministered with a rudimentary and callous efficiency that caused her to cringe. At last, they gave the order to stamp out the campfires, and the weary soldiers mustered to face the long, dark journey home to Epera. An armed guard accompanied her from the cart and led her outside to tend her needs, an event she dreaded having to experience again.

The temple bells were tolling in Sunira once more, although there was little life stirring in the forlorn city. She guessed they would be honouring their fallen. Her heart shrunk as she counted her grandmother and Joran in their number. Her mind reached for them as she had so many times in the past few hours, begging for some sense of their presence, but neither of them was within her narrow reach. Their souls had flown to the gods. She prayed the Mage and the High Priestess would allow them into their presence. She cast a quick glance backwards where her thick faced guards grouped, allowing her small privacy amongst the rocky outcrop of boulders bordering her view.

Facing violated Sunira, where traces of smoke still wafted from the blasted rooftops, she traced the sign of the Mage and the sign of the High Priestess on the fresh morning air. She shook off the rough hand that grasped her arm and interrupted her blessing. The urge to blast the soldiers away from her was hard to suppress, but through her pain, one constant thought lingered. They thought she was powerless. For now, it was better they continued to believe it.

Chapter Forty-Seven

Ten weary days later even the dull light of sullen Epera was enough to dazzle the eyes as the army put the grim black tunnels of the mines above Blade behind them at last and turned left to travel across the lower slopes of the Iron Mountains towards the Castle of Air. The fresh breeze was enough to reinvigorate tired legs. The men perked up as they anticipated returning home as heroes, complete with a rich store of desperately required grain and the runaway queen. Thin chests swelled with pride and snatches of song wafted to her on the brisk wind along with the jingle of tack, the rumble of hooves and cartwheels and the steady beat of marching feet.

Petronella clutched the sides of the cart as it jolted over a narrow path carved into the mountainside and tried not to look down. The height was dizzying. Stones and scree dislodged by the wheels tumbled into the void, and she clenched her teeth against her overactive imagination as she envisioned the cart losing a wheel and plummeting after them with her still in it. Overhead, birds in huge numbers raced the dark clouds across the sky. She could imagine them calling a welcome to her as her cart tracked slowly over the rocky slopes.

The fields in the valleys were still slick with oozing mud. Nothing had changed there. No livestock attempted to graze the muddy turf, and she could see no-one about at the isolated farms they passed as they cleared the heights for the mid-slopes. The land seemed blighted. Deserted of human life and silent, apart from the cries of the birds. If she craned her head forward, she could see, in the distance, the stern, blocked outline of the Castle of Air as it formed on the horizon.

Her ring gave a tiny pulse of energy on her finger, as if it, too, recognised home soil. She glanced down at it. The light from the diamond was shining through the weave of her glove. She twisted the ring around to hide the diamond in her palm and tugged the threadbare blanket more closely around her. It wouldn't do to let anyone see it dance to life on her hand.

At the end of the narrow track, the road broadened to allow more than single file, and Petronella's shoulders stiffened as her father cantered his mount back down the long column to ride beside her.

"Arion will be pleased at the success of his mission," he said. His acid smile did not meet his eyes.

"I'm sure he will be happy to fill the granaries and put a more fertile bride on the throne. Has he chosen one?"

Lord Darius glanced at her sideways. His dark eyes danced with malicious delight. "The king's wishes are not unknown to me."

"And so?"

Darius allowed a full-grown smirk to cross his bearded mouth. "His intended bride is the Countess of Wessendean, I believe."

Petronella rolled her eyes. Arabella. It was an obvious choice given the woman's undoubted fertility, but how the woman would crow.

"At least the Princess of Oceanis is safe from his intentions. She ascended to the rank of Seer. Blessed by their goddess, I witnessed her initiation myself. Did you know?" she said.

She stumbled as his fist shot through the bars of the cage and landed a crushing blow against her shoulder. Arm numb, she turned to him, her eyes blazing as fiercely as the ring hidden in her hand. His eyes held the same blank, reptilian gleam she had witnessed all those years ago when he turned on Jana. She was suddenly grateful for the bars that blocked his access to her.

"I will not hear of magic in Epera by word, or by deed."

He snatched at the reins and kicked his mount into an untidy gallop away from her. The animal's hooves kicked up clods of dirt. Petronella rubbed her arm where a large bruise was forming as she marked his progress.

She frowned as he put distance between them. She had caught a bare glimpse of his essence in those last few seconds. There was no magic inside him at all. But despite his denial of it, the taint of the shadow mage, warped and twisted, clung to him like a rancid perfume. Her brow furrowed as she recalled the ragged army who had wreaked such havoc on the citizens of Sunira and whose combined power had ended her own grandmother. *No natural magic in Epera. That's what you mean.*

Mind twisted with anguish, she slid down the sides of the cage and crouched in a corner with the blanket pulled close around her shoulders as an icy wind sprung up around her. Her grandmother was right. Despite his words, Darius, the trusted power behind the throne, was now in charge of the army and in control of what remained of Epera's magic. Her skin crawled as she wondered just what he was planning to do with it.

She entered the grounds of the Castle of Air in much the same way she had left it - under cover of darkness and in a horse-drawn wagon. Most of the army had peeled off to their huge barracks, and the provisions carts had diverted under heavy guard to the granaries of Blade on the way. Of the magical dark army who had ended Mistress Eglion, there had been no sign since they left the mines. A squad of the Palace Guard escorted her to the castle dungeons and sneered their disdain at her as they flung her into a tiny cell, slamming the door shut behind them with a clang that made her soul lurch.

She staggered to her feet, rubbing bruises. A bare light filtered in through a grate on the door from the torch thrust into a bracket on the corridor wall. Her breath froze in the air, and she shuddered, pulling the folds of her blanket around her as she took in her surroundings.

The bare stone walls oozed moss and water. There was a cot with no mattress and a three-legged stool rotten with damp. Rusty manacles decorated the far wall. As the guard's footsteps faded into the distance, she rubbed her wrists, thanking the gods they had not deemed her enough of a threat to warrant using them.

The only sound was the distant drip of water as it pooled in the coldest corner. Unutterably tired, she scraped ancient muck from the floor with the edge of a hide boot and folded her battered bag around the outline of the book that had somehow survived everything. Against all appearances, it made a good cushion as she settled down to wait.

The guards delayed several hours before they brought her a pewter flagon of water. She sipped it sparingly. Food was non-existent. She dozed off and on, trying to gather her strength and her thoughts against what was to come. Her blanket did nothing to block the chill of the place from her bones, and she eyed the torch hanging on the wall outside her cell with something like desperation.

She stood as close to the door as she could, attempting to get some warmth and longing for someone to talk to. The thought of heat turned her mind inevitably to Domita.

Reaching the Battonian with mind-to-mind communication was tricky. With nothing better to do, Petronella tried for over an hour until she gave up, with her head aching. She dozed. She paced. She waited. She starved. And she grieved.

The past, so clouded and remote before now, laid bare before her.

She had time now to remember her life before she became queen. Jana's face smiled at her, her grey eyes sparkled in the sunlight. Her quiet, haunted mother, Briana, dead years before, heartbroken after losing her eldest daughter, joined hands with her sister in her imagination. Joran's sparkling eyes and delighted smile broke her heart repeatedly as she retraced her journey over the last few weeks. Her memories of Mistress Eglion included pipe smoke, ink and parchment, and long hours of study and argument. She wished she had known who Mistress Eglion had really been and then smiled to herself. Grandmother or no, their relationship would probably have been the same.

"Wait for me," she begged them from the shadows. "I will join you soon."

The bitter touch of another's thoughts alerted her to the presence of Arabella even before the woman's slender figure appeared outside her cell door. Her former lady-in-waiting's magic-free mindscape featured a forbidding grey desert, punctuated by slivers of ice in stylish designs of silver and black.

Petronella stiffened her shoulders at the clatter of approaching footsteps and clutched her blanket around her to hide her ring. Four tall guards surrounded Arabella's slight frame. She wore sumptuous silver velvet, with a delicate lace veil crowning her elaborate blond curls. A delicate perfume clung to her, and she lifted a lace-edged handkerchief to her nose as she approached the cell door. Petronella narrowed her eyes and glowered at her through the bars.

"Why have you come, Arabella?"

Arabella tossed her head, grey eyes alight with triumph. Her diamond earrings reflected the red light of the torch. "I wanted to see you one last time. Not so fine and righteous now, are you?"

Petronella raised one eyebrow and shrugged. "My duty was to provide the king with an heir, and I failed. It was not for the want of trying. You may have my throne after me, and I wish you much joy of it. It is a cold seat, let me warn you."

Arabella's sudden smile was soft. It transformed her sharp features into something approaching beauty, and it startled Petronella to see the woman's mindscape warm and mellow as she thought of the king.

"You love him. I always thought you only wanted the throne."

Arabella's eyes snapped to hers, and she scowled. "You know nothing about it. Know nothing queen. You were always too feeble to live. Arion doesn't need a weakling like you. He needs someone who is on his side. Who wants what he does. And I already have a family with him. Not true-born perhaps, but still his own. We can make a legitimate heir and heal the land. I am not a useless barren article who sticks her nose in a book and is no use to anyone."

"And do you hold his love, Arabella? What if he turns that love and desire to another as he did with Alice? Will you try to murder her, as well?"

Arabella's chin jutted. "I will be the queen. I can do whatever I want."

"It's good to know the future Queen of Epera considers cold-blooded murder a small price to pay for her security. How long do you think he would let you live once he found out what you had done? You are not safe on the throne, Arabella, any more than I was. No matter whether you have an heir with Arion. He is not a man whose judgment is sound. Not anymore."

Arabella's lips thinned, and hatred blazed in her eyes. "You can keep your stupid opinions to yourself."

"The truth is always hard to hear, is it not? I am only trying to warn you. You can go now. You wanted to see me. I met your wish. I have no further desire to extend our conversation."

Arabella drew herself up and looked down her nose. "You don't give me orders anymore."

"As long as I still draw breath, I am the Queen of Epera. You may leave."

Petronella stood her ground. She gave Arabella the tiniest mental *shove* and her lip curled in satisfaction as her rival took an unbidden step back. A flicker of confusion crossed her pale brow and her velvet clad shoulders crept towards her ears. Petronella stood, one eyebrow raised in what she knew was a smirk, until the small group receded into the shadows down the long corridor.

Alone again, she leaned against the door, watching the flames of the torches make shadows on the dripping wall. Her heart ached with loss. It would be time soon. It was only the slightest comfort she found she could not hate Arabella.

Chapter Forty-Eight

The guards marching along the corridor awakened Petronella from an uneasy sleep and her head lifted at the jangle of keys in the lock of a cell not her own. She pressed herself against her door as a cell door creaked open down the corridor and the small party escorted her former first lady out.

"Felice," the old woman's head raised from her contemplation of the flagstones at the sound of her voice. She limped down the corridor surrounded by her guards and jerked to a stubborn halt in front of Petronella's cell. The guards tried to move her, but Felice stood her ground, as immovable as a rock, her dark eyes alight with love. Petronella glared at them.

"You will not even let her say a goodbye? What monsters are you?"

Her eyes blurred with tears as she stretched her gloved fingers through the grating to grasp her friend's hand. Felice's once-rich clothes were filthy and hung on her frail form like ragged curtains at a grubby window. Her rings dangled on fingers grown thin with deprivation, her formerly plump cheeks drooped, but her eyes, warm, rich, and kindly, were the same, as was the scent of flowers and honey surrounding her. Felice smiled to see her, as composed now as she had ever been.

"Petronella, my dearest child."

"I will demand to speak to Arion. He must not do this."

Felice lifted one shoulder in a dismissive shrug. "He has decided. Nothing you can say will stop him now. I scared him too effectively at our last meeting."

Petronella's brow quirked. "What do you mean?"

Felice's eyes dulled, but she managed a half smile and shook her head as she withdrew her hand from Petronella's clutching fingers.

"You will not mourn me," her old nurse commanded, as the guards lost patience and jerked her forward. "Death is not the worst thing that can happen. Arion is already experiencing much worse than that. You will see. And Petronella..." Her voice faded and Petronella craned to see her as the guards tugged her further down the corridor and the shadows claimed her. "The blessing of my Goddess, The Empress upon you. Do not give up."

Petronella stared down the corridor for as long as she could until the sound of their footsteps faded. The dank air in her cell was still fragrant with honey and flowers. Heart aching with guilt and loss, she slid down the door to crouch on the slimy floor with her head in her hands.

She cried for a long time, and when she finally raised her swollen eyes, the first thing she saw was the flower lying on her stool. It was strong and fully grown, with a mint green stem and a pure white flower crowned with azure blue. The light from it glowed.

She swallowed, glancing around for witnesses before she reached for it with fingers that trembled. The stem was alive and vibrant in her hand. She cradled it gently in her open palms and the rich, earthy aroma of the Kingdom of Pentacles grew ever stronger the longer she held it. Minutes slid by and her mind blazed with wonder as a new flower, beneath her own, began to bud.

Chapter Forty-Nine

Petronella spent a long time in the darkness in the shadows of her cell with her knees drawn up, gazing into the heart of her flower. Felice was dead. The world had lurched around her a mere hour after she had said goodbye, bringing her to her knees with sorrow, but the bloom still shone with its otherworldly light, and she pulled her blanket around it to shield its glow from watchful eyes. It was Felice's last gift to her.

The bud beneath the main flower was plump, ready to flower. Heart full of memories and eyes smarting with tears, she stroked it with a gentle finger, but it wasn't until she tried to count back through the days of the last month, she realised her courses had not arrived. It was hard to concentrate. She had spent such a long time in darkness and confinement on the journey through the mines, the passage of time was difficult to calculate. As far as she could tell, she had lain with Joran two weeks ago, so by that reckoning, she should be experiencing the familiar cramps in her belly. She put her hand there but was aware of nothing but a pulsing warmth from the ring on her finger and a slight tightening of her breasts.

Keeping a watchful eye out for the guards, she slid the glove from her hand and caught her breath. The ring was glowing like a torch, so bright it highlighted her surroundings in much more detail than she liked. The bloodstains on the wall behind the manacle station, for instance, were a sight left decently clothed in darkness.

She turned the jewel on her hand, bemused. She had grown used to it flashing to life at times of need and sparkling in the sunshine of the kingdom of Cups, but this was a different sort of light. A warm, steady glow, as if the diamond was smiling as she stared into its heart.

She bit her lip at the overwhelming rush of emotion that flooded over her. Still keeping a wary eye out for the guards, she placed her hand low on her belly. The jewel blazed to life and a flash of welcome warmth rushed through her as she crouched in the dank straw, mouth open with shock. The sound of marching footsteps marked the approach of the guards, and she snatched the glove back on.

They opened the door merely to replace her jug of water. There was a slice of bread. White. Newly baked with grain stolen from Oceanis. She wolfed it down with dismay at its origin, but the new life in her belly was more than enough to justify eating it. Swallowing the last morsel, she paced the cell, restive as a captive bird.

She was pregnant. At long last, she had proved she could conceive. Hope blazed inside her for the first time in years. She needed to tell someone. Try to get a message to Domita somehow. The grim-faced guards were no good. They would not risk their rations to help her, but she had to do something before it was too late, and they snuffed out the kingdom's only chance.

It was hard enough to concentrate with her excitement bouncing around her brain like a circus acrobat. Gritting her teeth, her mind reached for Domita again, but it was no use. Her communication bounced off the molten fire of Domita's fiercely held mental defences. Brow dotted with perspiration, Petronella withdrew and took a swig of brackish water as she cursed her inexperience. She was still too new at this to penetrate the mind of a different race, and there was no-one to help her now Mistress Eglion and Joran were gone. Her thoughts flashed over prospective candidates, and she gave herself a big mental kick for ignoring the obvious possibility. Concentrating with all her might, she reached out.

Dominic Skinner's mindscape was vast and full of imagination. Ideas popped and swelled in the young adventurer's brain like fireworks going off in every direction at once. It was a bright and colourful wonderland of possibility, lit with youthful ambition and energy. She smiled as she entered. His optimism and friendliness were like an oasis in the desert. He was tending a horse with a blade of straw between his teeth, but his thoughts were roaming freely. Catching hold of one of them was like trying to grab the lashing tail of a kite in a high wind, but Petronella chased one down, the one centred on her and wondering how she was doing.

"Dominic."

She sensed his caution and his hopeful scepticism as she pushed her thought down the line to him.

An indrawn breath at the other end. *"Your Maj?"*

It was weak and tentative, but it was enough. *"Yes, Dom. It's me."*

Another gasp, and she chuckled at the excitement fizzing through the communication towards her.

"Is it magic, Your Maj? Are we doing forbidden magic?"

She sent her laugh down the link to him as well as her thought. *"We are. I learned a lot of things in the Land of the Cups."*

"It don't feel bad to me."

"It isn't. I've got something to tell you."

"Is it about Lady Felice? I know she's dead."

His landscape dimmed momentarily as he thought about Felice, and she felt her own sadness communicate itself to him with no need for words.

"It's not that, Dominic. It's something that might make up for it a little. I am to bear a child."

She could barely hold on to their communication as his mind processed this new information. She screwed up her eyes at the brightness of the mental colours flaring across his mindscape.

"By the Gods, Dom. Calm down."

"Sorry, your Maj. It makes sense now."

"What does?"

"The trees around the castle are all in bud, an' it's the wrong time of year. Don't think anyone's noticed apart from me."

"Are you still with the army?"

"I am, but I am in the castle. They made me groom to Lord Darius."

"Can you get to the falconry?"

"Easy."

"Send a pigeon to Domita. I don't know where she is. Send a bird to Shoreborne, one to Sunira and one to Goldfern. Don't tell her I'm pregnant, just ask her to come here, if she can. Will you do that? As soon as possible?"

"Aye, your Maj"

"Please hurry, Dom. I don't know how long I've got before..."

His thoughts hardened as the inference hit him.

"Goin' now."

"Thank you."

Exhausted, she withdrew her thoughts from his mindscape and blinked into the relative darkness of her damp cell. Taking another sip of water, she pressed her face against the bars of the door. No-one marching down the corridor. Yet.

Her brow creased in thought as her mind drifted once more to Joran and the ache in her heart his absence had created. She smoothed her rough garments over her belly. Your father was a brave man, little one, she thought. And one day I will tell you all about him.

Her ring throbbed in sympathy with her thoughts, and she rifled through her filthy bag for the battered book. Propping herself against the saturated wall, she hefted it to her lap and used the glow from the ring as a light as she peeled the damp pages apart with as much patience as she could muster.

As ever, it was slow going, but the frown eventually faded from her grimy face to be replaced with a nod of recognition as her finger retraced the ancient script. She heaved a sigh as she reached the end of the paragraph, having read it through twice, and leaned her head against the damp wall. Icy water trickled unheeded down her neck.

It was all so easy to understand now.

The magical power of Epera flowed in the blood at the discretion of the Mage and, in the king and queen's case, became more powerful by the captured energy of their combined rings. The text was clear. A Trueborn Queen of Epera could only bear an heir got from a Trueborn King. Which meant Mistress Eglion was correct in doubting the evidence of her own eyes. At the last, Francis had doubted the rumour. He could not destroy Joran, his precious, first-born son.

Her grandmother's voice was echoing in her head as she bent over the text once again with a sad smile tugging at the corners of her mouth.

"The answers are always there, Petronella. You only have to look."

Chapter Fifty

Hunched against the cold, curled asleep with her book as a pillow, Petronella groaned when the guards rattled her awake. She dragged herself upright and covered her gloved hands with the blanket almost by habit as they shoved the door open and thrust a torch into the cell. The lurid light glowed on the damp stone.

"Up. It is time. We are to take you to the king."

The guard's voice was rough and expressionless. Petronella jerked to her feet with her hands clasped protectively over her belly. Her fingers shook, and she leaned against the wall as a surge of dizziness rolled through her head. The guard grabbed her arm, his fist bruising as he tugged her forward. It took her several seconds before her sleep clogged mind focused, and she remembered she was not completely powerless.

"Take your hands from me. I am your queen," she snapped.

The guard smirked. "Not for much longer. Queen Arabella will soon take your place and at least we know she can bear a babe for the land."

Eyes narrowed, Petronella focused her attention on the man's feet and gave him a small *push*. He yelped as his feet skidded on the grimy floor, and she gained a small degree of freedom. She glared at him with her chin raised as he closed the distance between them again, but he took her arm more gently this time. He watched her as he did so, as if he didn't quite trust her.

The journey to the Throne Room took them along dirty corridors lit with rush lights and tallow candles, up endless stairs and into the sullen, almost deserted corridors of the castle itself. Petronella's legs trembled with exertion and her overwhelming hunger. Her lips clamped together as she battled the new nausea that had appeared over the last few days. Under the filthy, outsized tunic she wore, her breasts were swelling.

An overcast light filtered through countless windows as they passed. A stiff breeze played with the branches of the trees on the distant hillside. The rain had stopped. Her gaze flicked around, all her senses on alert, starved for the sight of walls more distant and decorated than those of her dark cell.

The guards formed a solid wall around her. There were eight of them, three to each side, one in front, one behind her. Their pikes formed a metal wall, and the air rang with their footfall. The few servants they passed regarded her in silence from their places by the walls. Their skeletal faces wore expressions ranging from sympathy to downright hatred.

The servant's passages gave way to wider corridors hung with tapestries and decorated with suits of armour. She kept her eyes forward as they passed lesser members of the court who straggled in the same direction. Their heads pressed close together as they gossiped. Numberless pairs of eyes raised to follow her progress, and she shivered as their curious stares pricked her shoulder blades. A small foray into the mental landscapes of the nearest made her retreat, shivering, into herself. Their minds were small and sharp and filled with malicious beaks that liked nothing better than to rend and tear. There was not a magical bone amongst them.

The small party drew to a halt facing the massive oak doors of the throne room and Petronella swallowed, her mouth dry. She tipped her head back, her eyes following the decorative carving on the doors as if she had never seen it before, and she almost laughed out loud at the symbol of the Mage that formed the centre of a repeated image first carved centuries before. The sight gave her courage and a sliver of hope. Magic and the Mage had ruled here for centuries, and they would again. Somehow.

Her heart thudded with unease as the doors opened before her and the guard flanked her to the centre of the throne room. The entire court had gathered to witness her demise. Their stony stares were almost enough to penetrate fragile defences flung up with a thin veneer of pride. They wanted to see her broken and brought to her knees. She would not give them the satisfaction. She tried not to look at the ceremonial sword the executioner held with casual elegance against his black clad shoulder. His hooded gaze turned smoothly in her direction, but she ignored him in the astonishment that swept over her as she clapped eyes on her husband.

He lounged on his silver throne as ever. A large glass of some dark red wine dangled in his fingers. He drank deep of it as she crossed the expanse of tiled floor towards him. They shoved her to her knees in front of the throne, and she raised her head to stare at him.

No-one she had seen so far carried any extra weight, but Arion was skeletal. His dark hair, newly flecked with grey, hung in draggled waves to his shoulders. Dark shadows hollowed his cheeks, his black eyes dug deep pits into the dark. His lips were dry, stained blood-red with wine and flaked with patches of flaking skin. Her nose wrinkled at the scent of sweet decay wafting towards her from his direction. It had accompanied him for years but was now impossible to ignore. The hand holding the glass of wine was shaking as he raised it, but his left hand was so swollen the leather glove he wore could barely stretch over it.

Swallowing her gorge, she risked a quick glance into his mindscape.

It was horrible. A world full of tangled black brambles, obsidian flint daggers and endless burning cold. The physical pain in his hand, arm, and head was astonishing. How he bore it, she could only guess.

Logic and reason were gone from him, overwhelmed with tiredness, defeat and a deep, bitter sadness that had a savage and vengeful edge to it, barely contained.

Dangerous. An eagle in chains, brought down and ready to tear.

She withdrew and bit down on a sob. Her eyes stung with tears as he locked his gaze on hers. There was a silent entreaty there, beneath the haze of pain-killing drugs. She couldn't read it accurately. Her gaze slid to Arabella.

Expression steely as ever, clothed in her favoured silver grey, she stood like a sentinel at his side. She held a decanter ready. Petronella guessed it contained more painkiller, although it was clear from what she had witnessed the brew did little good. Her brow contracted. What could Arabella possibly hope to gain? Surely, she could see Arion was dying. Was the throne her goal all along?

Her father stood on the dais on Arion's left side, between Arion's throne and her own vacant seat. The inference was obvious. This was the new power base. His dark gaze clashed with hers with a determined hatred that took her by surprise. He was twisting a large silver ring surmounted by a black stone around his finger. Her eyes widened as she recognised it as a match of the necklaces worn by the tattered dark army who had done for Mistress Eglion.

She had to gird herself for the quick dip into his mind and what she saw there turned her cheeks white with shock. She braced herself with one hand on the tiled floor as the room twisted around her.

He was powerful. His mindscape an overbearing mass of molten metal and lust for revenge. She could watch for only a few seconds as she saw him raze cities, entire countries, with his armies. His ambition was boundless. The Dark Army was the beginning. Sunira just the start. He had his sights set on Shoreborne and beyond that, the fertile hills and lush valleys of the Argent and the wild desert land of Battonia. He wanted it all. Would ravage the mountains of the gods until the gods did his will, and then he would destroy them as well. Even the Shadow Mage. Gone. Everything magical. Instead, one nation. In his image. Of Arion, and of Arabella, of Epera or Arcanis itself, he thought not at all.

She snapped back to herself and clapped a hand against her mouth as she fought against the desire to be sick. The surrounding silence had stretched too long. The king was speaking. She had missed it.

"What?"

"...dereliction of duty. The sentence for treason is death, to be carried out immediately," Arion said. He raised the glass to his lips. Around them, the muttering in the court rose on a fevered wave of speculation and died back to a tremulous, dreadful silence.

Her father's expression was plump with smug satisfaction as the guards yanked her to her feet and forced her into the middle of the room. Arabella took a half step forward, her eyes glowing with greed. Petronella's guard pressed her to her knees, and the executioner raised his sword.

"Wait. You cannot kill me; I bear a child!"

Her voice rang to the ancient rafters. The crowd gasped, and a furious wave of chatter washed around the room.

"You cannot bear a child. You are barren. We all know it."

Arion's voice was bleak and tired, but there was a question there as well, hidden in his pain.

Gritting her teeth, knowing they might execute her for witchcraft anyway, Petronella struggled from the grasp of the soldiers to her feet and ripped off the black glove she wore.

The Ring of Mercy glowed like a beacon on her finger. She felt more than saw Arion wince as the diamond light pierced his skull. Power throbbed through her hand and into her fingers. The executioner took a couple of steps back, his sword dropping to his side. Doubt and confusion rippling across their gaunt faces, the soldiers followed sui. Arabella gaped, her normally white cheeks flushed with rage. Her father's face paled with shock before the familiar scarlet of anger flooded over him. His dark eyes bored into hers with a promise of death as he closed his free hand around his own ring. A pulse of dark energy surged towards her, through her and onwards out of the room. She swallowed her own anger and raised her chin higher. Let him send for his army!

"She's a witch. Seize her," Arabella's harsh, treble voice cut like a blade of winter wind through the tension in the room.

Unsure of what she was trying to achieve, Petronella raised her hand. Their fear of any kind of magic helped her. Everyone in the room ducked as if she was about to throw some sort of thunderbolt.

"I am no witch. This is the lost power of the Kingdom of Epera. This is our birthright. Our pathway back to the land."

"She's a witch. And any child she carries cannot be the king's. She's a traitor. An adulteress and a witch. Take her." Arabella's voice was as loud as hers. Strident with self-righteousness.

Petronella winced as a powerful hand clamped her shoulders and pressed her to her knees. She raised her hand again, concentrating on the magic coalescing at her fingertips. Outside, a rising wind lashed at the trees and sent the birds squawking into the sky. Power and rage surged through her like lightning before a storm, and she extended a trembling finger in Arabella's direction. She had the satisfaction of seeing Arabella's eyes widen in terror, but a shrill boy's voice from the direction of the doorway stopped her in her tracks.

"Your Maj. Don't. It's the Ring of Mercy. Don't do it!"

She twisted on her knees towards him and held out her arms. "Dominic?"

He scrambled towards her, dodging the fists and long arms of the soldiers with youthful agility. In his wake, Petronella's heart soared as the sight of The Grayling swooping behind him. The bird circled once around the room, high above their heads, and tears pricked her eyes as he gave voice to her with his familiar squawking chatter. Trembling, she held out her right arm, and the Grayling came to her gloved fist, his grey wings bating to stillness. He reached out to peck her ring and settled more securely on her arm. She welcomed his familiar, slight weight as her other arm formed a protective circle around the shaking boy.

Dominic took a shuddering breath and faced his king. "She ain't no traitor, Sire," he gabbled. "She's tryin' to save ye. An' the Kingdom too."

Arion's face closed. He passed his glass to Arabella and took out his knife.

"Say that again, boy," He stood. Tall and merciless, his shadow wavering before him.

His dagger glinted in his fist, and Petronella shot to her feet. Her ring hand lashed towards him even as the knife flew from his hand. The blade fell to the floor and skittered uselessly along the tiles. She swept him a look of utter disgust.

"A child, Arion? How many lives are you willing to take before you understand? The magic of Epera is gone from you and any child of yours you might sire. Your father lost his right to use it when he unjustly killed his first wife. I understand your fear of it, but the land, our land, is still under magical control. That will never change. You cannot alter it. And you will never get a child on me because your own magic is lost. Do you understand?"

His face constricted as her words slashed through him. Dazed, her stared at her. His hand dropped to his side, and a frown creased his brow as he searched the floor for his prized dagger.

"Your ring. It never came to life like that before." His voice was hushed and wondering. He sounded like a man in a trance.

She shook her head. "My mother ensured my magic would remain suppressed for most of my life. It only resurfaced on my journey to Oceanis once I stopped taking Heartsease tea." Her accusing gaze flashed to her father, who only gave her a crocodile smile. He appeared unmoved by this revelation in front of the entire court. Fear pricked her. What was he planning?

"My ring has given me nothing but pain. For years." Arion lifted his injured hand.

"Since first you wore it?"

"Yes."

Petronella waited as he tugged at the swollen glove swaddling his left hand. Arion flinched as he worked it over his sausage-like fingers and dragged it off. Sweat beaded his forehead, his face white with pain as he finished, and the onlookers drew in a choked breath as the ripe, sweet scent of decay and death wafted over them. Petronella pressed a hand against her stomach and swallowed a wrench of nausea. Arabella took a few quick steps back and buried her nose in her scented handkerchief. Arion's hand was a swollen black object, tipped with fingernails turned yellow and green with rot. She could barely see his ring, all its power turned inward and embedded in a prison of poisoned, angry flesh.

"You understand the Ring of Justice was never yours to wear?" Petronella asked. Her voice was gentle now. Her ring pulsed with a soft wash of energy that brought tears to her eyes.

"But I am the King of Epera." He sounded lost. Plaintive. Like a child afraid of the dark. Her mouth twisted in grief for him.

"No, my dear. You are not. Your father had another child, to his first wife, who was born before he lost his power. He is the true king."

"Not the king? Never?"

"No. I am sorry."

Arion's face dropped. Shock, anger, resignation, and acknowledgment swept across it in quick succession, overlaid with his pain.

"What? This is ridiculous." Her father strode down from his position next to Arion to tower over her.

His rage was dizzying to witness. He snatched for his own dagger and grabbed Dominic away from her. The Grayling lashed out with his beak and tore a chunk from his grasping hand. Lord Falconridge swore and dropped the lad, who scuttled away with his chin high, and his small fists clenched. Falconridge glanced up for the Grayling, who had found a handy perch high in the rafters and was watching him. Petronella squared her shoulders.

"Time for the truth, father. I know what you have done. You couldn't have Gwyneth, could you? She loved Francis. All the time, she loved him. No matter that he was older than her. No matter that you were younger, and fit and handsome. You couldn't turn her, could you? And you could not stand it. All that poison you dripped in Francis's ear. All the poison you have dripped in Arion's ear as his trusted tutor and advisor ever since. And they believed you, didn't they?"

"You can say what you like, girl. No one will believe you. A disgraced, adulteress queen." Darius's mouth was as thin as a steel trap.

"But you miscalculated. Did you think Francis, even in his rage, was evil enough to kill his firstborn son?" Petronella continued as if he had not spoken. "Even at the last, he doubted the truth of your words. Mistress Eglion saw him carry the child from his wife's bedchamber. She told me she thought he was dead. But he could not have been dead, because only the true King of Epera can get a child with me."

"So where is he now? This true King of Epera? Your lover?" Darius's voice was a sneer.

"Dead." Her chest constricted as the words left her lips. "Defending Sunira from the soldiers you sent to destroy it."

"Correction," Domita's voice sizzled with triumph from the door as she shouldered it open. Flames blistered the air around her, and smoke wafted in from the corridor. Distant screams still echoed someway behind her. The courtiers were quick to draw back against the walls of the immense chamber as she advanced, fire crackling from her hands.

Petronella jerked around like a puppet on a string, and her own mouth fell open. Joran's face was white, and he was leaning on a strangely familiar staff, but he was alive. And whole. And here. Her world splintered and rearranged itself in a split-second, but her father wore a grim smile that told her he had other ideas.

He advanced, drawing his sword. Blood dripped over his fingers as he tightened his grip on it. A wave of black energy poured from his ring hand. His face wore a taunting grin as he directed his attention behind Joran and Domita down the corridor where the Dark Army was advancing. Domita's flames roared to a blaze, barely held in check. The nearest courtiers tumbled over themselves to put distance between them. Domita's eyes were alight with her familiar, fox-like grin. Her expression promised death to any who stopped her. Darius strode forward, face set, uncaring.

"He won't be king for much longer."

"Hold."

Arion's voice was louder than she had ever heard it. Darius risked a glance over his shoulder as Arion shuffled down the few steps to where Petronella stood.

"My love," Arabella's voice held a jump of fright. Her gaze flashed to Darius. Joran, his face a grim mask of hatred, dropped the staff with a clatter and drew his sword instead. Petronella could see the effort it took. Perspiration broke out on his brow, and his sword arm trembled, but he stood his ground. Domita's lips thinned, and she readied her flames for attack.

Arion reached out to her with his tortured hand. She swallowed, willing herself not to flinch as he lifted it towards her. Tears flooded her cheeks as she waited for him to speak.

"I only ever wanted to please my father. To be a righteous king." His voice was hushed, meant for her ears only, but the throne room was an echo chamber with few soft furnishings. His words reached the ears of his courtiers, who muttered among themselves. The hushed voices raised the short hair on the back of her neck. Her ring pulsed with her heartbeat. She reached out to him, clasping his hands with both of hers. The damaged one burnt with an icy heat. Her ring pulsed a deep beat of power in her belly. His black eyes bored into hers. Caverns into the dark.

"What do you want of me, Arion?"

"End it. End the pain. Please. I know you can. Before I kill anyone else. I cannot control myself."

Time slowed. Petronella's voice trembled. Her whole body shook with fear.

"I do not want you to die. I don't want to kill you. You surely cannot ask me."

"I ask you. Take my ring. Give it to my brother. Do a better job."

He released her hands and stood back. Tears lit his black eyes like jewels, but he nodded to her.

"Please, Petronella. I cannot stand the pain anymore."

"I do not want to do this."

"I know. I forgive you."

Her mind tumbled back over their years together. The many days and nights they had shared, first in companionship and then in pain and fear, as their shared dreams withered along with the kingdom.

She swallowed, her mouth dry, and locked her gaze with his as she whispered. "I too."

Heart thudding, she raised her hand. Her ring blazed with a sudden, wild energy that carried the blue light of healing in its heart.

"Arion of the Eagles. King of Epera. May the Mage receive your soul." Her voice echoed around the chamber as she extended her shaking fingers towards him. "In all Mercy, let the Mage release you from your pain."

The path of light from her ring blazed a connecting path through the blackened mass of the Ring of Justice. Arion staggered as the bolt hit him and crumpled to the floor with the merest of sighs. Arabella dropped the pewter flagon with a shriek of anguish. Lady Violet fainted.

Petronella dropped her hand and stood over her dead husband with tears streaming down her face. Her ring resumed its steady light.

She was barely aware of the Ring of Justice as it left Arion's diseased hand and tinkled to the tiles, but Darius was quicker. Ignoring Joran, his eyes alight with possibility, he dropped his sword and fell to his knees to scrabble it from the floor.

CHAPTER FIFTY-ONE

As quick as Darius was, The Grayling was quicker. His angry cry split the air, and he dived in a blur of grey and black. Snatching the ring, he flew with it to the rafters before Darius had time to blink. Cheeks blazing with fury, he turned on Petronella, his face a mask of hatred. She had no time to react as his hand grabbed her throat and squeezed.

Under all his velvet and fur, he was incredibly strong. He lifted her easily. Her filthy boots scrabbled for purchase on the slippery floor, and she clawed in vain at fingers holding her in a vice as solid as stone. Panic gripped her. This was what he had done before. Jana had died the same way, except he had beaten her with the butt-end of his dagger as well.

Her voice useless, her mind reached for Joran, but there was no answer to her desperate plea. The courtiers at the edge of her sight stood motionless in the paralysis of spectacle. They could have been actors at the playhouse in Blade, on stage for entertainment only. She choked; her vision was blurring.

Dominic launched himself towards her father as he shook her like a mastiff with a rat. Darius's free fist lashed out. It connected to Dominic's jaw with a jolt that snapped the boy's head back on his scrawny neck. Dominic crashed to the floor. He didn't get up.

Darius's dark army reached the Throne Room unimpeded by the guards, who scrabbled in terror to get away from them. They surrounded Domita and Joran like a pack of hungry wolves at the periphery of her vision. Flames lashed from Domita's hands to scorch the enslaved magicians, but they pressed forward, closing their circle. The ebony stones dangling from the chains embedded in their diseased skin glowed with a dark, malevolent light. From a distance, it appeared each member bore a dark hole near their heart. Pulled inward, useless, Domita's flames vanished without effect the second they encountered the black diamonds. Joran, at her side, was slashing at the nearest, but they simply ignored him. They did not bleed, nor crumple. Instead, they closed ranks, tightening the circle. Corrupted magic still poured from Darius. It filled her mind with cold despair.

Domita screamed her rage, throwing flame after flame into the fray, but there was nothing she could do. The Dark Army simply absorbed and suffocated her powers, growing stronger all the while. Joran's face was a mask of frustration. She knew he must be talking to her, but his voice did not reach her. Somewhere, Arabella was laughing, a high, maddened note on the edge of hysteria.

Her world was greying. Its edges were fraying, her lungs bursting as she fought for air. This was what she got for opposing her father. This was always going to be her end. At the limit of consciousness, her head dropped, and all the fight went out of her. Her ring pulsed once on her hand and flickered out.

Her disembodied self hovered at a vantage point over the scene as her father grunted his satisfaction and dropped her like a sack of rubbish to the hard floor. His attention turned to his circle of enslaved magicians, and she heard Domita scream, a shrill, high-pitched sound of terror. Joran gave a shout of warning, and somewhere, high above her ghostly head, the Grayling joined their cry, swooping from his perch towards her body.

Francis was strong in his magic then. He could ride in the mind of an eagle if he chose.

Mistress Eglion's storytelling voice fluttered through her tired mind with wistful clarity.

I have no power. I am not strong.

You have the power... not good, but excellent.

Joran's voice. Somehow penetrating her consciousness. Was it a memory or his voice in her head? She didn't know. Couldn't think. She was fading, fading.

It is our choices that make us what we are...

In desperation, she *reached* for her falcon, willing herself across the space between them.

The Grayling's mindscape blazed with sharp, dazzling colour. He missed nothing. Questioned nothing. The twitch of a blade of grass, the whisper of the merest breeze against the edges of his feathers, the barest squeak of a defenceless mouse. Fearless. Free.

Her soul made a mad leap that closed the distance between them. Her body sprawled on the floor, a pile of discarded rags. Arion lay close beside her, a dark pool of cloth, his head thrown back to expose his throat. His ruined hand formed a black claw, like a question mark, against the sign of the Mage picked out in blue on the tiles of the floor. The courtiers hovered at the edges of the room, mere shadows. Ghouls at the feast.

Her father concentrated the force of his will on the Dark Army. They were raising power between them. The vortex of energy as it twisted like a dark tornado around their circle, ever building, was easy to see with her sharpened senses. A wild wind grew. It tore at Domita and Joran, trapped within the ring of magic wielders and unable to break free.

Domita's power was fading, the wind was stripping it from her, swallowing her flames into itself. Still weak from his injury, exhausted and at the end of his strength, Joran lowered his sword. With a shout of triumph, her father closed his free fist.

She struck.

Straight as an arrow, she launched herself into joyful flight. Her claws slashed through her father's cheek on her swoop into the circle, and she drew blood with savage delight. She poured herself into the swirling vortex of energy, the Ring of Justice she carried in her beak carved a brilliant pathway in front of her. Her wings beat as fiercely as her savage little heart as she battled the howling storm. The wind tore at her. Tried to shred the feathers from her wings. She battled on, forcing herself onward, downward. Dark magic crackled against her, but the ring protected her. She dropped it with a hoarse croak of triumph at Joran's muddy feet.

Hovering, gliding on the vortex of air as it lifted her up and tried to batter her away, she forced her thoughts to him.

"It is yours. Take it."

He gazed up at her as she battled to stay above him. His blue eyes were cavernous in his milk-white face.

"Take it. Please take it, before it's too late."

"I don't want to be a king."

"For our child, Joran,"

"Are you dead, Petronella?"

"I do not know. Take it, please."

He bent, leaning on his staff for support, and picked up the blackened ring. It flared to life in his palm, and he ran a finger over it with unmistakable reverence. She waited, her wings a blur in the racing air, struggling to stay above the dark circle. She was losing her strength. His face was infinitely sad as he turned the jewel once more on his palm. And then he shook his head and threw it to her.

CHAPTER FIFTY-TWO

Petronella inside the Grayling was not as fast as the Grayling himself when thrown something from a hunter's fist. Carrying her soul safe as her unborn babe inside him, he flashed through the air like a comet to snatch the ring and came to land on her unmoving chest.

He pecked her hand with a savage bite that drew blood, and the pain was enough to jerk her back into relentless life. She snatched a shallow, rasping breath and reached for the ring with shaking fingers. The Grayling dropped it into her gloved hand and swooped back to the safety of the rafters in a flurry of feathers.

Swallowing heavily against the crushing pain in her throat, she sat up. The vortex of energy was still swirling, although her father had to remove some of his attention to attend to the deep gash in his cheek. Blood poured from the wound to stain his expensive clothes.

She struggled to her feet, the ring still in her fist.

Her father glared at her through blood-shot eyes. "I will kill them unless you give me the ring."

"That is madness. You cannot wear it. You have seen what happened to Arion. Let them go, Father." Her voice came out as a hoarse croak, more bird than woman.

Her father's eyes glowed with a manic light that had no foot in sanity. "I don't want to wear it. I will destroy it, once and for all. The power in the land belongs to me now. I will do with it what I will."

He raised his hand, and the Dark Army started a low chant that grated against her ears like nails down a slate board. She risked a glance into the vortex. Domita was still struggling to use her flames, her face set in a snarl of defiance. Joran leaned on his staff, watching her. His face was white, exhausted, but some glint of his smile lingered at the edges of his lips. He nodded at her and raised his left hand. Handling the Ring of Justice had left its own mark on him. The symbol of the Mage was unmistakable, etched in silver on his palm.

The embedded chains clasped around the rotting necks of the enslaved Eperan Blessed caught her eye once more.

Steeling herself, she faced her father and plunged her power deep into his mindscape.

Time stopped.

He fought her. Far stronger internally than she had imagined he might be.

His will was iron. Inflexible. His mental barriers built fortresses of grey steel against a grey sky filled with racing clouds. It was a sullen place. The atmosphere poisonous and oppressive. Nothing grew here. A freezing wind raised dust across her phantom feet as she plodded towards the stronghold, bending her shivering back against the pressure that forced her out.

"What are you so afraid of, Father?"

Her mental voice echoed around her in the strange, barren landscape. There was no reply. She had expected none. He could not hear her out here, as oblivious to her now as he always had been. Focused only on himself.

Swallowing against the pressure in her dry throat, she forced herself, footstep by dragging footstep, towards the fortress of his inmost thoughts.

Up close, his defence was huge. It stretched to the sky and to every horizon as far as she could see. She pressed her ring-bearing hand against the steel wall, wincing at the searing layer of frost that clung to it.

"Let me in, Father."

A rush of autumn leaves swirled around her from nowhere. Her mental voice was not her own. It was higher, more bell-like. Astonished, she looked down at herself and saw she was wearing the same riding habit she had been wearing the day of Jana's death. The leaves tumbled in a dusty pile at her feet. Her bruised throat clenched.

"Please Father, it's cold out here."

She banged her small fist on the icy metal, feeling the vibration ripple through the structure from its tip to its roots. Heart aching, she struck again and again, harder each time, bruising her fist, feeling the blows like iron hammers against her own heart where her memory and fear of him lay.

"Please Father, do not shut me out."

Silence.

She banged once more, as hard as she could.

"Please."

She was crying now. Sobbing as she had as a child, and somewhere at the back of her head there was an old clamour, an ancient, primeval cry for help and strength.

"Please. I want my father."

There was a long pause. Slowly, with a creak of rusted hinges, a door opened. She stepped through.

The cave was smaller than she remembered. A young boy, handsome as honey with dark curls and snapping black eyes, sat alone in the middle of the floor. A carved wooden box lay open in front of him. Focused on the contents, he didn't look up as she approached. Moving closer, she could see the box contained his treasures.

Delicate as butterflies, his long, slim fingers sifted through them, naming each of them in turn.

"This is from the wing of Jezebel, my falcon," he murmured, almost as if he was reminding himself. "This is the collar of my hound, Fortune. This is the lace of the dress my mother was wearing the day they buried her."

He glared up at her as she leaned closer and shut the box with a snap that made her jump back, fearing for her fingers. His gaze was feral.

"They are all dead. Everything is dead."

He rounded on her, eyes blazing, and she stumbled away, terrified at his ferocity, to encounter the rough stone wall at her back. She followed his gaze as it wandered past her, out of the entrance and down the hillside. She recognised the pathway that led to her childhood home. A group of people, two adults and two older children, were on their way up. They did not speak out loud, but their gestures and smiles told her a mental conversation was taking place. Her attention switched to her father. He had backed up against the opposite wall and was looking around for somewhere to hide his box. Eyes darting, he stuffed it into a crevice but was a fraction too late in stepping away. The leader of the small band, a well-dressed elder of about forty, with a narrow circlet of silver decorating his brow, ducked into the space.

"Hey, ho. Here's where the cripple is hiding. What have you got there, lad? Stealing?" he said. The group tittered, although the youngest, a young girl of around twelve, shook her honey blonde head in reproach. Petronella frowned. Something about her was familiar.

"I have stolen nothing. Don't you call me that." Darius's voice was high and strained, his young fists clenched at his sides.

The leader of the group sauntered over to him and flicked at his head with a disdainful finger.

"Why not? That's what you are. A misfit. Forsaken by the gods."

The younger girl sighed and put a hand on his arm. "Francis, stop it. He's only eight. 'Tis unkind."

Francis sighed and patted her hand. "Only you would think so, gentle Gwyneth. For the rest of us, someone might well have drowned him at birth like an unwanted pup for all the use he is to the kingdom. With his lineage, too. He will never amount to much. Such a shame."

Darius bristled. His mouth contracted in a tight line, and his young chest swelled. Petronella's fists clenched in alarm and pity as his cheeks flushed with familiar rage.

"I will do something great. You will come to rely on me one day. And you will fear me. And you will never, ever laugh. Mark my words."

"Fear you? Really?" Francis said, one dark eyebrow lifting in derision. "Perhaps I'll send for you when I am king. See what you are made of. You could be useful. A clerk or some such."

His courtiers chuckled, but Gwyneth's thoughtful gaze caught Petronella's attention as Darius leaped past them, graceful as a deer, dashing tears from his hot cheeks to race down the path and back to the manor. The scene shifted and dissolved, and she faced her father as a young man in his prime now, kneeling by her own bed. Queen Gwyneth sprawled across the twisted sheets. Her green eyes sightless, staring at the ornate canopy above her, an expression of surprise on her delicate, oval face. In Gwyneth's time, the velvet had been emerald green, embroidered in gold with crescent moons and waves.

"Gwyneth always knew there would be something to watch out for with you, didn't she?" she said.

Her father sneered.

"Stupid woman, like all the rest. Never knew what was good for her. She should have taken me when she had the chance. As it was, she stayed loyal. To that... that... old..." words failed him.

He turned to her, black eyes blazing. "She was the only one," he roared. "The only one who ever had a kind word for me."

"Then why kill her, Father?"

His face was mutinous. "I didn't kill her."

"You may as well have. You were the one who spread the rumour she had been unfaithful to him."

His face crumbled with remembered loss. "I didn't think he would kill her. I wanted him to kill the child, and then she would have turned to me for comfort."

Petronella raised her eyebrows to the heavens as she took in the abandoned cradle by the fire.

"That sounds like a dream to me."

His mouth contracted.

"I loved her. And afterwards, I hated Francis. Nothing mattered, but that I got the power to bring him down."

"He brought himself down, Father. He lost his power and gave away his son, never knowing whether the child belonged to him. Why were you not satisfied with that?"

"I didn't know what had happened. Not at once. And then he was obsessed with getting his power back. Couldn't survive without it." Darius's face quirked at the irony. "I told him I would help to avoid him finding out who had spread the rumour about Gwyneth, but when I eventually found what we had been looking for, he didn't want it. Wouldn't pay the price for the power. He laughed at me. He used me."

"Ah."

Her heart clenched as she put the last of his story together.

"Jana was the price."

In the cave once more, autumn leaves swirled. Her father laid his head down on his dead daughter's broken body. His shoulders shook with despair and grief and her heart broke one more time for them both as he shouted his anguish at the uncaring sky and cried his soul away.

"You. You can never replace her. Get out."

She lurched away as the iron force of his will clanged the doors shut in her face. He hurled her out of his mindscape with a furious force that left her sprawled on the floor, the vaulted, painted ceiling twisting above her. Nausea twisted her gut as time snapped back to normal speed. Somewhere, there were birds calling.

Her eyes flung open. The Grayling watched her from the rafters, his soft, anxious chatter cluttering her ears. Mind reeling, she staggered to her feet.

Her father's blood-stained face was pale with shock. His teeth clenched in a snarl.

"You are a witch. Give me the Ring of Justice."

He made a swirling gesture with his ringed hands, and Petronella's eyes widened in horror. The vortex of energy that encircled her friends had not dissipated during her visit to her father's mindscape. Still trapped by magic near the entrance to the throne room, Domita and Joran choked as oxygen left the deadly circle and the Dark Army closed in.

"No, Father. You cannot do this. You have already done more than enough. It is over. I do not want to kill you."

"I am no longer your father. I am your God, and I will have my revenge on you and your Gods' blasted magic. My magic alone will rule now."

Faces turning blue as they gasped for breath, Domita and Joran fell to their knees. Their chests heaved for air. Joran's sword clanged by his side. Domita reached out with her flames in one last feeble effort to fight.

Power pulsed through the Ring of Mercy on the ring finger of her left hand. The Ring of Justice throbbed in unison in her right palm. She shook her head.

"Please, no. Don't make me do this."

She almost didn't know who she was talking to, her father, or her god. Her father gave a shout of triumph as the Dark Army raised their voices in a scream of anguish that crawled a shiver down her spine and their swirling, poisonous energy combined to bury Domita and Joran.

The two warriors collapsed to the floor together. Petronella set her jaw and shook her head.

"Mage, protect and forgive me."

She rammed the Ring of Justice on to the forefinger of her right hand and stiffened as the power arced through her brain like lightning to the Ring of Mercy on her opposite hand.

For a second that could have been centuries, she was both mountain and sky. Roots and wings. She was the rushing, tortured Cryfell, the heart and mind of the starving people. She was the blighted crops and the poisoned livestock. The breathing rock and the icy mountain air. The birds and the butterflies, the deep, dark forests. At that moment, all lived and breathed within her. All blighted. All tainted, but not without hope. Not while there was a child to be born. A child of the Eagles and the Falcons. A child of the Swords.

She blinked. It seemed to take forever.

"Darius, Lord of Falconridge, I order you. Stop in the name of the Mage."

Her voice was ancient and deep. Old as the mountains that birthed it. The stained-glass windows rattled. Eyes wild, Darius ignored her. His eyes glinted with satisfaction as his army did his will. Domita and Joran lay still as stones on the floor of the throne room, held in place by the implacable force of the dark circle. He stood like a man transfixed with the success of his own power. A jerk of his head and the Dark Army turned their sights on the rest of the court, who shrank back in terror.

"Any who defies me will die." The black gaze that snapped to hers was purely mad. The father she had known was gone. Corrupted. Evil. The wall of stained energy crept towards her, tasted her flesh. She took a disgusted step back. Its touch was sour and dirty, ancient and aching with malice.

Shaking her head, fresh tears staining her dirty cheeks, she raised both hands in her father's direction.

"I am the Queen of Epera. I renounce the power of the Dark Mage. Return it whence it came and let in the light."

She clapped her hands together and braced herself against the shock wave that blasted around the room and sent the courtiers to the floor in untidy, shrieking heaps of velvet and fur.

Darius staggered as the combined power of both rings hit him full on. The ancient, priceless windows blew out in an ear-splitting crash that was probably heard down in Blade. The power continued upwards above her head, outwards into the furthest, deepest, highest, most secret places of Epera.

Darius screamed as the Mage light roared back to find him. It filled his mouth, scorched his eyes, scoured him from head to foot. The black diamond melted on his hand as his hold on the Dark Army collapsed, and they staggered away from their circle. Darius fell as Petronella lowered her hands. He was dead before he hit the floor. The delicate clink of a hundred silver chains accompanied his landing as they, too, released their hold on the enslaved Blessed of Epera.

Eyes still dazzled with light, Petronella spared barely a thought for her father as she sprinted across the throne room to where Joran and Domita lay on the cold tiles.

The Grayling swooped down from his perch and gave them each a hard peck on the arm. When they both yelped, he ruffled his wings and took off again with a satisfied clatter. A rustle of wings above her head raised Petronella's eyes to the windows where birds of every persuasion were swooping into the throne room and turning in dizzy, delighted circles above her head.

Petronella fell to her knees and reached for her companions.

Domita coughed herself to a seated position and managed a wobbly smile, her usually tanned face milk white. She borrowed Joran's staff to lever herself to her feet.

"I am sorry, Petronella."

Joran's voice was soft in her mindscape, and she turned her gaze to him, her eyes wet with tears, grateful beyond words to have his voice in her head once more.

She shook her head.

"I do not quite understand. I would not think any man would resist the opportunity to be a king."

He gave her his beautiful smile, and her heart lifted with relief. *"That is the point, my love. I will serve you with my heart, mind, and soul. But I will never take your power away from you."*

She rolled her eyes at him and bent to press a gentle kiss against his lips before she allowed her attention to travel to the rest of the court. Young Dominic still lay out cold on the floor.

"Master Farron, your attention here, please. And Lord Colman. Fit a guest room for this young man. The finest one we have. We have much to thank him for. Please see to Arion and my father. Let Arion lie in state in the old Chapel. We will hold their funerals in due course."

The two men picked themselves up from the floor, dusted themselves down, and bustled to their tasks. Due reverence accompanied the removal of Arion's body. The detail selected to deal with Darius handled his remains with dubious attention, as if he could still burst into life. Mister Farron bustled over to patch Joran up where he lay with his cloak as a pillow. Dominic revived as feathers burnt under his nose, an act of first aid that had the courtiers choking and Domita staggering to a broken window for some cleaner air.

"You keep getting beaten up on my behalf, Dominic," Petronella said, lending him an elbow as he stumbled to his feet.

"Did we do it?" he asked, blinking around the throne room through the one eye that wasn't swollen shut.

"We did. I am guessing it was you who let the Grayling free."

He grinned. Lopsided through his swollen jaw. "Saw 'im when I went to send them messages. 'E was sad. Thought it might help."

She enveloped him in a hug and ruffled his hair. “Oh Dominic. You won’t believe how much.”

Her mouth curved in a smile as he left the chamber in the care of the Lord Chamberlain, who surprised her with a much lower than normal bow.

The courtiers stared at her from the edges of the room as if she had grown two heads. Weary now, she scanned their mindscapes. A multitude of emotions, from disbelief to envy to shock to admiration, bounced back to her. The throne stood empty, and she forced her tired legs to move in that direction. All eyes turned to her as she ascended the stairs and took her seat. The silver back of the throne rose above her. The blue velvet cushions were more comfortable than they appeared.

She waited until she had their attention.

“Our kingdom is now once more under the protection of the Mage, as it should be. You are more than welcome here if you choose to accept and acknowledge this. Those who do not are welcome to leave now. I will not persecute you.” She paused and let her gaze meet every eye in the hall. “I would urge those who may believe otherwise to keep their beliefs to themselves. As you can see, I am not a defenceless queen, and I will execute justice as I see fit.”

Her eyes travelled to the ragged knot of men and women who had comprised her father’s Dark Army. Their mental landscapes were a bewildering mixture of magical abilities, long suppressed. They appeared not to believe they were free. Guilt, hope and longing filled their mindscapes. She lingered amongst them for a long time, testing her options.

“You have my forgiveness,” she said. “I will not follow you, punish you or harm you. I understand the Shadow Mage forced you into the acts you have committed. You are welcome to stay here, or return to your families, whatever you decide. I would ask you to lend your talents to the healing of our country. I will reopen the library for your studies, and we will rebuild our shrines to the gods in due course.”

She stood. The court regarded her with something like wonder on their faces. A few, scowling, left the room, the Count Dupliss amongst them. She made a mental note to keep him in her mind's sight.

"Arabella."

The woman jumped. She was making for the door, and the weight of failure, outrage and hatred filled her grey eyes as they leapt to her.

"Guards. See this woman to my dungeon. Provide her with the bare necessities. I will deal with her later. There is an old book in there. Please bring it to me."

The guards rushed to their task. Petronella nodded icily at the executioner.

"Your services will no longer be required. On a permanent basis," she informed him, with some irony.

"As for the rest of you," she cast a steely gaze at the rest of the court, who gathered in stupefied silence as they processed the change of circumstances. "There will be a place here for those who deserve it. Our Court in future will welcome all those I invite, both Blessed and Citizen, from every land in Arcanis, with no distinction. I thank you for your service. You may retire."

The court, as one, bowed.

When they stood once more, she blessed them with the sign of the Mage as a dismissal before joining Domita at the window.

"I have so much to thank you for, Domita," she said.

Domita's face lit with her familiar grin. "Some of it was quite fun." She said with a shrug.

"You saved Joran."

"I used my fire to cauterise his wound, but it was Alice who saved him, not me. Or, one of the Blessed in Sunira with help from Alice. He did nearly die. I thought he would more than once, but he hung on. He must truly love you. By the way, this is for you." She held out the staff. "One of the Blessed in Sunira retrieved it. 'T'was Mistress Eglion's, but I think it now belongs to you."

Petronella took it. It was heavier than she had supposed. A buzz of power thrummed through her palm, and she blinked as the owl and ivy carving rearranged itself. Flowers, falcons and owls joined to adorn one side. The gnarled handle remained the shape of the tree that graced the Mage's clearing. A new symbol of twin, interlocking rings formed the Mage's symbol that flowed down the ancient hawthorn on the opposite side.

Domita watched it, mouth curved in a smile as the new carvings solidified.

Petronella turned it over with respectful hands.

"By the Gods, that is impressive."

Domita rolled her eyes.

"After what you have just done, you think that is impressive? It's just acknowledging you as the new Seer of Epera."

Petronella's mouth quirked. "My grandmother must have been wrong. I can't be the Seer and the Queen. I don't know nearly enough."

Domita jerked her chin at the breathless guard who appeared at the end of the room. He held the heavy leather tome at arm's length as if it might bite him as he hurried towards them. Domita grinned.

"Mistress Eglion gave you a book."

Petronella held out her arm to receive the volume. Smiling, Domita turned to the window, where a fresh breeze was shepherding the heavy clouds before it and light chased shadows across the courtyard walls.

"Oh, look," she said. "The sun has come out."

Epilogue

Epera, Castle of Air

Candlelight glittered on the remains of the evening meal.

Petronella pushed aside her plate and gazed around the hall with sleepy eyes. The burden she carried dragged at her belly, and she rubbed the ache in her back that had been growing in recent days. Tearing a strip of meat from the discarded joint in front of her, she handed it up to the Grayling, who perched on the back of her chair. He claimed it with a small chatter of thanks.

Joran put his hand over hers on the table, and her ring gave a gentle pulse of acknowledgment.

"Is all well with you, my love?"

"It is. Although I shall be glad when the confinement is over. "

Joran nodded, his hand drifting to caress the mound of her belly where it swelled under her robe. The babe kicked at his palm, and she laughed at the wonder on his face.

"Will you never grow tired of that?"

He grinned. "Never. Our heir is lively tonight."

A thoughtful frown crossed Petronella's brow as she considered his words.

"Yes," she agreed, "but not as much as normal. I don't think there is much room for moving about in there anymore." She glanced across at him. “I had word this morn that the last of the grain delivery from Oceanis has arrived. Did Lord Colman give you his report?”

Joran nodded. “As of this morn, the granaries are full. We can be sure of having enough to go round this season.”

Petronella grimaced. “Thanks to the Gods. But it has taken too much time. I fear we are too late for some.”

“You have done all you could in the conditions, my love.” He stroked her cheek, smoothing her frown with his thumb. “And made yourself ill with worry. Let's think of happier things. Shall we proceed with the main event?”

Turning her mind from her nagging doubt with an effort, Petronella put her hand on her swelling stomach. “I think we should. Before it's too late and my labour starts.”

Joran waved to the servers to refill the cups of the company. Petronella rose to her feet. The courtiers turned to the dais, their faces questioning. They looked slightly better fed these days, but hollows still lived in many cheeks. Lady Violet sat in her accustomed place surrounded by admirers, but she was thinner now, since she had miscarried Arion's child. Petronella had let her stay. She could find little point in taking petty vengeance on her former husband's mistress.

“Lords and Ladies. As you know, I am about to be confined for a while before our child, our new heir, is born...”

She squeezed Joran's hand as it crept into hers, and her court cheered.

"I believe we are expecting a special visitor this evening.”

At her signal, the vast double doors opened, and Domita gave a squeal of excitement.

“Alice!”

She was up and running in a flurry of russet before Petronella could finish.

“By the Gods,” she muttered. By her side, Joran chuckled and raised his glass to his princess.

Alice hugged Domita and hurried up the aisle to Petronella, her youthful face wreathed with smiles.

"Gods blessings to you," she said, holding Petronella at arm's length and admiring the width of her belly. "I've brought you someone else who asked to travel with me."

She gestured behind her, and the door opened once more to reveal a young woman with dark skin and warm brown eyes. A voluminous headdress scattered with gold crowned her cascade of dark curls, and a gown of forest green undulated around her curves. She strolled down the banqueting room in a familiar cloud of warm earth, honey, and flowers.

Petronella's eyes pricked with tears as she held out her hands in welcome to the new arrival. The woman dipped into a deep curtsy, her eyes alight with laughter as she extended her palms, face up. Petronella's lips lifted in a smile, even as her heart twisted with remembered grief. Two flowers bloomed in the young woman's hands. Snow white and tipped with azure blue.

"I am Felice's niece, Lady Fortuna de Winter. I ask if you would consider me for the position of nurse to your child."

Petronella nodded, dashing at the tears that welled in her eyes at the mention of Felice. "In honour of Lady Felice, you are welcome to my household."

Domita beckoned a page. "Find chairs for Lady Fortuna and Princess Alice," she hissed.

Petronella smiled her thanks as Fortuna and Alice joined her at the board.

She turned her gaze to the court, their faces gaunt but grateful after weeks of steady food deliveries. Her lips tightened as she caught sight of young Guildford of Wessendean's scowl, his twin Felicia watching Dominic with unusual interest.

Her voice rang clear over the chatter. "Master Skinner, come forward."

Dominic hesitated before rising, his clean blue doublet too big for his narrow frame. His cheeks flamed as he walked the aisle, the encouragement of slaps on the shoulder propelling him on the way.

"You may kneel," she said as he reached her, his cap nearly slipping from his hands.

The boy dropped clumsily, and she suppressed a smile. Reaching beneath the table, she drew the ceremonial blade Domita had prepared.

"Arise, Sir Dominic Skinner," she said, resting the blade briefly on his shoulders. "Master of Falcons in the Court of the Skies."

Dominic's blush deepened. "Your Majesty, you don't have to—"

Petronella shook her head. "I told you I would reward your service, and you have earned it. Besides, you are the only person besides me the Grayling does not try to murder." Her lips curved. "Speak to Lord Colman tomorrow. He'll explain your duties."

He bowed again, his face rosy with burgeoning pride, and scurried away from her presence, smoothing his new hat on his head as he went.

A griping pain low in her belly brought an indrawn breath, and she leaned against the table, reaching automatically for Joran's hand.

He clasped it, his sword-hardened palm warm against her own.

"Are you well, my lady?"

She couldn't answer him. Gazing out over the crowded tables, she watched Dominic return to his parents. They were standing to welcome him, arms around his shoulders. His mother beamed with pride. His father stood tall and spare at his shoulder. He glanced her way, and she stifled a gasp of horror as her belly twisted. She blinked, her stupefied gaze travelling from Master Skinner to his wife, and across the merry faces of her court. Somewhere at the back of her mind, she thought she heard laughter. Delighted, mischievous laughter. Mouth dry, she swallowed. The senior Skinner's face was gone, replaced by a grinning skull. His wife the same. Her gaze leapt across the rows, heart pounding. Face after familiar face vanished, to be replaced by the inexorable mask of death. She shook her head, vision blurring, and sank boneless to her seat.

"My lady? Petronella?" Joran's hand cupped her cheek, smoothing the start of tears. "Look at me, my love."

Her ring pulsed on her hand. Dreading what she would see, she cracked her eyes open, thanking all the Gods when his beloved face remained unaltered.

"Petronella, what's wrong? Is it our child?"

She gripped the table for support, her vision swimming. A faint laugh, harsh and mocking, slithered through her mind. The words a sibilant promise born on the breath of the north wind.

"Do you think you've beaten me? Think again. I can wait. And I will make you pay and pay again. I will take everything you are. Everything you cherish. Your children. Your husband. Your people, and your throne." Terror shuddered through her as the voice echoed in her mind. She retched, clapping a hand to her trembling mouth. Darkness hovered at the edge of her vision. A chasm waiting to trap her when she fell. She fixed her eyes frantically on young Dominic Skinner, smiling as he accepted the congratulations of his table companions. Catching her gaze, he snatched a tankard of small beer, tipping it to her in a toast. His face fell as he registered her frozen features.

"Your Maj? Are you well?" The tankard fell from his hand as his mind reached for hers. Gripped by the wrench of her belly, she had no thought of blocking him from her thoughts. No way of protecting him from the coldness and malice stalking the narrow corridors of her magical senses.

"Oh, Petronella, I see you watching him," the voice whispered, cold as the grave. *"Do you think a title and a sword will protect your little knight?"*

The laughter softened, almost playful, as though the Shadow Mage were toying with her. *"Prepare him well, my queen. He'll need every ounce of courage, every flicker of strength. I'll be watching. When the time comes, I'll test him to the limits of his endurance. And one day, your very throne may rest on his scrawny shoulders."*

The words coiled around her heart like a noose, their promise as chilling as frost creeping down the castle walls. The laughter faded, leaving silence and the tightening grip of Joran's hands on hers. At the other end of the hall, young Dominic stared at her in confusion, rubbing his head. She bit her lip. Hard. *He's heard it. He must have heard.*

"Petronella?" Joran's voice trembled. "What's wrong? Is it our child?"

Her lips barely moved, her gaze fixed on her former stableboy, secure under his father's proud arm, his new cap as blue as his eyes. He glanced away in response to something his mother said, a shy smile replacing his concern. The one bright light in a sea of shadows.

"My grandmother warned me. She said we hadn't won." Her voice cracked, a harsh whisper, fractured with fear. "It's here, Joran. The sickness. The evil. It's here."

The hall blurred, the haunting laughter echoing faintly in her ears. She looked again at Dominic, his boyish face lit with a quiet, untapped strength. Above her head, the Grayling soared from his perch, his chatter rising above the heads of the company. His call drew Dominic's attention. The newly minted knight held out his hand, uncaring of the savage clutch of the falcon's talons on his wrist as it came to rest. Laughing, he offered the bird a slice of meat. Stroked its freckled head with a gentle finger as it ate.

"He who holds the Grayling, holds the crown." Her grandmother's voice grew in her mind, cold and sure as the prickle of frost against a window. Petronella leaned into Joran's protective embrace and watched him. Dominic Skinner. Master of the Falcons.

He must be stronger than the shadows, she thought, her hand drifting protectively to her belly as her world twisted and darkened.

He must be.

THE END

Petronella's battle is won. But the war has only just begun.

The Shadow Mage promised vengeance. The sickness has returned. And the weight of the kingdom now falls on the shoulders of a boy who never wanted to be a hero.

In Book 2, Dominic Skinner must prove he's more than a tanner's son with a sword.

Four years after Petronella's rise, Epera teeters on the brink once more. When the queen's legendary falcon—the Grayling—vanishes, Dominic is thrust into a deadly conspiracy that threatens everything Petronella fought for.

The prophecy is clear: *"He who holds the Grayling, holds the crown."*

And the shadows are gathering.

Continue the Saga of the Swords

Read 'Page of Swords'

"From the first page, I was hooked and could not put this book down."
- Goodreads Review

Dominic's journey as Epera's unlikely hero begins here. Read the opening chapters below...

Enjoy!

CC.

Page of Swords Excerpt.

Page of Swords Excerpt Chapter One

Epera 1608. Castle of Skies.

High on the slopes of the northern mountains, the Castle of Air sheltered its sleeping inhabitants in a fortress of ancient stone. Early morning mist kissed the hard edges of the towers and turrets, lapping insistently at windows and battlements. Weary gate guards hunched their shoulders against the dew and longed for their rough pallets. Torches hanging on iron brackets sputtered and died as the sun crested the eastern hills to greet the morning.

The harsh, triumphant cry of a lusty cockerel echoed around the castle mews, and startled young Sir Dominic Skinner, Master of Falcons, from his stupor. Clutching his head, he levered himself upright. Nausea nagged his stomach as he plucked straw from his face. He squinted lopsidedly into the grey light, trying to work out where he was. An empty wineskin lay at his side. Stiff with dried mud, his breeches scratched his thighs. A dull ache throbbed on his cheekbone, beating in time with his pounding head. His left eye, sticky with sleep, refused to open. He winced as he probed it, tracing the outline of a decent bruise. The familiar essence of horse and dung and the proximity of the cockerel decided his whereabouts for him. The stables. A longtime place of refuge. Somewhere, an impatient hoof stamped, and the cockerel greeted the morning once more from atop the nearby dung heap. Swallowing heavily against his gorge, mouth stale, Dominic rolled to his knees and creaked upright. His second-best woollen cloak laid tangled at his feet. Barely even recognisable as a hat, his favourite cap languished, crushed and dirty beside it.

Guildford. It was slowly coming back to him. Yestereve, he'd played Primero. Gambled against Guildford of Wessendean, the King's bastard. Guildford was two years his junior, twice as broad, and probably two hand-spans taller. The young noble hadn't enjoyed losing to a former commoner, and his fists were brutal, as were those of his friends. Patting his sore ribs, Dominic grimaced at the flaccid pouch that had held his winnings.

"Bastards," he mouthed under his breath.

Limping to the door, he creaked it open and blinked at the stable yard. Somewhere nearby, the hounds barked, whining for exercise. More horses joined the stamping chorus. A group of grubby stable hands erupted like a colony of dung beetles from their quarters across the courtyard, rubbing sleep from their eyes. The cock crowed again, loud enough to wake the dead. The rising sun made his eyes water.

Dominic shrunk into the shadows with another groan and did his best to straighten his clothing. He was due in the mews. Work did not wait, and there was a hawking expedition to prepare for. Tomorrow, there would be a jousting tournament in celebration of Prince Ranulf's third birthday, followed by a lavish feast. There were people to instruct, hunting birds in need of his care, and lessons to attend later in the day. He almost envied the menial tasks of the stable lads in their dusty britches and soiled shirts. Three years ago, at the tender age of twelve, he'd been one of them. Ragged, starving, tired, and overworked. But at least he'd fitted in. He'd known who he was, and so did everyone else.

A grimace of discomfort shadowed his face as he straightened his back. Things were different these days. He was a member of the nobility, knighted by Queen Petronella herself. Gritting his teeth against the pain in his ribs, he bent to the straw-strewn floor to retrieve his battered cap. He took a moment to smooth the jaunty falcon feather that decorated it before replacing it on his head. Raising his chin with an effort, his gaze clashed with the dark brown stare of a lad he'd never seen before. He wore the uniform of the stable yard and balanced a pitchfork over his sturdy shoulder. Contempt hardened in his eyes as he took in Dominic's battered headgear, and his face twisted into a mocking smile when he noticed the swollen eye.

"Who does he think he is? Jumped up little weakling. Thinks he's better'n us. Deserves every beating he gets."

Dominic's face blazed scarlet as he caught the edge of the boy's thought. His Blessed gift of telepathy had developed slowly over the last three years. Petronella had woken it during her incarceration in the castle dungeon. Once the novelty wore off, he hated it. It was unreliable and uncontrollable. There were days when he could swear the whole of Epera gathered to shout at him and drive him mad. At other times and, usually, when it would have come in handy, the gift remained stubbornly mute, taunting him with its silence. His uncle, Terrence Skinner, said the gift would settle for him on his sixteenth birthday. Dominic cast his one good eye at the rose-pink sky and counted the days. Two to go.

Shoulders slumped, he trudged to the kitchen courtyard well, where he dunked his sore head in a bucket of moss-tainted water. Hunger joined his other maladies, and his heart sank. He would have to brave the cook and beg for some food.

Hoping to avoid attention, he slid into the kitchen via the battered courtyard door. Harassed kitchen servants glanced at him from the edges of their eyes, as ever uncertain what to do with him. Shouting voices and the bustle of early morning energy echoed off the low ceiling and clanged from the edges of huge iron pans. The air was already thick with the smell of small beer and bread. A reek of hanging meat drifted underneath it from the butcher's quarters. Perspiration bloomed on his forehead in the heat from the massive fireplaces, already stoked for the day. He reddened at the wrinkled nose of a nearby scullery maid as she caught the stench of the stable that hung around him.

"I suppose you'll be needing some ale?" Dominic shrunk under the one-eyed gaze of Marjorie Ashburn, the castle cook, as she loomed before him. She wiped rough red hands on a cloth hooked over her belt and poured off a tankard from a nearby barrel. "Here. Rough night, was it?"

He took the drink with a shrug of his narrow shoulders, dreading the inquisition to come. It was the price he paid for her bounty. "I've had worse."

"From what I hear, you bring it on yourself, lad. Can't keep your mouth shut when you've taken too much wine."

Dominic scowled and winced when the action reminded him of his black eye. "Who said that?"

"Never you mind."

"I want to know."

"Well, I'm not tellin' you. If you don't want to be the subject of servants' gossip and easy pickings for young Guildford, lay off the wine and stick to beer." She gave him another hard look. The twisted skin around her empty left eye wrinkled. "Or learn how to fight better."

"Easy for you to say," he mumbled, swiping a hand across his mouth. The ale stung a cut on his lip that he'd not noticed.

Marjorie shrugged, her bosom jiggling. "Easy for you to learn if you just put your mind to it. A bit of training with Sir Dunforde, and you could joust and wrestle and sword-fight with the best of them."

"Huh, the size of me compared to the rest of them? I don't think so."

He finished the drink and handed the empty tankard back to her.

"My thanks, Mistress," he said. Pulling his cap firmly over his ears, wishing it was as concealing as his old tunic hood, he turned to leave. Marjorie clamped an iron hand on his shoulder.

"You'd better eat something. Wait here."

She marched across the kitchen, retrieved a ladle, and used it to knock a dawdling scullery maid into action.

"Get you going, wench, fetch more water."

Rubbing her head, the girl scurried past Dominic to the courtyard, rolling her eyes at him as she passed.

Dominic shrugged. Marjorie ruled the kitchen. If she took to you, she'd feed and bully you. If not, a knock on the head with a ladle was as much as you might expect in the way of affection.

Saliva flooded his mouth as the cook returned with a small loaf of rye bread and a hunk of Argentian cheese.

"Break your fast with this, lad. You need feeding up."

He took the food with a nod of gratitude, his thoughts already running ahead to the many duties waiting for him in the mews.

"You'll think about what I said," the cook warned as he headed for the door. "Strong wine is no good for a lad like thee."

Dominic's eyes narrowed, and he turned around, squaring his shoulders. "When you are a courtier, strong wine is hard to avoid," he said pointedly.

The woman bristled, setting her jaw. "Oho! Quite the gamecock this morning! Gentleman, are you? Master of Falcons, are you? Then what are you doing beaten up, sleeping in the stables, and looking for comfort in my kitchen, young man?"

Squashing the bread in his fist, Dominic turned on his heel for the sanctuary of the mews. Marjorie's voice and the titters of the kitchen scullions dinned in his ears as he retreated, face scarlet, ears burning.

"What are you goin' to make of yourself, Dominic Skinner?" she bellowed after him. "Servant or noble, it's up to you."

Page of Swords Chapter Two

Face flushed with impotent rage, Dominic strode the length of the stable yard to the tall wood building that housed the castle's hunting birds. The echoing courtyard bustled with mews staff scurrying about their daily duties. A group of workers carrying out repairs to a nearby roof muscled a heavy ladder across the cobbles. Dominic winced at the sight of it. Heart racing with trepidation, he stopped with his hands screwed into fists as a young stonemason bounded up the narrow treads and shinned onto the relative safety of the roof. Swallowing heavily, his attention turned to a knot of falconers gathered in front of the high gable wall. Thurgil, the oldest of them, held his hand to his brow, squinting against the sunlight. Dominic frowned. Something was wrong. Spirit sinking, he followed their collective gaze upwards. Guildford's half-trained tiercel perched on the apex of the roof, jesses dangling from his leg.

"Well, what are you going to do about it?" Thurgil demanded over his shoulder to young Trinian, his apprentice. "You're the one who let it go."

The boy, a skinny ten years of age, trembled in his shoes and sucked blood from a gash on his thumb.

"'Tweren't my fault. It bit me."

"What about your glove? What did I tell you yestereve? The bird don't know you yet, and it's only half-trained. You don't go handling them without yer glove."

"I forgot. We could borrow that ladder?" the boy suggested.

"No ladders!" Dominic's voice coming from behind jerked Thurgil's lined face towards him. Trinian blanched under his habitual grime. "T'weren't my fault, Sir Skinner," he gabbled.

"Don't be daft, lad. The bird'll fly if we come at it like that," Thurgil said, scratching his head. "It's touch and go now. Tetchy it is."

"Was it fed?" Dominic squinted up at the falcon. His brain felt like a stone in his skull as he tipped his head back. "Some of them are already in moult."

Thurgil shook his head. "Not yet. Master Guildford wants to train with it. We've not fed it today."

"Fetch a lure and his hood, then."

Thurgil clapped his apprentice on the shoulder, a hefty shove that caused him to stumble to the door. "Make haste, lad. Afore the bird remembers he's wild and we never get him back."

Above their heads, Guildford's falcon observed the activity in the courtyard. His head turned skywards to the swooping castle starlings who circled the battlements, preparing to fly, his wings lifted. Dominic drew a breath and let it out slowly into the sound of a pigeon and its gentle coo. The falcon's head lowered, searching for the source of the sound.

Trinian scurried back, lure in hand. Dominic took the looped cord from him and retreated into the courtyard, where he had more space. He swung the lure in a figure of eight. Guildford's bird followed the passage of the bait, and the busy courtyard stilled to watch the entertainment as he soared from the gable. Dominic turned with the lure. The bird swooped, missed, and circled once more, gaining altitude and speed. Another pass. Dominic turned again, the bird following. Another five passes, and then he let the bird snatch the bait and take it to the ground. A murmur of appreciation rumbled around the watching servants. Armed with the hood, young Trinian lurched forward. Dominic held out a hand to stop him.

"Steady. Let him eat; he's earned it." He took the blind and approached the hungry bird calmly, crouching in front of him as the falcon snatched at the dead chick it had won. Intent on his meal, the falcon didn't flinch as Dominic waited patiently for it to finish. He offered his wrist to the bird, who stepped forward willingly and submitted to the hood.

"That was well done," Thurgil said as Dominic preceded him into the mews and returned the falcon to his perch.

Dominic grinned, wincing through the pain in his ribs swinging the lure had awakened. "You taught me well, Thurgil," he said, "none better."

Thurgil returned the smile, although his eyes creased with concern at the bruises adorning Dominic's face. Jaw set, he returned to his duties, trailed by Trinian, who followed in his footsteps like a faithful hound.

Avian eyes followed Dominic with interest from their tethered perches as he made a circuit of the aviary. Strolling along the row of cages, rubbing his bruises, Dominic found a measure of peace as he noted their condition. Satisfied that most were sound and content, he conferred with Thurgil, who issued a series of instructions to the men and women of the falcon mews. United in their mission to care for the precious birds, his fellow falconers spread to their daily tasks with quiet competence.

In a thoughtful mood, he exchanged his velvet cap for an old tunic and hood. He offered his fist to the Grayling and attached the jess to his falconer's glove. The Queen's bird would not be required on the forest hunt planned later in the day. For that, they'd be hunting with goshawks, which were better suited to ground prey. But the Grayling was about to moult and needed to fly. It was just the excuse he needed to remove himself for a space.

Bidding a good day to Thurgil, he left the confines of the castle. A little-used path to the high moorland that skirted the foothills beckoned. The chill of the morning dew soaked his feet. Calf muscles burning with effort, his breath rasped in his lungs as he panted his way further up the gorse-wrapped slope. Attached to his wrist, the falcon swayed with the rhythm of his stride, its wings raised for balance whenever Dominic slid on the damp grass. They stopped at the top of the steep hill, and Dominic turned to survey the view, catching his breath.

Stretched in stony magnificence below him, the Castle of Air could almost be a toy fort set up for his pleasure. Queen Petronella's blue and grey standard billowed from its mottled turrets in the breeze that swept the mountain pass. More pennants and banners surrounded a narrow area freshly set up on the flat ground just in front of the drawbridge. Servants began a steady procession from the castle, manhandling benches between them. Easily identified by their more colourful clothing, a group of squires followed the servants. They were setting up for the celebratory joust in honour of young Prince Ranulf's third birthday on the morrow. Watching the activity, Dominic sank on his haunches and pulled his hood up. An old habit from the days when he'd scurried about his duties at the behest of Old Harold, the stable master. The thick cloth muffled clouts across the back of his head and could be mistaken for a sack in dull light. Chewing his sore lip, he shrugged his bag from his shoulder. Marjorie's offering and a flagon of small beer lay inside. He unpacked his breakfast one-handed. The Grayling put his head on one side, watching his progress with interest.

"Your turn, my friend?" Dominic said.

Free from constraint, the falcon soared from his fist. Catching a rising swell, he ascended into the fresh blue air. Dominic broke bread, ate cheese and drank as the bird hunted and the castle prepared. Above him, the Grayling circled, watching for movement. Dominic scrambled to his feet, shading his eyes from the sun to follow his swooping progress over the wild hillside as he sighted his quarry. When the falcon brought down a fat partridge, Dominic raised his flagon in salute and took another swig of ale.

Guilt stabbed at him. By rights, he should still be down at the castle in the mews, supervising matters in the falconry, ensuring every available bird was ready for the hunting party later in the afternoon. He was a courtier now, with a well-paid position. Old Harold, still the stable master, had no authority over him anymore. Dominic Skinner, stable boy, was now Sir Dominic Skinner, Master of Falcons. He sighed and took another swallow. It was a good thing, of course. His mother had chirped her pleasure a hundred times the evening he received the honour. His father had regarded him with his wise, steady gaze and wished him good fortune. A pang of pure loss pierced his chest at the memory, and he scrubbed at the tears that threatened, forcing them down with the heels of his hands. Ellen and Tobias Skinner lay in the crypt in the castle temple. Swept away in the tide of sickness that overcame the population in the first grim year following Petronella's ascension to the throne. The Starving, they called it. Grain had flowed back to Epera in the weeks that followed the Queen's victory over the Dark Army, but feeding the desperate population took time. Weakened and still hungry, few had the resources to fight the new sickness. Ellen and Tobias had succumbed within days of each other.

The Grayling swept low over his head, and Dominic's good eye turned to the right. In the distance, the city of Blade dominated the valley, smoke already wafting from its many chimneys as the citizens there started another day. The Temple of the Mage once again dominated its skyline as the stone masons sweated to rebuild it to the queen's command. The snaking path of the rushing Cryfell tumbled from the western mountains. It sparkled clear and pure at this altitude. But Dominic was the son of a tanner and of Blade. Those pristine waters would soon foul with the detritus of a city recovering from the dark days of its recent past.

Struggling with a sudden, overwhelming tiredness, he pressed his lips together and forced his attention to the future. The dark days were over. He'd be sixteen soon. A man. He was Master of Falcons and the owner of a thriving tannery inherited from his father. Perhaps everything would become clearer, and his memories of blood and terror would fade. He shook his head free of the dark mood as he packed up his belongings and scoured the sky for the Queen's precious familiar. A shrill whistle brought the Grayling back to him. Dominic stroked his plumage. The Grayling observed him, head cocked. Comforting somehow. A clutch of bloody feathers stuck to his beak, and he waited patiently as Dominic plucked them away.

"Well, lad, it's just you and me now. Are you fed and flown?"

Talons tightened on the thick leather glove Dominic wore, and the bird stretched his magnificent wings to their fullest extent. His freckled breast glowed in the sunlight, and Dominic took a moment to admire him. The Grayling lowered his savage beak and grasped Dominic's finger. He shook his head, a light tug, and released. Dominic allowed himself a wry smile. "Besides me, you are the only person the Grayling does not try to murder," Petronella had said. And then she'd elevated him to the nobility and made him Master of Falcons, and his parents glowed with pride.

The Queen had meant his position as a reward for his service. But three years on, Dominic still struggled to believe he was worthy of her faith in him.

Page of Swords Chapter Three

The edges of a headache clung to the inside of his skull as he returned to the bustle of the mews with the midday sun high overhead. Grateful for the shade after the brightness of the morning, he ushered the Grayling into his cage and turned for the door, eager for dinner. He clapped Thurgil on the shoulder as he passed. The tall falconer was leaning on a cage, scratching his thick black beard.

"Ready to eat, Thurgil?"

"Noticed anything about Lady Wessendean's merlin?" Thurgil asked in return.

Dominic looked at the bird, perched asleep, with her head under her wing. His face creased in a frown. "I could see she was sleepy this morning. Lady Wessendean has not hunted with her for a couple of days. Has she eaten?"

"Nay. That's the thing."

The two falconers left the mews for the Great Hall. Dominic's stomach rumbled as the familiar smell of roast boar and freshly baked bread rose to greet them. As tradition dictated, they bowed towards the royal dais as they entered. Heavily pregnant with her second child, Queen Petronella sat in state at the top table. Her husband, Joran to her right. Domita Lombard, her First Lady to her left. The rowdy courtiers crowded the narrow tables set at right angles to her, and the chat and gossip dinged his ears. Receiving a nod and a smile from the queen, the two men took their seats at the board. Greeting their fellow diners, they helped themselves from the laden platters lining the centre of the table.

"She'll be coming into moult," Dominic said.

"Aye, but so's the Grayling and some others. They don't want to sleep the day away. Seems strange she's so low." Thurgil picked up a flagon of ale and filled their tankards.

"She's maybe sickening. Should I mention it to Lady Wessendean?" Dominic wiped his face with his sleeve, smearing fat across his cheeks.

"Should do, I suppose." Thurgil scratched his beard, dark eyes thoughtful. "Lady Felicia can't hunt with her today, that's certain."

"I'll tell her this afternoon in the library."

Ever hungry, Dominic filled his stomach with roast boar, his gaze drifting to Felicia of Wessendean. Neatly robed in sky blue, the maid nibbled daintily at the contents of her platter several seats away from her usual place alongside Guildford. She seemed engrossed in her food, her shoulder subtly turned from her twin. Dominic frowned. Normally, the Wessendean twins formed an impregnable duo at mealtimes, surrounded by the sons and daughters of other noble Citizens. Seated in his usual place, Guildford had filled his pewter plate with enough food for three people. His square jaw chomped through it with relentless efficiency. Under cover of his own meal, Dominic noted how many times the lad's eyes turned to his sister. Searching for what? Recognition? Approval? He nudged Thurgil with his elbow.

"Guildford and Felicia have had a row. Look at that."

Thurgil turned his gaze to the pair and grinned, showing a row of crooked teeth. "Aye, seems to be so."

Ignoring the surrounding conversation as much as her brother Felicia turned the page of a small book, and Dominic cursed.

"God's take it. My books are still in my chamber."

Even as he watched, Felicia pushed away her tankard and left the board, sketching a bare curtsey to the queen as she left the room for lessons. Guildford followed her without even a token acknowledgement of the pregnant monarch. Nodding at his nearest neighbours, Dominic tore another strip of meat from the dripping joint. Swinging his legs over the bench, he received a tired smile from the queen as he bowed. Hurrying as much as he could, given the sorry state of his bruised body, he headed for his remote tower chamber at the end of the western wing.

"What happened to you? You're late. I've told you before about keeping the others waiting." Terrence Skinner, his saturnine, dark-eyed uncle, peered impatiently over his glasses.

"My apologies." Breathless after his run across the massive castle, Dominic slumped into a hard wooden chair and tried to compose his mind to study. The Great Library dwarfed him on every side. Tall oak shelves crammed with books and scrolls loomed above his head. Lamplit, the surrounding air smelled of dust and parchment. Other alcoves contained various groups of scholars, with a selection of tutors in attendance. Terrence's desk commanded a space near the vast central fireplace. As Chief Librarian, he ensured the smooth running of the largest collection of knowledge in Arcanis. Besides his normal teaching, his duties also included the transfer of magical knowledge and ability to the Blessed population. Whether or not they wanted it. Dominic had been studying there for only three years. A mere sliver of time compared to that of his younger classmates, Guildford and Felicia of Wessendean. He'd barely been able to read at first. Had endured hours with the youngest students, shoulders clenched with mortification as he rubbed mistakes from his slate. His skill at forming letters was still rudimentary, his embellishments shaky, his spelling atrocious. But mathematics was alright. He could manage that. Just.

Struggling to ignore Guildford's smug expression, he pulled parchment and quills from his bag. The boy sat directly opposite Dominic and was busy sharpening a quill with a wicked-looking blade. After one quick, gloating glance that took in Dominic's battered visage, he kept his face down, concentrating on the task at hand. Dominic's swollen eye narrowed painfully at the satisfied twitch of Guildford's lips, half hidden under the dip of his stylish hat. Flanking him, his twin, Felicia, massaged her forehead, and shot him an impatient glare. Her pale hair dulled beside her brother's gold magnificence, but the siblings shared the same grey eyes and scattering of freckles across their narrow noses. Guildford's face glowed with sunlight, evidence of long hours in the saddle. His meaty forearms threatened to split his sleeves. Felicia's skin shone paler than the moon, her expression habitually remote. A dowdy hen beside her brother's brash cockerel.

The Wessendean twins. Illegitimate son and daughter of the late King Arion. Grinding his jaw, Dominic forced his attention to arranging scrolls, quills, and ink. The old table rocked a little as his uncle took his own seat.

"So," Terrence said, "The Art of Enchantment: A Journey into the World of Mathematics for Young Apprentices".

"Oh, no." Guildford's groan of dismay ended sharply with an elbow in the ribs from his sister. He ignored her and dropped his quill to the knife-pocked desk. "What about those of us who are Citizens, Master Skinner?" he demanded. "What can studying that," he flicked a disdainful finger at the leather-bound tome in front of his tutor, "have to do with us?"

"Plenty, if you would only apply your brain," Terrence said. "Not being able to use magic should not prevent you from a basic understanding of trigonometry."

Guildford rolled his eyes. Terrence ignored him.

"Now, Felicia," he said. "Perhaps you can explain the first theory?"

Obedient as ever, Felicia replied, her soft voice hushed as a falcon's wing, haunting in its melody. Dominic kept his eyes down with an effort. The lads in the mews called Felicia plain. He could never understand it.

At the end of her reply, Felicia sat straight, upright as a pine tree against the hard back of her chair, hands neatly folded. He blushed as her direct stare clashed with his. The tiniest smile curved around her rosebud mouth.

"Dominic?"

Terrence's voice. He started.

"Sorry?"

"If I could have one ounce of your undivided attention, perhaps you could explain the second theory?"

Felicia stifled a giggle under her hand. Guildford sat back in his chair, hands behind his head, legs sprawled wide, and smirked at him.

Dominic stumbled through the previous day's lesson while Guildford stifled an ostentatious yawn. He floundered as the younger boy cracked his knuckles and gazed at the ceiling, tipping his heavy chair on its back legs.

"Forever waiting for the peasant to catch up," Guildford mused, seemingly at the sky. His chair tipped further and then suddenly lurched backwards with a crash that took Guildford's ink and parchment with it. Felicia slid sideways with a cry of dismay, but failed to avoid the pool of ink that flooded the heavy table. Opposite them, Dominic clutched the edge of the desk as though he were drowning. His breath came in sharp pants, hatred clutching his chest like the Grayling's talons. His hands tingled with energy. The pressure in his head clanged like a temple bell.

Terrence observed the chaos with a quizzical expression and tipped back in his own chair, finding the balance point with a skill born of much experience.

"The art and science of balance," he declared. "Clearly a lesson for another day."

A quick gesture of his hands righted the fallen inkstand and collected the scattered parchment.

"I suggest you find a cloth and clear up the mess. Felicia, go with him. The ink will stain your gown," he said.

Face crimson with temper and embarrassment, Guildford extricated himself from the chair. A chorus of jeers erupted from students clustered in the vicinity as he clambered to his feet. Dominic winced as the young noble barged past, elbowing him in the shoulder as he went.

"I know you did that. I'll get you later. Just you wait," he hissed.

"You can try." His headache easing slightly, Dominic stifled his own smirk and stared down at his hands. He flexed his fingers, marvelling at the energy fizzing under his skin.

"Feels good, doesn't it?"

His uncle's voice, as mild and unassuming as if they were discussing the weather, made him jump.

"I didn't...It wasn't..."

Terrence quirked a cynical eyebrow. "Yes, interesting, but perhaps not surprising. Your telepathic gift we know about. Now, we can add telekinesis to the mix. The Mage has surely Blessed you. Just like your grandfather."

"I didn't mean it, not really," Dominic stuttered.

Terrence rolled his eyes, dark against his pale face and snow-white hair.

"Oh, I think you did, young man. Intention is everything. I should know."

He raised a finger and rotated it in Dominic's direction. Dominic yelped as his clutching fingers left the table, and the heavy chair spun like a dancer beneath him. He grabbed the seat and stifled nausea. His uncle's face was a study in nonchalant concentration, seen in spare glimpses on every giddy rotation. The mocking laughter of older students studying at nearby tables drummed in his ears.

"You can stop whenever you like," Dominic gasped, his belly roiling. "I'm going to be sick."

Terrence folded his hands in his lap, and the chair shuddered to a halt, facing the wrong way. Dominic staggered to his feet to haul it back to the desk.

"Are you going to show me how to do that?" he demanded.

"In good time. Come, let us walk." his uncle replied. He removed his spectacles and polished them on the sleeve of his gown as he preceded Dominic away from the central fireplace. Clambering to his feet, Dominic followed his uncle further into the stacks, trying to match his long-legged stride. Away from the cluster of desks, the air grew chill, the shadows watchful.

"It is interesting to find latent telekinetic power within you. Powerful as well, to move the entire chair with our young would-be king sitting in it and no training at all." Terrence continued, once they were out of earshot of the other students.

"Then I'm glad I have it," Dominic said, rubbing his sore face. "I'm sick of him and his friends using me as a punch bag and stealing my money every chance they get."

"Ah, so that black eye is the outcome of your little game of chance last night?"

Dominic stared at the stone floor under his shuffling feet. He shrugged.

"Tell me, did, perchance, your telepathic ability have anything to do with the fact that you won every game? Don't think that went unnoticed."

His toes curled in their worn boots. Another shrug.

"So, you, a member of the Blessed, used your ability to gain an advantage over a Citizen?" Terrence's voice was as quiet and relentless as sea ice.

"Could have done. He deserved it. Always laughing at me and calling me a peasant." Dominic mumbled the words past his bruised jaw.

They stopped in the history section. Carved in the Mage's pattern, a small, unassuming dark oak door in the far wall snared his attention. Dominic glanced around with a frown.

"What? Why are we here?"

Terrence leaned against a shelf and waved a hand at the immediate vicinity. "Do you notice anything about this section?"

Convinced something hidden behind the ancient door was watching him, Dominic barely heard him.

"What's in there, behind that door?" he asked.

"Nothing that needs concern you. I asked you a question."

Dominic shrugged. "Too easy. The wood is paler, not so intricately carved. These shelves are not as old as the others."

"Correct. You need to listen to me carefully now, Dominic."

Dominic dragged his attention from the mysterious door and met his uncle's serious gaze.

"I'm listening."

"When I was a lad in this very library, studying architecture, I used my gift to bring down the original shelving in this section on top of a Citizen. He was a member of the King's Guard. I injured him badly. They arrested me for it and sent me to the mines."

Dominic's eyes widened. "I knew they took you. I never knew why."

Terrence nodded, his face as shuttered and remote as a statue. His long fingers trembled as he fingered the neck of his robe. Dominic frowned at the ridged and rippled knot of scar tissue that encircled his uncle's throat. He'd never noticed it before.

"Lord Falconridge had sent the King's Guard after me. I was trying to protect the Restricted section." Terrence paused, his gaze resting momentarily on the door that so captured Dominic's attention. "That room contained Epera's magical knowledge. If the soldiers had found it, the Gods know where we would be now. As it was, I trusted the law. I knew I had hurt a Citizen, and I went with the soldiers. They hanged my father when he threatened the King to save me. Used him as an example of what would happen to the Blessed if they attempted to use their magical abilities against the new regime. I was the first ever sent to the mines. Lord Falconridge used the Skinner family to prove a point."

Open-mouthed, Dominic stared at the door, marvelling. His head twisted, looking at the heavy shelves laden with literature. Terrence's fingers still fidgeted at his neck, tugging against a chain that now existed only in his memory. Dominic blanched in realisation, and he took an involuntary step back. His uncle saw it. His mouth thinned, and suddenly he seemed old. Stooped with years and bitter with injustice. Unnerved by the chill in the atmosphere and the fact that his tutor's eyes had turned entirely black, Dominic whimpered as Terrence raised a hand. Heels sliding across the flags, Dominic heaved a breath against the sudden constriction in his chest as his Uncle's Blessed ability forced him hard against the nearest shelf.

Locked in the past, Terrence remained on the spot, cheeks ashen, clenching, and unclenching his free fist. Terrified, Dominic's eyes darted away, all his instincts telling him to run. Skewered in place like a butterfly by the power of his uncle's will, his legs refused to obey. He swallowed as Terrence's remote gaze snapped towards him.

"Yes, nephew. I was part of that darkness once. Trying to protect what I believed was right. I paid a bitter and terrible price. In the silence of the mines, the hatred and injustice in my heart made me easy prey for the Shadow Mage. I am the founding member of what became the Dark Army. A subject of Lord Falconridge's early experiments as he sought to harness its power and turn us into weapons for his own purposes. The Shadow Mage still has my soul in his claws. I battle him to stay in the light every day of my life."

Open-mouthed with horror, Dominic swallowed, his skin crawling. "You were part of the Dark Army?" His mind reeled, remembering the devastation at the battle of Sunira and then later, in the castle throne room. The Queen had almost died facing the power of the Dark Army with only the power of her newfound magic to help her. Dominic had tried to come to her aid and received a broken jaw from the fist of Lord Falconridge, her father, for his trouble,

Terrence clenched his fists, his whole body shaking as he fought to remain in control. His eyes regained their usual dark brown, although terrible memories churned within his gaze. The horror inflicted on the peaceful inhabitants of Sunira. The merciless, unescapable command of the Shadow Mage. Dominic gasped as the pressure against his chest lifted, and he stumbled away from the shelf, rubbing life back to his limbs. His uncle cleared his throat and his eyes softened. He held out a hand, half in comfort, half in supplication. Dominic stared at it. The power it wielded at his uncle's mental command. He shuddered, and Terrence lowered his arm stiffly to his side. His voice was sad when he spoke. Burdened by years of self-reproach.

"That's all in the past, lad. And it is my burden to bear, not yours. For now, you need to understand this, above all other things. A member of the Blessed should not use their abilities to injure or kill a Citizen who cannot retaliate in kind. We are powerful. Gifted with skills beyond their understanding. The Mage considers it unjust. It is not a fair fight."

Dominic's face creased into horrified pity. "But you still have your gifts," he pointed out, his throat dry.

Terrence swallowed, massaging his scarred throat. "That was the Queen's choice. She had the right to judge all of us for our crimes. She understood we were under the control of the Shadow Mage. We had no choice. She could have ended us where we stood. Instead, she spared us," his voice dropped, almost as if he was talking to himself.

"Perhaps that was the worst punishment. Letting us live in full knowledge of our deeds."

Dominic nodded. Unbidden, his voice narrowed to a whisper. "What would happen to me if I used my ability against a Citizen? Would the Shadow Mage come for me?"

Terrence chewed his lip and shrugged his broad shoulders. "The Queen banished the Shadow Mage. I doubt he would come for you. His influence remains within those who once wielded his power. We were bound to him, you see. But times have changed. I see no reason you should ever have to use your powers in that manner."

"But if I did?"

His uncle raised a chalky eyebrow. "Persistent and so full of questions, are you not? Old King Francis is the best example of that. He lost his powers and became a Citizen when he used them to murder his own wife. It was that terrible act of injustice that paved the way for an entire nation to plunge into darkness. So be warned."

"How do I get even with Guildford, then? What can I do?"

Terrence leaned in, pushing his spectacles further up his nose. His eyes glittered, huge and predatory, behind the glass. "You shouldn't use your magic, lad. Not if you want to keep those gifts. The Mage gives them to those he deems worthy. Those who can wield them with honour and discretion. He can also take them away."

"But Guildford's stronger than me. He beat me up and stole my money."

Terrence smiled, a rare expression on his habitually sad face.

"You got that money by trickery. So, really, all he did was punish you and take it back. There are better ways to vanquish your enemies. Learn the lesson, my boy. Learn it from me."

He whirled abruptly, the edge of his robe swirling on the flagstones.

"Come. Back to your studies."

Brain churning, his respect for his last remaining relative mixed with a healthy dose of pure fear, Dominic obeyed. But his head kept turning, glancing behind at the low door. There was someone behind it. Watching him. He could feel it.

Ready for Dominic's full adventure?

You've seen him take his first steps as Epera's hero. Now witness his complete transformation from tanner's son to legendary knight in this gripping coming-of-age epic.

Get Page of Swords for $3.99

Or find it at your favorite retailer: https://books2read.com/page-of-swords

Dominic's journey continues through Knight of Swords and culminates in the epic finale, King of Swords. Don't miss a moment of this unforgettable saga!

WHY DOMINIC?

You've walked with Petronella through her transformation from over-looked daughter to queen. But her story is only one thread in a much larger tapestry.

In Book 2, we shift our lens to Dominic Skinner—the Page of Swords—whose choices will ripple through the kingdom and determine whether Petronella's hard-won power can survive what's coming.

Petronella's fight continues. But to understand what she's truly up against, you need to see the battlefield through Dominic's eyes.

The Saga continues. The stakes are higher. The enemy is closer than you think.

Continue the Saga → Find it at your favorite retailer: https://books2read.com/page-of-swords

Also by Christine Cazaly

Books from the Tales from the Tarot series

SAGA OF THE SWORDS

Queen of Swords

Buy on all platforms: https://books2read.com/Queen-of-Swords

Page of Swords

Buy on all platforms: https://books2read.com/Page-of-Swords

Knight of Swords

Buy on all platforms https://books2read.com/Knight-of-Swords

King of Swords

Buy on all platforms https://books2read.com/King-of-Swords

Seer of Epera *(prequel)*

Buy on all platforms: https://books2read.com/Seer-of-Epera

WAY OF THE WANDS

The Unbound Flame (Knight of Wands)

Buy on all platforms: https://books2read.com/the-unbound-flame

COMMENCING 2025

A New World. A New Magic. A New Destiny.

The Unbound Flame (Knight of Wands)

Way of the Wands • Book One

In the harsh desert kingdom of Battonia, where the sun scorches and survival demands strength, magic flows like wildfire through those brave enough to wield it.

Here, the Wands rule—elemental forces of creation and destruction, passion and power. But when a tyrant king seizes the throne that rightfully belongs to another, one divided family must unite to reclaim their birthright and restore their shattered realm.

Enter a realm where:

- Magic burns as bright and dangerous as desert fire
- Love ignites in the heat of rebellion
- A shattered family fights to reunite and reclaim their crown
- Hearts and kingdoms hang in the balance

From the author who brought you the emotional journey through Epera comes a passionate new adventure of love, magic, and the unbreakable bonds of family.

Because some flames can never be extinguished...

The Unbound Flame Way of the Wands Book One.

For more information on this series —join Christine's mailing list at https://christinecazaly.com

If you loved the Saga of the Swords, please consider leaving a review. Your words help other readers discover these stories, and every review means the world to this author. Thank you for being part of this magical journey.

amazon.com/Christine-Cazaly/e/B0BBJW5VWS?ref=sr_ntt_srch_lnk_2&qid=1661516964&sr=8-2

facebook.com/christinecazalyauthor

bookbub.com/profile/christine-cazaly

goodreads.com/https://www.goodreads.com/author/show/22759981.Christine_Cazaly

Facebook https://facebook.com/christinecazalyauthor

GoodreadsChristine Cazaly (Author of Queen of Swords) | Goodreads

BookbubQueen of Swords (Tales from the Tarot) by Christine Cazaly - BookBub

Instagram https://www.instagram.com/christine_cazaly/

AmazonAmazon.com: Christine Cazaly: books, biography, latest update

WANT TO BE THE FIRST TO KNOW?

For updates, recommendations and giveaways, join my newsletter and get Carlos and the Mermaid, a FREE short story, set in Oceanis, the Kingdom of Cups. It's inspired by the tarot card Five of Cups. You can join my newsletter at https:/christinecazaly.com

Join my newsletter for progress updates and to be notified when my next books are due for release!

Carlos and the Mermaid (A Tales from the Tarot short story)

ACKNOWLEDGMENTS

Massive thanks and love to my wonderful husband, Jim, whose support is astronomical.

Thanks to my wonderful editor, Gary Smailes of Bubblecow, whose objective eye, advice and help added so much to the finished story.

Also to my brilliant beta readers, Joy, Adrian and John, who all had different strengths and perspectives on the story as they saw it and helped to bring it to life. Double thanks to Aly, best friend, cheer-leader, beta reader and eagle eyed proof-reader combined. Thanks for your help in adding the final polish!

Last, but not least. Thanks to my wonderful dog, Bingo, for all that unconditional love, support, patience and company when I couldn't play ball. You are the best dog in the entire world.

CC x

About the Author

Christine Cazaly is a Tarot reader and writer of the Tarot inspired series Tales from the Tarot, that follows the lives of the sixteen court cards of the minor arcana. When in the real world, she's a qualified ballroom dance teacher, leading an enthusiastic band of eager learners.

She is lives in West Yorkshire, England, with her long-suffering husband, three gorgeous cats, and a mad and very loveable Bordoodle called Bingo.

Apart from the day job, you'll most likely find her writing, reading Tarot, walking with the dog, creating handmade soap and (in order to save her own waistline) baking for her friends.

Christine Cazaly is the pen name she promised her six-year-old self many moons ago.

Connect with Christine on facebook, or sign up to her newsletter at https://www.christinecazaly/contact

Printed in Dunstable, United Kingdom

76280969R00245